Catherine Parr was ... in the
United Kingdom. For many years she taught in
both the state and private sectors, before
moving to France in 2001 with her husband.
She lives in a hamlet at the foot of the
Montagne Noire between Carcassonne and
Narbonne. She is the author of
'Clouds over the Montagne Noire'

Carcassonne Dreams

Catherine Parr

Artwork by C Frankau

To my husband David
and all my wonderful family

CHAPTER 1

Nothing in Orla O'Sullivan's behaviour had prepared her family for the terrible time when she had begun to whine that she was too fat. It seemed to happen almost overnight, and mealtimes suddenly became battlegrounds with bitter words, recriminations and tears. Her mother Theresa was anxious and tense as she watched her pushing the food around her plate, saying she was full after a couple of mouthfuls and refusing to touch anything that had the least morsel of fat in it.

She frowned now at Orla's almost full plate of battered fish and peas, and at the knife and fork lying tidily together on it.

'This is getting ridiculous,' she said in exasperation. 'Will you look at Padraic, now. He eats everything I put in front of him. Only seven years old and he eats a lot better than you do.'

Padraic was offended. 'No, I don't eat everything. I hate sprouts and I hate cabbage and I don't like that stinky cheese you make me eat, and I...'

'Well, you still do a lot better than your sister. No wonder you're always tired, Orla. You need food to give you energy. You're just wasting away. I could understand it if the food was horrible, but if I take the time to cook you could

4

at least show that you appreciate it and not be throwing half of it away. Mary's never as fussy as this.'

She stood up and stretched across the table, collected Padraic and Declan's empty plates and balanced Orla's nearly full one on top.

In the kitchen they all heard the plates banging down on the draining board.

'Can't you try a bit harder to eat, child?' her father said. 'You're getting Mammy desperate about you now. And look at all that good food, just thrown away.'

His face was concerned and Orla could see her sister Mary glaring at her. This happened at nearly every meal. Her mother's impatience and her father's gentle persuasion were a thrice daily battle. But there was nothing she could do. She had a horror of seeing a piled plateful of food that Mammy expected her to eat. There was simply too much of it, too much fat, too many calories, and she knew even before she picked up her knife and fork that she would never be able to finish what was put in front of her.

'I do try to eat, Daddy, honestly. It's just that there's too much, that's all.'

'No, you're not trying,'' Mary put in. 'The only thing you're trying is everybody's.....patience.'

She only just stopped herself from saying 'everybody's bloody patience,' but knowing her mother's views on bad language, she was glad that she had, for Theresa was returning with a large plate bearing a home made chocolate cake, double layered and sandwiched together with apricot jam.

Up at University College, Dublin, Mary's daily conversation was peppered with expletives, but now that she was home for the Easter holidays she almost instinctively adjusted her terminology in front of her mother.

'And will I be cutting you a piece, Orla?' Theresa asked pointedly.

With everyone looking at her, she nodded miserably. 'Just a small piece, please,' she murmured and with tight lips, Theresa sliced a thin wedge for her.

Dutifully, Orla bit into it. She swallowed one mouthful and then pushed her plate aside.

'I'm sorry,' she said in a small voice. 'I can't.'

By her side, Padraic beamed, already leaning towards her with his spoon. 'Can I have hers?'

She scooped up the rest of her cake and deposited it onto his plate. He grinned widely and it was gone in three mouthfuls.

'You're trying, all right,' Mary said drily. She finished her own cake and scraped back her chair to clear the table.

Orla was well aware that food was becoming an issue for her, and it was Sister Bernadette who had started it all, or so she thought. Sister Bernadette took them for history. She was shorter and fatter than most of the other nuns and her temper was legendary.

Despite the excellent results year after year, the only thing she ever predicted for her current set of students was that they would all end up in jail, on the streets or worse. When they invariably proved her wrong she put it down to the prayers she had so generously offered up on their behalf. Naturally it had nothing to do with the endless hours of homework and essay writing and learning whole pages of stuff off by heart.

There was a rumour that she had once been married and subsequently divorced, but no-one really knew if it was true. At any rate, she had come into the convent late in life.

'It couldn't be true she's been married,' Kathleen said. 'Who'd ever have a misery guts like her?'

'Imagine coming home to a face like that,' murmured Lyndsey. 'She'd turn the milk sour.'

'Maybe she was beautiful when she was younger,' Kathleen suggested but without much hope in her voice.

'And maybe I'm a flying pig.'

'Maybe she's having a mid-life crisis, they all go completely insane at that age.'

'And maybe we should shut up now, she's looking.'

Sister Bernadette held a sheaf of essays in her hand and waddled her way around the class, flinging them onto desks and commenting loudly on their deficiencies.

'Orla O'Sullivan, if you think this essay is acceptable then I'm here to tell you that it is not. There's a whole raft of spelling mistakes in it, it's too short and you've added no detail at all. Didn't you hear me say I was looking for detail? I wanted to hear all about Cromwell and his confiscation of Catholic holdings. Did you hear me say that? Well, did you?' She planted her stout body by Orla's desk and glared down at her.

'Yes, Sister.'

'And you didn't think it was worth putting any in, is that it?'

She ducked her head to hide the tears that were starting to form. Sister Bernadette was a great one for yelling at you in class for no reason at all. Other teachers like Sister Magdalene would take you aside after the class, and then explain, nicely, what you had done wrong and then she would wonder out loud what would be the best way of correcting the unfortunate lapse.

But this was never Sister Bernadette's way. She was continuing now, pushing her thick glasses more firmly onto her chubby face before she said, 'In all the years I taught your sister Mary she never gave me an essay like this one. You'd do well to take a few leaves out of her book. And don't be telling me you can't do it, because I know better.'

By now the tears were spilling over. Her head went still further down and Sister Bernadette took that as a gesture of defiance. 'Can't you even look at me when I'm speaking to you, child? You'll stay in after school tonight and write me a decent essay. One that your sister Mary wouldn't be ashamed of, do you hear?'

She nodded dumbly, but inside she was burning with resentment. It was always the same. At home and now at school. Mary this, Mary that. Mary who was so brilliant at everything that she hardly seemed to put any effort in. Mary who had always brought home glowing school reports. Orla's were usually good enough and her father was pleased that the nuns thought she was doing her best.

Her mother had read her last one with a slight frown. 'Only a grade C in geography? Have you not been paying enough attention in class, Orla? Or did you not do enough revision, is that it?' The voice was very stern.

She defended herself with just a hint of truculence. 'The exam was so hard, Mammy. I did revise, honestly, but I swear, there were some questions we hadn't done in class. No-one could answer them. It wasn't just me.'

'Well, I expect to see at least a B next term, so you'd better start working a bit harder in future. If I see another report like this one then you can say goodbye to those nights at the discotheque. Your work comes first. Do you hear me, now?'

'Yes, Mammy.' She was outwardly meek. She was used to these outbursts and they rarely lasted long.

'And while we're about it, I've just been up in your bedroom. Why can't you hang your clothes up properly? You can get yourself upstairs this minute and put your wardrobe straight. I'll be up there in fifteen minutes and if it's not tidy by then there'll be trouble.'

'Yes, Mammy.' Evidently her face did not match her tone.

'And you can take that insolent look off your face right now, young lady.'

She marched across the room and went out, seething with suppressed rage but not daring to slam the door as she wanted to.

Once in her room she wrenched open the wardrobe door to see just what on earth her mother was so annoyed about.

She spotted it at once, and she rapidly selected the two coat hangers holding skirts that had slipped off the rail and put them back in the correct place after her trousers. Trousers and jeans had to be hung up on the right, followed by skirts, blouses and then dresses. Theresa had a habit of checking regularly that everything was in its correct place and with that in mind, she finally placed her shoes back into pairs on the rack at the bottom.

Once the wardrobe was in a state that she hoped would satisfy her mother, she pulled open the top drawer of the chest that held her underwear. She snatched out the whole lot and piled everything up in a heap on the floor before she began to sort it out. She folded everything tidily and tucked her handkerchiefs back into their lacework sachets, before finally rolling up her tights and packing them away in the pale blue drawstring bags. Mammy hadn't mentioned her drawers but she was just as likely to inspect those as she was the wardrobe.

Mammy liked everything neat. Her favorite, much quoted proverb was 'a place for everything and everything in its place', and to that end the whole house was as kept as orderly as was the small reception office where she worked at the doctor's.

Padraic never seemed to come in for the full force of Theresa's wrath. He was never sent upstairs to tidy his room. Theresa routinely did it for him. To her, girls were future housekeepers and needed to be firmly brought up with that in mind, whereas naturally, a boy could not be expected to cope with household chores.

It had never been openly acknowledged, but Declan was certain that Theresa had been disappointed at the successive arrival of the two girls.

During her first pregnancy she had been wont to pat her bulging stomach and talk about 'the boy' and how the family would be complete when he was born. Declan was relieved when he had finally made his appearance seven years ago. He was beginning to have terrible visions of a long string of girls to support and their weddings to pay for and wondering how he would possibly be able to afford it on his postman's wage.

Reluctant to go downstairs until her mother's temper had cooled, Orla wandered into the bathroom.

She pulled open the top drawer of the vanity unit and took out Mary's lipsticks, her tiny round pots of eyeshadow and the tube of mascara that was supposed to thicken and lengthen the lashes in a couple of simple strokes.

During the holidays Mary had a part time job as a cashier at the local supermarket and she was allowed to spend her earnings any way she liked. Orla had pocket money, but Theresa always demanded to know what she spent it on, and make up was on the list of forbidden items.

She crept to the bathroom door and tilted her head to one side, listening intently, and from

Mary's room there came the faint sound of music.

Sure that she would not be disturbed, she daringly tried a light beige foundation, rubbing it in with her fingers until her freckles were barely visible. She applied the deep brown eyeshadow, and then some bright red lipstick. Liking what she saw, she carefully unscrewed the wand of mascara and with deft stokes, applied it to her pale lashes. She lifted her chin and smiled at her reflection. Most definitely, an improvement. The face that smiled back at her was far more glamorous than it had been five minutes ago.

She was so intent on regarding this new, unaccustomed version of herself that she barely had time to react as the door opened.

Mary strode over to her and her voice was horrified. 'Orla, what on earth do you think you're doing?'

'What do I look like?' she demanded, turning to face her sister and tilting her head.

'That's not the point, Mammy will kill you. Get it washed off.'

'But does it suit me?'

Mary regarded her speculatively. 'Since you're asking, yes, I suppose so. Gives you a bit more colour in your face. But you can't possibly go down looking like that. You know what Mammy said. No make up until you're eighteen.'

'I'm nearly eighteen, what difference does a few months make?'

'None at all, as far as I'm concerned, but it does to Mammy so if you know what's good for you, you'd better get it cleaned off, pronto.'

Orla was already splashing at her face, wishing she looked more like her sister who was petite with gorgeous reddish-gold silky hair that framed her face, a beautiful oval shaped face with no spots on it and a flawless complexion.

Her own hair was long and auburn, but she had inherited Declan's curls and the least bit of moisture in the air turned it into a mass of frizz. She had tried all the products that promised a smooth and shiny silkiness, but either the products were wrong or she didn't have the right kind of hair, because none of them worked on her. Padraic had the same hair type too but on him it looked fine, with a mop of reddish curls framing his chubby face, and being a boy he didn't care anyway what his hair looked like.

Both Mary and Padraic were well rounded, which was testimony to their mother's excellent cooking skills. Theresa had grown up as the only girl in a family of four brothers and had learned to cook from an early age.

'And while we're here, just let me tell you Orla, Mammy's getting to the end of her tether with you and your everlasting dieting. Why can't you just eat food like normal people?'

'Because I don't want to be a fat slob like you,' she retorted with spirit.

She turned around, her face clean now, and jabbed a finger at her sister's slightly bulging thighs encased in her tight jeans.

'I'm voluptuous, darling, that's what I am,' Mary said, looking down at herself with evident approval. 'That's what the fellows like, a bit of arse, something to get hold of.'

She smiled, a contented, secretive smile as she thought of Aiden up at university, who liked her curvy flesh in a manner which her mother neither knew about nor would have approved of.

'Jesus, if Mammy could hear you talking like that! She'd kill you!'

'She's not here, is she? And don't you go tittle tattling to her, either, madam. And you can put all that lot back where you found it.'

Regretfully, she replaced Mary's beauty products back in the drawer, thinking how unfair it was that she couldn't wear make up. All her friends did, at least when they went to the discotheque. If she was as old as Mary it would be different. If she had non frizzy hair like Mary she was sure that in some indefinable way, her life would be better.

But it was hopeless. She couldn't change the colour of her hair, that was for certain. Mammy would kill her if she started using dyes on it. But she could be thinner than Mary. That would be easy. All that took was a bit of effort and some exercise, and she was determined to start the very next day.

In the first week she was thrilled to find that she had lost two pounds. Then another one the following week. Food stopped being a pleasure and became something to confront, to categorize into good and bad. There was no in between, there were no middle ground foods. There was good food, like lettuce, cucumber and tomatoes which she continued eating, and then there was the bad stuff like ice cream, butter, cheese and full fat yoghurt. Then came the really disastrous foods like biscuits and sweets and the wonderful apple and cinnamon pie that her mother was so excellent at making.

She weighed herself incessantly, obsessively. Each evening she stood naked in the bathroom and mentally calculated how many calories she would burn up whilst asleep, and then she would weigh herself again in the morning, but always after going to the toilet. Urine was liquid, it was heavy and there was no point in weighing that too.

She quickly became very focused and disciplined about the whole thing. If she didn't lose more than a pound in one week, she would do an extra half hour of exercising every day to make up for it. She was happy when she saw the results, the thighs that were an inch thinner, the hips that were narrower and the stomach that was completely flat.

At school Kathleen teasingly started calling her 'Skinny Orla', which pleased her enormously.

There was huge admiration in her voice. 'Would you just look at her? She could be a model.'

Lyndsey, who was herself a little pudgy, put her arms around Orla's waist and turned her round slowly. 'How are you doing this? It's not fair. I've been on a diet for months now and I haven't lost anything.'

'Ah, you have to try,' she said with just a hint of smugness. 'It's no problem, you just have to control what you put in your mouth, that's all.'

It was clear that neither of her friends believed her and she continued to be the object of admiration and envy of the other girls who were nearly all convinced that they were too fat.

After two months of this regime she weighed just over seven and a half stone, but she was beginning to feel lethargic most of the time. Everything was too much effort, including her schoolwork which she skimped as much as possible.

Then there came a turning point. She had studied all the charts and she knew that in theory at least she was underweight for her height, but standing in front of her bedroom mirror, twisting herself round, she was convinced that she was not thin enough. She was not making enough effort. She knew she could do better. She had to do better. She looked down at herself in disgust and ran bony hands over her thighs. She frowned. They were too fat, and she thought she could detect a slight bulge in her stomach.

She increased her exercise regime. She got the earlier bus so that she could get off three stops before it reached the convent and alternately jogged and sprinted the last couple of miles. Once at school and in lessons, she took to clenching her buttocks, in and out, in and out. Nobody noticed and she could keep it up for an hour or more. At home she did press ups in her bedroom until Theresa intervened.

'Would you come downstairs and stop shutting yourself up in your room, Orla. If you've done your homework then come and watch TV, or read a book, or anything you like, but just be a part of this family for Heaven's sake.'

At night she turned up the radiator in their bedroom until Mary complained.

'Holy Jesus, would you turn the bloody thing off? I'm sweating here. I can't sleep if the place is like a greenhouse.'

'I'm cold. I need it turned up full.'

'If you're cold it's because you're not eating enough to keep a fly alive,' she retorted.

She was not exaggerating when she complained of the cold, for she really was. She wriggled her toes around at the end of the bed, hoping to warm her feet so that sleep would come. She also clung to the hope that a hot bedroom would make her sweat during the night and burn off some extra calories.

'That's not true, I do eat. You see me doing it every day, don't you?'

'Well, if you're eating then tell me why are you only seven stone something?'

'How do you know what I weigh? And anyway, I bet I'm the same as you.'

'Of course you are, eejit, but you're taller. A person of your height should be a lot more than seven and a half stone. And I know because Mammy told me this morning.'

'What!' She sat bolt upright and glared at Mary. 'Mammy has no right to be telling everyone what I weigh. It's no-one else's business.'

'Then why don't you start eating properly and then maybe she'll stop making you get weighed every day? And you could start thinking about somebody else for a change instead of yourself all the time. You've got Mammy and Daddy worried sick about you, do you know that? Mammy was crying this morning.'

She didn't tell Orla what she had witnessed. She had been setting the table for breakfast in the dining room and her parents were in the kitchen. She heard sobs and she stayed quite still, listening.

'Declan, she's wasting away. I'm so scared for her.' And then, in a different tone of voice, furiously: 'She has no right to put us through this. Has she any idea how we feel? Doesn't she care how it's affecting us? Can't she see that everyone's worried to death about her?'

'Shush now.' The words were soothing. 'She's going to get better. Stop your fussing.'

There was a silence. Mary had gone back upstairs, unwilling to intrude, but she knew, as Orla didn't, just how her eating pattern was destroying their parents.

'Would you stop getting at me! I can't help it.'

'I'm not getting at you. I'm just telling you how you're making all our lives a misery with your everlasting diet. And of course you can help it. You're the one who decides what to put in your mouth, aren't you? Just think about it. And for God's sake turn off the light, some of us need to sleep.'

Orla sat up and flicked the switch by her bed. She lay down, but trying to get comfortable was a nightly ordeal as she had no cushion of fat to come between her and the rather hard mattress. Both her body and her mind hindered sleep. She was furious that Mammy had told Mary what she weighed.

What neither Mary nor her mother knew was that every time she was weighed she wore her new padded bra. Inside each cup was a small white cotton bag, and into this she had slipped as many two euro coins as she could fit in. They were tightly wedged together and she had checked carefully that there was no clinking when she walked. It didn't add much, just a few grams, but at least it helped. She made sure, of course, that she also drank at least four glasses of water just before her daily weigh-in sessions. Again, not much difference, but it counted.

She lay down, eyes wide open and listening to Mary's breathing until it became deep and regular. She was deeply disturbed. She knew that her dieting had gone way beyond normal limits. On one level she was acutely aware of just how idiotic it was but there was another, overriding part of her that just couldn't stop. Something was taking over her life, it was driving her, telling her that she was too fat, making her count every calorie and burn up as many as possible during the day.

Not long afterwards her five foot ten frame had shrunk to seven stone. Her eyes looked enormous in her oval face and her normally glistening auburn hair looked like straw. Worse still, when she brushed it she looked at her comb in panic. It was tangled with long strands of her hair which had begun to fall out as her weight plummeted even further.

Her periods became erratic and finally they stopped altogether. She noticed a fine, downy hair on her arms which by now were hardly anything but bone covered by a thin veneer of skin. She was constantly exhausted now, from the minute she woke up, but she forced herself to keep going, to believe that everything in her life was normal and under her own control.

Theresa was desperately worried about her and one morning she issued her ultimatum.

She was making great sweeps of the steam iron over Declan's blue shirt, but looking at Orla with the air of someone who had made up her mind and will brook no dispute.

'I'm taking you with me to the doctors tomorrow,' she told her. 'This has gone far enough, Orla. If you don't start eating properly there'll be nothing left of you.'

'I don't need a doctor. I'm not sick. There's nothing wrong with me.'

She stood the iron on its edge on the board. 'You might not think so, but just tell me, is it normal to weigh the same as a twelve year old child, at your age? Well, is it or isn't it?'

'I'm not the same as a twelve year old.' She was determined to defend herself. 'It's just that I'm not hungry all the time, that's all. It's nothing to go to the doctor about.'

'You can stand there arguing about it all day, Orla, it won't make any difference.'

She hung Declan's shirt on a hanger and scooped up the pile of ironed clothes to take them upstairs.

'You're coming into work with me tomorrow and I'll get Doctor Costello to have a look at you. If we get in early he'll see you before his first patient.'

She brushed past Orla on her way out of the room before she had to listen to any more objections. She wished that Declan would appreciate how serious this was.

'Sure, she's skinny, but don't they all want to look like sticks nowadays? Better say nothing about it. The child will grow out of it.'

But Theresa was far from convinced, and she put the phone down thankfully when Doctor Costello told her to bring Orla with her the next day, and he would see her before his scheduled appointments.

'Thank you so much, Doctor. It's good of you, and I wouldn't trouble you unless I thought it was getting out of hand.'

'Will Declan be able to come with you?'

She was bewildered. 'Why would you need to see him?'

'Well, in cases like this, it's often best to see both parents as well.'

'I'll do my best,' she said, 'but he won't be pleased. He thinks she'll grow out of it if we leave her alone.'

Doctor Costello shook his head. 'No, if Orla's having real problems with her food then it becomes a whole family affair. Just you tell him from me that he needs to be here as well.'

It hadn't been easy.

'What does the fellow want with me? It's Orla he needs to see, isn't it?'

'Declan, she's just as much your responsibility as mine,' she retorted. 'If Robert says we should both go then the least you can do is show willing. It's not going to take all day, it's only an hour at the most, and it's early morning.'

'I don't know about getting time off, it's short notice,' he grumbled.

'Tell them you've overslept. No-one's going to know any different.'

There was a definite reluctance, but finally he agreed. 'As long as I'm back for nine o'clock then.'

They were in the surgery promptly at eight the next morning.

After examining Orla, the Doctor's face was very grave as he asked her to wait in a small side office.

He waited until she closed the door behind her and then spoke, and his voice was very low when he said, 'Theresa, why didn't you bring Orla to see me before this? She's very seriously underweight. Didn't you realise that?'

'Ah, we thought she'd get over it,' Declan said, a shade too easily, and the doctor looked at him sharply.

'This isn't something she's going to get over without some help. Orla is verging on severe anorexia and if she continues in her present pattern it's going to be very hard to help her. We need to act now and get her back to a healthy weight before things go too far.'

He explained further, settling himself back into his black leather seat and regarding them both from under his pale eyebrows. He told them that the illness of anorexia was not only about food, but there could be underlying issues such as Orla using food as a mean of taking control of her life.

'If it's not about food then what is it all about?' Declan was very impatient. Of course this was all about food, that's why they were here. What else could it possibly be about?

He told them more about the disease. 'Anorexics often feel that they have no control over what is happening to them,' he said. 'Refusing to eat properly gives them the sense that they have the power to control their body, which is, of course, the essential thing about their lives. Sometimes it can be triggered by some kind of trauma, or even a family upheaval such as divorce. Do you know if Orla's worrying about something? Has she experienced any trauma recently?'

This was the wrong approach. Declan had no clue what the doctor meant by trauma, but he understood divorce.

'Theresa and I have been married twenty-four years,' he said brusquely. 'There's never been any divorce in our families, and there never will be.'

Theresa began to wonder uneasily if something she had done had set all this off. Was Orla unhappy in some way that nobody knew about? Could it be the convent? Was everyone expecting too much of her? The worries circled round in her mind and she began to fell guilty that somehow, she and Declan must be at the root of it all.

When they left they had a slightly better understanding of the disease which hitherto had only been a name and a couple of television programmes which they had watched without much interest, and without the faintest inkling that they themselves would ever be affected.

'What did he say about me?' Orla demanded crossly on the drive home. She was still mutinous.

'Oh, for the love of God, what do you think he said?' Theresa was exasperated. She swivelled her head round to look at Orla in the back seat.

'You're anorexic, you need to eat properly and put weight on and it's gone too far. From now on, you're going to eat whatever I put on your plate and we'll be having no more of this nonsense.'

She spoke more sharply than she had intended. The doctor's explanation had made her more anxious about Orla's condition than she had been already.

After this, with her mother so patently angry with her and watching every mouthful, she made an enormous effort and ate all her meals, resenting every mouthful she swallowed. But soon afterwards she would disappear into the bathroom. Her parents would hear the shower, never suspecting that it was masking the sound of vomiting, as she got rid of the meal that her mother had so cruelly forced her into eating.

This morning she leant over the toilet bowl and forced a finger down her throat until she retched and had the grim satisfaction of seeing most of her breakfast disappear down the pan.

At the sound of loud bangs she hurriedly wet her hair until it dripped over her face and opened the door cautiously, clutching a huge white towel to her throat.

Mary was still in her striped pyjamas and she was very impatient.

'You've been in there forever. Would you come on out of it, I have to get a shower or I'm going to miss my bus.'

'Alright, I'm coming,' she said crossly, towelling herself vigorously. 'Give me time to get dried, will you?'

'And I know you've been throwing up in there. You can't fool me Orla. I can smell it a mile off.'

She was anxious suddenly. 'You won't tell Mammy, will you? Please?'

'No, I won't, but only because she'll worry about you even more than she is already. You have to stop this. You're off your head. You're driving us demented with it all.'

From outside, Mary heard the shower switch off to a drip and muted noises as Orla got into her clothes. She finally whisked into the bathroom as Orla passed her quickly without looking at her and disappeared into her own room.

She wrinkled her nose at the faint smell of vomit that permeated the room and taking a small perfume bottle from the glass cupboard, she pressed at the inflatable mesh top and sprayed a light mist into the air. At least if Mammy came in the whole place wouldn't reek of sick.

She sighed deeply, thinking about Orla, as she undressed preparatory to taking her shower. In spite of their occasional spats, the two sisters were fond of each other in a non demonstrative way, and Mary was only too well aware that the incessant dieting was showing signs of spiralling out of control.

Theresa felt helpless. Seeing the girl losing weight was a daily torture to her. She slept badly for the first time in her life. As soon as she got into bed the thoughts whirred in her brain. Where had it all started? Was there anything she could cook that the girl would eat? Should she force her to eat? Indeed, *could* she force her to eat if the child refused? Was there anyone she could turn to for help?

In desperation, she went to see Father Hagan, who promised her that he would call round that same evening. The elderly priest told Orla that it was a sin against God to abuse the body He had given her, but it didn't help. Outwardly compliant, she listened with tightly compressed lips to the old priest whilst studying her hands, but inwardly she was furious. How dare Mammy get this old man to come and preach to her? What business was it of his what she chose to eat or not eat? She bit her lip in an effort to prevent herself from giving voice to her objections, and as Mammy was sitting opposite with her eyes fixed on her, she could only remain silent until he stood up and prepared to leave.

'And so, you will think seriously about what I've been telling you, Orla?' He placed a benign hand on her head in a gesture that combined both blessing and farewell, and she only just managed with a huge effort to stay still and not shrug his hand away.

'Thank you so much, Father,' Theresa said as she showed him out.

'Now, don't be worrying yourself over all this,' he told her. 'God's ways are strange, but he's got the child under his care and I'm certain it will all work out in the end.'

He shook her hand heartily and turned to give her a cheery wave from the gate.

Orla was furiously resentful of all this interference in her life. Partly to show that she wouldn't be ordered about and partly because it had now become an unbreakable habit, she redoubled her efforts at dieting until she was barely taking in enough calories to sustain a five year old.

CHAPTER 2

The noise coming from room twenty-two was terrific, but the moment that Peter McGuire, Deputy Head of St. Wilfred's Comprehensive, stuck his head round the door, it ceased abruptly. He went in and gazed around, frowing a little as pupils sat down, retrieved books and pens from the floor and generally tried to appear studious.

'What's going on here?' he demanded. 'What lesson should you be having?'

It's French, Sir, with Mrs. Saunders,' said Daniel Trotter. 'She ran out in the middle of the lesson.'

His frown deepened. This did not sound at all like Liz.

'Any idea why?' The class looked blank, until Frances Soames raised a timid hand.

'Well?'

'I think she was upset, Sir,' she volunteered. 'She just suddenly rushed out. We were watching a French film.' She indicated the large television screen on the wall, which now showed only a flickering blank image. Peter strode over to it and flicked it off.

'Right, well, you can all get out some paper...' He walked to the whiteboard at the front of the class and wrote in large letters: *Vouloir, Devoir, Savoir.* 'I want five sentences from every one of you, a minimum of ten words, using each one of these verbs. And if I hear another sound coming from this room there'll be trouble. Is that clear?'

There was a murmured assent from the reluctant class, but his authority was too well established to be questioned and they set to work. Satisfied that there would be no more disturbance, he left them to it and set off in search of Liz.

She was not in the staffroom, and he was puzzled. It was most out of character for her to leave a class like that, and he knew that something untoward must have happened.

At the top of the stairs, he paused and looked out across to the staff car park, and he could just discern a figure, sitting in a pale blue Fiat.

He was outside a minute later.

Her head was slumped forward and her hands covering her eyes. He rapped on the window and she jerked her head up. She was crying.

'Liz, open the window,' he said, and she reached across and the window slid down a fraction.

'Peter, I know what you're going to say. I shouldn't have left them alone, but it's not the right time just now. Just leave me, will you?'

He strode around to the passenger side, jerked the door open and sat beside her. 'I'm not leaving you in this state,' he said firmly. 'And forget about the class, I've set them some work.' His face was screwed up with concern.

She looked at him; the kindly face with its slightly grizzled beard, and bushy eyebrows. He was easy to talk to, as he was with all the members of staff if they had a problem. But this was nothing to do with school.

'Is it something I can help with?' he asked, but she shook her head.

'No. Not really,' she said in a low voice. 'It's something I have to work out myself.'

She stopped and fumbled in her handbag for a tissue. 'It was that stupid bloody film,' she said. 'God knows why I chose that one. I should have known.'

He waited for her to go on.

'There was a scene; a man hit his wife, and...it brought it all back. I just couldn't stay and watch it.'

He was still puzzled, but his eyes opened wide as she flung her handbag onto the floor and started to unbutton her blouse.

'No, it's not what you think,' she said wryly, and she lifted her blouse.

He drew a sharp breath as his eyes fell on the purple, swollen bruise on her stomach.

'Bloody hell, Liz. What's happened?'

Then he said slowly, 'Don't tell me Douglas did that.'

Her fingers were shaking as she rebuttoned her blouse, and she said, 'That was four o'clock this morning. He'd been up drinking half the night and he objected when I got up to go to the toilet. Said I was disturbing him.'

'Has he ever done this before?'

She laughed, a bitter sound that was almost a cry. 'He's been doing it for years. Last night was just the latest.'

'For God's sake, Liz, why didn't you say something? I had no idea. Why do you stay with him?'

She sounded very weary. 'I don't know,' she said in response to his last question. 'But I am going to leave him. I've given him chance after chance. He says he'll change. He's always so desperately sorry afterwards, but he's gone too far this time. I want a divorce.'

Peter was staggered. He would never have suspected that the outwardly confident, capable and calm Liz Saunders would have had marital problems on the scale that she was now revealing. Hesitantly, he leaned towards her and took her hand.

'Do you want to tell me a bit more about it?'

She smiled wanly. 'Hadn't I better be getting back to my class?'

He shrugged. 'They'll be fine. But I didn't mean that. What I mean is, perhaps you can tell me more about it later on? Tonight, perhaps, if you're free?'

She was decisive now, and sounding much more like herself. 'No, not tonight. I'll have to stay at home. He'll be in one of his penitant moods, and I've got to tell him it's over.'

She smiled at him. 'But thanks, Peter,' she said. 'You're good to be supportive. I only wish Douglas could be...'

He interrupted her. 'If not tonight, what about tomorrow?'

'If you like,' she agreed.

'Brilliant. Why don't you come over to my house? I'm not a great cook but I can cobble something together for us. That is, if you can get away?'

She searched in her bag and brought out a small mirror. 'God, I look a sight,' she said ruefully. She brought out a powder compact and dabbed at her face before she looked at him.

'I'll be glad to get away. I'll tell him I've got a meeting.'

'Lovely. I'll dust off the recipe books.'

She powdered her face and reapplied a little lipstick, and they walked back into school together.

Peter was, in fact, exaggerating when he spoke deprecatingly of his culinary skills, and the following evening, after they had both enjoyed his main course of beef stroganoff and raspberry tart, he asked the question which had been uppermost in his mind since yesterday.

'Tell me, Liz, why have you stayed with him for so long?'

She crossed her legs, thinking hard. She was still not sure how much to reveal, but suddenly she made up her mind. He had a right to know, after being so kind to her.

'I don't know,' she said finally. 'In the beginning, when it all started, I stayed for Martin's sake. Douglas is his father, after all. I didn't want him to grow up as a child from a broken home, but then it got worse, and I did leave him for a while and I took Martin with me. He was about nine then. We stayed in a refuge for battered wives, but he found out where I was and he kept ringing me. Saying how sorry he was, begging me to come home. He really did sound as if he meant to start over again, and I was idiotic enough to believe him, so I went back.'

'But now that Martin's left home – he's at college now, isn't he?'

'He's up at Newcastle, studying medicine of all things.'

'So, you've no real reason for staying in an abusive relationship, have you?'

She sighed. 'No, I suppose not. It just got to be a habit. I was forever thinking that one day I'd leave, but the time never seemed to be right.'

That was the beginning of a relationship which deepened over the next two years. As her divorce proceeded Liz found herself leaning more and more on the older man for his quiet sympathy and later on, for his practical help. He accompanied her to the solicitors, and was with her when she finally received her decree absolute.

'Quiet, you lot!' Peter strode down the corridor to room twenty-eight and his voice boomed over the chatter of the line of teenagers. 'Right, in you go.'

He waited for Alan Booth who was the last to slide into his seat, before he sat down at the staff desk.

'Nicola, are you with us?' Nicola Sayer swung round in her seat to face him, looking astonished. 'Yes, sir.'

'Good, because I need everyone's full attention, and that includes yours.' He ignored the pained look on her face and continued. 'Now, you've all had the programme of events for the trip, and don't forget, deposits must be in by this Friday at the latest. No deposit, no trip. Understood?'

He smiled faintly at the chorus of 'Yes, Sir,' flicking his hands through hair that was thinning a little on top and showing the first betraying touches of grey.

'We'll go through the main points again. You know where Carcassonne is? Alex?'

'South of France, Sir.'

'Be more specific. The south of France covers a vast area. Where exactly is it? Gillian?'

'To the east Sir, in Languedoc-Roussillon.'

'Good. Now, somebody tell me what Carcassonne is famous for.' He pointed a finger into the welter of raised hands. 'Ben?'

'The Cathars, Sir.'

'And they were? Ruth?'

'A religious sect, Sir.'

'That's a start. Can you tell us a bit more?'

Ruth hesitated. Peter waited patiently, knowing quite well that she was nervous, but one of his most capable students.

She consulted the notes on her desk and then looked up and said, 'They date from the eleventh century, and they didn't use church buildings. They refused to eat meat and they believed that men and women were equal.'

'That's a good start, Ruth. Anyone else? Yes, Pauline?'

A tall, dark haired girl said, 'There were wars, Sir, starting about 1200, and thousands of people were murdered.'

'They were indeed. Any idea why?'

But the class had reached the limit of their knowledge, and so Peter perched himself comfortably on the edge of a desk at the front of the class, and continued:

'Basically, the Catholic Church was opposed to the Cathars. The Catholics considered that the natural order of things was the feudal system...'

Here he broke off to walk to the whiteboard and he wrote 'Feudal System' in large letters, before he faced them again, saying, 'The Cathars also refused to pay tithes to the Catholic Church...'

He wrote 'tithes' on the board before saying, 'That's a very basic account, but before we go to France I want you all to find out as much as you can about the Cathar religion. We'll be visiting two castles, the *Chateau de Montsegur* and the *Chateau de Lastours*, so you need to collect as much information about them as you can. And if you're not sure about tithes or the feudal system, you need to familiarize yourselves with both those terms. Now, for the rest of the lesson we'll go over some vocabulary that you'll find useful when you get to France. And please remember, if you haven't given your deposit in by Friday you won't be going. You can give it to me or to Mrs. Saunders. Neil Brooks, if I hear that stupid noise again, you'll go straight outside.'

'Is she coming, Sir?' His face showed both apprehension and disgust.

'You don't think I'm taking twenty students to France on my own, do you? Of course Mrs. Saunders is coming.'

'I'm not going in her group, then.'

Peter's eyes narrowed just a little and he frowned. His class, who knew him very well, correctly interpreted the change in his facial features as a warning and the rest of the lesson was quiet and orderly.

He took no further notice until the end of the session, when the group had jotted down the dates of the Cathar invasions, the key figures and made a list of vocabulary that would help them during their visit.

As they were filing out, he beckoned to Neil.

'A few words with you, please.'

His mates grinned at him, recognizing the formula for what it portended. Neil waited by the staff desk until the door closed.

'So, what was all that about? Not a very polite way to talk about a member of staff, was it?'

'Sir, she hates me!' His voice was high and protesting and he looked at Peter with wide eyes.

'Oh, come on, I very much doubt it. What makes you think that?'

'But she does, Sir. She gave me a D for my last essay, and there was nothing wrong with it, Sir, I swear. My mum checked it.'

'Checked it? Doesn't your mother teach French over in Normanton? Wrote it, perhaps?'

He had the grace to blush faintly. 'Well, she helped me a bit, sir, but I know it was right.'

'So why do you think Mrs. Saunders gave it a D? She must have had a reason.'

He drooped his head and looked at Peter from under raised eyelashes.

'Said she couldn't read it, Sir.'

Peter nodded. 'Ah, now we're getting somewhere. Go and fetch me your file.'

When Neil brought it and handed it over, he leafed through the crumpled pages with the mounting exasperation showing in his face. Finally, he lifted his eyes to Neil and said,

'There's nothing wrong with my eyesight as far as I know, but I can't read most of this. If this is an example of what you gave Mrs. Saunders then she was quite within her rights to mark you down.'

His voice betrayed nothing whatsoever of his inward amusement.

He brought his gaze back to Neil now, as he said, 'A piece of advice. If you want Mrs. Saunders to mark your work as you think you deserve, then you'd better improve on your presentation. For a start, I suggest that you type everything up in future.'

'Aw, Sir, I can't. It takes ages, and anyway, my computer won't do accents.'

'All computers have accents,' he said firmly. 'You'll find them under 'special characters'. How do you think I produce worksheets for my classes?'

There was a reluctant half smile of acceptance, as he said, 'OK, I'll try, Sir. Can I go now?'

'Alright, off you go. But think about what I've just told you. You're a bright lad, you know, and I don't want to see you with a poor mark at the end of term just because you can't be bothered making a bit of effort.'

Neil closed the door behind him, and Peter sighed as he sat down at his desk to go through the list of final preparations for the trip to Carcassonne. He made a mental note to make sure that Neil was placed in his own group instead of Liz's.

Neil left the room without having the slightest idea that Mr. McGuire and Mrs. Saunders had been lovers for the past two years. Nearly every member of the staff was aware of their relationship, but as far as they knew, none of the pupils. Neither of them ever betrayed it by an incautious word or glance, and on the rare occasions when it was necessary to refer to each other, their manner was totally professional.

Peter was quite certain of his love for Liz, but so far, neither of them had discussed any long term plans. He was fully aware that she needed time to adjust to her new life without Douglas, and so he had kept his deeper feelings to himself.

Liz had a busy life. Her weekends were taken up with marking, preparing lessons, shopping and cleaning her neat terraced house, but today she had to find time to send a cheque off to Martin.

She sat at the desk she had set up under the stairs and pulled her laptop towards her. She tapped in her bank codes and after noting that she was well within the monthly spending limit she allowed herself, she opened her handbag and took out her cheque book.

She had stopped buying him birthday presents as soon as he had started medical school, but she always managed a cheque. He was forever in need of equipment and textbooks, and fifty pounds would be useful. At least he only had one more year before his finals, and then he would be earning. He was a smart boy and she had no doubt at all that he would graduate. His photograph stood in a small silver frame on the pine desk, and she smiled again at the handsome face, the shock of blonde hair falling over his forehead and the impish grin on his face.

Since her divorce, he spent alternate holidays with his father and herself, and they always managed to get away somewhere, even if it was just a ramble in the Dales or a short break in a B&B at the coast.

The cheque would need to go off today. Though well into April, the day was chilly and she zipped up her jacket and changed into her ankle boots before she set off.

As she covered the quarter mile to the Post Office, she wondered how he was getting along with Douglas's wife Phoebe. He had already told her that his father's alcohol abuse and its subsequent consequences were a thing of the past, as Phoebe apparently didn't allow any drink in the house.

This was a revelation to her. Without ever having met Phoebe, she had a grudging admiration for any woman who could have brought about such a turnaround in Douglas's habits. She wondered if she could ever have been strong enough to do it. Then she inwardly laughed at the idea. One of the punches that Douglas had landed in her stomach was the result of her attempt to suggest that he cut down. But, she recalled, she had been stupid. Stupid to suggest such a thing when his temper was already fuelled by the three whiskies he had drunk.

An hour later the cheque was posted and she was back at home, consulting a list she had made the previous evening, and rapidly packing her small suitcase for the school trip to Carcassonne.

She usually enjoyed all the school trips abroad, but this one was clouded by the knowledge that it would be the last time she and Peter would be away together. He was taking early retirement at fifty-five. She had thought about it for months, hardly daring to examine her feelings. The thought of Peter no longer being in her life not only depressed her but gave her an actual physical ache in her chest whenever she let herself think about it.

He had never married although there were occasional hints of past relationships. She didn't probe and he never elaborated. They lived for the moment, each of them revelling in the time they spent together and each of them, secretly and separately dreading the moment when it would end.

The trip went well, with only one or two anxious moments, such as Lynne Oliver managing to get lost in Minerve, so that the coach was held up for half an hour before they found her in a book shop, immersed in scanning the titles.

Peter had to intervene in a tussle between Kevin Delaney and Simon Monks over who would partner Christine Jones on their trip to Lastours, but once that was settled and Christine herself made the final decision to go with Simon, things went smoothly.

The pupils were lodged with host families, and Peter and Liz boarded with their counterpart Monsieur Georges Libault at the Lycée Saviot. His home was an ancient *Maison de Maitre* with double doors of oak leading into immense rooms, all of which were furnished with massive pieces of furniture dating from the nineteenth century. The dingy wallpaper too, Liz noted with slight disapproval, looked as though it dated from roughly the same period.

Until now they had spent the evenings with Georges and his wife Clothilde, appreciating her fine cooking and finishing the evening chatting. Georges produced a superb bottle of vintage wine which Peter shared and Liz refused politely. Mostly they compared their respective jobs and the demands made on them, each party being fully convinced that their own classes and working conditions were far worse than those of the other.

But tonight was their last evening and Monsieur Libault had to leave them, politely regretting his imminent departure and wishing them a safe journey back to England in the morning. Reluctant to impose themselves on his wife, they strolled outside to the immense garden that stretched away to a patch of woodland.

They walked silently, but each of their minds was filled with a tumult of unspoken words.

At the edge of the woods they emerged into the fading sunlight to find a patch of grassland interspersed with slabs of grey rock. Below them, a shallow stream sparkled as it rushed over glistening rocks before disappearing round a bend and out of sight.

'I feel like Steinbeck's George and Lenny,' Peter remarked as he sank down to rest his back against a smooth boulder.

He removed his sun hat and fanned his face, grateful for the waft of cooling air on his skin. 'This must be something like the brush they came upon when they were looking for the ranch.'

She laughed, instantly responsive. 'It can't have been very different,' she agreed. 'I'm sure it's every bit as hot and there's the stream.' She paused, and then said in a slightly horrified voice, 'I just hope that doesn't make me Curly's wife.'

'Liz, I love you so much. Will you marry me? Liz, would you be my wife?'

There was no reply and she continued to stare down at the trickling brook, but this was not surprising since he had only spoken the words in his head. *Go on, say it, say it! Ask her! But what if if she refused? He would feel so humiliated. Had he read more into their relationship than there actually was? Did she feel the same way? Could she possibly love him as much as he loved her?*

To her surprise, he turned to her and took her hand. His voice was very quiet.

'No, not Curly's wife,' he said slowly. 'Liz, I hardly know how to say this. I've asked you in my mind a hundred times, but I've never had the courage to actually say it. But I'm saying it now. You're nothing like Curly's wife, but I'd be very happy and very honoured if you would become mine.'

His face was creased with anxiety, which turned to a grin of pure happiness as she leaned towards him and kissed him.

'I was wondering, actually,' she said, 'when you were going to get round to asking me.'

A few months later, Peter stood up during the morning coffee break.

'If you've got a minute to spare,' he said, 'Liz and I have got something to say to you.' He beckoned to her and she stood by his side, unusually embarrassed. He took her hand and in the sudden silence, he made his announcement.

'The only person who knows of our decision so far is Mike.' He nodded towards the head teacher who gave him an encouraging nod as he continued. 'Well, the thing is, Liz and I will be getting married next month.'

There was a buzz of interest, and he waved a hand to stop the murmurs. He gazed round at the raised, questioning eyebrows, and rushed on.

'As you all know, I'm coming up to retirement very shortly. I have to decide what to do with all that time I'll save not doing any marking...'

He grinned round at the chuckles that followed, 'and so we've decided, Liz and I, that we'd both like to make a fresh start, and we'll be doing it in France, together.'

This time he was unable to stem the burst of comments.

'Peter, that's fantastic news.' Kitty Branley, geography, grasped his hand and then turned to kiss Liz. 'You're both going to be so happy, and I don't mind admitting, I'm frantically jealous of you!'

'Going to live the dream, eh?' This was Neil Acton, one of the newer members of staff in the

Maths department. 'Don't blame you. You might get some decent weather anyway.'

'Do we get free holidays?'

'What part of France?'

He laughed and shook his head at Len's request for a holiday and replied with a grin to the last question.

'Down in the South. We both like the Carcassonne area so we're going to start looking for a couple of gîtes to let out, hopefully nothing too expensive, and we'll take it from there.'

Mike stood up and raised a hand for hush that had immediate effect. Into the silence he said, 'I'm sure I can speak for everyone when I say congratulations to the pair of you.'

There was a spate of applause, and he continued, 'We all know what a valuable contribution both Liz and Peter have made to this school over the years, and we all wish you the very best of British, or should I say, French luck in your new venture.'

This time he let the applause ring out until the bell announced the end of break and there was a general shuffling of papers and collecting of books as the staff left for the rest of the morning session.

It took them eighteen months to sell their respective houses and do the thousand and one things needed for a move abroad, but finally they were able to rent a small apartment in the centre of Carcassonne on the third floor of a block overlooking the Place Carnot.

Before they embarked on what they both knew could be a daunting search for a new home, they spent a few days as tourists, looking down over the colourful, buzzing market stalls and finding their way around the grid of surrounding streets. Finally, they decided they would have to begin. Liz bought a small blue notebook and in her neat handwriting she made a list of their principal requirements. They sat by the marbled fountain with tiny cups of strong coffee and went through it.

'One letting gîte would be fine,' Peter said, 'but the ideal would be two to let and a small house for ourselves.'

'We don't want to be too far from their airport, either,' she said, taking a sip of the strong black liquid. 'Don't forget we'll need to pick Martin up when he comes for the holidays.'

'Guests too, possibly,' he said thoughtfully. 'Not everyone will want to hire a car.'

It took a lot longer than they expected. In easy, fluent French, they were able to explain exactly what they were looking for but as the days and weeks went by, the initial enthusiasm and sheer joy of being in France began to wane. There was a plethora of gîte complexes, but all of them were either way above their budget, in completely the wrong location or too small for their needs.

They spent weeks traipsing around modestly priced houses in varying states of neglect and decay, from those requiring complete modernization, to buildings that scarcely warranted the word, being little more than crumbling walls and the last dilapidated remnants of a red tiled roof. Many of them were situated in splendid rural isolation with breathtaking views, but sadly lacking in such small niceties as mains drainage, electricity and an adequate water supply.

'What about this one?' he suggested. They were in the third estate agent of the day, leafing through a folder of properties the agent assured them were all 'habitable'. 'It's within budget and there are three houses.'

'That's because all three of them need complete renovation,' she said firmly. 'And look where they are. Totally isolated. No Post Office, no restaurants, no bank. We'd have to drive miles for the shopping.'

She soon realised that they had different ideas regarding finances. Peter was ready to spend to the limit of their budget and she had trouble persuading him that this was unfeasible.

'Whatever we buy, we'll need spare cash to make improvements. We need to be realistic.'

They thanked the estate agent and left the small office. Another two weeks passed and they were no nearer finding the right property.

'We have to be patient. I know the right place is just waiting for us somewhere,' he said when they were finally in bed after yet another fruitless day of viewing.

'Pity we can't find it then,' she said. She was feeling jaded and just a little despondent at their failure. 'I'm desperate to get our furniture out of storage and start living properly again. This all feels so temporary and I want to be settled.'

He pulled her close to him. 'We're not giving up,' he said firmly, 'and we're not going to start

46

getting all depressed over it. We'll find the right place.'

'It had better be soon, then,' she said sleepily, and she flicked off the light.

After another week during which both their spirits were flagging, they turned into a narrow street in the old town and at the very end of the road they found themselves looking into the window of the *Leblanc Immobilier*.

'Bingo,' Peter breathed. 'Look at this.'

She followed his pointing finger and she smiled; a broad, happy smile that showed all her white teeth. 'Let's get in there."

Monsieur Leblanc was small, dark and dapper, with closely cropped black hair and large framed spectacles.

They were both excited when he took out the pages from his folder and passed them across the desk. This was the first complex they had seen so far that looked ideal, at least on paper.

'I can take you this afternoon,' he said. 'The houses, they are on the market since a long time, you will have a good price.'

He spoke in halting English but as he realised that these people were more than competent in his own language he switched to French.

They followed him, sweating a little as he led the way to his Citroën. He was dressed in a navy blue suit which was a little too big for him on the shoulders, and as Liz noticed, with trousers that were badly in need of pressing. Nevertheless, it gave him a businesslike air even though both Peter and Liz thought silently that he must be terribly uncomfortable in the sweltering thirty degree heat and that he would have been better dressed like themselves in shorts and shirts.

He expertly negotiated the narrow Carcassonne streets and drove out of the town and on through the countryside until finally they climbed a steep hill in the medieval village of Caunes-Minervois and he parked outside a complex of three bungalows.

Originally, he told them, the houses had been built for a family and two sets of parents, both of whom had died, so that the owners no longer needed all three and had moved into a flat nearby. They got out and followed him into the first house, as excited as two children on their first visit to the seaside.

He led them into the shabby salon. It was dingy with peeling brown paintwork and scuffed tiles. The clinging cobwebs on the walls and ceiling caused Liz to murmur, 'Shades of Miss Havisham,' but there was no comment from the estate agent.

The walls of all three bedrooms were covered in once bright poppy wallpaper which was now faded and starting to peel off. The beds had lumpy mattresses and Liz shuddered inwardly at the thought of the origin of the stains on them.

They stood in the centre of the first bedroom, staring around them until she nudged Peter, pointing upwards at the patch of damp in one corner at the top of the wall.

'That could be coming from the roof,' she said, but Monsieur Leblanc was unconcerned.

'It is perhaps one or two tiles,' he shrugged. 'It is a small matter to replace them, and my cousin is an excellent builder who will do this for you at a small price.'

He was speaking as if the sale was a foregone conclusion, but years of experience told him that although this couple might raise a few objections for form's sake, they would buy in the end. He had not yet played his trump card which was the garden, and he was sure that when he did, they would be unable to resist.

He was pleased that these people were English. He had grave doubts about his chances of selling this property to the French, who were very rarely in need of three houses on one plot. Foreigners, however, often wanted to open bed and breakfast businesses or hire out gîtes to sustain their new lifestyles, and he knew that here was the best opportunity for a sale that was likely to come his way for quite some time.

Peter was unconvinced that a couple of roof tiles would be enough to fix what appeared to be a severe case of damp, but he said nothing, as they both followed him into the bathroom.

The walls here were mouldy, with a dilapidated bath encrusted with years of grime, and the stainless steel of the taps was barely visible under a veneer of thick hardened scum.

'We can do a lot with this,' Peter said, far too cheerfully in Liz's opinion as they both leaned over to inspect the stained sink. She gingerly lifted a tattered cloth in front of it and grimaced when she revealed a mass of ancient pipework thick with dust.

'Peter, I thought we'd agreed. We don't want a renovation project. Have you seen the state of this?' She spoke in English and in a low voice so that the estate agent wouldn't hear, and jerked her head at the rusting pipes.

'It's cosmetic,' he said urgently. 'And don't forget, this is the only property we've seen so far that's within budget. If we can get it at this price, there'll see plenty left for decoration.'

'Ah, the price, it is exceptional,' the estate agent cut in. He had understood the word 'price' and now he was beaming at both of them, his instinct telling him that now was the time to show them round the land that came with the houses.

'We will look at the outside now. You will be enchanted. It is perfectly placed, and with just a little work on the houses you will have a truly magnificent property with room for all your friends to come and visit you.'

They trooped after him into the bright glare of the sunshine and Liz gazed round her.

The garden was a vast expanse of rough terrain interspersed with the remaining brown leaves of clumps of irises and fading dull purple stalks of lavender. They walked past twiggy bushes of rock roses bearing fat brown seed heads, and tangles of honeysuckle bright with red berries. A little further on was an overgrown hedge split into two by a rusting archway, and they ducked under it to find themselves in a small orchard.

'Cherry trees!' Liz exclaimed delightedly. She fingered the long oval leaves, saying, 'Peter, we could make out own jam for the guests,' and he grinned.

'You have the *abricotiers,*' Monsieur Leblanc told them, pointing them out as proudly as if he had planted them himself. 'Here, you see, you have a *figuier*, and there are many....' He was still searching for the translation when Peter put in, 'Apple trees.'

On the ground lay the brown, shrivelled remains of last year's apples, some of them thick with ants, and they spotted a scurrying lizard as he darted away at their approach.

'Now,' Monsieur Leblanc said impressively, and he waved an arm expansively, taking in the sweep of the countryside. 'Tell me, what do you think of this?'

They both stared out beyond the garden, and Liz caught her breath.

From their position high up on the hillside they gazed in wonder at the vista of neat vineyards, olive groves and dense woodland, fields of golden sunflowers and swathes of gently waving wheat. In the distance they could glimpse the faint peaks of the Pyrénées mountains showing pale grey against a cloudless blue sky.

'Peter, this is heavenly,' she breathed, and Monsieur Leblanc smiled complacently as he had a mental vision of his substantial commission cheque.

'The place, it is perfect,' he assured them. 'This village has everything. There is the abbey, you have all the shops you will need, there are restaurants, bars, a bank and a Post Office. Your friends, when they come to visit you, they will be enchanted.'

Liz turned to him. 'There's no swimming pool?'

'Ah, for this price, alas, no. But it is a small matter to have a pool. Come with me.'

He led them back out of the orchard and back under the archway to the very centre of the garden, from where all three bungalows were visible.

'This is the very place,' he said dramatically, and he spread his arms wide. 'Exactly here you will have the perfect swimming pool. It will be magnificent.'

They looked round at the scene and nodded in total agreement, both of them visualizing a crystal clear pool, surrounded by three superbly refurbished gîtes. He was right. It was the perfect spot.

Back in their sparse apartment they made the decision that would change their lives, and three months later they held the keys to the gîtes that were going to sustain them in a way of life neither of them had seriously contemplated until a few months ago.

The restoration took over their lives.

'God, and I used to think teaching was tiring,' Peter exclaimed after yet another day of wallpaper stripping.

'Think what it's all for.' Liz was encouraging. She looked round at their own lounge, furnished with pieces taken from both their houses so that if the place was still shabby, at least it was comfortable. 'In another few months the whole place will be transformed and then we can start letting.'

He gathered up an armful of soggy strips of torn wallpaper and stuffed them into a bin bag. 'I'm so glad we decided to stick to renovating the gîtes and not our own house,' he said thoughtfully. 'I don't think I could stand doing up another property at the moment.'

'And don't forget, we can't really afford to do it yet,' she reminded him. 'Once we start taking rental money we can start thinking about it, but not before.'

The key phrase, which they used over and over again, was 'once we start letting the gîtes.' When that happened everything would fall easily into place. They would finally be able to relax and enjoy their new life. They were both fired by the same vision. At the end of a long day in the sun, with guests happily enjoying their holiday, they would sit in the garden by the pool. Peter would have a glass of wine, and they would chat about the guests and discuss the bookings they had taken and the money they had banked so far. They might even be able to afford a short break themselves in low season. Italy, perhaps, or northern Spain, or a nostalgic trip back to the UK where they would visit friends and let them know, without appearing to be bragging, of course, how well their new life was going.

That was the dream. The reality at present, however, was an endless round of work, shopping and overseeing the installation of new kitchens and bathrooms. It filled every single moment they had.

Monsieur Leblanc's cousin had been to inspect the houses but the estimate he sent in made them open their eyes in horror, and finally after scanning through the *Pages Jaunes* they found a builder in Carcassonne who gave them a reasonable estimate for the construction of en-suite shower rooms for each of the six bedrooms.

'These people must think Christmas has come early,' Peter murmured as they wandered around the electrical shop for the third time that week. The vivid yellow and blue delivery vans soon became a familiar sight outside the property as washing machines, freezers and fridges, ovens and microwaves were unloaded. They were in total agreement that everything for the two letting gîtes had to be top quality, and with that in mind their savings dwindled by thousands of euros in the first two months.

'I've never spent so much money in such a short space of time in my whole life,' Liz said after she tapped in her pin code for the fourth time that afternoon.

'I could get used to this,' he smiled. 'Makes you feel like a millionaire.'

'We do need to be careful, though,' she said a little nervously. 'I know we've got savings but they won't last forever.'

'But isn't it brilliant,' he replied, 'to actually need something you've always secretly wanted to buy but didn't have a use for?'

He grinned delightedly but Liz was slightly apprehensive as they signed away yet another huge cheque for the new seven-seater people carrier that would be so handy in picking up their future guests and their luggage from the airport.

They quickly learned to coordinate their shopping with opening hours, familiarizing themselves with which shops opened after lunch at two o'clock, and which were closed until three.

They spent hours searching the web for holiday letting websites, and planning down to the last euro how much they could charge for each gîte per week.

'If we get this totally right,' Liz said excitedly one evening, 'we should easily have enough to live on until I get my pension.'

'It shouldn't be a problem,' he said easily. 'It's a balancing act really, between what we spend on advertising and the returns we get from letting. Get that right and we're laughing.'

Neither of them had any concerns. It was all going to be fantastic. They would charge a higher price in the peak booking periods of July and August, and they would be open the whole year. A total of thirty weeks booked on both gîtes would provide them with a good standard of living, and the spare money would be put into a savings account to finance their own holidays.

'That's if, of course, we get any free weeks,' Peter said. 'We can't really tell until we start letting. We might be busy the whole year round and just not get the time to go away ourselves.'

'Well, it certainly beats marking books for a living,' she said, and he was in agreement, even if there were the occasional moments when he missed the chatter and the gossip of school life.

They had their first disagreement over the swimming pool. Liz brought home a catalogue and decided that an above ground pool would be eminently suitable and would come well within their budget, but Peter had other ideas.

'If you had to choose between staying in a property with a traditional pool or one with a giant paddling pool, which one would you go for?' he challenged her.

'But they're so much cheaper,' she protested. 'Think of the money we'd save. An in-ground pool is going to be at least twenty thousand euros, and we can get an above ground one for a fraction of that.'

He was not convinced and they had what constituted a real argument over it before in the end Peter had his way and the swimming pool was now the highlight of the garden. The construction of it had swallowed another massive chunk of their budget.

It was Peter's pride and joy. He delighted in spending hours there, cleaning it, adding pH plus and pH minus granules to achieve the correct balance, and chlorine tablets until the water was sanitized, sparkling and extremely inviting.

Liz planned the garden down to the last detail, and Peter marked out the gravel walkways where she indicated, and created round and oval shaped flower beds. They planted them with hibiscus bushes and small palm trees and surrounded these with bedding plants of geraniums, petunias, white alyssum and lobelia.

It all looked idyllic, but as the weeks passed by they began to fully appreciate that the hot, dry Mediterranean climate was totally unsuited to their choice of plants.

'The geraniums have died now,' she said in disgust. She dug up a clump and flung them into the new wheelbarrow. 'If we don't water everything twice a day there'll be no garden left.'

'This lobelia won't last long either.' He heaved a full watering can over to the fading plants and soaked them. 'We can't go round the whole place with watering cans every day.'

'There's no choice,' she said shortly. 'Unless we want a garden full of dead flowers for the guests to look at.'

'We could put indigenous plants in instead,' he suggested. 'Cacti, perhaps.' He was hesitant and he put the watering can down and looked at her. 'Or why don't we put in one of those watering systems you see in people's gardens?'

'What! Are you joking? I've seen them in the catalogues, they cost a fortune.'

'So will replacing all these plants,' he said morosely. 'We have to do one or the other.'

After a major discussion they settled on a complex, wholly electronic watering system which drained their finances almost as fast as the water it sprinkled twice daily onto the plants.

The hours of hard work and all the expense would be worth it, they thought, when the guests started arriving.

Each gîte now had French windows overlooking the pool, and both were equipped with ultra modern furniture, large televisions and DVD players. A splendid houseware shop in one of the industrial zones close to Carcassonne airport provided them with classic, plain white dishes to complement the highly modern kitchens with their stainless steel appliances.

The smart new en-suite shower rooms were fully tiled with double sinks, the fluffiest of white towels and the most expensive of shiny new taps. The bedrooms had pristine white walls, comfortable beds with lightweight duvets with pale blue and white striped covers, Egyptian cotton sheets and pillowcases and high quality bedside lamps.

Both gîtes were as perfect as good taste, time, energy and money could make them. They advertised widely, choosing a mixture of holiday rental websites, printed brochures which they posted to all their friends, and at huge expense, they had their own website created.

They checked their emails regularly, eager to know who their first guests would be. At first they were just a little despondent when there was nothing positive, but increasingly, as the days passed with still no result, the disappointment set in until finally, they were frantically checking the emails every half an hour. But after four months, all the planning, the huge expense and all the work looked as if it was a complete waste of time. There was not a single booking.

CHAPTER 3

Entertainment was one of Belinda Carstairs' passions and her parties were a miracle of organization and diplomacy. Her guests were all members of the rarefied world of art; some of them painters and others owners of galleries. Belinda always knew who was having an affair with whom and the guest list was always extensively vetted to ensure that no embarrassment would be caused by the wrong people turning up together.

She hired the best caterers to provide trays of high class canapés, the alcohol was in plentiful supply and she had a gift for recalling her guests' favourite drinks so that each person would have an ample supply of whatever suited him or her.

Her spacious London flat had a magnificent view over the Thames. She had it professionally cleaned, both before and after each party, so that the cream leather sofa and chairs were immaculate and the long glass tables holding cream lilies in fluted vases sparkled. A collection of original paintings, some by renowned artists, relieved the stark whiteness of the walls.

Her hairdresser had left an hour ago and the blonde hair was carefully arranged in loose curls which framed her face and just touched the nape of her neck.

Just before the first guests arrived she sprayed her neck and wrists lightly with her own bespoke perfume which had entailed three consultations in a London perfumery. She put a wrist up to her nose and sniffed, satisfied that the scent suited her perfectly, before she wandered around checking that everything was immaculate. As she nibbled absently on a tiny smoked salmon and hollandaise tartlet, probably the only food she would allow herself that evening, she hoped that Prinny would turn up.

They had been at school together and for part of their school career in the same dormitory, and had sustained a lasting, if rather casual friendship ever since. When Prinny moved into her London flat, Belinda had offered her a part time job at her small art gallery in Knightsbridge.

She had always been ambitious and now owned not only the art gallery, but two of the most prestigious antique shops in Bayswater and Notting Hill where her clients included the wealthiest of London and European society.

In appearance and manners Prinny was perfect for the job, as Belinda knew she would be. She charmed and flattered the women clients and flirted mildly but discreetly with the older men, so that people often finished up taking home an expensive work which they had never intended to buy at all, together with a glowing memory of the enchanting lady who had sold it to them.

Prinny's baptismal name was in fact Hermione Roseanne Hammond, and her initials gave rise to the nickname 'Princess,' which in turn was shortened to Prinny. Not many people were aware of her real name, and now only her mother ever called her Hermione. At thirty-eight she was still single and Belinda saw it as her sacred duty to try to remedy this unfortunate situation. She had hesitated over the choice of men before finally, she had invited Luc de Rouget.

Belinda needn't have worried about Prinny turning up. At that moment she was on her way but she was feeling jaded. She had spent hours that morning browsing the shops in Oxford Street without finding a single thing that she could possibly wear.

After a light salad lunch, she went to Selfridges and found a black lacy dress full in the skirt and with a nipped in waist that would accentuate her petite figure perfectly. She hesitated between this one, a pale yellow sequined dress and a beautiful creation with a strapless top and a mid calf skirt in a floaty green fabric. Totally unable to make up her mind, she consulted her tiny platinum wristwatch and decided that there simply was no time to visit any other shops. She bought all three dresses on the basis that she was sure to wear them all sometime. She was only left now with the problem of which one would be the best for tonight. Finally she decided on the black lace, and once she had paid the bill which ran into four figures, she left the shop and called a taxi.

'Come and meet Luc, Prinny. I really think the boy doesn't know anyone here except for me. He's just started working at the Bayswater shop, you know, and he's absolutely invaluable. Such a genius. He only has to look at an object and he can tell you its provenance. He's got a real gift for finding antiques. We call him our French national treasure.'

'He's French?' Prinny was startled. 'But I can't speak...'

'Oh, darling, he's completely bilingual. Just the teensiest hint of an accent, you know, but it sounds divine. Such a marvellous husky voice.'

Prinny allowed herself to be gently steered towards the sofa and quite suddenly, unexpectedly, she felt her stomach give a lurch. Luc was quite simply the handsomest man she had ever seen in her life. His hair was as black as her own, and cut short into the nape of his neck. His face was finely chiselled with full, sensuous lips, a slightly uptilted nose and a small chin.

'Please, Madame, to sit down.' He rose politely and with a sweeping gesture he indicated the place on the sofa beside him. She sank back into the deep leather cushions.

'So, what part of France are you from?' she asked. Somehow, she expected him to say Paris. It was the part of France she knew the best, and this debonair, sophisticated man would surely have his roots there.

'I am from the Aude,' he said, and at her questioning, raised eyebrows, he explained further. 'It is in the South of France...'

'Oh, you mean Monte Carlo? Antibes? Cannes?'

He laughed gently. 'Ah, no. These places are far away. I am from the Languedoc-Roussillon region. The Aude is one of the departments there.'

He could see from the polite, interested but vacant smile that the name meant nothing to her, and he continued: 'It is one of the largest wine producing regions in France. It is to the west of the famous places you have mentioned.'

'Ah, I see,' said Prinny, who was very little the wiser. She steered him onto safer topics. 'And what brings you to London?'

He shrugged. 'I wished for new experiences,' he said lightly. 'Where I live, it is very beautiful, but there is so little to do. I did not wish to be like my brother, a *vigneron* for the rest of my life...'

'A what?'

'A *vigneron*,' he said patiently, as if he had answered the query many times before. 'My brother grows grapes to make into wine. But, it is a hard life. He works all the day, and sometimes during the night and I think it is not the life for me. I...I am interested in the...how do you say...the antiques, the *objets d'art*, and so I come to London and I find a job with Belinda and I am happy.'

She smiled. 'So you don't miss France? Your family?'

'A little, it is true,' he admitted. 'But, it is easy to go back from time to time. I see everyone, I have all the....glossop, you say....?'

'Gossip, actually,' she laughed. 'Glossop's a place. I'm not quite sure where, but I've heard of it.'

'Ah. You see, my English, it is not fine, but I improve.'

By the end of the evening, and after Prinny was well primed with her favourite Laphroaig whisky, the two of them were still together, with little time to spare for the other guests. Belinda stooped and kissed her approvingly as she left.

It was the beginning of a relationship that would change her life forever. The first evening that she invited him to her Portland Square flat, she was grateful for the heavenly scented small bunch of white freesias that he pressed into her hands as he kissed her, but she was intrigued by the plastic carrier bag he held in his other hand.

She peered inside. 'What on earth are all those for?' Her smile widened. 'You've brought vegetables? Darling, I do hope they're not for me.'

'I did not wish to arrive without the ingredients,' he said easily, as if it was the most natural thing in the world to arrive on a date with a bag of fresh vegetables.

She was bewildered. 'Ingredients for what?'

'But...*naturellement*, for the soup. I thought you would wish it, if we spend the evening together.'

'Making soup was not quite what I had in mind,' she murmured, and she took his hand and pulled him through the hallway and opened a door.

The kitchen was bright with stainless steel appliances and glowed softly with back lit lighting from the glass cupboards. Shiny dark blue work surfaces held nothing more than a juicer and a coffee maker.

'Now, tell me,' and she tilted her head and smiled up at him. 'Does this look like the kind of place I spend a lot of time in? This room and I are barely acquainted, darling.'

She took the bag from him and emptied it onto the sink draining board. 'And this is?'

'A swede,' he informed her, and his deep throated, infectious laugh filled the room. He picked up a golden skinned onion. 'And this is...'

'Oh, darling, I know an onion when I see one, but honestly Luc, I wouldn't even begin to know what to do with it. All I know is that they make you cry, and I'm afraid I don't want to have to redo my eye makeup tonight.'

She put the swede and the onion back into the bag, and then said, 'I rather thought we might go to Claridges. We'll get a far better meal than if I tried to make soup.'

'If that is what you would prefer,' he said. He was a little puzzled. At home, he was sure that any girl would have loved the present he had bought. But, he shrugged inwardly, these English women were different in so many ways. It was hard to understand them.

After a few short weeks, she was totally besotted with Luc. She had never known that it was possible to have such intense feelings for another human being. She thought about him every waking moment. The mild flirtations with the gallery clients became a thing of the past. Somehow it seemed like a betrayal to even feign an interest in any other man.

It was easy to persuade him to give up his tiny flat in Southwark and move in with her. She would lie awake and look at him, his chest gently heaving and falling as he slept, and she would gently stroke his black hair.

She loved him more with every single day they were together. He was gentle, sometimes ironic and had a mischievous sense of humour. She became a frequent visitor to the Bayswater antique shop, and during his lunch hour, which often stretched illicitly well into the afternoon, they would wander hand in hand through Hyde Park. On wet days they would shop together and they never returned without several bags full of designer shirts and trousers for Luc and dresses, shoes or tops for herself. She even accompanied him when he wished to visit the museums and he astonished her with his knowledge of English antiques.

Everything in her life took on a glow that she had never experienced, and the days passed in a haze of pure joy.

She loved their breakfasts together, when she served him with freshly baked croissants from the local bakery and a top quality plum preserve. On other days they ate oak smoked kippers or honey roasted ham, and finished with coffee which she now learned to make herself in her so far unused shiny coffee machine.

He was the best thing in her life, and with every day that passed, she became more convinced that she wanted to spend the rest of her life with him. And yet, she felt a gnawing fear. She was thirty-eight and Luc only twenty-five. She began to panic that he would he find someone younger and leave her. Her other anxiety was what her parents would make of him, and in particular, her mother. She decided that they would have to make the journey to her parents' Surrey home and that it would have to be soon.

He was very enthusiastic when she mentioned it. 'It is normal to wish to meet the parents. In France this is done quickly. I will wish to present you to my mother also. But for this we must wait a little, until I go home again.'

She looked at him, quickly and sharply. 'But London's your home now,' she said. The anxiety showed on her face. She was never quite certain that Luc considered London to be his permanent residence and she had an unspoken fear that one day, he might decide to go back to France.

He took her in his arms and kissed her. 'Wherever you are, this is my home,' he said lightly. She was not convinced, and tried to dismiss her fears. She thought instead about her mother's probably reaction to him, but that train of thought gave her no more satisfaction. She sighed deeply.

As the taxi sped through the rural countryside Luc began to relax and enjoy the scenery. He had never travelled extensively in England and his innate artistic temperament was stirred by the tranquil picturesque villages, expansive sweeps of meadow and lush farmlands.

His enjoyment was short lived and his stomach tightened with apprehension as they approached the house.

They drove through massive wrought iron gates and on through a sweeping driveway bordered by mature rhododendrons. Every time they passed a small, honey coloured cottage he expected the car to stop, but they drove on until finally they pulled up outside the most magnificent house he had ever seen. Not even the large properties he had entered in his search for antiques bore any comparison to this one. It was a Georgian mansion, solid and imposing with three storeys of symmetrically placed casement windows and a curved flight of stone steps leading to a surrounding balustrade and an elegant entrance framed by fluted columns. He caught a brief glimpse of a distant lake, and gardens laid out in formal rectangles and squares, bright with summer bedding plants and bordered by neat low boxwood hedges separated by wide gravel walkways.

He thought the man who answered Prinny's knock looked too young to be her father. This must be the brother Rupert she had mentioned. He was dressed quite informally in dark grey chinos and a white shirt.

No introductions were made, however, and he was a little bewildered when the man took their coats and Prinny merely said, 'Thank you, Hawkins,' before she led him through a square marbled hallway and opened the door into the longest salon he had ever seen.

Mrs. Hammond stood up to greet them. He saw that she was small and dark haired like her daughter, and dressed in a beautifully fitted deep purple dress with low heeled court shoes of exactly the same colour. At her throat was a three stranded necklace of pearls which he strongly suspected were not fakes. She leaned forward to shake his hand and inclined her head graciously.

'Do, please sit down, Mr.… er…Monsieur…'

'It's Luc, Mummy,' Prinny put in a little impatiently. She already knew the mood her mother was in, and as she had feared, the conversation was awkward right from the start.

'And so, Herminone tells me you live in France?' He was confused.

'Luc calls me Prinny, Mummy.'

'Oh, really?' The question was imperious, as if Luc had been caught out in over familiarity with his betters, and Prinny gritted her teeth.

'Like everyone does, except you, Mummy,' she reminded her, hoping that her voice did not betray her irritation.

'I live in London at the moment…'

'But you weren't born in London, surely?' She spoke slowly, with a bright encouraging smile as if addressing a very young child.

'I was born in the South of France.' Luc was regaining some of his confidence. He had dealt with supercilious antique buyers for months now, and this woman with her patronizing air was not going to defeat him. 'Near to the famous city of Carcassonne. It is one of the most beautiful regions of my country. We are between the mountains and the Mediterranean. Perhaps you have heard of it?'

She turned to her daughter, the crease between her eyes and slightly lifted eyebrows giving her the puzzled air of one seeking obscure information.

'Wasn't that the place little Mrs. Foster went to last year? Some kind of jaunt organized by her church? I seem to remember she was frightfully excited about it, wasn't she, dear? I must ask her when she starts serving.'

'Heather!' The short word from Prinny's father caused her mother's eyebrows to rise slightly, but it had the effect of curbing her slimly veiled hostility.

'Perhaps it was, Mummy.' She sighed. This was even worse than she had anticipated.

He managed not to gasp when they all went through to the dining room. He had never seen a dining table as long, as highly polished or as weighed down by silver and crystal. A series of matching porcelain vases held yellow and white rosebuds, gypsophila and pale green ferns. Gilt sofas upholstered in pale turquoise were placed between high French windows which were framed by heavy drapes.To his intense astonishment, he recognized a tulipwood and rosewood cabinet by Jean-Francois Oeben, and it was at that moment that his heart sank as he fully comprehended how far he was from Prinny's social background.

The starter course of ham and asparagus tartlets was superb. Luc bit into his second and brushed a couple of crumbs off his lips.

Mrs. Hammond leaned across to him, her voice icily polite. 'These tarts are so messy, aren't they, my dear? Would you like a tissue, or perhaps you might use your napkin?'

Prinny saw her father's lips tighten. He hated it when Heather was in this mood, but he said nothing. Much better to keep the peace, he thought wearily. But Prinny had reached the end of her patience.

'Mummy, I'll take the plates back,' she said. 'Could you give me a hand?'

'But darling. Mrs. Foster will be in...'

'I'd rather do it myself,' she said shortly. She balanced her own and her father's plate, and firmly passed Luc's to her mother, who pushed back her chair and rose to her feet with a deep sigh.

Mrs. Foster was in the kitchen, loading a silver tray with veal cutlets and porcelain tureens of vegetables. She looked up, surprised, when Prinny shot the plates into the sink with a resounding thud that all but cracked them.

'For goodness sake, Hermione, whatever is wrong?' Her mother was alarmed. Prinny jerked her head in Mrs. Foster's direction, who nodded imperceptibly and scuttled off to wait until she could have her kitchen back again. She wondered what had happened, but she liked working for the Hammonds, and respecting their privacy was unfortunately one of the requirements of the job.

Prinny's hands went to her hips and she faced her mother squarely. 'You know what it is,' she started furiously. 'You're being impossibly rude to Luc.'

Her mother's face was slightly flushed. The words had gone home, but she defended herself vigorously.

'I'm not being rude, darling. But honestly, please tell me, you're not serious about this boy, are you?'

'He's not a boy, Mummy, and if you must know, then yes, I'm very definitely serious.'

'But darling, you must see, he's utterly unsuitable for you.' She spread her arms wide. 'I mean, who is he? Who are his family? What is he doing here?'

'He's working here,' she snapped, 'Like thousands of other French people in London.'

'Yes, well ...' The sentence trailed off, her mother's tone implying that this was a regrettable situation that had to be endured since it could not be cured. 'And what do his parents do?'

'His father's dead and his mother works for local government. He *is* aristocracy, you know. His family goes back a long way, just like ours.'

'Impoverished aristocracy. There are thousands of those all over Europe,' she sniffed...'Well, I really don't want to sound priggish, but you must admit, Hermione, when all's said and done, he is a foreigner. Daddy and I always hoped you'd find someone of our own class when you were ready to settle down.'

'No, you're not being priggish, Mummy,' she flashed furiously. 'You're being racist, if you want the right word.'

'Racist?' The voice was high and indignant. 'Now you're being ridiculous, darling. No-one could possibly accuse me of racism.'

'What else would you call it, then? You're objecting to Luc simply because he's French. What's that if it's not racist?'

'Oh, darling, you completely misunderstand me. I've got nothing against the boy....against the man,' she amended as she caught Prinny's eye. 'But surely, you must see that all he's interested in is your money. He's....'

At this last remark, Prinny exploded. 'That is totally outrageous!' she shouted. 'Luc is not in the least interested in money. He loves his job, and he love me. Loves me for who I am, not for what I've got.' She glared at her mother, and then went on, 'But that's just it, isn't it? You'd say that about anyone I went out with. Unless, of course, it happened to be a member of the royal family, and I'm sorry, Mummy, but there just aren't enough of those left around for me to marry!'

She was shaking with rage now, and her mother tried to backtrack as she realised how upset she was.

'Darling, I didn't mean that,' she said weakly. 'I don't think he's the right choice for you, that's all. Surely you must see that? And after Rupert made such a good marriage. Daddy and I were so thrilled with Lucinda...'

'Quite,' she said acidly. 'Rupert's wife is exactly what you both wanted, isn't she? Country set, jolly type, face like one of her damned horses. Well, you should be satisfied. She's given you two grandsons, hasn't she? The family name will carry on, so what does it matter if I marry where I choose? I don't see how you can possibly object. He might not be exactly what you had in mind for me, but he's my choice. And do you think you might manage to be polite to him for just one evening? You needn't worry,' she finished bitterly, 'it won't be for long and I won't be bringing him here again.'

She snatched up the prepared tray of food and took it as far as the kitchen door. When her mother opened it for her she gave her a bitter glance before taking it through to the dining room. Her mother followed her, raising her eyes to the ceiling at the outburst. When they arrived it was to find Luc chatting easily to Mr. Hammond. He rather guessed what had gone on in the kitchen and he felt rather sorry for the young man. Heather seemed to be doing her best to unnerve him.

Luc was more at ease now, and smiling as he recounted details of his family.

'My sister Marie-Claire, yes, she is married. Her husband is Guillaume...'

'Ah, the French version of William, I believe.'

'This is so. He has a shop, he is a butcher...'

Unwittingly, Prinny's eyes slid to her mother's face, which showed no change of expression, although she thought she detected a faint shudder.

'And my brother Maurice, he is older, and he has many vineyards.'

'Oh. So he works in the *fields*...?' She took a final mouthful of the superb raspberry cobbler served with Mrs. Herbert's home made ice cream, and looked across at Luc, who nodded enthusiastically while her father suppressed a groan.

Prinny was sufficiently annoyed with her mother to refuse a liqueur after their coffee and said that they really should be going.

Luc shook hands with Mr. Hammond, and returned Mrs. Hammond's limp handshake as they departed.

The minute the door closed behind them, Prinny's mother balanced her coffee cup on the edge of the sofa and looked at her husband with lips that were a thin line of annoyance. 'Well really! A Frenchman! And not a penny to bless himself with either. She seems to think he's not a fortune hunter, but she's being incredibly naive. I thought she'd know better at her age. Of course that's what he's after. And when I think of all the young men she met during the season. Men with proper backgrounds, too. Why on earth did she have to pick on a poverty stricken foreigner, for Heaven's sake?'

'Perhaps she loves him?' The suggestion came mildly and it was crushed immediately.

She flung her arms wide and the cup fell, splashing the coffee onto the carpet. She was incensed. 'Look what you've made me do now,' she snapped. 'And you're talking utter nonsense, George. She couldn't possibly. It's simply a silly infatuation and I hope it won't last much longer.'

'She isn't getting any younger, though, is she? And if she's happy with this young man... he seems personable enough to me...'

He sensed that his wife's objections to the young Frenchman were not as serious as they sounded. Like himself, she was inordinately proud of the family name and its history, and there had been several tense months of speculation and anxiety when Rupert had brought home young ladies whose background had failed the unspoken criteria of suitability. Since his marriage to Lucinda she had become far more relaxed.

Lucinda's credentials were impeccable. Educated at Roedean School, she was the second daughter of Earl Hubertson and had all the social graces expected of a young lady of her strata. She had consolidated her acceptance into the Hammond family by the birth of her two sons, the eldest diplomatically named after her father-in-law and the second, Frederick, now three years old.

All this did not prevent Mrs. Hammond from now venting her frustration over her daughter's choice of partner.

'George, you have absolutely no discernment. No real idea of what is acceptable and what isn't. I tell you, this ridiculous little affair will be over in a month and she'll find someone suitable. Give it a little more time and you'll see I'm right.'

Luc had never imagined that a simple wedding could take months of such intense planning.

Prinny and her mother had seemingly endless visits to a prestigious bridal shop in Knightsbridge, but the details were kept a huge secret.

There were several visits to a tailor in Savile Row to be fitted for his morning suit. He was quite pleased to discover that the wedding would take place in the morning. It would leave them the rest of the day to enjoy themselves quietly, he thought.

When he found out that the ceremony was scheduled for two o'clock in the afternoon he began to have doubts about the sanity of the English as a nation.

He sat at the huge dining table with Prinny and her mother to discuss the wedding breakfast, and here he thought he could make a contribution. Why not give the guests the very best croissants they could find, with pots of home made jams of different varieties? And as a special treat, maybe pain au chocolate for the children?

His enthusiasm was quenched completely when Prinny's mother regarded him despairingly from behind the spectacles she wore for reading.

She sighed deeply and said, 'They will already have *had* breakfast, Luc. This is the *wedding* breakfast.'

Now he knew they were totally insane.

The wedding day itself was one of the most confusing of his whole life. He had attended many of his friends' weddings in his own small rural community and had always fondly imagined that when he married, his own would follow the same pattern.

After the civil marriage which would take place in the Mairie, there would be a church ceremony and then the guests would spill outside into the glare of the hot sunshine and make their way, chattering and laughing, to the reception.

At a summer wedding this would invariably be outside. Everyone would gather around makeshift trestle tables, covered for the occasion with a white paper cloth. Neighbours and friends and distant relations, some of them not seen since the last wedding, would greet each other with delighted kisses and huge embraces.

Children of all ages would race around the table and tumble on the grass, dashing up to the table to snatch bites of food as they fancied. The food would be simple but well prepared. Some guests would bring their own just to help out in case of insufficiency. There would be pizzas and salads, dishes of crisps, fat ripe figs and melons cut into quarters. Raffia baskets of fresh bread would be spread at intervals, along with bottles of red wine and diluted syrup for the children.

However hot the day, the men would be dressed in dark suits, with jackets that would be removed later in the afternoon and they would mop sweat from their brows with large white handkerchiefs especially ironed by their wives for the occasion.

All the local weddings he had ever been to followed this pattern. They were joyous occasions and long remembered in a rural society that had few entertainments.

None of this could possibly have prepared him for the reality of an upper class British society wedding in the gentle English countryside, at which he was one of the most important and one of the most ill at ease of participants.

In Luc's home society, a wedding was the celebration of the union of two families brought together by the marriage of their offspring. Here, he felt, it was an extremely grudging acceptance of himself into theirs.

In France, as he had no living father, his brother Guillaume would have been a witness at the ceremony. Here in England he learned that he would need what was intriguingly called a 'best man', but his tentative suggestion that Guillaume could perform the function was summarily dismissed by his prospective mother-in-law.

'Nonsense, he would never be able to follow the ceremony,' she had snapped, and sadly, he had to agree with her.

Now, standing beside him while he waited for his bride was Prinny's brother Rupert, whom he had only met once before, very erect and smart in his morning suit and top hat.

He flashed an encouraging sideways smile at Luc. 'Chin up, old man, soon be over now.'

He was confused by Rupert referring to him as an old man, but he obediently jerked his chin a little higher as the organ music reverberated and echoed around the ancient church as Hermione Roseanne Hammond walked down the aisle to become his wife.

If the ceremony had been frightening and confusing, the reception afterwards turned out to be a nightmare.

Prinny had paid for his mother, Guillaume and Marie-Claire to come to London and there had been a long discussion over where they should stay.

'Dunstan House would be ideal,' she suggested. She was very enthusiastic. 'It's not too far away and I'm sure they'd love it.'

As soon as Luc saw the photographs of the five star luxury hotel on the Internet he shook his head sadly.

She was amazed. 'Why on earth not? It's a lovely place. I've stayed there myself lots of times.'

'It is not the right place for them,' he said slowly. 'I think they will feel...' He searched his vocabulary for a word meaning 'overawed', and finally he said, 'They will not feel good in their own skins.'

She was used to his lapses into odd phraseology and she understood what he meant. Finally they found a convenient one star bed and breakfast and made the reservation.

His brother Maurice had not even replied to the invitation. His internal reasoning was the fact that it was impossible to leave the vines at that time of year. They needed spraying. In reality, his decision was prompted by sheer terror. He would have to take an aeroplane, he understood, and the mere thought of that was enough to set him shivering.

Then of course it was a foreign wedding and he would not understand a single word, which was too daunting to even contemplate.

Amongst his hectares of vines, totally alone except for the rabbits and the birds, he was completely at ease and he felt secure, but in England, he knew for a certainty that he would be wandering around like a lost soul.

And now, as the reception was well under way, Luc was sure that Maurice had made the right decision. He permitted himself a tight little rueful smile as he realised that he himself was every bit as ill at ease as his brother would have been.

Guillaume now stood very close to Marie-Claire, his portly figure snugly encased in his best suit. The jacket was a shade too tight across the chest and the trousers were a little shiny and inclined to bag at the knees, but Marie-Claire had pressed it well so that he would be sure to look his best.

Marie-Claire herself was wearing her best dress, the one she had worn to her cousin Fabien's wedding last summer where it had been much admired. She had made it herself from a crisp blue cotton. It buttoned to the waist and flared out gracefully over her well padded hips, and as an afterthought, she had added two large patch pockets of a contrasting red fabric onto the short skirt. Her wide feet were planted into the shoes she wore on her rare shopping trips to Carcassonne. They were of a sturdy, serviceable dark brown leather with a nice low heel so that they were comfortable for walking.

They both gazed around them, utterly bewildered by the chatting, laughing groups on the impeccable green lawn, holding champagne flutes and seemingly having a wonderful time.

They were not ignored. Not in the least. The guests were all far too well bred to let this happen, and from time to time a figure would detach itself from a group and come towards them with a bright smile. The women were exquisitely perfumed and dressed in the most amazing creations Marie-Claire had ever seen. All of them wore fantastic hats.

Everyone who approached them, recognizing immediately who they were, started a conversation in French, some more fluently than others, but when Marie-Claire's face beamed and she replied rapidly in her heavy accent, they looked confused and started to back away, murmuring, *'Bon après-midi'* as they took a hasty but dignified retreat back towards their own party.

Prinny was magnificently dressed in a perfectly fitting billowing ivory dress of duchess satin, ruched in the bodice and decorated with pearls. Luc kept close to her while his gaze wandered around. There were far fewer children here than there would have been at a French wedding, and each one of them was exquisitely turned out; the girls all wearing dresses of white lace or of delicately embroidered pale blue or pink silk and the boys in impeccably white shirts, ties and well cut dark trousers.

Puzzlingly, none of them seemed to belong to any of the adults, but instead were being decorously entertained by young ladies dressed in flat heeled shoes and a brown uniform, all of whom seemed to know each other very well indeed and who kissed rapturously when they met. It was all very odd.

Suddenly he felt an almost overwhelming longing for the peace of the French countryside, for the small village of Caunes-Minervois where he had grown up and where he knew almost everyone and they knew him. This elegant gathering where he knew almost no-one could not have been any further removed.

Of the four de Rouget family members present, Arlette was the most composed. She was far from being completely at ease in these strange surroundings, but it was after all her own son's wedding day and she was quite determined to play the part expected of her.

Taller even than Luc and with her black hair combed into a chignon at the nape of her neck, she was elegantly dressed in a simple but well cut dress of lavender silk. She had found a hat in Narbonne with a large brim which she had trimmed herself with a band of ribbon of a slightly darker shade of lavender. She was the equal of any of them there, she told herself sternly, and with that thought she left Guillaume and Marie-Claire and set out to prove it.

Slightly fortified by her second flute of champagne, she wandered over to each group, holding out her hand and introducing herself in slow, careful French in the hope of being understood.

'*Bonjour, je suis la mère de Luc.*' And with a slightly sad shake of her head, '*Je ne parle pas anglais.*'

Having established that, firstly, she was the mother of the groom, and secondly that she didn't speak English, she forced them to cast around in their minds and dredge up long forgotten French vocabulary, and they would have a short conversation about the weather. Once she had firmly placed them at a linguistic disadvantage she smiled at them, nodded her head graciously and moved onto the next group. She ignored the audible sighs of relief that she heard as she moved away.

The day finally came to a close as the sunlight faded and guests kissed each other and made their elegant way to waiting Rolls- Royces, Mercedes and Bentleys.

It was over, and for better or for worse, he was married.

After a two week honeymoon in Venice they returned to the flat in Portland Square.

It was three days later when Luc took the phone call from Guillaume. Prinny could hear sharp exclamations and questions, but since they were all in rapid French she understood only from the tone of voice that something was wrong.

Luc had his hand clapped to his mouth when he walked into the lounge.

'What's wrong?" she asked sharply. "Is it Guillaume? Are the children alright?'

He shook his head. 'No. It is not Guillaume or the children. It is Maman. She has had a stroke.'

CHAPTER 4

'I have to tell you the truth, Mrs. O'Sullivan. There's no easy way of saying this, but I'm afraid there is a chance that Orla may not live.'

Doctor Hannigan looked at the couple seated opposite him; Declan, powerfully built with curly auburn hair and a florid face, and his wife.

He knew Theresa quite well. She was the receptionist at Doctor Costello's small village practice and he was well aware that under normal circumstances she was capable, meticulous and confident, but now her emotions were evident in the white knuckles that clutched at her black handbag, in the normally well set brown curly hair that was uncharacteristically straggling around her face and the tense body that sat on the very edge of the leather seat.

The two of them stared at him, thunderstruck by his words.

It can't be true, Theresa thought wildly. *No, please God, not Orla, not my little girl. Don't take her, dear Lord. I couldn't stand it if she goes. I can't lose her.*

Declan's face was red and angry, but Theresa was a deathly pale and the tears were flowing down the side of her nose. She pulled a paper tissue out of her handbag and wiped them away.

'What can we do for her?' she whispered. 'Is there anything at all that we can do? Please say she won't die.'

Doctor Hannigan shook his head slowly. 'We're doing everything we can for Orla,' he said. 'We're feeding her intravenously...'

'You're doing what?' Declan asked roughly. He couldn't take in what the doctor was telling them. Orla was only seventeen. She was, she had been, such a beautiful little girl. This sort of thing happened to other people, to people whose lives were chaotic, to people in films and on the television and to pop stars. It didn't happen to people like themselves who lived in a tiny village in Ireland.

'Feeding her through a tube inserted into her nose,' he explained. 'She's too weak to take anything orally...by mouth,' he added, as Declan was looking bewildered again. 'She's being nourished ever hour, and all we can do is monitor her closely and hope that her body will respond.'

'We can pray for her,' Declan said. 'That will do more for her than tubes stuck up her nose.' He shook his head in disbelief at what they were hearing. It wasn't long ago since Orla had been full of life; happy and confident and the nuns up at the convent had predicted a fine future for her.

Today, as Doctor Hannigan was giving her parents the worst news of their lives, she lay in Ward 12, known as the Little Sisters' Ward. She was barely conscious, only vaguely aware of a white globe of light above her head, abruptly blocked out by a lined face, and then of pain in her nose and throat as a tube was passed into her stomach. She gagged and retched, and then she flopped back onto the pillow, exhausted by the effort.

She tried as hard as she could to sit up but it was impossible. Even raising her arm was much too hard. She had no strength left in her wasted body to do even this simple thing.

It was at that moment when she realised that it was possible that she might die, and the tears ran silently down her sunken cheeks as she murmured, 'Mammy, I'm sorry. Oh, Daddy, I'm so very sorry.'

Her tortured mind showed pictures of Mammy silently weeping by her coffin, and Daddy unable to hide his grief, before mercifully, the grotesque, tormented images vaporized into clouds and she slept.

Declan left Theresa at the hospital. He had taken time off work but he had his shift to do. Theresa stayed all day, looking down on the pitifully thin body, praying for her and willing her to get better. She had to leave in the evening and she bent down and kissed the shrunken cheek.

Every single day she returned and sat at the side of the bed. Sometimes she prayed but mostly she watched over her daughter with an intense longing for the girl she had been before.

Declan joined her in the evenings when Mrs. Kelly was looking after Padraic, and four weeks later the doctor had some news for them.

He asked them to come into his office and Theresa's heart was thumping hard when she followed him in and sat on the brown leather chair in front of his desk.

He settled himself behind his desk and leafed through the papers in front of him before he spoke. Theresa silently willed him to get on with it, to tell them the news. She felt she would burst if he didn't speak soon, but finally he cleared his throat and looked up at them. His expression was grave and they were unprepared for the words.

'We think that Orla is past the danger point now,' he said.

'Oh, thank God, thank God!' She could have kissed him, but instead she reached across the desk and grasped his hand. 'You have no idea what that means to me, to us all,' she said. 'She's really going to get better? You're sure?'

'It isn't quite as simple as that,' he said carefully. 'The feeding programme she's been on has stabilized her, but she has a very long way to go before we can say that she is completely recovered. You can see for yourself that she's nowhere near a normal weight yet. All we've done here is to stave off the very worst, to keep her alive, but I'm afraid that we can't say that we have achieved a cure. The fact that she has put a little weight on doesn't imply a full recovery.' He looked at them to see if they understood him. They both nodded.

Theresa looked hopeful and so he continued. 'There has been a lot of research into the illness, and we think now that a part of the brain called the insula cortex may be damaged in some cases of anorexia.'

Declan was appalled. 'You mean that Orla is brain damaged? Is that what you're saying?'

The doctor shook his head. 'Not in the sense that you mean,' he said. 'There's no problem with her intelligence or her memory. The insula cortex is a highly complex structure of the brain and if it is dysfunctional it can cause some abnormality in the thinking processes that govern pain and reward, as well as in the perception of body image.'

He could see from their expressions that he was losing them, and so he stopped his explanation abruptly and put forward a suggestion.

'We won't be discharging Orla just yet,' he said. 'Even though she's out of immediate danger, she needs to stay with us until she gains a few more pounds, but when we do discharge her I feel that she would benefit from a specialist residential treatment programme. They would be able to provide her with motivation enhancement therapy and cognitive remediation, and that would be of a great help to her. There's a centre close to Dublin and I know one of the doctors there. If you are both in agreement I could contact him and see if he has a place for Orla. But of course, it is your decision.'

'We want the best for her,' Declan said gruffly. 'We'll do whatever it takes.' Then he added a little fearfully, 'Would it be very expensive, do you think?'

'Oh, no, not at all. Not if we refer her. The only expense you would incur is in visiting her, of course. It's so far from here you'd need an overnight stay in a hotel whenever you go. We do feel that a patient with anorexia needs the support of the whole family, and if Orla is admitted then it would entail you making regular visits.' He looked questioningly at the couple, who seemed more positive than they had been for a long time. 'Would you have any friends in Dublin? Anyone who could put you up for a couple of days?'

Theresa and Declan looked at each other. 'There's Maura's sister,' Theresa said doubtfully, but Declan shook his head.

'I wouldn't say we know her that well. She's not someone you could be ringing and asking could we stay with her. No, we'll find a cheap hotel and that way we'll be no bother to anyone. Even if it's not in the centre we can get a bus to this place. Where did you say it was?'

He went to a small filing cabinet and brought out a brochure which he handed to Declan.

Theresa leaned towards him and together they looked at the brochure. The front image showed a modern, white painted building set in a gently sloping lawn, with flower beds in the foreground and mature trees beyond them. The impression was of a well kept hotel rather than a clinic.

'It looks a good place all right, 'Declan said, slowly turning the pages. 'But I see they have psychiatrists there,' he said wonderingly. 'Why would she need a psychiatrist? She's not mad, she just doesn't want to eat, that's all.'

'The problems that Orla is having with food are very complex,' he explained carefully. 'It's much more complicated than her just wanting to be thin. Anorexia is a very serious illness. I'll be the first to admit that we are a long way from fully understanding the whole of it, but the centre will help her to understand why she has these issues, to get her to start thinking normally about food. The psychiatrist is just one member of the team and they'll all be working together to help her to recover.'

'It's a long way,' Theresa said, 'but if you really think it's the best for her, we'd be very grateful if you could arrange it.'

CHAPTER 5

In a small village just south of Carcassonne, Arlette's eyes moved across the room in the convalescent home in Conques-sur- Orbeil, hating its sparse clinical cleanliness. Her mind was still numbed by the catastrophic change from being an independent woman with a responsible job to suddenly being dependent on other people for the most basic of her daily functions. A stranger fed her, another stranger washed her and yet others mopped the floor, brought in clean towels, took her blood pressure and wheeled her out into the grounds because it was the proper time, whether or not she wanted to go.

Everyone was kind, she thought wearily, and the doctors and nurses were briskly efficient, but their forced brittle cheerfulness grated on her. What was there to be so happy about? Possibly they fondly imagined that it would have a brightening effect on her and lighten her long days, but in fact it had the opposite effect. If she was so bad that she required artificial lifting of her mood, then perhaps she was in an even worse state than she had thought.

If just one of them could have said, *'Yes, Arlette, you've suffered a severe stroke. This is as good as it might ever get, and it's very, very tough on you,'* then she was sure she would have appreciated the honest assessment. But then, she tried to be reasonable. Their manner was the same to just about everyone and unlike some of the patients, she at least had regular visits from her family.

Guillaume and Marie-Claire could only manage Sunday afternoons when the butcher's shop was closed. They came alone the first time, leaving seven year old Guy and nine year old Hélène with a neighbour. But she had finally managed to convey using the strangled noises that used to be her voice, that she would like to see them.

And so they had brought the children but it had not been a success.

Hélène stood by her bed and her eyes were wide with incomprehension.

'What's wrong with Mamie?'

Maire-Claire had tried to be matter-of-fact.

'Mamie's not very well just now.'

'Is that why she can't talk properly?'

'Yes, partly.'

Hélène understood. She herself had been ill, that time when she had woken up with red spots all over her tummy, but it had got better.

So she was confident now when she bounced her head at Arlette and said, 'Don't worry Mamie, you'll be better soon.'

She was rewarded with a lop-sided smile from her grandmother.

That short conversation had its effect on Arlette. Hélène's calm assumption that she would improve had filled her with a kind of grim determination. She would get better. She had to, but she knew that as long as she was in this place, recovery was unlikely. She had to be at home.

This much they understood, but they were embarrassed. Who would look after her? Guillaume was irritated when Marie-Claire was showing signs of considering how it could best be done.

'Where could she go?' he said, annoyed. 'And don't think you could take care of her on your own. I need you in the shop, it's not a job for one person. We couldn't manage with the children and my mother as well.'

He was feeling not only irritated but he had twinges of guilt. It was perfectly true that their house was not big enough. Downstairs was taken up by the shop and the storeroom behind it, and their flat upstairs had only enough bedrooms for the four of them. Still, that did not alter the fact that his mother was stuck in a convalescent home and hating it.

Maurice came more often. He called in most evenings after he had finished working in the vines, and he sat by her bed rubbing her hand. He said very little but then, he had never been the garrulous type. His bony little wife Liliane was better company, and entertained her with anecdotes of the neighbours.

Luc and his English wife never came at all, and out of all her three children, Luc was the one she most wished to see. She knew that he could not be expected to jump on a plane from London every week just to see her, but she fretted. She knew that Guillaume phoned him regularly and kept him up to date on her condition, and perhaps unfairly, she now wanted him back in France.

She knew it was wrong, but as soon as he had been born she had preferred him to Maurice and Marie-Claire.

Perhaps Maurice had sensed her preference, even though she had tried hard not to show it. He had been an aggressive child, given to tearful tantrums when he couldn't get his own way and he would lash out at whichever of Marie-Claire or Luc he could hit first. Marie-Claire often gave back as good as she received, but Luc was never as good at defending himself against his brother and she often had to step in and separate them. If she could choose which of her children she would prefer to look after her, she knew it would be Luc.

Before her stroke, she would never have dreamed of asking him to return to France. She had accepted his wish to go to the UK, knowing that objections would be futile. He was an adult, and she felt sure that his pleasant, easy charm would secure him an entry into whichever society he chose to align himself with.

And what a society he had joined. She felt that he had grown away from them. She realized that he belonged in London now with the smart set of people who had been at his wedding, but at the moment her main wish was to have him back again. With Luc there, she felt that somehow she would get the strength to overcome this catastrophe, but without him she would be lost.

She fully recognized that she was no longer the capable, well adjusted woman she had been, and despite a part of her recognizing that she was being unreasonable and selfish, there was another, the main part, that felt frustrated enough for her to ignore her pricks of conscience. She would make it as clear as she could that she wanted Luc. She needed him now and she would try everything within her power to get him back.

Prinny lay on her back in bed, waiting for Luc to emerge from the shower. He was as fastidious as she was herself, and his morning shower was never shorter than fifteen minutes. Eventually he came back into the bedroom and lay beside her. Their lovemaking at night often spilled over into a morning session, and she turned to face him.

But instead of fondling her, he said, simply and without any prelude, 'Maman does not say so, but I think she would like it if we moved to France to be with her.'

His mother was no better and she was now bedridden for most of the day. There had been a long and involved telephone conversation the night before with his brother. It was conducted in rapid French, so even if she had listened she would have been no wiser, French being one of the many subjects at school that had eluded her.

She said carefully, 'You mean, for a short break?'

She watched him closely as his handsome face turned away from her. He could not meet her eyes when he said, 'No, I mean, I think we should go and live with her. She is not recovering well from the stroke, and she wants her family to take care of her.'

She looked at him, searching for some sign that he was teasing her, that this must be one of his lighthearted jokes. She found none, and her eyes widened with surprise and horror.

'Oh, Luc, no! I couldn't possibly. I couldn't live in that little backwater. There are no shops, no restaurants, nothing. I wouldn't know anyone, and whatever would I do all day? Come to that, what would you do?'

He was serious now. 'Prinny, she is my mother and she is counting on me...'

'On me, you mean,' she said bitterly. 'If we go over there who's going to take care of her? It won't be you. You'll be out at work all day. I'll be on my own with no-one to talk to.'

'But you would know the neighbours,' he said, turning his palms upwards as if to imply that everything would be simple. 'It is not completely isolated. It is a village, there are other people there.'

'I don't know, Luc. This is too hard. I can't make up my mind about something like that in a minute. I need to think about it. And have you thought about anything practical? What about your job? You can't simply leave it.'

'There are galleries in Carcassonne, in Limoux, in Narbonne. I am sure I can find something,' he said easily.

She looked at him in astonishment. 'Luc, this is quite absurd! I can't believe you'd want to give up everything we've got here to go and live in France.'

But to Luc it was simple. In his world it was taken for granted that any female members of the family would provide aid to an ageing or ill parent, but he could see now that she was not in the least convinced that they should uproot themselves.

She sat up in bed, propping herself up on the pillow with one elbow and staring at him. She was incredulous and shocked beyond measure as she realised that he was absolutely serious.

'It's a ridiculous idea,' she said firmly. 'And if your mother needs nursing, why can't we pay for a live-in nurse? Why does it have to be us, for Heaven's sake?'

'I have asked this already to Guillaume,' he said. 'But Maman does not wish for a stranger. She will not mind so much if it is the family. And besides, I think she would like it if I were there. She only wants her family at this time, and I cannot see how I can refuse her.'

'What about the rest of them?' she asked a little desperately. 'What about your brother? Can't Maurice do anything for her?'

'It is not possible,' he said. 'He is out in the vineyards all day. He already has a hard life...' He did not add that his mother had already refused any help from Maurice. Of all her three children, he was the last one she would have appealed to for any kind of help. In fact, she strongly suspected that even his wife did not find him as appealing as she had when they first married. There had been occasions when Liliane had been to her house wearing heavy makeup that Arlette felt was used to conceal evidence of Maurice's outbursts of temper. Liliane had made no complaint to her and she had not brought up the subject with her daughter-in-law, but nevertheless, she would

98

not have been at all surprised if their marriage did not last much longer.

'And Marie-Claire?' She was determined to find at least one member of Luc's family who could take on the burden of his mother.

'She is too busy with the children, and besides, she has to serve in the shop. Guillaume needs her for most of the day when the children are at school. She could not look after Maman as well. There is only us, Prinny. Truly. Maman hates being in the convalescent home and they will not permit that she goes home unless she has someone living there to take care of her. Maurice says that is all she talks about. We need to go, Prinny. Maman needs me.'

She sat bolt upright in bed now and faced him angrily. 'What about me?' she flashed at him. 'I need you too, Luc. Don't I mean more to you than your mother?'

'You are everything to me,' he said simply, 'but this is why we both have to go.' His voice changed and he spoke softly and persuasively. 'It might not be for long. As soon as Maman is well enough we can come back....'

The word 'home' hung in the air, and with a sudden jolt, she realised that he did not, and never had, considered London to be his home. Coming to the UK had been a huge, bold experiment and clearly, he was tiring of it.

She got out of bed and wrapped a vivid Chinese silk robe around herself before she said quietly, 'I have to think about it. It's a huge decision, Luc. It would mean selling this flat, and we haven't been here very long. I like our neighbours. I get on so well with Emma and

Susannah. I'd really miss them if we left.'

'I thought we could rent the flat.'

'You have been busy planning, haven't you?' she said bitterly. 'You seem to have it all worked out already. You've made up your mind that we're going, you haven't even had the decency to talk it over properly with me and now you expect me to jump at the idea. Well, it isn't going to happen, Luc. It's simply too much to ask.'

But even as she spoke the words, she felt a gnawing fear. Deep inside herself, she acknowledged that if she refused to go, he might leave her. It would be a battle between his love for her and his longing to go back to France, and she was not at all sure that she would win the fight. She couldn't bear to think about it.

She walked to the door and before she left she turned to him, saying, 'I haven't time to talk about it now, but I warn you, Luc, we'll be staying here. Nothing on this earth would persuade me to go and live out there, so you might as well get used to it.'

They were due at one of Belinda's cocktail parties that evening. On the short drive there she mentally rehearsed what she would say to Belinda. Surely she would back her up. With a little judicious hinting from herself she might even tell Luc that the idea was completely insane and that he would be far better off staying in London. She knew that he had an enormous respect for Belinda, and she was confidently counting on her support.

It was a huge shock, then, when Belinda offered her a whisky and said, 'Prinny, darling, Luc's been telling me about his poor mother. And I think you're simply marvellous to want to go and look after her.'

She was outraged. 'Is that what he's told you? I don't believe it.'

'But why not? Prinny, darling, please don't tell me you didn't *know*. Hasn't he discussed it with you? I thought you'd both decided to go.'

She got no answer, as Prinny threw back her head and drained her whisky in one long gulp, banged the glass down on the nearest table and and strode away, leaving Belinda staring after her as she thrust her way though the crowd of guests to the kitchen where Luc was chatting.

On the way, Sally Renfrew stopped her and put a slightly unsteady arm around her shoulder.

'Prinny, it's been ages, darling. Now just tell me this isn't true, will you? Luc says you'll both be moving to France so that you can look after his mother.'

She shook off Sally's arm more brusquely than she had intended, saying, 'Nothing's definite yet. We're still thinking about it.' She tried to keep the fury out of her voice but Sally sensed the tension. She tried to appease it.

'I wish I was so self-sacrificing,' she said. 'Rather you than me, Prinny darling, but I'm sure you'll be a huge comfort to Luc's mother.' Having delivered her opinion, she smiled at her charmingly and left to search for another gin and tonic.

Luc was having an animated conversation with Melissa Darwin, whom he knew very well. She was one of Belinda's best clients.

'Prinny! Luc's just been telling me about his mother. How wonderful of you to offer to go and look after her.'

'Oh, we haven't quite decided yet,' she said firmly, and she shot a warning glance at Luc that he correctly interpreted as a furious message to keep quiet on the subject.

But it was too late. Gregory Wallis joined them and said, 'I hear you'll be leaving us to go back to France, Luc. So you won't be here for my silver wedding party. A pity, Eileen was looking forward to you both being there.'

'We might be able to make it,' Prinny said desperately before Luc had a chance to speak. 'It's only in the early planning stage yet, and we may decide to stay in the UK after all.'

Gregory looked surprised. 'Oh, I thought Luc said it was all arranged?'

She bit her lip to stop herself from blurting out that nothing was arranged, and that she was furious with Luc for even hinting that it was.

'Not quite. There's a lot to sort out, as you can imagine. I'm sure we'll be here for a while yet.'

By the end of the evening she was sick and tired of people wishing them well in their new life in France, but she was surprised how many of their friends were congratulatory, and by how much they admired her for wanting to go and take care of Arlette.

She was too well bred to make a scene in public, but the minute they were in the taxi she let fly.

'How dare you tell people we're going,' she exploded. You know we haven't decided on anything yet.'

He refused to meet her gaze and stared out of the window at the bright lights as they passed over London Bridge.

'Luc,' she said sharply. 'Will you answer me? You had absolutely no right to tell all our friends. What's everyone going to think if we decide to stay here? I'll finish up looking like a fool and people will think we don't care about your mother.'

There was no reply and she thought he was sulking. Then quite suddenly she saw his shoulders were shaking, and when he turned to her his face was wet with tears and he fumbled for a handkerchief.

'Prinny, I'm so sorry,' he said, and there was anguish in his voice. 'I thought it was the best way. I have already decided. I am going back to France.'

She was awake nearly all night, alternately tossing in bed and getting up to see if another whisky would help her to sleep. Finally she fell into a fitful doze, punctuated with nightmarish scenes of being totally alone in a hilltop village with nothing to do except look after his mother.

She knew now with a sickening certainty that he would leave her to go back to his home, and that nothing she could say or do would make the slightest difference.

She cursed herself for being such an idiot not to have recognized just how homesick he was. She should have seen the signs. Now it was too late, and with the dreadful knowledge that she might soon have to say goodbye to him, her thoughts began to undergo a slight shift.

It would be something rather wonderful, she thought, to be a help and a comfort to a sick woman. And if she did go, then naturally it would be a temporary situation.

Much as Luc had protested that his mother needed a member of the family, she felt sure that once she was in France, she would persuade her to accept a trained nurse instead of herself, and then she and Luc could look for a larger house. She would have the approbation of all her friends, with very little inconvenience to herself. After all, everyone said that the region was beautiful, and there must be *some* good shopping, surely. Perhaps she would be able to get up to Paris from time to time, and there were always regular flights back to the UK.

At the back of her mind she was well aware that she was desperately trying to conceal from herself the real reason for even contemplating moving to France. She simply could not bear the thought of living the rest of her life without him. He was every bit as determined to go to France as she had been to stay in London, and as she drifted off into a deep sleep, she realised that her decision was finally made and that wherever he decided to go, she would follow him.

The once weekly lunch with her former neighbour Emma Ward was an established part of Prinny's life, and one that she knew she would miss enormously when she moved. Even when Emma had moved from Portland Square down to Kent, they rarely missed their weekly lunch in London and two days later, Emma was waiting for her in the top floor restaurant at John Lewis in Sloane Square.

Prinny took the lift, acutely aware of her new shoes which were nipping her toes unmercifully.

'Prinny, darling, you look wonderful.' They kissed the air close to each others' cheeks; neither woman would have appreciated her face being stained by bright red lipstick. Prinny thankfully sank into her chair and kicked her shoes off under the table.

Between dainty bites of her avocado salad, she related the details of her decision.

Emma was appalled. 'But Prinny, you can't! My dear, it will be a terrible life for you. Where on earth would you shop?'

To Emma this was of prime importance and Prinny shrugged. 'I'd have to come back here, I suppose. There won't be anything over there, that's for sure.'

'Even so, we'd miss you so much. Darling, do reconsider. Surely someone else can take care of Luc's mother? Why on earth should you give up everything you love here and go and live in the back of beyond?'

She laughed, a high pitched sound that only just escaped being a cry. 'No-one could expect it, it's too much.'

'I have to consider Luc. It's his mother after all, and if we don't go then she'll be stuck in the convalescent home for ever. Luc will fret about her and I'll feel so guilty all the time.' Even to herself she sounded a little too self righteous.

Emma was adamant. 'You shouldn't let Luc make the decision,' she said firmly. 'It's your life, too, remember. It sounds to me as if he's already decided and that he's dragging you along with him. Can't you just say you won't go?'

Emma was appealing to her, Prinny knew that, and briefly, it did occur to her that if she had followed her mother's advice, she wouldn't be in this situation now.

'Actually, I think he's homesick,' she said baldly.

'Yes, I rather thought it might be something like that. And that's not all. Personally I think he's ashamed of being homesick. I mean, it's not terribly macho, is it, telling people you can't live in England because you're missing Mummy? Let's face it, Prinny, he's using his mother as an excuse to go back to France.'

She pushed her plate aside with half the salad uneaten. 'But he will go, Em, I know he will. And I couldn't bear it if he leaves me.'

A small smile on Emma's face made Prinny say, 'What's so funny?'

'I was just being thankful that his mother doesn't live in Outer Mongolia,' she grinned. 'We'd never see you again. And the shopping would be even worse than in France.'

She had to laugh but Emma sensed that tears were not far away, and she pressed her point.

'Prinny, do think about it seriously and don't make any rash decisions, please. Don't do anything you're going to regret in a few months' time.'

She sighed deeply. 'The terrible thing is, is that I've already decided to go, and I think I'm regretting it even before we get there.'

Two months later when Luc came home from work he flopped down on the sofa and she handed him his customary gin and tonic. She herself stuck to whisky. Usually she restricted herself to a single measure before their meal, but tonight she allowed herself a second and swallowed it in three gulps.

She warned him that her parents might not be keen on the idea of their leaving England. 'Daddy won't make a fuss,' she said. 'He never does, bless him. But Mummy won't like it.'

'When did your mother ever like anything?' he asked with a slight shrug. And so it proved to be the case when she decided she would really have to tell her.

Their flat was now rented to a young couple who would move in the following week and their flights were booked.

Fueled by the whisky, she dialled her parents' number and waited with increasing trepidation until her mother picked up the receiver.

'Hermione, darling. Whatever are you thinking of? Can't the old lady go into a home somewhere? Surely even the French have some kind of arrangement....'

She could almost see her mother's outraged, tight-lipped expression.

'Mummy, you've met Arlette and she isn't old as you very well know. And perhaps I'm thinking of someone else instead of myself for a change?'

'Oh, nonsense,' she said roundly. 'No-one will think you're being selfish if you decide not to go. And what am I meant to tell people when they ask about you? It wouldn't be so bad if you were going to Paris, or even one of those places on the Riviera, but no-one has even heard of this Languedoc place. What am I supposed to say to everyone?'

'Why not start by telling them all to mind their own business,' she flared. 'I'm sorry, Mummy, but we're going and that's that. Your friends will just have to get used to it and look us up on a bloody map.'

Her mother was every bit as offended as Prinny thought she would be. There was a long silence, and then her mother said, 'Well, if you've made up your mind then I don't suppose anything I say will make the slightest bit of difference. I just hope you're not expecting us to come out there and visit you in that god-forsaken place.'

'No Mummy, I'm not,' she shouted and she slammed the receiver down.

Her mother had never accepted Luc as her husband, and that was the whole crux of the matter. Had he been from a background as wealthy as her own, she was aware that even the fact that he was French might have been overlooked, but as it was, her mother simply considered him unsuitable and that was that. She would never change.

Her mind flew back to her time at school, when she had written a list of the girls she wanted to invite to her tenth birthday party.

With a slightly amused smile her mother had scanned the list and crossed out half a dozen names on the basis that they were 'unsuitable.' The criteria for suitability was never made clear to her but her mother was never in any doubt. This one was suitable, that one wasn't.

She remembered her embarrassment when Anne Thompson had asked her why she wasn't invited. Prinny had attended Anne's part only the previous month. She had mumbled something about only being allowed to invite twelve friends, but Anne had looked at her with utter scorn and contempt, and had not spoken to her since. The same happened every year when her birthday came round.

Finally, for her eighteenth party, she had put her foot down and invited anyone she liked, and her father had backed her up. Still, the memories were not pleasant, and to dispel them she turned to her favourite method of obliteration. A stiff whisky usually did the trick, and so she tried it again.

They were ready to move much sooner than she had expected. Once it was certain that they were going, Luc became more animated with each passing day. He actually infected her with some of his almost pathetic enthusiasm for going home at last, and she remained cheerful until the very morning of their flight. Only at the very last minute when they heard the taxi hooting from the street below, she walked into the bedroom and threw herself on the bed, sobbing like a child.

Emma and her daughter Susannah actually travelled down to Stansted Airport to see them off.

Prinny clung tightly to her friend. 'Ring me,' she begged tearfully. 'I'm going to miss you so much, Emma. Promise me?'

'I promise,' she said, hugging her back. 'And as soon as you're settled, let me know and we'll arrange something. We'll come and visit. Don't you worry about a thing. Everything's going to be fine and you'll love it.'

She and Susannah waved to them for as long as they could, until they were swallowed up by the crowd making their tortuous way through to the departures lounge. Then they turned to go home.

'I just have a terrible feeling about all this,' Emma said. "I'm sure she's making the biggest mistake of her life.'

CHAPTER 6

Tumultuous applause filled the small theatre. Row by row the audience rose to their feet, clapping hands above their heads until the whole auditorium rang to the sound of cheers. One or two of the more enthusiastic parents whooped and there were even a few piercing whistles.

On the stage and in the powerful glare of the footlights, Guy Elliot, Romeo, grasped the hand of his Juliet. Ecstatic, they glanced sideways at each other and grinned for a mere second before they stood very erect and strode forward in unison to take their third curtain call. The atmosphere was electric and the few seconds before the curtain descended were the most thrilling moments of Susannah Ward's whole life.

Back in the dressing room they could still hear the fading applause, and the place was buzzing with laughter and excitement as they changed out of their costumes. Susannah slipped out of her long dress and smiled at two of the juniors who were looking at her in awe. Her contemporaries crowded around her.

'Sue, you were fantastic!'

'That was brilliant, Sue.'

'You were super in the dying scene, Sue.'

Mrs. Delaney, head of drama, was suddenly amongst them, her beaming face heavily made up and smelling of a pungent perfume which wafted around Susannah when she came close and embraced her. Susannah, slightly embarrassed to be hugged by a teacher while she was still in her bra and knickers, hugged her back quickly and smiled.

'Susannah, my dear, that was one of the best performances of Juliet I have ever seen.'

She returned the smile and said, 'Thank you. I loved every minute of it. I just wish we could do it every week.'

Mrs. Delaney pushed aside a messy heap of clothing from the bench reserved for the cast and sat down heavily. She looked up and said, 'You really should think about doing this professionally you know. You were easily as good as Olivia Hussey.'

They had watched Zeffirelli's film several times whilst rehearsing their play and Susannah had based her own performance on Olivia's.

'I can't possibly have been as good as that,' she demurred politely, but secretly she treasured up the remark. *As good as Olivia Hussey. Wow!*

'I know a great performance when I see one, my dear. And I really do want to speak to you and go through some of the options. There are so many theatre schools nowadays and you will have to make the right choice. I have a free period after lunch on Tuesday, so get your form mistress to excuse you and we'll have a little chat. I really do believe you have it in you to become a splendid actress.'

Back in the staffroom, Mrs. Delaney's pronouncement that Susannah Ward was destined to become the world's next Kate

Winslet was not received with the acclaim she felt it deserved.

Mr. Stettin raised his eyes from above The Times. 'She'd also make an exceptional physicist,' he said tersely. 'I've spoken to the parents several times but I'm wasting my time. They're adamant that she'll do medicine.'

Miss Langley, newly qualified and a little ill at ease amongst the older members of staff, said rather timidly that she felt that Susannah would make an excellent historian. 'She's analytical and she has the most amazing ability to organize information and come up with factually based conclusions.'

When no-one remarked on this, she bent her head once more over the book she was correcting, wishing she had never spoken.

That had been the previous week. The euphoria was still strong but somewhat regretfully, she tried to put it out of her mind as she settled herself comfortably in the garden with her maths exercise book and flipped through it carelessly, searching for any topics she might need to revise for her A levels in June. A quick glance showed her that was nothing in the book that she did not thoroughly understand. Nor was there in any of her other textbooks. She was predicted A stars in all her subjects, and had a conditional place at Newcastle University to read medicine.

She closed the book and threw it onto the grass, uncomfortably aware that sometime soon she would need to talk to her parents. Most definitely, she did not want to study medicine.

On an impulse, she took her mobile out of her jeans pocket and called Monica.

'Sue! Well, have you told them yet?' Monica Lewis was not the only person to know about Susannah's ambition but she was her closest friend and the only one who was fully aware of just how badly her parents would react to the news. She knew that Mrs. Delaney had given Susannah a whole list of drama school websites to look at, and which one she had set her heart on.

'Not yet, but...'

'Sue, you'll have to say something soon. The A level results are due out and you'll have to confirm with Newcastle.'

'I'll tell them today.'

'You're mad, you've been saying that for weeks.' She was very impatient.

'I will, honestly.'

'Let me know how it goes, then. And good luck.'

'Thanks. Oh, and Monica, if you want any help with the physics, give me a buzz and we'll go through everything.'

'Brilliant. I might even take you up on that. Somehow I understand it better when you tell me. It's a teacher you should be, not an actress.'

With that, she hung up, and Susannah glanced up towards the top of the house to the dormer window where her mother was painting. She knew that the longer she put this off, the harder it would be, and she stuffed her phone back into her pocket.

Despite her good wishes, Monica was not at all sure that Susannah would persuade her parents to allow her to go to drama school, and her father was astounded when she related the conversation.

'I can't see Henry approving of that idea,' he said. 'What on earth is the child thinking of? And Emma will be livid.'

'You really don't like Sue, do you, Daddy?' Monica asked him. She had been aware of a slight coolness in his tone whenever her friend was mentioned, but he had never openly voiced any disapproval.

'I don't *dis*like her,' he said. 'I've always thought she was a bit on the frivolous side. Every time she's been here she's spent hours in the bathroom, and she can't seem to pass a reflective surface without stopping to admire herself. To be perfectly honest, I'm not sure what kind of a doctor she'd make even if she does go to Newcastle. She's got the intelligence, but a doctor needs to put the patients first, and I don't know if she's capable of that yet. I can quite imagine her pausing during a resuscitation to check that her nails haven't got chipped.'

'Oh, I think you're being a little harsh there,' her mother protested mildly. 'Susannah is very beautiful, but she works hard and I'm sure she would make a good doctor.'

'She never had to work that hard,' Monica put in. 'I remember Professor Griggs saying she had an almost photographic memory. She caught up with the rest of us in no time, even though she didn't come to Queens until sixth form. Not like me,' she added glumly. 'I'd love it if I were like her.'

'Well, I certainly wouldn't want you to be like her,' her father said dryly. 'And I fancy beautiful is the key word there. That's her problem. She's got the looks and the brains, and the trouble is, she doesn't quite know which of them to choose between.'

Meanwhile, Susannah was taking the stairs two at a time to her mother's studio in the attic. She was definitely nervous. She knew that it was going to be difficult but she was determined to get it over with and bring her parents round to her point of view.

She had hesitated over whether to tell her father first or her mother, and finally she had decided to tackle her mother on the correctly assumed basis that the opposition here would be more intense. Her father would cave in eventually if she persisted, but Emma was possessed of an obstinacy that matched her own.

Her mind flew back to her choice of A level subjects, which was the last time that she and her mother had seriously clashed, and her mother had won that time.

One if her many talents was drawing, but any tentative suggestions that she pursue it academically had been dismissed out of hand. What she needed were the useful subjects. Emma had been unyielding on that occasion and so she had regretfully abandoned art and textile design in favour of maths, further maths, biology, physics and chemistry. These were the serious subjects, the ones which would start her on the path towards the medical career that her parents had fondly imagined that she would take up after leaving school.

The attic space had previously been used as storage, until Emma had decided that she really needed a proper studio with good light. Now, the light streamed in from four Velux windows and she spent hours up here working on huge canvases. When Susannah entered, she was daubing bright yellow ochre into clouds. In the foreground, two people were walking hand in hand towards a villa that had a very Mediterranean look to it. The woman had sleek black hair cut short at the nape of her neck and wore a dark red trouser suit. The man wore tight jeans and had his arm around the woman's waist. In the background a range of mountains showed peaks tipped with snow.

Susannah perched herself on the edge of a high stool and looked at the canvas more closely. 'Even from the back,' she said, 'that looks a lot like Prinny and Luc.'

Emma looked up and smiled faintly. 'That's good, because that's exactly who it is. I've got far too much snow on those mountains, though.'

'It's excellent, mum.' Her mother tilted her head and regarded the canvas speculatively. 'I don't feel that I've got her figure quite correct yet. I've made her too short, I think.'

'Prinny isn't very tall,' she said. 'She's smaller than I am, anyway.'

Something in her tone of voice made Emma turn round. She laid her paintbrush on the small table beside her and she peered at Susannah's troubled face.

'Is something wrong?'

'No, nothing.'

Emma wiped her brush with a soiled rag. 'There must be something, Sue.'

She looked down at her nails and then the words came out in a rush. 'It's nothing much really. It's just that I don't want to go to Uni, that's all.'

She looked at her mother from under lowered eyelids, fearing the reaction that she had expected and which now exploded.

'That's *all*?' she repeated incredulously. 'But you always wanted to go to Newcastle. How many times have you said it's one of the best universities in the county for medicine? What else have you been working for?'

She looked up and glared at her mother. 'No, Mummy, *you* said that. I never said it. You and Daddy were forever predicting my future as a doctor. I only went along with it because I didn't want a row about it, but now it's actually time to decide, I just don't think it's for me.'

Emma sat down heavily on the stool beside her canvas, her face a study of incredulity and dismay.

'Not for you!' she repeated. 'Good Lord, Sue, why on earth not? I thought you *did* want to do medicine..you never said...'

She shrugged. 'Like I said, it wasn't worth arguing about it. I knew you wouldn't like it.'

'Of *course* I don't. Everyone expects you to be a doctor. It's a fantastic career. It's well paid, you'd be helping people. You can't suddenly change your mind like that and let everyone down.'

There was no reply. Susannha bit her lip and stared at the floor.

Emmas persisted. 'So, if you don't want to do medicine, what *do* you want?' She waited expectantly.

Susannah took a deep breath. This was not going to go down well.

'I'd rather be an actress,' she blurted, 'and really, it's a good career. There are all sorts of possibilities. Once I get established I could be on television, or there's the theatre....' She was excited now and warming to her theme when Emma cut her short.

'An actress!' She almost screamed the word. 'I don't believe I'm hearing this. You can't possibly mean you're not going to University at all. Susannah, you've done some idiotic things in your life, but this is the most ridiculous idea I've ever heard of. There is no *question* of you not doing medicine. You've worked hard, there's no reason at all why you shouldn't get your predicted grades, you've been accepted at Newcastle and that's where you'll go. You've had the best education a girl could want and you're talking about throwing it all away to start acting.'

Her painting, which had absorbed her completely until Susannah's appearance, was forgotten and she stared at her daughter with a mixture of puzzled apprehension and sheer anger.

'It's my life. I should have the right to do what I like with it.'

The sulkiness in her tone only served to infuriate Emma even more.

'Well, shouldn't I? Why do I have to do everything that you and Daddy want all the time? You never let me choose.'

'But you've already chosen. There's absolutely no reason why you shouldn't do medicine.'

She screwed the caps back onto the tubes of yellow ochre and white and flung them down onto a brightly colored saucer. 'I'm going downstairs. Your father will be home soon and we'll see what he has to say about it. I can't paint any more, anyhow. I've totally lost interest after all this.' She glared at her daughter, evidently blaming her for her temporary lack of inspiration as well as for the bombshell she had just dropped.

She slipped out of her painting smock, threw it over a chair and jerked her head towards the door. As the two of them went down to the drawing room, Emma was thinking rapidly. She knew that the ignominy of Susannah becoming an actress when she could be a doctor would be too much to bear, for both herself and for Henry. Susannah was a bright girl, possibly even brighter than her elder brother James. It would be sin it throw away all that intelligence. She suddenly had a terrible mental vision of Susannah, barely existing on benefits or touring the country staying in third rate accommodation, or even, just possibly, being sucked into the seedy world of pornography if she could find no other jobs. She had to persuade her that the idea was monstrous.

Susannah's mental images were totally different. She saw herself at the centre of a film set being admired by other members of the cast and directors, and even by the cameramen who would be so impressed by her performances that they would hardly be able to concentrate on their work. The crowning glory would be starring in a major film. And of course, she wouldn't be staying the the UK. After completing a couple of successful films here she would move to California where her stunning looks and exceptional talent would assure her immediate acceptance and parts in the current blockbuster movies. It could happen, she was sure. She hadn't expected her mother to be happy about it, but if she could persuade her father then she was quite sure that in the end she would get her own way.

Henry, at that moment, was standing on the 6.50 from London Waterloo. He was wedged between a corpulent lady laden with shopping bags and two men dressed like himself in discreetly striped suits, polished shoes and carrying briefcases. He hated this daily commute, and tried hard not to blame Emma every weekday evening when he forced his way into the heaving carriage; but then, trying hard to please Emma was fast becoming a way of life.

The morning journey was bearable, as he got up at half past five in the morning to catch the 6.15 and could be reasonably sure of having a seat, but every evening was the same terrible squash. He couldn't help thinking back to when they lived in Portland Square. The flat had been ideal, and he could be at his desk in Canary Wharf in under half an hour.

That was before Emma decided that the flat was not large enough, not grand enough, and a whole list of other inconveniences which she aired with ever increasing bitterness until he felt obliged to give in and move down to their current house just outside Leatherhead.

By definition, his career as a lawyer meant conflict. He loved the work, but when he left it to come home he wanted to leave the human bickering behind him in the office and courtroom and find peace. And so to please Emma and for the sake of a calm domestic life, they had moved. Emma had loved the farmhouse as soon as she had seen it, although the term farmhouse was misleading. Two hundred years ago, the house had actually belonged to a farmer, but successive owners had transformed it into a modern, luxurious property which bore no relation whatsoever to its original function. True, there was the massive inglenook fireplace complete with basket of logs, but the fire was never lit. Underfloor heating and concealed radiators rendered it totally obsolete, but still, Emma loved the cosy feel it lent to the drawing room and so it stayed.

When they moved in, the kitchen had been ultra modern with sleek, high gloss red units, stainless steel sink, an expensive wall mounted double oven and microwave. Henry, Susannah and James had thought it wonderful, but Emma disagreed.

'It doesn't match the rest of the house in the least,' she said firmly, and she had had the whole room stripped out and replaced with a stone flagged floor, rustic pine units and a matching dresser, a Belfast sink and a hugely expensive Aga stove in a dark green. Their existing crockery was wrong too, she decided, and she packed away the white and gold bone china plates and bought a dinner service in heavy duty ceramic decorated with hand painted pine cones. The expense had been colossal and in Henry's opinion, completely unjustified, but once again he had said very little and given her free rein to revamp and spend as she chose.

In the drawing room, the expensive brown leather chesterfield sofas from their London home had been replaced by comfortable chintz fabric ones, and she had searched for weeks to find vases that exactly matched the deep crimson and pale greens in the fabric. Now, several of these were placed around the room holding arrangements of deep red roses and white lilies. The polished oak flooring was partially hidden by a Persian carpet in subtle shades of cream and beige, and she had found elegant rosewood coffee tables and a matching wall unit in an exclusive London boutique. The walls held several of her own landscape paintings that she had completed in Provence.

Money was no problem. By anyone's standards they were very comfortably off, but Henry's parents had struggled to educate their bright son and send him to Cambridge and his innately thrifty nature baulked at the thought of waste.

The minute he entered the drawing room he sensed the tension in the air. Susannah didn't even look up and there was no greeting. Emma's expression said clearly that she was extremely annoyed about something, and Susannah's face was an image of her mother's. It was extraordinary, he thought, how similar they were in appearance. Emma was an older version of her daughter. They had the same pale blonde hair and deep blue eyes fringed by curling lashes, and at the moment, the same stubborn, exasperated expressions.

'Anything wrong?' he asked lightly. Whatever it was, he hoped it wouldn't involve another house move. He felt that he could cope with anything at the moment except that.

'You'd better tell him,' Emma said shortly.

Susannah shrugged. 'It's nothing much. It's just that I don't want to go to Uni.'

The reaction was instantaneous. 'Not go to University! Sue, what on earth do you mean? I thought that was what you wanted. What else have you been working for? Do you mean you'd prefer a different university? It's not too late, is it, if you want to go somewhere different?'

'No. I don't want to go to any of them. I've changed my mind, that's all.'

'No, that isn't all, not by any means,' Emma said. 'Tell your father what you do want to do.'

'I'd rather be an actress.' There was a short silence while Henry digested this, and she continued hopefully.

'Of course, I know I'd have a lot to learn first, I'd need to work at it. But there's the ALRA school in Wandsworth, I could go there....'

'The what?' Henry was confused.

'The ALRA,' she explained patiently. 'It's the Academy of Live and Recorded Arts. Miranda Hart went there, you know, and look how successful she is. They teach all sorts of techniques. You can learn from real professionals; they have directors giving classes, and at the end of the course you do a showcase...'

Emma cut in furiously, 'The only work you'll be doing is in medical school. I've never even heard of this acting place. I'm not going to let you throw your life away doing third rate acting jobs. Half the time you'll be out of work anyway. All actors are, it's a well known fact. And what would you do in between acting jobs? You'll have to take anything you can find, just to keep yourself, because I can tell you now, my girl, don't expect your father and I to subsidise you while you're out of work, because we won't.'

She sat bolt upright in the armchair. 'But mum, it's my life we're talking about. I should have the right to do what I like with it. Well, shouldn't I?' She looked from one to the other of her parents.

'What you do with your life doesn't just affect you, though,' Henry said. 'As your parents it affects us too. And our friends. And there's James to think about. How do you think he would feel if his patients or his colleagues found out that his sister was an actress?'

'So what if they do find out?' she cried. 'It's not a crime, is it? There's nothing shameful about acting. I'm not thinking of becoming a drug addict, for Heaven's sake. And you've seen me acting. You both said I was brilliant as Juliet. And Mrs. Delaney said so. She said I'd got the looks and the talent.'

Henry was frowning now, trying to be reasonable but knowing that his patience was likely to be sorely tested shortly. 'That was a school play,' he said finally. 'Yes, I know you were very good in the part,' he added hastily, 'but tell me, how many girls did Mrs. Delaney try for Juliet?'

'There were four of us.'

'That's my point exactly,' he said firmly. 'You were the best out of four girls. No,' he said as she opened her mouth to protest, 'I haven't finished. You must see, Sue, that as a professional actress, just supposing that you make the grade, you'll be competing against hundreds of girls. And believe me, they'll *all* be good looking and they'll *all* be talented.'

'It's not about me, though, is it?' she said bitterly. 'It's about you and mum. You want me to be a doctor so that you can show off to your friends and to people at work. Just like you boast about James. You don't care what I want. It's all about everyone else.'

'No, Sue, that's not what it's about.' Henry tried hard to keep his impatience under rein but his bushy dark eyebrows met and his face darkened as he said, 'Your mother and I have given you the best possible start in life. We've paid for good schools and you've always done very well in your studies.' He nodded towards her, and his voice rose with his next words. 'We're proud of that, you know, but we didn't spend a fortune on your education so that you could start acting. We might as well have sent you to the local comprehensive in that case.'

'That was your choice,' she countered instantly. 'Isn't it time I had a choice, too?'

'But wouldn't you rather do something useful with your life?' Henry urged her. 'As a doctor, you could be, you will be, saving people's lives. Isn't that worth aspiring to?'

'There are thousands of doctors,' she retorted. 'No-one's going to die just because I'm not one of them.'

Emma's pent up anger now showed in her voice as she said sharply, 'Don't you think you owe your father and I anything? Don't we even get the slightest bit of gratitude?'

Susannah protested, her voice raised now. 'That's all you think about! Gratitude! Why on earth should I have to be so grateful? You've only done what all parents do for their children. Suddenly it sounds as if I have to pay you back for educating me. And in any case, you're an artist. That's what you chose to do. How is it that suddenly *I'm* not allowed any choice in my own life?' She was red in the face now and furious with both of them.

'I haven't got your brains, Sue,' Emma said bitterly. 'I only wish I had. And I didn't go to the best schools in the country, either.'

Henry felt they were getting nowhere. 'Look, let's just leave this for now, shall we? Sue, calm yourself down. We'll discuss this later, but I do want you to think seriously about...'

'But I've already thought...'

'No,' he said, and it was a firm enough command to silence her. 'Later, I said. I don't want to hear any more about this right now. I don't know about you two, but I'm ready for some dinner.'

Emma got up and left, and shut the door with a force that clearly spoke of her frustration, and Henry sighed wearily. The peace and tranquility he sought at home after a long day in the office seemed very evasive indeed at the moment.

Dinner at the large farmhouse table in the kitchen was almost silent. Emma dished out the lamb casserole she had prepared earlier in the day, and it was followed by a pear and ginger tart of her own making. She was an excellent cook and from their infancy, James and Susannah's diets had formed a vital part of their upbringing. Sweets were strictly rationed, and she saw to it that they had the freshest of vegetables, wholemeal bread, plenty of fish and lots of fruit. She liked to think that this had contributed to their academic success, but now, she thought bitterly, Susannah looked like throwing the whole thing away at this crucial part of her life.

Without being asked, Susannah got up and began to fill the dishwasher. Emma ignored her, but she was thinking of ringing Prinny and asking her advice. She and Susannah had been quite close when they were neighbours in the Portland Square flats. And besides, it was a while since they had spoken and she was genuinely curious to know how the sophisticated Prinny was faring living with her husband and his mother in a tiny village in the south of France.

Leaving Susannah to finish loading the dishes, she went back to the drawing room and settled herself on one of the large chintz sofas. Henry was opposite her on a matching sofa and his head was hidden behind The Times.

'Henry, do put that paper down. We have to talk about this.'

With a sigh, he folded the paper. 'Em, don't let yourself get worked up over this. It won't happen, you know. She'll soon realise that she can't support herself on her earnings.'

She was incredulous. 'You mean you're actually going to allow her to go ahead with this. Henry, it's insane! You have to tell her she can't do it.'

'She's eighteen, Emma. She's not a child any more. I can't tell her what she must do or mustn't do any longer. We've directed her life so far, and so maybe she does have a point. Perhaps she should make her own decisions now.'

'You mean you don't care what she does? After all we've done for her and she pays us back like this. She'll finish up in some tacky digs somewhere, keeping Heaven knows what sort of company. Is that what we've paid for all these years?'

'Emma, stop it! You're getting hysterical about the whole thing. It's not going to come to that. Just calm down, will you? We need to think rationally about it and try to come to some sort of solution, but you ranting about it isn't helping.'

Emma got up. 'I'm going to ring Prinny,' she said. 'She might have something useful to say. I can see I'm not going to get any sense out of you.'

When the telephone rang in France, Prinny hesitated between answering it, or rushing into the bedroom once again to respond to Arlette's insistent call. She answered the telephone.

'Emma! How lovely to hear you. How is everyone?'

She listened intently as Emma told her about Susannah, and added, 'Prinny, I'm asking a huge favour. Would *you* speak to Sue? She won't take any notice of me or Henry, but she always looked up to you. Do you think you could persuade her not to be such a little idiot?'

'Oh, Emma, you know I'd love to help, darling. But don't overestimate my influence with Sue. She's at that age where they all think they know everything. And besides, I don't know what a single phone call would do.' She paused for a moment, and then she said, 'Do you know, I've just had the most splendid idea. Why don't you come over for a while? If I'm going to talk to Sue, it would be much better face to face, I'm sure. Do you think you could manage it? Just for a couple of weeks?'

She heard the relief in Emma's voice. 'That sounds absolutely fantastic. You have no idea how much I'd love it.' And then, doubtfully: 'But where could we stay? I thought you said Luc's mother's house was only a small one. Are there any decent hotels nearby?'

'Oh, darling, absolutely not. The nearest good hotels are in Carcassonne, and that's miles away. Or should I say kilometres, now that I'm living the French life? But I could have a word with Liz for you...'

'Who?'

'Liz and Peter McGuire. They've retired here. I believe they were both French teachers in England. I got the impression that they met at school. Liz has been married before and there's a son, I think, but he doesn't live with them. They're about ten minutes away. They run two gîtes and I'm sure they would be suitable. Every time I go over there Liz is in the throes of cleaning something. And you'll adore Peter, he's such good company. Luc and I sometimes go across there for an aperitif. That is of course, when we can get away, which isn't often nowadays.'

The faint bitterness in her tone prompted Emma to ask, 'And how is Luc's mother?'

'Not too good, I'm afraid.'

'She's in hospital again?'

'Oh, no. She's here. She's been in a convalescent home but they wouldn't discharge her until there was someone at home to look after her. She hated being away there, and I really do think she's pleased to be back, although to be quite truthful, it's very hard to know. She can't speak very well.'

'And you're looking after her on your own? Isn't anyone helping you?'

'Practically on my own. Luc gives me a hand sometimes when he comes in from work but he's usually tired and all he wants to do is flop, so I can't count on him. No, there's just little me, I'm afraid.'

There was a definite weariness in her voice, and Emma briefly contemplated the life she must be leading now. If only she had listened and taken her advice, she wouldn't be in this situation now. But even with these thoughts, Emma still felt sorry that circumstances had changed so much. Prinny belonged in London, working part time and spending money in her favourite shops.

'You poor thing! It sounds horrendous.'

'Oh, it's not too bad.' Just too late, Prinny realised that she didn't want to give Emma the impression that she was unwilling to do her duty, but honesty forced her to add, 'I must admit, though, I am getting Harrods withdrawal symptoms.'

'You must be, I'm sure. And what about our lunches in John Lewis? I do miss those.'

'Me too, darling. You wouldn't believe it, but there are no good shops here at all. I have to do most of my shopping online now. That goodness we've got a good Internet connection here, or I think I'd go totally mad.'

Emma laughed. 'Darling, I can't wait to see you again. Let me know when you've spoken to your neighbour and I'll get the flights booked.'

'I'll go as soon as Arlette is asleep,' she promised. She put the receiver down and stared at it for a long moment before heading off to the lounge again to pour herself a small whisky.

The moment she had drained her whisky she headed for the ground floor bedroom. A faint, nauseating smell when she opened the door told her that once again, she would have to change Arlette's incontinence pad, and she sighed heavily. She wished that Luc was home. Not that he would ever contemplate doing anything practical for his mother, such as washing her, changing her sheets or cutting her toenails. No, all that was Prinny's domaine, it was a woman's job. Luc would be safely in the antique shop in Carcassonne. It hadn't taken him long to find a job and he spent days out hunting around the countryside, buying antiques that were then sold on with a high mark up from the tiny shop.

She tried not to show her disgust when she approached the bed. The stench was worse here; a nauseating mixture of urine, faeces and sweat. Arlette regarded her from black eyes, and mumbled something.

'I'm sorry I'm late,' she said. 'I had to answer the phone. It was a business call.'

Arlette had heard the gist of the conversation. Business callers were not usually addressed as 'darling,' she thought wryly. But she was totally dependent on Prinny during the day, and she dreaded upsetting her to the point where Prinny might neglect her even further than she felt neglected already.

'Could you change me, please?'

She was ashamed now, and humiliated that her daughter-in-law was performing these menial tasks, doing things for her which she could no longer do for herself. Mentally, she was as alert as she always had been and this made the effects of her stroke even harder to bear. She knew what she wanted to say, but the words refused to formulate themselves. Even to her own ear, the garbled phrases sounded ludicrous and she wasn't at all surprised that Prinny became impatient at her attempts to communicate. They had told her, both in hospital and in the clinic, that in time she may regain some of the movement in her facial muscles, but for now she was left with the most severe difficulties.

The paralysis had affected her left side and her mouth was grotesquely twisted, making mealtimes an agonising embarrassment. She knew that when she started eating she was going to dribble her food, and no matter how hard she tried, how much she willed herself to eat normally, the muscles would not respond and the food slipped out. Each time that Prinny entered with a laden tray her anxiety levels shot up, knowing that here was just another ordeal. Drinking was a messy procedure too. Prinny would hold a cup to her lips and she would try her hardest to suck up the moisture, but inevitably half of it dribbled down her chin and onto the large square towel around her neck.

Even worse than the eating was the incontinence. Recently she had developed a hacking cough and this simply made things much worse, as each spasm would trigger a bowel movement which she was totally unable to control.

'I am sorry, Prinny,' she said, when Prinny rolled her over and began to clean her up. She was apologizing for putting her daughter-in-law in this position, for bringing her over to France when she knew that she would rather be in

London, and for being so incapable that it was necessary.

She was humbly grateful to be here instead of in the convalescent home, but at the same time, her fiercely independent nature made it an agony for her to have to submit to being cared for. Wearing incontinence pads was the final humiliation and in her darkest moments she prayed that it would all be over soon.

Liz was wondering, as the sun beat down on her, if they had made the most dreadful mistake of their lives. The Taxe Foncière bill had arrived that morning. At first she had stuffed it under a pile of papers on the living room table, but now she ripped the envelope open.

The bold black figure at the bottom of the bill made her open her mouth in horror. She had known it was coming, but the sight of the amount was too much for her. She crumpled the bill in hands that were suddenly clammy with sweat.

Peter was by the pool. Even with zero bookings, he kept it in pristine condition. It was an occupation. At school he had been one of the liveliest members of staff, cracking jokes in the staff room that could have them all in such stitches that it was hard to compose their features before going back into class. She strongly suspected, even though neither of them would dream of admitting it, that he was lonely here.

The only people they knew were neighbours Luc de Rouget and his wife Prinny, who apparently looked after Luc's mother who had

had a stroke. They didn't talk about her much. She had the distinct impression that both she and her husband changed the subject if she mentioned his mother. She suspected that all was not as it seemed but didn't feel she knew the couple well enough to probe deeply into their affairs.

They sometimes called round to join them in an evening aperitif, but Liz was reluctant to confide in the woman. They had absolutely nothing in common. Back in the UK, Liz was sure, neither Peter nor herself would have become friends with them, but out here, English neighbours assumed a greater importance than they would have done at home.

She had a feeling that Prinny's chatter was fulfilling her desire just to talk to someone who understood what she was saying, but as her conversation was mostly confined to shopping and the lack of any decent outlets, Liz's function seemed to be to listen and murmur appropriately as Prinny bewailed the fact that there was nothing at all once one left Paris.

Liz herself could have found enough clothes for the rest of her life from the shops in Carcassonne, but she refrained from pointing this out. From Prinny's aggrieved tone of voice, it sounded as if the local shops would be totally inadequate for her needs.

So, Prinny was useless as a confidante. She was sure that the petite woman with her designer outfits would be the last person to understand her troubles but the desire to talk was overpowering. She had no-one but Peter to confide in. Between them, they had to come up with some kind of a solution.

He turned round with wry smile as she approached.

'I've added more pH plus,' he said. He stared down into the azure blue water and Liz could feel the sadness behind his words. 'Should be fine in a couple of hours when the filtration kicks in.'

He avoided looking at her. She knew that he was frightened of her starting the topic of conversation that had been uppermost in both their minds for a long time. If neither of them mentioned it, they could go on as they were, hoping that something would change, that somehow a miracle would happen. Only as long as they were never spoken of, the huge and frightening problems would somehow be diminished.

She looked at the pool with no enthusiasm.

'It seems fine to me.' And then, after a hesitation. 'Do you think anyone's ever going to swim in it?'

His face was hidden as he screwed the top back onto his jar of granules, but his back stiffened, a sure sign of his disturbance.

'Peter, we have to do something.'

He did not reply and she persisted. 'The Taxe Foncière bill arrived this morning.'

'How much is it?' he asked without turning round.

'It's two thousand seven hundred and eighty.' Her voice rose. 'Nearly three thousand euros, Peter! What are we going to do?'

He turned to face her, and his face was screwed up with concern when she started to cry.

'We can't go pretending that things are going to be alright.' She was clutching the crumpled bill and she waved it in a gesture of hopelessness, her whole body now jerking as the sobs engulfed her.

'Liz, please. Please stop crying. Something's bound to turn up. It always does in the end.'

'What something?' she sobbed. 'We're at the end already, Peter.'

She seated herself on one of the loungers and opened out the bill, smoothing it with fingers that were still shaking. 'It's due on the sixteenth of August. If we pay this, there'll be nothing left.' She looked at him and her eyes were wide with fear. 'We won't even be able to buy food, Peter!' At this, the tears started afresh.

'Don't be so melodramatic. We've still got my pension, we're not going to starve.' His words came out more harshly than he intended. It was a measure of his helplessness. Suddenly he took her into his arms and pressed her close, rocking her gently as her sobs subsided.

'I'm not being melodramatic. It's a choice, isn't it? If we pay this there won't be enough left for the week's shopping. We both know that, so stop trying to pretend that everything's alright, because it isn't.'

He stroked her hair and hugged her tighter. 'I'm sorry. I didn't mean to upset you. We'll find a way,' he murmured. It's not going to beat us, we'll.....oh, my God, not now!'

She jerked her head up, startled by the abrupt change of tone, and to her dismay, she saw Prinny opening the gate and advancing towards them.

Peter was quick to make his escape. He usually found Prinny quite amusing in a lighthearted way but today he felt he couldn't possibly cope with a jovial conversation with her. His huge strides covered the path in a minute, and Liz heard the door slam as Prinny was beside her.

She made a supreme effort and even managed a wan smile as they greeted each other with the traditional kiss on each cheek.

Prinny saw at once that something was amiss, but she did an excellent job of ignoring it on the basis that asking someone what was wrong was usually both crass and liable to upset them even more. Instead of risking a blunder with any tactless remarks, she simply looked up at her and said,

'Liz, darling, I know it's probably quite out of the question, but I don't suppose there's any chance that you and Peter have a couple of free weeks in one of your gîtes, do you? I used to live next door to my friend Emma, and she was wondering if she and her daughter could possibly come over for two weeks in July. Of course, I know it's short notice...'

One of the most useful skills that Liz had acquired in her whole teaching career was the ability to control her facial features when the occasion demanded. Whenever her pupils had made dubious jokes, passed lewd comments or otherwise behaved in a completely inappropriate manner, she had learned to suppress her immediate emotions and react as the situation called for. This ability was never more important than now, at this very minute, when it was imperative that Prinny didn't suspect how much this booking would mean to them. She arranged her face into a slightly worried, doubtful frown and Prinny reacted as she had confidently expected.

'Oh, dear, I suppose you haven't anything left, then?'

Her mind was racing. The booking might not even happen, she reminded herself and so she said, carefully non-committal,

'Do have a seat, my dear. I'll go and have a look at the booking calendar and see what's still available,' and as Prinny sank gracefully into a deck chair, she smiled at her and left.

In the kitchen, Peter was moodily examining the freezer, mentally calculating how much longer their stocks would last. He felt totally guilty. He had inveigled Liz into this new life. It was he who had been the driving force, encouraging her to take early retirement and now they were in a huge mess that seemed to have no solution. He was still evaluating the contents of the freezer when she burst in, her face alight with excitement. She grabbed him by the waist and swung him round.

'Hey, what's all this for?' He was laughing now as she began to waltz him round crazily.

'We've got a booking!' she shrieked. 'Someone's actually coming to stay. For two weeks, would you believe!'

'You're joking. Who?'

She lowered her voice, even though Prinny was still in the garden and couldn't possibly overhear them.

'It's some friend of Prinny's,' she said rapidly, as she reached up to a cupboard and took out files and papers. 'Where's the booking calendar? I'm supposed to be seeing if we've got any free weeks. Honestly, free weeks. Would you believe it! Ah, here it is.'

She laughed almost hysterically, and snatching up the calendar, she left Peter looking dazed and rushed out of the house with it.

On the way back she managed to compose her features into the serious expression of someone who was concluding a routine business deal.

'Yes, you're in luck,' she said calmly. 'We just happen to have two weeks free in July. But of course, it is high season, and with so many enquiries they could easily be booked up soon.'

As she had correctly predicted, the reply was forthcoming.

'In that case, I'd better ring Emma straight away,' she said, and to Liz's delight, which she succeeded in concealing, she took a mobile phone from her handbag and dialled.

Tactfully, she walked away, ostensibly to pull out a weed from the gravelled path, and she tried not to rush back when Prinny waved at her. She made herself saunter as nonchalantly as she could, and had a bright, polite smile on her face when Prinny said, 'That's settled, then. Emma was so pleased. She's going to book the flights today.'

CHAPTER 7

'I don't need a wheelchair, I can walk,' Orla said, but she might as well not have spoken since the nurse took no notice of her and just wheeled her down the long corridor and into room twenty-seven.

She was dismayed when she saw the two beds. 'Can't I have a room to myself?'

'We have no single rooms vacant at the moment,' Nurse O'Grady said primly. 'You were lucky to get in here at all at such short notice, we have a waiting list of over six months. It's only thanks to Doctor Hannigan that you got a recommendation and we were able to take you.'

She looked around the small room. Evidently there was an en-suite shower room and for that she was thankful. A large, solid looking wardrobe with a mirrored door took up most of the space on one of the walls, and for the rest, it was not much different from the hospital ward. A small chest by each bed, two green leatherette armchairs and a wall mounted television. Large framed prints on the walls failed to make the place look homely, as had been the intention.

Nurse O'Grady left her, and as she walked out, a girl came into the room.

Orla's first thought was how terrible she looked. She was tall, but with an emaciated face and arms like two twigs. Her knees stuck out beneath her short skirt and the legs were almost as spindly as her arms. She had long brown hair tied back in a ponytail, which only served to emphasize the hollow cheekbones in her face. For the first time, Orla looked at someone else and thought, *she's far too thin.* And she wondered briefly if that was what other people thought when they looked at her.

The girl pulled a book out of a drawer in the bedside table and sat cross legged on the bed next to Orla's.

'Are you the new girl? They said someone was coming. I've been on my own up till now.' The tone was neither friendly nor unfriendly, she just sounded uninterested.

She levered herself off the bed and walked across to the wardrobe where she looked at her reflection and smiled. 'I've put nearly a pound on!' she said, and there was a note of triumph in her voice.

'Is that good?' Orla was very doubtful.

'Of course it's good. Listen, whatever your name is...'

'Orla...'

'I'm Bridget O'Reilly. Yes, well, listen Orla. There's only one way to get out of this place and that is to eat and put weight on. Once your BMI is normal they'll let you out, but if you keep losing the weight you might as well be here for the rest of your life. We're watched every blessed minute of the day. It's not like being at home. You can't get away with putting weights in your bra...'

'Oh, did you do that too?' Orla was delighted.

'Of course I did, doesn't everyone? But that's what I'm saying. There's none of that here. You can't do any exercise. They bring you books and jigsaw puzzles and sewing and knitting and God knows what else to keep you sitting in an armchair all day. So the only thing to do is to play them at their own game. The minute you put on enough weight you can go home, and then it's down to you again, with no one telling you what you should be eating and what you should be doing. And I can't wait,' she said bitterly. 'Once I'm out of here it's all down to me and I'll decide for myself what I eat and what I don't eat.'

All this was such familiar territory to Orla that all she could do was nod enthusiastically in complete agreement.

With Bridget's help and constant advice she became an accomplished liar in an incredibly short space of time. Yes, she told Nurse O'Grady, the lunch was delicious, she adored meat pie and yes, she felt so much better now. She had so much more energy and she was ready to continue a healthy eating programme for the rest of her life. The nurse smiled at her, pleased that the child was responding so well to her treatment.

She saw Doctor Clive Dunne twice a week. She rather liked the little man who was informally dressed in jeans and a grey shirt. He spoke very calmly and tried to get her to talk about her feelings towards food, her relationship with her family and her feelings of inadequacy when she compared herself with Mary. He was an excellent psychiatrist with ten years' experience behind him, and he knew with a certainty that Orla was routinely giving him the answers that she knew were expected.

Now he sat opposite Derek Moore in the small office the staff used for their weekly assessment meetings.

'If you'd like to begin, Clive,' Derek suggested, and Clive pulled an open file towards him.

'Shona Devlin,' he began. 'She's almost ready to be discharged now. BMI twenty-three, she's eating normally and she's well adjusted. The family are very supportive and I see no real reason to keep her here much longer. Would everyone agree with that?'

'Sure, she's more than ready,' Derek agreed. 'We'll keep her for another week just to get the family prepared and then she can go home.'

'Next, then. Orla O'Sullivan. She's still worrying me, I don't feel there's been much real progress.'

'Orla?' Derek raised his eyebrows. 'I thought she was doing very well. Why do you think there's a problem?'

Clive took a sip of his coffee and placed it carefully on the desk. 'She's not opening up to me at all,' he said slowly. 'She's giving me all the right answers, but I get the feeling she's telling me what she thinks I want to hear, and I don't feel that I'm getting to the root of her problems at all. I think she's just playing along with us. There's no real change of heart there.'

'We can only keep on trying then,' Derek said. 'How do you find the family?'

This time Clive didn't hesitate. 'Oh, they're behind her all right,' he said. 'The mother has a better idea of how deep the problems are, but to be honest, I think she's partly the cause of it all. From what Orla's told me, I get the impression that she's a very controlling personality. Lots of family rules and the children doing as they're told. We know, of course, that anorexics often come from that kind of family situation. They use food as a means of regaining control of their own lives, and...'

'Yes, yes,' Derek cut in a little tersely. He was apt to find Clive irritating at times. He was just two years out of university, and in Derek's opinion he was competent enough but lacking in the intuition that comes with years of experience.

'We are all aware of the theories, Clive, but unfortunately, identifying a cause doesn't equate to finding a cure. Wouldn't we have the answers to all the diseases on God's earth if that were the case?'

Clive looked crestfallen, and he instantly regretted his uncharacteristic outburst.

'What about the father?' he asked, more calmly this time, and Derek responded immediately, with only a faint note of resentment in his voice.

'He's supportive alright but he's got a very simplistic view of anorexia. He thinks it's just a matter of persuading Orla to eat and once we've done that everything's going to be fine.'

'Have another try, Clive,' Derek said. 'We can't fail her. This might be her only chance of recovery. Real recovery, where she herself recognizes that she has to change.'

'Do my best,' Clive said, but there was a note of doubt in his voice and he sighed. He really feared that Orla O'Sullivan was going to be the biggest challenge of his career so far.

Meanwhile, Orla and Bridget were sitting together in the dining room, both of them forcing down chicken with a cream sauce, cheese topped mixed vegetables and garlic bread. This was followed by apple and ginger sponge and custard. At home, neither girl would have even contemplated finishing their plates but here they made a huge effort, even to the extent of appearing to enjoy it. If it added to their weight then it would be worth it to get out of the clinic.

Their treatment included cookery classes. It was hoped that by getting the girls to cook, they would not only want to eat the results, but at the same time they would learn about the nutritional values of different foods. Side by side, the two of them learned how to cook chocolate puddings, how to roast a chicken, make light as a feather Victoria sponges and rich fruit cakes.

Clodagh Boyle was a part time domestic science teacher at the local school and she came into the centre twice a week. She was small and wiry with short cropped black hair and a no-nonsense manner about her. She taught them how make a variety of different sauces to accompany their dishes. Cream was very much encouraged, it was added everything that could possible take it, and full fat cheese was often sprinkled on top of a dish to make it more interesting.

'More fattening, more like,' Orla murmured as she dutifully grated a lump of cheddar on top of her cottage pie, and Bridget laughed.

'Remember, the more calories, the quicker we get out of here,' she reminded her. 'Keep grating.'

'That looks fine, Bridget.' Clodagh leaned over the bench and took a spoonful of Bridget's pie. 'Tastes as good as it looks,' she said approvingly. 'Nicely seasoned too, and there are very few calories in cottage pie.' She strode swiftly across to the other side of the room to rescue Shona Devlin's pie which was in danger of burning black in the oven.

'She's lying through her teeth,' Bridget murmured. She grimaced at Orla and the pair of them stifled a giggle.

'If we eat it all up like good girls maybe we'll be out sooner than we think,' Orla said.

'She'll force it down our throats anyway so we might as well eat it.'

The calorie laden diet they were eating resulted in both of them gaining weight and after a few weeks, Orla's BMI was nudging the normal range.

Theresa and Declan visited each weekend, leaving a reluctant Padraic to spend the two days and nights with Mona Kelly. She was delighted to have him, but Padraic was not happy. His normal Saturdays were spent with Donal and Kevin, the thee of them wandering round the village, but Mona would only let him play in her vast back garden and he was bored.

After they had forced down a three course Sunday lunch, the girls walked together in the grounds. These were spacious and well laid out with meticulously clipped lawns, wooden benches at intervals, some of them paid for by grateful parents, and plenty of gravelled walkways and flowerbeds planted with roses, dahlias and petunias. The girls' favourite place was beneath a massive cedar tree whose branches cast a deep shade.

They soon found out that they had much in common besides their anorexia. Sister Bernadette was apparently a carbon copy of Sister Clare in Bridget's convent.

'Do you think she was the reason you had problems?' Orla wanted to know, but Bridget shook her head.

'No, it wasn't her,' she said. 'It was all explained to me in therapy. I was fine until a couple of years ago, and then things just started to go wrong.'

She sounded very sad and Orla waited patiently for her to go on.

'It was Maureen, you see.' She sounded far away and it was as if she was talking to herself, and thought that Orla must know all about Maureen. She waited patiently but it was a full minute before Bridget spoke again.

'Maureen is...was my sister,' she said. She didn't look at Orla and her eyes were fixed on the lawn. She tugged at blades of grass as she spoke. 'She was coming home from the nightclub in our village. It was raining really hard and she was driving two of her friends home. We don't know exactly what happened, but the police said the car went out of control and it skidded.'

She stopped again, and Orla ventured, 'So, she had an accident, was that it?'

Bridget nodded. 'Yes, there was an accident. Her car went off the road and it turned over. She was killed. Instantly, the police said.'

'Oh, my God, how terrible for you.'

'No,' she said quickly. 'Maureen's the one it was terrible for. And Mammy and Daddy. They kept having rows about it. Daddy said that if Mammy had picked Maureen up she would still be alive now, and Mammy kept saying that Daddy should have put his foot down and not allowed her to go out so late. They were forever arguing and shouting at each other. It was awful.'

'And now?' Orla said tentatively. 'Have things got any better, I mean, between the two of them?'

'No, they never got any better. They got divorced about six months ago. Daddy moved out of the house. He lives in a flat now.'

Orla was hesitant. 'And do you see him at all?'

'Oh, yes. I spend the week with Mammy but I go to Daddy's at the weekend. It's not so bad really,' she said with determination. 'It's like having two homes instead of just the one.'

Orla nodded. She could see that Bridget was trying to make the best of a situation that sounded very bad indeed, and she had a quick twinge of guilt when she thought about her own parents. They had not lost a child, but she knew that they were worried about her.

As if she was reading her mind, Bridget suddenly said, 'I know they're worried about me, but I can't help it. There's just something inside me that keeps saying I have to be thinner.'

'Ah, you're not exactly fat, you know.'

'And look who's talking,' Bridget countered swiftly, and they both began to giggle. Orla was pleased to see that Bridget was cheering up a little. She knew exactly what she meant about there being something inside her telling her to be thin. She had just the same feelings herself, but it was a little disquieting to hear someone else voicing them.

The two girls were inseparable. There was no-one else in the clinic who could possibly become a good friend. Shona Devlin was only thirteen, and although she seemed a pleasant enough girl, she was very shy and lived for her family's visits. She was always depressed when they left and hardly spoke to anyone for days afterwards. Deirdre Ryan, a tiny girl with a cloud of auburn curls was from Dublin and appeared to think that she was a cut above girls like Bridget and Orla whose homes were in the country.

It was a month later when Bridget bounded into the bedroom. Orla was trying on the new dress that Theresa had brought with her last weekend. It was too big, of course, but if she put on a couple of pounds, she thought the red shirt dress would suit her.

'What do you think?' she started, but then she stopped as Bridget grabbed her round the waist and leapt into a wild dance.

'Hey, Bridget, stop it! You're making me dizzy!' she cried as they whirled round, 'What is it?'

'I'm going home! They're letting me out!' she whooped. 'Isn't it glorious? They're discharging me next week.' Orla disentangled herself and collapsed onto her bed.

'But, I'll be on my own,' she wailed. 'Do you have to go?'

'Don't be an eejit, you'll be out if here yourself soon. And we'll keep in touch. I'll ring you, and we can text. And when you get home maybe we can meet up.'

She sat beside Orla and took her hand. 'Listen,' she said. 'Try really hard to put a bit of weight on and you'll be out of here before you know it. If I've done it then so can you. It's not that hard. It's about telling people what they want to hear. However you feel yourself, don't let them know, do you hear me? It's the only way you can get control back in your life. Once you're home you can do as you like, there'll be no-one practically force feeding you and no more therapy sessions. You'll be a free person again.'

'Couldn't you stay just until they let me out too?' she asked, but without much hope.

'They wouldn't let me, and to be honest, I don't want to be in this hell hole a minute longer than I have to be.' She gripped Orla's hand compulsively. 'Maybe we can meet up in the holidays. I'm not too far away in Ennis.'

Bridget's father's car rolled into the driveway the next day. Orla watched sadly as they embraced, and Bridget slammed the car door shut. She tried to return her excited wave, but managed no more than a limp floppy gesture as the car drove away.

Bridget kept her promise, and for the next few days the texts flew between them. Orla recounted her interviews with Doctor Dunne, and how she was managing to persuade him that her eating patterns were set for the rest of her life, and Bridget let her know how great it was that no-one was watching every mouthful she swallowed.

By the end of the following week the texts were fewer, until three weeks later they were barely communicating at all. Orla was saddened by this, but supposed that Bridget was so taken up with her own life that she had forgotten about her. The only thing she could do was to follow her advice and eat everything put in front of her, so that she too would be discharged.

At the treatment centre, Theresa learned to let go of her feelings of guilt about Orla's eating disorder, and several sessions taught them both that forcing her to eat was not the right solution. They learned with huge relief that the illness was curable, and that they themselves could play a large part in her recovery by listening to her and by understanding the true nature of her illness.

To Declan all this was a revelation. He was now fully aware that the clinic was their best hope that Orla would recover eventually, but that this would take a long time and they would need to be vigilant.

He was delighted when the day came when Orla was finally discharged.

'Let's hope this is the last of it,' he said with huge relief in his voice. His big florid face was a beam of delight, but Theresa was more cautious. 'The great test will be when we get her home,' she said thoughtfully. 'They stand over them the whole time here and make sure they eat. We don't want to get her home and have her refusing food again.'

Orla dialled the number and a man's voice spoke. He sounded very weary, and she said hesitantly. 'Hello? Is that Mr. O'Reilly? Could I speak to Bridget please?'

'Who is this? Is this some kind of joke?' The man's voice was rough.

'I'm Orla. Orla O'Sullivan,' she said desperately. 'I was in the clinic with Bridget, and I just wondered how she was, that's all.'

'Oh.' This time the man sounded a touch less aggressive, and his tone was sad. 'I'm sorry. I didn't realise who you were. Yes, I remember you now. Bridget spoke a lot about you when she came home...' He tailed off and Orla got the impression that he was trying to speak.

'So, could I speak to her, please?'

This time the silence was so long that Orla wondered if he was still there. Then he said, 'No, I'm very sorry, Orla. I'm afraid Bridget passed away two weeks ago.'

She put the phone down, carefully and precisely as if it might smash, and she stood there, stunned as if by a physical blow. Then she turned away and walked mechanically into the bathroom. She leaned her head over the toilet bowl and vomited. Somehow she made her way to her own room and lay shivering on the bed in a foetal position.

If only she could see Bridget, just once more. She realised with a sudden clarity that she had loved her. More than she loved her own sister Mary, in fact. She missed their easy companionship, the giggles they used to have together and the outwitting of the staff at the clinic. Bridget, who was always there to talk to, to confide in, to tell those truths about their illness that they would never admit to anyone else. Bridget who understood what she was going through because she was on the same journey herself.

And then, one night, she did see her. She was standing at the foot of her bed. For a brief moment Orla didn't know her. This was not the Bridget of the clinic - the emaciated, sunken-cheeked girl with the spindly legs and matchstick arms. This was a pleasant faced girl with rounded cheeks and silky smooth, glossy hair that framed her face and curled under just above her shoulders.

'It's you,' she murmured. 'It really is you, Bridget.'

The girl at the foot of the bed came close and bent down. She kissed her cheek gently.

'Are you better now?' Orla asked, and the girl nodded slowly. 'Yes, darling, I'm completely better now. I'm happy. Very happy, and you will be too. Very soon now.'

She tried to reply but the words refused to come. Bridget was walking away from her now and getting fainter.

'Bridget!' she called in anguish. 'Oh, Bridget, come back! Please, Bridget, please. Don't leave me here alone!'

'Orla!' Another voice spoke and this time much nearer to her ear. She opened her eyes to see Mary half sitting up and glaring at her from her bed. 'What's going on? What are you shouting for?' She was sleepy eyed and definitely very annoyed at being woken up. 'Get to sleep, will you. And stop making that row.'

She turned over away from her sister but she was afraid to close her eyes. She desperately wanted Bridget to come again, and yet she was terribly afraid of that happy, healthy girl at the foot of her bed.

'Daddy, do you think there are ghosts? Real ones, I mean?' Declan looked at her with a puzzled frown. 'Well, there's the Holy Ghost, of course. Is that what you mean?'

'No. Not that. I mean, more, well, people... you know, people who are dead. You know they're dead and then you see them. Is it true? Are they really there?'

Declan came close to her and put his arm around her shoulder. She looked so despondent and forlorn and she sounded sadder than he had ever known her.

'What is it you're telling me, child? Have you seen someone, is that it?'

She nodded, yet diffidently with a face that was confused and bewildered. 'It was Bridget,' she said. 'She really was there, Daddy. Truly. She was standing by my bed.' It was suddenly all far too much and she started crying softly. Declan's arm tightened around her and he held her close.

'No, darling, it wasn't a ghost,' he said gently. 'You were asleep and you were dreaming, that's all.'

'But she was real, Daddy,' she protested through her tears. 'I know she was there, and I'm frightened...'

'No, pet. It's like this. Listen to me and dry your eyes.' Obediently, Orla raised her head. 'This can happen, in the time when you're falling asleep. You're in a different kind of state, you're neither awake nor asleep, it's a kind of in-between state. And when you're grieving for someone like you are, you can sometimes dream so vividly that you think the person is there. You honestly believe they've come back. But it's not true. It's just your mind playing tricks on you, that's all it is. Do you hear me? It's nothing to worry about, and now you've told Daddy all about it, you won't have that dream again.'

He was treating Orla as if she was much younger, but she was comforted by his words and she didn't resent it as she would have done a year ago.

'Thank you, Daddy,' she said. 'I can see that's how it was.'

'Honestly? You're not just saying that to please your old Daddy?'

She managed a weak smile then. 'No, I'm not, and you're not old.'

'Ah, but I'm far too old to be making cups of tea every minute of the day. Do you think you could put the kettle on?'

She grinned now and went off to the kitchen. Declan watched her go, and his smile faded. He knew she was reassured, but he was worried about her. She had been through so much already, and Bridget's death had hit her hard. He would have to talk to Theresa about it, just as soon as she got home.

Between the two of them, Declan and Theresa knew almost everyone there was to know in the village. Declan brought them their post and Theresa arranged their doctor's appointments with the smooth efficiency that Robert Costello had valued for the last five years. Files were never misplaced when Theresa was working, and she was totally at ease with the computer software he used, where detailed notes on every patient were meticulously kept up to date.

There was little they didn't get to know, but they always swore that no gossip in the village would come from either of them.

Both of them kept quiet about Helen Daly's husband who saw Doctor Costello about his huge problem with the drink, and neither of them mentioned outside their own home that Declan had found old Mrs. Hughes sprawled awkwardly on the floor after she had slipped on her hallway mat.

He had a large parcel for her, and he knocked on the door with the customary heavy raps he always used. He knew that she must be in the house; she never went out before half past ten when she took her usual stroll to the shops, and so when there was no answer he cautiously opened the door. He heard the moaning immediately and dropped his heavy bag immediately. She was lying just outside her lounge doorway, clutching at her side.

'You won't say anything to our Keith, will you?' she had pleaded. 'He wants me to go into the Home, I know he does, and if he gets to know I've fallen he'll put me in there. You won't tell him, Declan, will you?'

He had soothed her with assurances that he would say nothing to anybody, and made her a cup of strong tea with three spoonfuls of sugar before ringing Theresa to ask her to call an ambulance. Both of them kept her short hospital stay to themselves, and her son Keith was none the wiser when she returned in two days time with nothing worse than a bruised hip.

Being a postman was not Declan's first job, but it was the one he enjoyed the most. Before that he had worked in a factory making parts for industrial printing machines, and even further into the past he had been a window cleaner. He liked the open air, even the freezing cold days in winter when the paths were slippery and the frost sparkled on the hard ground. It didn't pay too well, but between them, they had enough to live on. He was happy if he had his two pints in The Wanderer in the evenings.

'Get yourself a job, earn your money fairly and spend it on what you like,' he would tell the children. 'Have a good time and don't be counting the cost. Life's too short to be pinching the pennies.'

But Theresa took a different view. When Padriac was born and Declan had wanted them to take out a massive mortgage on a four bedroomed house in Grange Avenue she had put her foot down.

'Doctor Costello lives in Grange Avenue,' she said, 'it's not for people like us.'

'Are you telling me we're not good enough to live on the doctor's street?' he blustered.

'No, that's not what I'm saying,' she said calmly. 'Not at all. I'm talking about a little thing called a mortgage. We'd be paying out hundreds a month on a house there. And what would happen if we lost our jobs, have you given that any thought? Before we know it there'll be the bailiffs coming knocking at the door and we'll be on the streets like poor Maura Flanagan.'

'Oh, that wouldn't happen to us.' He was very confident. 'And isn't Maura fine now, living with her sister?'

'It can happen to anybody,' she said darkly. 'And Maura's one on her own. No-one's going to take in a family of five like us. And she isn't fine. She and Christine are at each other like two cats the whole of the day. But what can you expect with two women sharing the same kitchen?' She did not add that Maura Flanagan was still taking the tranquillisers that Doctor Costello had prescribed. Some things were much better left unsaid.

In the end, of course, Theresa had her way and they finished up living in the small cottage by the side of the main road running through the little town.

'This is fine, it's exactly right for us,' she said. 'Three bedrooms; one for the girls, one for us and Padraic can have the single room when he's ready for a bedroom of his own. And we're nice and central here. I can walk to work, you can be at the Post Office in ten minutes on your bike, and the bus stop is just up the road for the convent.'

Secretly, he was relieved. It would have been a terrible thing to be burdened with a massive mortgage. Theresa was usually right about these things. She had not changed much since the day they were married. After Padraic's birth she had not managed to lose the extra pounds and she was now chubbier than the slim girl of their wedding day, but in other ways she was exactly the same warm hearted, generous and practical woman she had been since they were married. It was Theresa who expertly organized their daily lives, seeing that the children were well dressed, even on their limited budget.

'I don't know how you do it, Theresa,' Mrs. Ryan once said. 'The three of them are always so well turned out.'

'My children have each got four sets of clothes,' she told her. 'One set for school, one set for home and two for Mass. As soon as they are home from school they change, their uniforms are hung up and that way they last much longer.' She was proud of the orderly and thrifty way in which her house was run.

This morning she was at the small supermarket in the village. Really, she thought, picking up a bag of frozen peas, the prices here were getting ridiculous. She knew for a fact that this particular brand was cheaper in town, and it was a shame she didn't have time to go. She put the peas in the trolley anyway. Orla actually admitted to liking them, so she was easily prepared to pay the extra if it meant seeing the child eating. She gave a lot of thought to meals nowadays, and Orla was eating quite well. Although she was still thin she had regained some weight and her hair was looking far better; healthy and shiny instead of lanky and straw-like.

Theresa always prepared meals that Orla would not only enjoy, but which were genuinely low in calories so that there was no possibility that she would reject them. But still, she was troubled. Her daughter was no longer the happy and confident girl she had been before her illness and there was a mute sadness about her that told Theresa that their problems were not over yet. She knew that, although she rarely spoke of her now, Orla was still mourning the loss of Bridget. She sighed deeply and added a bag of carrots to her trolley.

'Theresa!' She stopped her trolley just in time to prevent it running bang into Branna Cullen. 'I thought you always went to the town to shop? Run out of something, have you?'

Theresa always called Branna the neighbour from hell. If she got so much as a sniff of gossip she would elaborate it into a world class drama. She had already passed remarks about Orla, wanting to know if she was suffering from a debilitating illness.

'She's got very thin lately, hasn't she? You want to keep an eye on her, Theresa. They grow so fast at that age, don't they? She puts me in mind of little Cathy Nolan, you remember her?'

As a chance remark to a worried mother this was spectacular in its tactlessness. Since Declan and Theresa had been to Cathy Nolan's funeral two years ago after the child had contracted tuberculosis, Branna's comment infuriated her. Little Cathy Nolan, indeed! Orla was nothing like her. Everyone knew that Cathy had been a delicate child for years before her illness, and there were those who were surprised that she had lived until the age of thirteen, in and out of hospital as she had been nearly all her short life.

'Yes, of course I remember her,' she said shortly. 'But as Cathy never had a day's good health from being a baby there's no comparison really, is there? Orla's been a bit run down lately but there's nothing wrong with her. Nothing at all.' With this she turned her trolley sharply around and disappeared down the next aisle. Branna shrugged and threw two packets of butter into her trolley. She wondered what had got into Teresa lately. It wasn't like her to be so touchy.

Theresa used to enjoy shopping, but now it was fraught with doubts and uncertainties. Could she persuade Declan that the low fat cheese really tasted just as good as the full fat variety that he liked? He thought the treatment centre had solved all their problems but deep down, Theresa knew that not very much had changed. Perhaps a break away from home might be a good idea, she thought, and she resolved to talk to him about it as soon as he got home from work and Orla was upstairs doing her homework.

She picked up the low fat cheese, and a crisp cos lettuce and a cucumber. They already had enough tomatoes, and she would make a salad for tea, yet again.

As she was checking out at the till, Declan was well on the way to completing his morning round. He turned into Yew Tree Drive to see Mona Kelly standing by her open doorway. The days were few when Mona didn't meet him at the door for 'a bit of a natter,' as she called it.

There was nothing about the woman that was remarkable. She was one of those people who blended into the background. You could pass dozens like her in the village, but if she were not there, there would be hardly a family in the village who would not miss her. She passed her days quietly with her mother, the two of them doing the housework together and spending evenings watching TV or sewing. Although her mother was now in her late seventies, her eyes were still bright and there was nothing she enjoyed more than working on fine sewing. When Mary was born Mona had presented them with two exquisitely embroidered dresses for her, and Declan knew that she and her mother had together embroidered the kneeling cushions for the church.

In winter she wore a long grey coat and hat of a darker grey and for the spring and summer she had cotton dresses and two good suits which she wore with pale blue or white blouses.

The two women were on their own now as her father had passed away after a heart attack at the age of fifty-five. He had owned the local hardware shop and after his death Mona and her mother found themselves far better off than they had ever expected.

Kelly's hardware had been a byword in the village. If all you needed was one single screw then Eammon Kelly would sell it to you. There was no need to buy a packet of fifty and leave the rest to rust in a drawer in the kitchen. You could go into his shop and spend a pleasant ten minutes discussing the exact type of screwdriver needed to fix your window frame, and receive sound advice on the correct way to go about doing the job.

When he died, his widow sold the shop to a national chain, and although the village lost out on a valued retailer, Mona was able to give up her job as a dinner lady at the junior school and she and her mother had set off on a series of trips.

'I know it seems ridiculous to be gallivanting off to places,' she had told everyone, 'but mother has always wanted to travel.'

They had gone into the town to have their passport photographs taken and there was always great excitement choosing accommodation and booking air tickets. Together they had been to Venice and Rome, Switzerland, Austria and the South of France.

Today she stood at the doorway neatly dressed in a floral shirtwaister dress and flat, open toed sandals.

'And how is Orla faring nowadays?' she wanted to know, tilting her head to one side as she waited for his news.

Declan hesitated before he said, 'Well, to be honest we're still a bit anxious about her. She's not underweight any more but she's still got her worries about food. Theresa's wanting to take her away somewhere, give her a break, so to speak. She thinks it'll be a kind of reward for her.'

'And have you decided on anywhere?'

Declan was rueful. 'Not really,' he said. 'When we go away at all it's a day by the coast and I don't think that's what Theresa has in mind.'

Mona became excited. 'Declan, I know the very place. Why don't you take Orla to France?'

'France?' He was startled. 'Abroad, do you mean? But who would we know in France?'

To Declan, going on holiday meant visiting someone you knew, and preferably family. As a young boy, his parents had taken him and his two sisters each year to visit Uncle Liam and Auntie Keira in Cork. It was always a huge occasion, requiring several weeks of careful planning and consulting of train and bus timetables, pulling out and dusting off the battered suitcases from under beds, and not wearing best clothes because of saving them for 'the trip'. The idea that anyone would go away to an unknown place, with equally unknown people was a totally new concept.

He didn't have much time to reflect on this as Mona was saying, 'Come inside, Declan and I'll show you.'

Mystified now, he followed her into the tiny hallway and then into the lounge. It was a highly feminine room, with tapestry embroidered cushions on the armchairs and the sofa, and floral cretonne curtains at the windows. It reminded Declan of the fictitious Miss Marple's home that Theresa was so keen on.

'It's only Declan, mother. Have a seat Declan,' she said. 'Mother, do you remember where we put the leaflets about France?'

Her mother was sitting in an armchair close to the fire that burned in the grate despite the warm weather. She looked puzzled and Mona said, 'You know, mother, the gîte we stayed in?'

Declan carefully moved a cushion, richly embroidered with purple and yellow pansies, to the very edge of the chair and sat down, ill at ease. Chatting to Mona at her gate was fine, but he was uncomfortable in her living room. Mrs. Kelly closed her eyes and for a second Declan thought she had fallen asleep, but then she opened them and held up a finger. 'I know,' she said. 'They would be in the wardrobe, in the second drawer down. I tidied it out not so long ago. They're all in a blue envelope.'

Mona disappeared and returned presently with an envelope as her mother had said.

'Here it is, this is what I was looking for,' she said and she handed him a leaflet.

The photograph on the front showed a group of Mediterranean villas surrounding a deep blue swimming pool. The place looked hot, he thought, looking at the clear blue sky. In the background he could see mountain peaks. It certainly seemed attractive, and he opened the leaflet and read: 'Languedoc-Roussillon Gîtes.

Liz and Peter McGuire welcome you to our two gîtes in the heart of the Minervois countryside.'

'Gîtes. What would they be?'

She explained. 'Gîtes is the French name for a kind of self catering place. You know, you go and stay there and you do all the cooking.'

'And would you know this place, yourself, now?'

She nodded emphatically at him, her eyes bright with enthusiasm. 'Yes, that's the whole point. We stayed there a couple of months ago. It was a great holiday altogether. There's a fine big kitchen with everything anyone could ever want. Theresa would be in her element, and there's a big garden for Padraic to run around in, and there's even a swimming pool. Not that Mother and I ever went in it, you understand, but it's there in case anyone would want to. There's countryside you wouldn't believe, there's the seaside not too far away, and then there's this great castle thing called Carcassonne. Well, it's more of a tourist place really, but your Padraic would be in Heaven. They have all kinds of shops there with suits of armour and toy castles and knights.'

Declan was still doubtful. 'Sure, it sounds a good place to visit alright, but how would you go about something like that?'

'I'll tell you what,' Mona said. 'I've still got Liz's phone number. I could ring her up for you if you like and see has she got any room this year.'

Declan felt pressurized as he did when he and Theresa went shopping and were accosted by salesmen who talked at you until they persuaded you to part with your money for something you hadn't really wanted and didn't need. He had a strong suspicion that he was being carried along with Mona's enthusiasm. So he said hastily, 'That would be great Mona, but I'd need to consult with Theresa first. She's the one who decides these things.'

Mona was confident. 'Oh, I'm sure she'll agree. I've a feeling it could be the very thing for Orla. A completely new experience for her.'

'Well, I suppose it might help. Anything to take her mind away from her grieving...'

'Grieving?' Mona was startled. 'But what is she grieving for? I thought you said she was getting better?'

'Oh, she's still sad for this girl she met in the clinic. It seems they were great friends and they kept in touch afterwards but the poor child died recently.'

Mona caught her breath. 'Did she have some kind of an accident, was that it?'

He shook his head slowly. 'No. From what Orla says, the girl apparently stopped eating when she was discharged, and she died from malnutrition.'

'God, how terrible. You don't think that Orla will...?'

'Oh, no,' he said hurriedly. 'We're not thinking along those lines at all.'

'I'm very glad to hear it. But Declan, seriously, do think about this holiday. It will be the best thing in the world for Orla, I'm sure. In fact, if you like I can call in tonight after the Parish meeting and discuss it with Theresa.'

He demurred politely, but she cut him off with, 'Oh, it's no trouble at all. And it's not just Orla who'll benefit. You'd be amazed at how travel has opened up our lives. Hasn't it, mother?'

But Mrs. Kelly had closed her eyes again and was gently snoring, so Declan never heard from her how her life had been opened up. He smiled his thanks to Mona and left quietly.

Mona decided to go and have a word with Theresa, just as soon as she could after tea. Without being consciously interfering, she was possessed of a general wish to do good, and Orla, she felt, would not be the only person to benefit from a trip to France. She had an idea that Liz McGuire was finding life hard, and a booking for one of her gîtes would help a lot. She remembered Liz clearly; the tall, angular figure and wavy fair hair. She looked highly capable but Mona couldn't help remembering the day she had called at the McGuire's house. She needed to know what time the local post office opened, and so had strolled up to the house. She was immediately startled by the difference between their own gîte and Liz's house. Liz had invited her into a lounge that was sparkling clean, but shabby, with a worn fabric sofa, a low sideboard that was polished but scuffed at the bottom, and the whole place looked badly in need of decorating. Outside, the blue paint was flaking off the shutters and the wrought iron garden gate was rusting. She had tried not to look around her too obviously. Liz was not the kind of woman to appreciate any pitying glances, she was sure, but when she went back to their own gîte, she told her mother: 'It seems to me that Liz and Peter have spent everything on the gîtes and can't afford to do up their own place. You should see it. Mother, it's falling apart.'

With a sense of complacency at doing another good deed, she nodded gently to herself. She was fond of Theresa, who never missed mass and brought up her family so well. They were pleasant, well mannered children and it would be a real pleasure to steer them towards a nice holiday in a beautiful region of France. She would go and see Theresa the minute Father Hagan finished his weekly meeting.

But it took all of her powers to persuade Theresa that a holiday in France would be a great idea, not only for Orla but for the rest of the family too.

'I don't like to leave the house empty for so long,' Theresa objected, but then Mary, who had been silent up until now, cut in eagerly with,

'It needn't be empty, Mammy. I could stay here. I've got a whole rake of revision to do, you know, and it would be so peaceful. I could get so much done if I was on my own.'

She carefully avoided looking at Orla, who was bringing in a cup of tea and a plate of custard creams for Mona, and whose lips had suddenly tightened as she understood what was behind all this.

'Well, I'm not sure. I could leave your meals ready in the freezer, but you'd need to look at the dates on everything. All the older things will have to be eaten up first...'

'I know that, of course I do.'

'I just wouldn't want you to run short if we do go away.'

'Mammy, I'm twenty-two. I have money. There are shops in the village. How do you think I manage up at Uni?'

Theresa did not look at all convinced and she turned to Declan. 'What do you think?'

'Oh, sure, she'll manage for a couple of weeks without us all round her.'

'I didn't mean that,' she said impatiently. 'I mean, the holiday. Do you think we should go?'

The question was only relevant in that she needed Mona to hear her consulting her husband. It would never do, she thought, for the whole village to realise that she herself made all the decisions, so she was barely listening when he said,

'Well now, it would be a change, all right.' He was still rather bemused at the suddenness of the whole thing, and actually not too sure where the place was, even though Mona had described it in huge detail.

''Mammy, *please* say we can go,' Oral pleaded. 'We've never been abroad, and you know it would be so good for me. I'd learn such a lot of French, I'm sure.'

Theresa's face softened slightly as she glanced over at her daughter who was still so frail and inclined to be nervy and jumpy. She had been through such a terrible time, and Theresa knew that she was still not sleeping well and being troubled by nightmares.

'We'll see,' she said. Orla's face brightened and Mary looked suddenly smiled to herself and looked hopeful.

When Mona finally placed her empty cup and saucer on the small table at the side of her chair and stood up to take her leave, she was convinced in her mind that despite Theresa's objections, the holiday in France would take place.

CHAPTER 8

'Quick now, that's our flight they're calling! Padraic, hold onto Mammy's hand like a good boy.'

Declan heaved himself out of the airport lounge seat and scanned the departures board.

'Theresa, have you got the boarding cards and the passports?' he called urgently over his shoulder.

'Jesus, Declan, that's the third time you've asked me. They're all in my handbag,' she said calmly. 'Unless someone's stolen them while I've been carrying it, of course. Stop your panicking, will you? People do this every day.'

Orla giggled, but Declan had not heard, he was making huge strides towards the boarding gate, following other passengers who were booked on the flight to Carcassonne.

It was the first flight for all four of them. Padraic had caught some of his father's nervousness and was unaccustomedly quiet, staring around him with huge eyes at the bustle of the place. Orla followed her mother's lead and was outwardly calm, although when she first caught sight of the massive plane she felt butterflies in her stomach. She greatly wished Kathleen and Lyndsey were here to see her doing something as glamorous as boarding an aeroplane. But Kathleen was spending a week at her grandmother's in County Clare and Lyndsey's family was at home. Her parents thought holidays were a huge waste of money and so the furthest Lyndsey had ever been was Waterford when the whole class was taken on a school outing last year.

The plane was crowded. Declan heaved their cabin cases into overhead lockers whilst people squeezed past him. Nearly all the seats seemed to be taken.

'Declan! There are seats down there further along the aisle, look,' Theresa said scanning the length of the plane. 'Take Padriac with you. There's a spare one here, look, Orla. Hurry up before someone else takes it.'

Orla saw the seat at the end of a row of three and she sat down. Once she was settled she felt herself relaxing, and she looked at the air hostesses with great interest as they made their through the cabin, slamming shut the overhead lockers and checking each passenger's seat belt. They looked so smart, she thought, in their royal blue uniforms, polished fingernails and hair neatly arranged in buns at the back.

In his seat further down the plane Declan held himself tensely, gripping the armrests during take off, but trying hard to compose his features into a nonchalant half smile that clearly told everyone who might be looking that this was routine for him and that he wasn't in the least bit concerned.

Halfway through the journey an air hostess rattled a laden trolley down the aisle. The elderly man in the window seat raised an imperious hand to order, and then reached across his wife and Orla to pay and collect his sandwiches. He unwrapped them and passed one to his wife who accepted it with no acknowledgment. Theresa shook her head when she was offered a selection from the trolley and as soon as the air hostess had passed them, she reached into her oversized handbag and unwrapped foil covered packets of egg and cheese sandwiches. She leaned across the aisle and passed two of them to Orla. 'I'm not paying their fancy prices for food,' she said. 'I don't know which are the egg and which are the cheese, you'll have to take pot luck.'

Orla glanced sideways and thought she detected a curl of the lip on the face of the old lady next to her. It could have been slight amusement at the glossy magazine she was reading, but somehow Orla got the impression that it was something to do with people who brought their own sandwiches onto the flight. She felt very young and inexperienced at the side of all these smart passengers who were so obviously used to flying.

The plane taxied into Carcassonne airport half an hour later.

Back in County Limerick, Mary snuggled up to Aiden on the sofa.

'They should be landing just about now,' she said gleefully. 'Just imagine it, three whole weeks and not a single person to bother us.'

He pulled her closer and they kissed.

'And for God's sake remember not to answer the phone,' she warned him, 'or I'll have to be inventing huge lies about the plumber calling round.' They giggled like two children at this, before Mary pulled him to his feet. They wrapped their arms round each other and Mary led the way upstairs.

In the arrivals lounge Theresa pulled two suitcases off the baggage belt and Padraic grabbed at his own bright green ride-on case that Theresa had picked up cheaply at the car boot sale the week before.

'Just you take care, now,' she warned him. 'Don't go banging into people with it.' She got a huge grin in return and he set off, weaving in and out of the arriving passengers.

They collected their cases and left the cool interior of the arrivals lounge into the bright glare of the afternoon sun.

'Jesus, it's hot!' Theresa exclaimed, looking around her. 'Now, where do you suppose we get the car from?'

Declan was fishing in his pocket for the car hire papers. If the flight had unnerved him, it was nothing to how he was feeling now the moment had come to collect the car. This was what he had dreaded from the minute the holiday was discussed.

'But they drive on the wrong side of the road over there,' had protested. 'You wouldn't know what you were doing.' But Theresa had been sure it would all be easy.

'Once you get used to it you'll be fine. Don't millions of people drive on the wrong side of the road in America?'

Declan's brow creased as he felt that somewhere there was a flaw in this argument but he couldn't place it for the moment and he was far too hot to puzzle it out, so he concentrated on wheeling his heavy case. It was not only the sun that was making his armpits run with sweat as he tried to remember the details of the route that Liz McGuire had thoughtfully emailed to them before they left. They saw the building as other passengers dragged and carried suitcases towards it.

'Orla, you'd better go in with Daddy,' Theresa suggested. 'You can explain everything in French.'

She was sunnily confident that the years of learning French up at the convent would have left Orla able to cope easily with trifles such as hiring a car, and as Orla opened her mouth to protest, she gently pushed her towards her father with a nod of her head.

'Go on, now,' she said. 'The quicker we get inside out of this heat the better.'

Declan needn't have worried. The dark haired man at the desk took his papers, asked in impeccable English for his credit card and reached up to a shelf behind him for the keys to the Mondeo they had reserved for the three weeks of their stay.

Declan found that memorising the route had been wasted effort. The car was equipped with satellite navigation, and with its help they left the airport and he successfully negotiated a couple of roundabouts, finding it strange to drive around them in an anti-clockwise direction. He found the dual carriageway he was looking for.

'Look out for signs for Mazamet,' he instructed them all. He was hunched up and gripping the wheel tightly. 'It's all I can do to drive this thing, I can't be watching for the signposts as well.'

Obediently they all peered out of the windows. 'Villemoustausou,' Orla read. 'Villegailhenc, Villedubert...they all seem to start with 'Ville...'

'We're looking for something starting with an M,' Declan growled. He was getting more flustered by the second, and was totally incapable of stopping himself from reaching for the gear lever with his left hand. He was thankful that at least the pedals were in the same positions as cars at home, otherwise he could see them all ending up in the ditch which flanked the road.

'There it is, Daddy!' Padraic yelled. 'It's straight on at this roundabout.'

'Well done, son. We're on the right road at least. I've been having visions of us getting lost and driving round in circles.'

They drove on. On their left they passed a canal where boats were negotiating a lock, and from there a straight road bordered at each side by tall plane trees whose canopy almost met above them.

'Yes, it must be the right road,' Theresa affirmed. 'There's a sign to Villegly. Liz said that was one of the places we'd go through.'

Once they had passed through the villages, fields of deep green bushes set out in straight lines flashed past them on either side of the road. Here and there in the fields were squat, one storey stone buildings, often in disrepair and with dilapidated roofs of rust-coloured tiles. Orla wondered what they were. They can't be houses, she thought. Not possibly.

They're far too small. Beyond the fields on her left she could see undulating hills in sombre grayish green set against the intense blue sky. At the summit of one if the hills was a tall mast which she was later to learn was Pic De Nore, the highest point of the Montagne Noire.

'Would you look at those!' Teresa exclaimed, twisting her head round as they drove on. 'Aren't they beautiful?' They were passing a field of bright sunflowers, their golden heads brilliant against the bright blue sky.

'And what are all these bush things in the fields?' Orla asked. The car was going too fast for them to distinguish the clusters of purple grapes, and none of them could identify them.

'Probably Liz will be able to tell us,' said Theresa. 'She seemed very knowledgeable about the whole place when I spoke to her on the phone.'

Padraic was gazing out as they made their way carefully through the villages. 'What are those wood things on the windows?' he wanted to know.

'They're called shutters,' Orla told him loftily. 'Maybe we can get you a pair, to put across your mouth and shut you up.'

'Orla, that's enough!' Theresa said sharply. 'The child is only asking. There'll be a lot you can learn about this place so don't be coming over all high and mighty now.'

She shrugged and Padraic's face lost its aggrieved expression and he jutted out his chin at her. 'See, you don't know everything.'

'For the love of God, you two, keep quiet will you? It's bad enough trying to control this car without controlling the pair of you as well.'

Rebuked into silence, Orla stared huffily out of the window. It was true that much of this countryside was unexpected and entirely different from the low and lush Irish countryside she was used to. They passed through a village with a long row of houses, some with chunks of their stucco facade flaking off, while others looked new, with bright window boxes bearing geraniums and petunias.

The journey was not quite as bad as Declan had feared. Apart from mounting the kerb two or three times and accidentally hitting the window instead of the gear lever, he finally negotiated the steep winding hill in Caunes-Minervois and brought them to a halt inside the gates of a cluster of neat looking bungalows.

A tall man with a grizzled beard was at the door of one of the houses as they drew in, and he moved towards them with a beam of welcome on his face.

'Peter McGuire,' he introduced himself. He grasped Declan's hand in a grip that only just stopped him from wincing. 'And you found your car alright? No problems with the driving? It can take a bit of getting used to if you've never driven on the right before.'

'Ah, no, nothing like that,' he said airily. 'A couple of minutes behind the wheel and I was fine.'

'Except when you nearly ran that lady over, Daddy,' Padraic reminded him, which earned him a nudge from his mother and an indignant glare from Declan.

Peter laughed. 'No harm done, then,' he said jovially. He turned to Orla. 'Pleased to meet you, too, young lady.' And then, disastrously, he added with another hearty chuckle, 'I can see we'll have to put a bit of fat on your bones while you're here.'

He was totally oblivious to the tense silence that followed his pleasantry or of Orla's suddenly compressed lips.

Theresa hurried to turn the conversation to less dangerous waters. 'We're so pleased to be here,' she said. 'And we're so much looking forward to the holiday. We don't get away much at home. What are all those bushes over there?' she asked, looking out towards the countryside surrounding them.

'You've come to one of the biggest wine producing areas in the whole of France,' Peter told her proudly. 'They're our local vineyards, it's the main source of income in these parts. Better get used to them, your gîte overlooks them.'

Before she could reply, a tall, fair-haired lady approached, closely followed by a young man who looked very like her, except that his hair was straight and he was a little taller.

'I'm so sorry I wasn't here to meet you,' she said. She was a little breathless. 'I was over at my neighbour's house and I didn't realise it was getting so late. I'm Liz, and this is my son Martin.' They all heard the pride in her voice as she made the introduction.

Martin shook hands with each of them in turn, but his gaze lingered on Orla as he took her hand. She was uncommonly pretty, he thought, with delicate features, flowing auburn hair, beautifully shaped blue eyes and a firm little chin.

Liz smiled warmly, taking them all in her glance. 'If you're ready I'll show you your gîte. We've called it Les Jonquilles. Not appropriate at this time of the year, but in Spring it really lives up to its name.' As they trooped after her, Theresa wondered what on earth she was talking about.

'Jonqilles are daffodils, Mammy,' Orla told her in a low voice as they followed Liz up a neat gravelled pathway.

'We were going to name this gîte Les Roses,' she continued, 'but really I'm not fond of them at all. Far too messy when the petals blow off, and so hard to weed around, don't you think?'

She looked back at Theresa, who only nodded. She was no gardener. As long as the house was totally neat and orderly, she left it to Declan to mow their tiny patch of garden regularly and rarely gave it a second thought.

She led them up a red flagged pathway towards a cream stuccoed bungalow. Shiny blue wooden shutters framed the windows, which Theresa noticed with approval were sparkling clean. They all felt excited when Liz turned the key in the lock of the gîte that would be their home for the next three weeks. It was like the beginning of some huge adventure.

She led them through a small hallway, painted in a pale cream and with beige tiles on the floor and from there into an immense open plan lounge, tiled in the same large squares. Facing a large television screen was a huge black leather sofa and two matching recliner chairs. Through an archway at the far end they could see part of a modern, white kitchen. At one end of the lounge was a massive fireplace with an over mantle of carved reddish brown marble, and beside it was a neat pile of logs, all sawn off at exactly the same length.

'You won't be needing those,' Liz smiled as she watched them. 'We get an average of three hundred days of sunshine here, and I don't think this year will be any different.'

Declan looked puzzled as he glanced down at the floor. 'Wouldn't you be having carpets in France, then?' he wondered aloud, earning him a glance from Theresa that combined annoyance and exasperation.

But Liz was not at all perturbed and she answered sunnily, 'Oh, no, you won't find very many carpets around here. They'd be too hot in the summer, for one thing, and most people use tiles. Much easier to keep clean, too,' she added, and Theresa nodded in evident approval. She rather liked the look of this tall, efficient sounding lady who seemed to hold some of her own ideas on hygiene.

As she left, Liz wondered if Mrs. O'Sullivan would be doing any cooking. The girl called Orla was painfully thin, she noticed, with a pair of legs that hardly looked capable of supporting her.

'She's like a rake,' she told Peter. 'The little boy looks alright, but I'd be worried about the girl if she was mine. She reminds me of some of those girls you read about, you know, the ones with that anorexia disease.'

'She's a bit on the skinny side,' he agreed, 'but a lot of them are like that nowadays. They all want to be models or something.'

Inside the gîte, they separated and found their bedrooms. Orla's room was clean and neat with a narrow bed covered in a striped blue and white duvet, with matching striped curtains and a single wardrobe in pale wood. A matching bedside table held a blue shaded lamp, and a pale blue braided rug partially covered the beige tiled floor. Once she had completed her short inspection she heaved her suitcase onto the bed and began to unpack. Doubtfully, she held up the pair of new white shorts that Mammy had bought her. She thought they looked a bit small and she quickly undressed and slipped them on. Far from being too small, the waistband gaped open and they were definitely baggy on her tiny hips. Satisfied that she did not appear to be putting on too much weight, she changed back into her halter neck print dress and stuffed the shorts into a drawer.

Theresa was in the kitchen, reaching upwards to open cupboards and examine the crockery. 'What do you think?' she asked excitedly. 'Isn't this just a great place? Will you look at all the pans they have here?'

As soon as they were all unpacked they went to explore the surroundings.

The garden was neat with gravelled pathways and oval flower beds enclosed in borders of stone. Opening the tall wooden gate, they found themselves in a narrow lane which led to the long steep hill that would take them to the centre of the village. The people they passed were dressed mostly in t-shirts and shorts, the children chattering loudly as they accompanied their parents, and the air was thick with French voices. For some reason Declan couldn't get used to the fact that the people really didn't speak English, and Theresa was mesmerized by the tiny shops. They could hardly move ten paces without her stopping to exclaim over more exotic produce.

'Will you look at these jars,' she said in amazement. 'See, Declan, they have fig jam. Imagine, figs, in a jam.'

'And all those olives,' he said, peering in at the window. 'They've all got bits of stuffing inside them.'

They passed a shop selling vases, clocks, bookends, tiny pyramids and soap dishes, all made from a polished brown marble.

'It must be some kind of speciality they have here,' Theresa said. 'Maybe a local stone that they use. Aren't they lovely, Orla? I wonder should we choose something here for Mona?'

'Remember the weight allowance going home,' Declan cautioned. 'They could well be too heavy, and besides we've got weeks here yet, let's not be spending the first day we're out.'

Orla was excited to recognize the names if shops she had learned at the convent. '*Boucherie, boulangerie-pâtisserie,* she murmured. 'So that's what they're like.' She peered into the window of the *pâtisserie* where croissants, baguettes, strawberry tarts, elaborately decorated cakes and meringues were displayed at prices that made her open her eyes wide. 'Mammy, they want fourteen euros for a cake!' she gasped. 'Who would ever pay that much?'

Declan was puzzled when they stood in front of the *Hotel de Ville* in the village square. It doesn't look like a hotel,' he said, staring up at the building with flags fluttering from the facade. 'There's no mention of the room rates or anything.'

'Ah, we've done that up at the convent,' Orla told him. She was proud to show off her knowledge. 'It isn't a hotel at all, it's a kind of tourist office and information centre.'

'So what do they call a hotel, then? he asked.

'Er, actually, they call it a hotel,' she said, and they both fell to laughing.

Padraic found nothing at all to interest him in the surroundings and he brought the subject back to the important issue. 'When can we go and see the dragons and the knights?'

The Cité of Carcassonne had been used as a huge incentive for him to go on a holiday that involved much trying on of new shorts and t-shirts and a trip to the barbers to have his red curls cropped closer than he liked.

'We'll be going there soon, Declan promised him.

'You always say that,' he grumbled. 'But when?'

'Padraic, we've only just arrived,' Theresa said firmly. 'Daddy will take us soon. Let's have a look around the village first.'

'I'm thirsty,' he complained. He knew there was no point in arguing when Theresa spoke like that and he looked hopefully up at Declan.

'Daddy, I can see a café, look,' he said, pointing towards the bottom of the hill. 'Can't I have a drink there?'

Even in the fading evening light the cafe was busy, but they found a table for four under the canopy of a massive plane tree.

Padraic sipped at orange juice but he was not happy. 'Will we be going to the seaside soon?'

'Would you stop your whingeing,' Orla flashed at him.

'But it's not fair! We always do what you want to do. Nobody cares what I want.' He slid off his hair and stalked off.

'Where are you going?' Theresa said. 'Don't be wandering off, now, you'll get lost.'

'I'm only going to that fountain.'

'Well, don't drink the water, then,' Orla told him. It says '*eau non potable*' and that means you can't drink it.'

She got a scowl in response and they watched as he trailed his fingers in the round stone pool.

'What's got into him?' Declan said. 'He's not usually like this.'

'He's got a point, though, hasn't he?' Theresa said. 'I mean, we're here for Orla and it's not exactly ideal for a boy of his age.'

'He'll just have to put up with it,' Orla said grumpily.

'Show the lad a bit of patience, Orla,' Theresa said quickly. 'If you think about it, he might be feeling a bit left out. Everything has been about you and your eating for years now, it's no surprise if he thinks no-one's taking much notice of him, poor little mite. We could go to

Carcassonne tomorrow. Liz says it's the best place to visit here.'

Padraic was mollified when he heard that he promised trip would be the next day.

Declan found a parking space by the banks of the River Aude. They made their way across a bridge flanked on both sides by ornate street lamps, and down into the narrow Rue Trivalle, made even narrower by the cars parked on both sides.

Declan looked at them with interest. 'Would you look at the plates,' he said wonderingly. 'Spanish, German, UK. God, the place must be popular alright.'

Orla stopped walking and screwed up her eyes. The massive walls of the fairytale Cité of Carcassonne loomed high above them, dwarfing the terraced houses of the street.

'Jesus, would you look at that!' Declan exclaimed. 'Never seen anything like it in my life. It's a giant's castle up there.'

'Like Jack and the Beanstalk,' Padraic put in.

'Look at all those towers.' This was Orla. 'They're like shiny witches' hats and they're all different. It reminds me of Rapunzel. You know, Rapunzel, Rapunzel, let down your hair. That one.'

'It's more like a set from a film,' Declan said. 'I don't know why but I think I've seen it before somewhere.'

'You have.' Theresa was excited. 'I knew it reminded me of something the minute I saw it. It's been on the television. Robin Hood, I think.'

'That must be it, then. Come on, let's get a move on. It's a fair pull up this hill and we want time to look round the place when we get there.'

The walk up to the Cité tested their stamina. Orla sat on a low wall half way up to regain her breath.

'See, this is what I mean,' Theresa said, looking down at her with a frown. 'If you ate everything you'd have more strength. A girl of your age shouldn't be out of breath climbing a little hill.'

'It's not a little hill,' she protested. 'And you're out of breath as well.'

'Don't start being cheeky, now. I'm not seventeen.'

'Jesus, will you all save a bit of breath and let's get to the top,' Declan said. He too was breathing heavily. He reached out a hand and pulled Orla to her feet and they resumed the treck.

A gaudy yellow train passed them, packed full of tourists, and across the road, a full coach park indicated that the place was popular with many different nationalities.

They trudged up the last few steep steps up to the castle, and Padraic exclaimed, 'There's a merry-go-round, look. Can I have a go?'

'Now what have I told you about asking for things?' Declan said.

He was aggrieved. 'But how would you know what I want if I don't ask?'

Theresa laughed. 'Oh, let him have a go,' she said easily.

'There's no-one taking the money,' Declan said nervously, but Orla pointed.

'I think you have to get a ticket over there,' she said, and she strolled over. Theresa passed her a ten euro note. 'Go and see can you get him one.'

Feeling a little shy, she took Padraic by the hand and they joined the queue. She was too nervous to speak, but she held up one finger and pointed to Padraic, and this seemed to be enough. A minute later he was hoisted onto the back of a gaudily painted horse and waving to them as the merry-go-round increased speed and revolved.

The crowds milled around them as they made their slow progress up the narrow cobbled main street and into the heart of the Cité.

The street was crowded with families, tour groups and school parties and the street hummed with conversations. Orla could hear voices she tentatively identified as being Japanese, Spanish and Italian, and there were others she had no idea of.

Theresa walked on just ahead of them. She was entranced by the shops and boutiques, daringly going into them to finger the tea towels decorated with images of Carcassonne, and to examine the garish red, yellow and orange pottery painted with sprigs of lavender and stylized olives.

There were shops with outlandish jewellery, a toy shop with traditional wooden toys, and at last they came to a boutique which filled Padraic with joy.

When they came out he was clad in a suit of plastic armour, topped by a knight's helmet and carrying a long plastic sword which he swished around him, making other shoppers step hastily aside.

They peered into the *Musée de l'Ecole*, which Orla proudly told them meant the Museum of the School.

'Of course it is.' Padraic was scornful. 'It's got desks inside it.' Orla give him a slight push, and he bean to whimper.

'Mammy, I'm thirsty, can't we have a drink now?'

'I'm not sure where,' Declan replied a little nervously. They passed the *Taverne du Chateau* whose pavement cafe was filled with tourists, but all he could hear was a babble of foreign voices and he hurried them along in the hope that somewhere in this heaving place they might find somewhere with a menu in English.

After they turned the corner by the *Hotel de la Cité* with its gay window boxes spilling out geraniums, they wandered until they came to a cobbled main square packed with tables under the shade of massive plane trees and parasols.

Theresa inspected the menus.

'It's in English,' she announced, 'and it looks like normal food with chips and everything.'

They were all tiring in the heat of the blazing sun, and thankful to sit at one of the crowded cafés. Shortly afterwards they were tucking into cheeseburgers with chips, and comfortably settled enough to be able to gaze round at the crowded scene. Orla was well aware that both her parents were surreptitiously watching as she bit into her burger. Neither of them remarked on it when she finished the whole plateful but she thought her mother looked pleased.

She started on her diet coke and over the top of the glass she saw Padraic turn round to wave a greeting.

'Who on earth are you waving to?' she demanded, and he beamed at her.

'It's that man from the house,' he said, and at that moment Martin walked to their table.

'I thought I recognize you earlier,' he said. He pulled up a chair from an adjoining table. 'Mind if I join you? I've left mum in town shopping so I thought I'd come up here for a drink.'

It was the truth, but like many truths, only half revealed. The part that he concealed was that he had heard Padraic announce that he was going to buy a whole suit of armour, and guessed correctly that they would be visiting the Cité. He had offered to take Liz into Carcassonne to do the shopping and then he had driven up, parked the car and scanned the crowds until he spotted them emerging from a chocolate shop before they made their way towards the outdoor eating square.

He chatted easily and confidently, but his attention was fixed far from his polite conversation. His original impression that Orla was pretty now ripened into the thought that he had never seen a girl quite so beautiful.

'Do you come here every day?' Padraic wanted to know. He was frankly jealous of anyone who could go to the shop with the knights any day they wanted, and he was intrigued when Martin laughed.

'No, not at all. It's fine for an occasional drink but it's far too crowded for my liking.'

'Oh, but it's a lovely place,' Theresa protested politely. 'We have nothing like this in Limerick. Nothing as old as this.'

'Don't let appearances fool you,' came the surprising reply. 'The foundations are certainly ancient; in fact, it dates back to the twelfth century but it was scheduled for demolition a hundred and fifty years ago.'

'Really? This beautiful place?' This was Theresa, most definitely interested.

'I love the pointed towers,' Orla put in rather shyly, and he edged his chair slightly closer to her.

'There are fifty two of them,' he said,' and every one of them is a different design.'

'They look like witches' hats,' she added, and he smiled. 'I think the whole place is wonderful.'

'Not everyone shares your enthusiasm,' he said ruefully. 'Some people think it's become nothing more than a tourist trap, but if you look around, you'll find some beautiful features. Have you been into the church yet?'

They hadn't, and so after the meal he offered to show them around, and on the way told them more about the ancient Trencavel family, the Cathar religion and the horror of the persecution that took place in the thirteenth century.

He looked at his watch as they emerged from the gloomy splendour of the Basilique Saint-Nazaire, and said, 'I'm afraid I'll have it leave you. I have to pick mum up in fifteen minutes.'

He turned to go, but before leaving he looked back and asked, 'Will you be coming to the barbecue tomorrow?' He tried hard to make the question a general one, but meant it for Orla.

As they looked confused, he explained. 'Mum and Peter organize a barbecue for our guests. It's a sort of welcoming party. I thought she'd mentioned it to you.'

'We'll be coming,' Padraic said confidently, and he laughed. 'See you tomorrow evening, then. We start around seven o'clock.' And with that, he waved cheerfully and hurried away.

CHAPTER 9

Peter looked at his watch. It was half past six. Luc's brother-in-law Guillaume should have been here fifteen minutes ago with the sausages and beefsteaks he had ordered for the barbecue, and still there was no sign of his white van. He poked at the blazing embers. The barbecue was ready and he was irritated at the delay. He knew that Liz would not be happy either. She liked everything to go to like clockwork, down to the minute whenever they had any kind of event for their guests.

She soon appeared laden with a tray of cutlery and she looked down the length of the long trestle table, covered with a white cloth.

'What are all those plates for? There'll be six of us, won't there?'

'No, there'll be ten altogether,' he said. 'The Irish family in Les Jonquilles are coming now. I saw the woman this afternoon and she's paid for all four of them.'

Liz was annoyed. 'Well, you might have said something earlier. I've only got enough baguettes for the six of us. I'll need at least another couple and the *boulangerie's* shut now. Oh, Peter, you are the limit. Why on earth didn't you say?'

'Oh, just cut the slices a bit thinner. There'll be enough.' His voice was calm, but Liz's tone showed her exasperation.

'There won't be nearly enough for ten people.'

She cast her eyes over the table, mentally calculating if the amount of food provided would stretch. There was the Camembert, several dishes of pepper-stuffed olives, a fine pâté de campagne and glass bowls of mixed salads with tiny bottles of vinaigrette as a dressing. The deserts were all wrapped in cling film in the fridge; she would bring those out later. She had been busy all afternoon but she was well satisfied with the results. She had made trays of tiny profiteroles with jars of chocolate sauce and two apple pies well flavoured with cinnamon. Luc's sister Marie-Claire had given her an excellent recipe for *clafoutis* and had gone into great detail about the best cherries to use. With the chops and sausages that Peter would barbecue later, there ought to be plenty, she thought, but all the guests would need bread. She set the tray down in the table with more force than was strictly necessary, annoyed by the oversight.

'I'll have to go up to Prinny's, that's all. She's probably got a couple of baguettes in her freezer and I can pop them in the microwave.'

She pulled her blue apron over her head, slapped it down on the table and was gone.

Ten minutes later she turned into the short drive to Prinny and Luc's bungalow. She rapped smartly on the door but there was no response and she tried the handle. The door was unlocked but this was no surprise. People in the village rarely locked their doors during daylight hours.

After another loud knock brought no reply she tentatively twisted the handle and opened the door, fully expecting Prinny to be watching TV or reading, or maybe she was attending to Luc's mother.

In the tiny hallway, she called out. 'Prinny? Are you there, my dear?' There was silence. She might be in the lounge, she thought, and she turned the door handle.

Prinny was there. She was slumped on the sofa. Her head was back, her mouth slack and gaping and she was snoring. Liz was surprised. Surely she couldn't be so worn out looking after her mother-in-law that she needed a nap in the afternoon?

She came closer, and she watched Prinny as she stirred slightly, her head slumped over to one side. Puzzled now, she bent over her, meaning to shake her gently and ask if she could take some baguettes. But when her head came close to Prinny's there was the unmistakable smell of alcohol. Her foot knocked against something on the floor and she looked down. She had nearly kicked over an empty bottle of whisky.

Liz was shocked. She would never have imagined that the self possessed, charming Prinny would have a problem with alcohol. She herself hated the stuff. She couldn't bear the lack of control it induced, and although they kept wine and beer in the house, it was Peter who drank it, and she wasn't even too keen on that.

She stood there in an agony of indecision. Was it worth trying to wake her up? And even if she did, would Prinny be in any state to hold a rational conversation?

She thought rapidly and then headed for the kitchen. The bottom compartment of the tall freezer held several baguettes. She helped herself to three and bundled them under her arm.

When she got back, Guillaume had obviously arrived with the meat as Peter was busy turning burgers and sausages on the barbecue and poking more sticks of wood onto the embers. The trestle table was humming with muted conversation from the guests.

'Good, you're back,' he said in a low voice. 'Did she have enough baguettes?'

He glanced at the long breadsticks that Liz was now slicing up. She nodded briefly. She would have to tell him about Prinny, but she needed to get him alone.

He loaded a tray with the cooked meats, added a plate of bread and set off around the table.

'Mrs. O'Sullivan, what can I give you? Sausages, a burger?' He had an easy geniality that made Theresa relax and smile as she said, 'Oh, please, call me Theresa. Yes, I'd love a burger.'

He flipped it expertly onto her plate and handed her a sliced bun. 'Help yourself to salads. And would you like red wine, white wine? Or if you're a teetotaller there's lemonade.' He laughed, evidently at the absurdity of teetotalism for anyone except Liz.

'No, thank you. I don't drink.' Her answer was a little frosty. 'If you've got some iced water?'

A little nonplussed, he said, 'Yes, of course,' and he reached over for the bottle of Perrier water that Liz had placed by her own plate.

A CD player was plugged into the kitchen and Liz had run an extension cable out to the barbecue area and fixed up speakers, and the merry accordion music lent a real French ambiance to the table.

Padraic accepted three sausages and two hamburgers.

'Don't be filling your mouth, now,' his mother warned him. 'We can do without you being sick like you were at Auntie Colleen's.' Padraic just grinned and stuffed half a sausage into his mouth and the others laughed.

'Orla, my love, what can I get you?' Peter asked, and he was suddenly aware of Theresa and Declan staring at their daughter. It was almost as if they were expecting the girl to do something extraordinary, and he was puzzled. What was so odd about offering the child something to eat? he wondered. Even Padraic paused, his mouth agape showing half chewed sausage.

When Orla accepted a burger, her parents glanced at each other, and when she cautiously bit into it there was an almost audible sigh of relief from the pair of them.

'You're doing very well there, Orla,' said Declan quietly. 'Can you manage a sausage as well, do you think?'

'I'd do a lot better if you'd all stop staring at me like I'm some kind of circus freak!' she said, low voiced and furious. 'Just leave me alone, can't you?'

'All right, all right,' he said hastily. 'No-one's staring at you, child. We're just concerned that you eat, that's all.' Theresa was frowning at him now, and he fixed his eyes on his own piled plate and started munching.

Peter moved around the table, offering food and filling up glasses. The cheerful music had loosened tongues and there was a steady hum of conversation.

Under its cover, Liz whispered urgently to him. 'Come into the house, I have to talk to you.' Surprised, he passed his tray over to Martin and followed her into the house.

'What's the matter?'

'It's Prinny,' she said. 'She's drunk. She was on the sofa, totally out of it.'

'Are you sure? She wasn't just asleep?'

'Of course I'm sure,' she hissed. 'I'm not blind. And there was an empty whisky bottle on the floor.'

He frowned. 'That's a bit of a problem, all right. How is she supposed to look after the old girl if she's senseless?'

'I don't know why you're calling her an old girl. She can't be much older than we are. And do you think we should tell Emma? They are supposed to be best friends, aren't they?'

'Goodness me, no. Think how Prinny would feel if she knows we've told her best friend that she's an alcoholic. Best keep it to ourselves.'

'I'm worried about Arlette, though. What if she needs help and Prinny's out of it?'

'Liz, what can we do?' He was exasperated now. He liked Prinny. He found her witty and amusing, and knowing Liz's views on alcohol, he was afraid that this would put a definite strain on their relationship. Then he recalled himself. Hs guests were all out there and he and Liz should be with them instead of debating their neighbours' affairs. 'It's really nothing to do with us. It's Luc and Prinny's problem. That is, if there really is a problem. She might just have had one drink too many. We all do that sometimes and it doesn't make her an alcoholic. Come on, let's get back. They'll have finished the burgers now and there are all the desserts to get out.'

'We don't all have a drink too many,' she said acidly. 'Some of us don't have a drink at all.'

But she was talking to his retreating back as he headed back to the barbecue. This was not the time to start a row. The guests had to come first and so she followed him.

She made a mental note to buy more baguettes before the next barbecue, but before she did that, she was going to visit Prinny.

She had an idea that the woman was not happy. Whenever she and Luc visited, Prinny was vivacious, witty and a great raconteuse. She threw her head back and trilled with high pitched laughter when she was telling a story, but underneath all the fun Liz sensed a tension. She was too bright, too edgy and nervous. The last time that she and Luc had been over for an apéritif, Prinny had drunk just a little more than Liz thought wise, and when she had said goodnight there was a look of pleading in her eyes. No words were exchanged but it was not in Liz's nature to ignore the mute message that she was almost sure had been given.

She set off down the steep hill, pausing to wave a greeting to Marie-Claire in the butcher's. She passed the tiny shop on the corner, only recently opened. In the window there were bottles of high quality sauces, cellophane wrapped spices in tiny jars, local honey, olive oil in beautifully painted glass bottles and a few bottles of wine. She smiled with delight when she saw the bottles of Le Clos towards the back of the window. That was Luc's brother's wine, and she hoped it was selling well.

Her knock was not answered for a minute or two, but there were faint noises coming from the house.

Prinny opened the door finally and looked cautiously at Liz.

'Oh, Liz, it's you.' It was not very welcoming.

'Do you mind if I come in? Are you busy?'

'Oh, no. No, please, do come in. I was just having a little tidy around. You know how it is when you're trying to look after someone. There's no time to do anything.'

As an excuse for the state of the lounge, Liz thought it a pretty poor one. She glanced around at the sofa, piled with dirty washing, at the massive oak dresser that obviously hadn't seen a duster for days and at the windows which could have done with some good hot soapy water on them. She ached to set to and give the place a good clean. But obviously this would be crass and tactless in the extreme. Prinny hadn't invited her to do so, but she sat down in a blanket covered armchair. She decided to start with the obvious question.

'And how is Arlette? Is she any better?'

'No, not really.' The tone was very flat. 'There's not much hope that she'll ever recover completely, although the doctors say she might improve in time.'

'That must be very hard, for you and for Luc.'

To her surprise, the end of Prinny's nose grew pink and tears started to form. 'It is hard. I don't know what to do, Liz. I don't feel that I'm helping her at all.'

'Oh, I'm sure you are,' she murmured comfortingly. 'It must be lovely for her knowing that you and Luc are here. It was wonderful of you to give up your life in London and come out here.'

'No, you don't understand. I didn't want to come. Luc put me in an impossible situation. Either we stayed in the UK and I'd feel guilty about that, or I gave up everything there to come out here and now I feel guilty that I'm not helping. I had no idea it would be like this. Day after day, and I feel so terrible. Just so guilty about it all.'

'But why on earth should you feel guilty? You've given up everything to come here. It was wonderful of you. You did what was right.'

Her head came up sharply and she turned a tear streaked face towards Liz.

'Who exactly was it right for?' she flashed. 'Right for Arlette, right for Luc? I know he really wanted to come and live in France again. It seems it was right for everyone except me! And sometimes I ask myself, if it had been the other way round; if I'd been ill, would Arlette have left France to come and look after me? Somehow, I don't think so,' she finished bitterly. 'And there's never a single word of thanks. Luc seems to think I can just go on and on looking after her, and I can't. I don't even feel as if it's my house,' she went on bitterly. 'I wanted to order new furniture. Even though the place is so tiny, it might not be so bad if it were completely refurbished, but Luc says his mother doesn't want me to. He says she's used to it as it is and she doesn't want anything changing.'

Liz reflected. 'I suppose after she's had such a terrible change in her life, she just wants to hang on to what's familiar.'

'Yes, well, she might be used to living in a hovel,' she said crossly, 'but I'm certainly not. Oh, Liz, I feel like I'm such a failure.'

Liz was bewildered. 'But surely, if you know you've done your best, then why should you think you're failing?'

'That's just it. I'm not doing my best. I can't even feel sorry for her and I hate looking after her. What kind of a person does that make me?' By now her tears were spilling over. 'Oh, God, I need a drink.' She got up and went over to the crowded cupboard. She poured herself a generous measure of whisky and drained the glass in two gulps. She bowed her head. 'That's better,' she said. And then apparently remembering her manners, she continued, 'Oh, sorry, Liz. Would you like a drink?'

Liz shook her head. 'No, I never touch the stuff. I can't bear it, not after...' She stopped, remembering that she was here to try and help Prinny and not to burden the poor woman with tales of her own dark days when she and Douglas were in the throes of their divorce.

Prinny started to speak, but at the same moment a low moan came from the bedroom.

She sighed heavily before walking away and calling back over her shoulder, 'Sorry, Liz, I have to see what she wants.'

It was a dismissal that Liz recognized as such, but curiosity made her follow Prinny out of the room and down the short corridor leading to Arlette's bedoom.

Prinny was already inside, and she turned the handle. When the door swung open she opened her mouth and gasped in horror.

The only word to describe the place was chaos. Arlette had been sick, and fairly recently by the look of the bed. There was vomit dribbling down her chin and on the quilted counterpane. Beside the bed on the floor was an untidy heap of soiled incontinence pads. Dirty clothes littered the bed and were piled high in top of a dresser. On the bedside table were several opened bottles of tablets, their contents spilling out, and a medicine bottle with no cap. The bedroom window was grimy like the ones she had noticed when she came in.

Prinny looked up at her entrance and her face flamed. 'I didn't know you were coming in,' she said. The tone was defensive and Liz knew she would have to choose her words very carefully. Prinny would be well within her rights to ask her to leave, and for the sake of the poor lady in the bed that was the last thing she wanted. So she asked quietly, 'Where are your cleaning things? In the kitchen?'

Prinny nodded wordlessly, her face still red with embarrassment, and Liz turned and left. She was furious with the woman. What was she thinking? How could she let poor Arlette spend her days in such filth as she had just seen? But then she reminded herself that Prinny was probably the least qualified person to take charge of a sick woman. What had Emma said about her? Something about her being from a very wealthy family. She was determined not to antagonise her, but she swore that before she left, the room would be sparkling. When she returned she was carrying a bowl of hot soapy water, several cloths, binbags and two tea towels. She gently wiped Arlette's face and received a faint smile of thanks. She could see that the woman was tired and she beckoned Prinny out of the room with a jerk of her head towards the door.

Back in the lounge there was a silence, before Liz said, speaking as gently as she could, 'Prinny, I think you could do with a bit of help with Arlette. I really don't want to interfere, but why is her room in such a mess? Can't you do something about it?'

She was genuinely bewildered. She herself took care of three properties, and in her wildest moments she could never have imagined letting any of them get into the state of the room she had just seen.

'I just can't bear seeing her,' she confessed. 'It's all so awful. I just hate going into that room and seeing her like that. And the terrible smells. I had no idea it would be like this. Oh, God, I need ...'

'No, you don't need a drink,' she said firmly. 'After we sort out Arlette's room I'll make us some coffee.' All she got was a slight grimace, but she knew she had won.

'I want us to wait until Arlette is asleep, and then we'll go in and get the place sorted. Where's your window scraper?'

'My what?'

Liz sighed. The woman had probably never cleaned a window in her life. 'Never mind, we'll use cloths instead.'

Fifteen minutes later they crept into the bedroom to find Arlette sleeping peacefully. Liz bundled the incontinence pads into a binbag and she told Prinny to take all the dirty washing into the kitchen. When she came back the two of them set to work. As Liz had surmised, Prinny had no idea how to clean a window.

'Do you mean to tell me you've never done this?' she asked quietly, as she expertly swept the cloth over the glass.

'No.'

Half an hour later, she looked round with satisfaction. Between them they had removed the soiled counterpane and replaced it with a clean beige quilt that Liz found in the cupboard. Prinny sorted out the pills and put them back into their packets. The floor was mopped, the window was shining and everything was tidy.

They went back into the lounge, leaving Arlette dozing peacefully.

'Thanks awfully, Liz,' she said a little shamefacedly. 'You're a real brick.'

The English must be the only nationality in the world, Liz thought, to give away their social status as soon as they opened their mouths to speak. *A real brick*, she thought a little contemptuously. No-one used phrases like that anymore. She wondered why on earth Luc had married this pretty, empty-headed little butterfly. Aloud, she said, 'It's a pleasure, but now we need to get the rest of it sorted out.'

She was startled. 'The rest of it?'

'You, and the housework, and looking after Arlette. You really do need some help, Prinny.' She gazed around at the room; the battered sofa with sagging cushions, the oak dresser piled high with mismatched crockery and unwashed glasses. 'This whole place needs a good clean. I'll make you a list,' she said. Lists were Liz's forté, she loved them. At home she kept lists for the cleaning of the gîtes, lists for the groceries and lists of household repairs. She even had a list of lists she needed to make. 'And another thing, she added just a little grimly. 'Your clothes.'

'My clothes?' Prinny was really alarmed now. 'What's wrong with them?' She looked down at her Christian Lacroix dress. Was there a mark on it? Was it torn somewhere?

'There's nothing wrong with it, but it's not exactly the right thing for cleaning, is it?' She looked at the gorgeous creation in a bright swirly pattern with its deep neckline and three quarter sleeves gathered from the shoulder. 'You're going to be using bleach and I'd hate you to ruin that.'

'Bleach?' She looked blank.

'You don't mean to tell me you don't know what bleach is?'

'No. I mean, I've heard of it, of course, but what would I want it for?'

In spite of her rising impatience, Liz did feel a little sorry for this beautifully dressed woman with the long red-polished fingernails and immaculately styled sleek black hair.

'Didn't your mother teach you any of these things?' she asked curiously. 'How to look after a house, how to cook, clean things? Didn't you have a job?'

'Oh, yes, of course. I worked part time in an art gallery in London. It was fun, I met heaps of lovely people there, and of course, that's where Luc and I met.'

'So, didn't you do any of the cooking at home, then? Or the cleaning?' She was determined to discover at least one useful thing that Prinny had done in her life.

But she was disappointed yet again. Prinny shook her head. 'Oh, no, of course not. We had little Mrs. Herbert to do the cooking. She was jolly good, and we had cleaners in daily from the village.' She paused. 'Mummy didn't need to teach me cookery. She didn't think I would need it. She thought it was important to be dressed correctly and to have good manners. You know, how to be a good house guest and what kind of little posies to send as thank you gifts. That sort of thing.'

'No, Prinny, I do not know 'that sort of thing,' she retorted a little grimly. 'I grew up in a back street in Manchester and in my world you went to school, you came home and you did your homework and if you were lucky you played rounders in the street with your friends and tried not to let the ball go over into Mr. Thompson's garden or he would kill you. My sort of world did not involve being a house guest, good or otherwise, so I wouldn't really know what you're talking about.'

'No, perhaps not,' she agreed, slightly shamefacedly.

'In my opinion, your mother would have been better teaching you how to look after a house.' Her eyes swept round the untidy room, and she asked curiously, 'What can you do?' She meant in the line of housework, and was unprepared for Prinny's enthusiastic reply.

'I'm frightfully good at tennis. I played in teams when I was at school, and then of course, my riding isn't too dusty, and I fence a little.'

Liz shook an uncomprehending head. 'I wasn't thinking of sports, actually. I meant looking after a house. Didn't you ever do any housework at home?'

'But there was no need, I keep telling you…there were people….'

'Well, there's certainly the need for it now. You can't carry on like this, that's for sure.' Then, as the idea occurred to her, she said, 'If you hate all this so much, why don't you and Luc hire a nurse for Arlette? You could get someone to come in every day. Or at least a cleaner. I'm sure someone in the village would be pleased to have a job.'

'That's just what I suggested,' she said gloomily. 'But she's told Luc she doesn't want to be cared for by a stranger. She said she had enough of that when she was in the convalescent home, and the only people she wants around her now are her family. That's why it has to be me.'

'What about her daughter? Why doesn't she take care of her mother?'

'Oh, she couldn't possibly live with them. The shop is downstairs and all they have upstairs are a couple of small rooms. There wouldn't be enough space and in any case both of them are busy all day.'

'Oh, I see. Well, in that case, we'll have to do the best we can. But tell me a bit more about Arlette. Can she speak to you?'

'She speaks, but only in French and often it's so garbled I haven't the faintest idea what she's saying.'

'That must be so frustrating for her. That poor woman. And what does she do all day? It must be so boring for her, in bed the whole time. But there's a wheelchair in her room. Doesn't she ever sit outside?'

'It's so hard, getting her out of bed,' she confessed. 'I can't do it on my own.'

'Well there are two of us now, so why don't we take her out? It's a beautiful day and she's stuck in this room.'

Prinny nodded a little wearily and they both went back into the bedroom.

Arlette was awake, the bed littered with books as if she had tried reading and was tired of it. Liz asked her gently if she would like to go outside and received a grateful assent. Together, they slid her long legs out of the bed and eased her into the wheelchair. Liz pushed her into the garden, found a shady spot under a tree and tucked the light cellular blanket around her knees. 'There now, dear, that's better, isn't it?'

She smiled as she kicked the brake on with her foot, but to her surprise, Arlette's face changed. She was unmistakably furious, and Liz immediately recognized her error. She had spoken to the woman as if she was in her dotage, and she realised with a sense of shock just how patronizing her words must have sounded. Before her stroke, Liz recalled, Arlette had held a senior position in the local government, and to be reduced to this must be unbearable.

Her voice was low, as she said. 'I'm sorry, Madame. I meant to say, are you comfortable?'

The effect of being respectfully addressed as Madame once more had its effect, and Arlette nodded, at once both accepting Liz's apology and acknowledging that she was indeed comfortable for the moment.

As soon as she was back inside she broached the subject of Arlette's care again.

'Didn't anyone from the convalescent home give you any advice? Did no-one tell you how to look after her when she got home?'

She looked up at Liz, her face crumpling and her voice wobbling as if tears were imminent. 'The nurses did say a lot when she was leaving, but it was all in French, and so I...'

'You just nodded and smiled, did you?'

Liz could understand that. Prinny was far from being the only English person in France to feign more understanding of the language than they actually had. A smiling nod of the head was usually enough to convey the impression of complete comprehension when in fact, that could be far from the case.

In the house, she collected the window cloths from the dresser and folded them into neat squares. 'I'll go and put these away in a minute,' she said, 'but Prinny, quite apart from the cleaning, don't you think it's time you learnt a bit of French? After all, you're not on holiday, you could be here for a long time. Do you ever speak to the neighbours, for instance?'

'Well, I say *bonjour* when I meet people, of course...'

'That's exactly the point. You're never going to get to know people if you can't speak their language.' She gave Prinny a quizzical look, before she went on, 'Didn't it ever occur to you that you'd need to learn?'

'I thought they might speak English,' she said a little wearily. 'They did when I came to France before.'

Liz was puzzled. 'Who did, exactly?'

'Everyone, of course. The waiters, the people on reception, even the chambermaids understood nearly everything.'

Comprehension dawned. 'Oh. You mean in a hotel?'

'Yes. It was a long time ago, though,' she added, as if this might explain the lack of English she was experiencing now.

'And just where was this hotel?' Liz sighed inwardly.

'It was in Juan-les-Pins. We went to see some friends of Mummy's. Such a gorgeous place.'

'But, my dear, there's a vast difference between what was, presumably, a five star hotel on the Riviera, and this region. Naturally they'll speak English in a good hotel. That's part of

214

their job, to make everyone feel at home. But this is the Aude. The vast majority of people here are *vignerons*. At the very best they'll have learned English at school, but there's no way you can expect them to speak English to you.'

'Yes, but Luc can speak French.' She spoke slowly and distinctly, as if explaining a difficult concept to a young and not too bright child. 'We don't both need to.'

Liz felt her patience ebbing away, but she controlled herself and tried to speak calmly. 'Have you ever thought about what would happen in an emergency? What if Luc's not here?'

'I'd ring you, of course,' she said brightly.

'And if I'm not here? Out shopping, in the garden?'

'I've got your mobile number,' she said triumphantly, and despite herself, Liz had to smile.

'Yes, I know. But seriously, Prinny, you can't always count on somebody else being there. You really should learn yourself, even if it's just the basics.'

'Oh, I suppose it would be better,' she said a little crossly. 'But French is so hard. I really tried with it at school, but there are all those gender things. All that '*le*' and '*la*' business. I never could decide which to use.' She looked at Liz and gave a wan smile. 'You'd know about those, of course. And Luc, well, he never seems to have a problem with them.'

'No, well, he wouldn't, would he? He knows instinctively, just like you know how to speak English without having to think about it.'

She paused, still clutching the window cloths. 'How would you feel if I gave you some lessons?'

Prinny gazed up at her in consternation. 'Really? But I'm hopeless at it.'

'I'm sure you're no worse than some of the juniors I've taught. Honestly my dear, I do think you need it, and it wouldn't be any trouble. I have done it for the last thirty-odd years, you know.'

'I could try, I suppose.'

Liz gave her no time to reflect and change her mind. 'Good, that's settled then,' she said briskly. 'We'll start with a couple of hours a week, whenever you're free. Perhaps when Arlette is having a nap?'

'Yes, alright,' she agreed reluctantly. 'But I warn you, I'm totally useless at it.'

'You won't be when I've finished with you,' Liz assured her. She gave her a grim, half ferocious smile and took the cloths back to the kitchen.

When she came back, she returned to the most pressing concerns. 'Now, you know which tablets Arlette needs, don't you?'

'Yes, they're the ones on the side table. She has one every four hours.'

'Right, then, in that case, I'll be off. And I'll come back in the morning and we'll see if we can get a routine going with the housework. Oh, and there's just one more thing, Prinny.'

She leaned over to the coffee table and picked up the bottle of Laphroaig. 'Do you really need this?' she said gently. 'It isn't helping, you know. Can I take it away with me?'

She hesitated and looked up pleadingly. 'Oh, Liz, I don't know. It's so hard sometimes.'

'But this,' and she waggled the bottle in front of Prinny's face, 'this is only making you feel worse, I'm sure. Do let me take it, my dear. You'll feel so much better without it.'

She capitulated, as Liz had thought she would. 'Alright, then, take it away.'

'You're sure?'

'Yes.' She was impatient now. 'I'll be fine, honestly.'

She was rewarded with a wide smile and they kissed briefly before Prinny closed the door behind her. She leaned against it and heaved a great sigh, and then she went into the lounge. She opened the left hand cupboard of the huge oak wall unit and smiled faintly at the four unopened bottles of whisky. She opened a bottle of twenty-five year old Glendronach and poured herself half a glass. She sank down into the sofa and drank it in three gulps.

The next morning, still slightly hung over and with a thumping headache, she found a small brown paper parcel in her postbox. She was intrigued; she hadn't expected any post, and she took it into the lounge, fumbled with the string and eventually succeeded in cutting it.

A long white envelope contained several lists, each headed with a day of the week, and underneath were some garments. She held one of them up between her finger and thumb, very gingerly, eyes half focused and looked at it with horror. It was an overall with a note pinned to it.

'I was going to suggest that you wear old clothes to do the cleaning,' Liz had written, 'but thought you might not have any....'

'How right you are,' she murmured to herself.

'....so I found these. I bought them last month in Narbonne market for myself, but I thought they'd be just the thing for you when you're cleaning.'

She returned her gaze to the first overall. It was made of nylon in a bright blue, with gaudy roses in a hideous pink shade.

She shuddered and took out the next one. It was a twin of the first but in a ghastly shade of purple, with printed ivy leaves on it. Her first instinct was to bin them both, but then she reflected. If Liz should call in she would have no real excuse not to be wearing them, and, she supposed, at least they would protect her clothes. She laid them aside and looked at the lists. Monday was for washing, and there were detailed instructions concerning separation of colours, water temperature and ironing. Tuesday was apparently the right day of the week for changing bed linen, and Wednesday for cleaning fridge and oven. Each task had a list of apparently obligatory cleaning products which, Liz wrote, she would find on a separate list.

She sighed and shook her head as she took the cut glass decanter from the top of the sideboard and poured herself a double whisky. The woman was only being kind and trying to help, she supposed, but really, to expect her to wear those dreadful articles was almost too much to contemplate. Once she had drunk her whisky

218

and felt the familiar warmth flow through her she bean to feel slightly better, and after the second glass she was almost ready to wear the overalls. After the third glass she put on the blue one and decided that the colour quite suited her, after all.

CHAPTER 10

'Susannah, do you think you might just put a smile on your face when Prinny and Luc meet us?' Emma was exasperated by the sulkiness which had started on the day she had told them about her future plans and had not abated a jot since then.

'I'm alright, and I'd be a lot better if you'd just leave me alone and stop getting at me,' she snapped.

Emma's face was rigid with anger and she felt like slapping her. She controlled herself in time for the landing. It was no use at all letting herself become so irritated. They were here on holiday and she meant to make the most of it. Deliberately, she tried to put Susannah out of her mind and think about Prinny instead. There was a good chance that she would be late meeting them, as she had often been on their London outings.

But she was wrong. When they had shown their passports and made their way outside, she spotted the tall figure of Luc first, standing by the tiny figure with sleek black hair who was perched on the low wall with her back to them.

'There she is!' Her mood lightened as she saw her friend. 'Prinny!'

The woman turned round at the sound of her voice. She teetered over to greet them on navy high heeled shoes and dressed in a simple navy linen dress with a narrow white leather belt that showed off her petite figure beautifully.

'Emma! Darling! How wonderful to see you!' The two women embraced, and then Prinny turned to Susannah.

'You're looking marvellous, darling.' Susannah returned her embrace but with a slight air of reservation. She was fairly sure why they were here, even though Emma had insisted that it was nothing more than a short trip to see Prinny and cheer her up.

Luc came forward and bent forward a little tentatively to kiss both of them. He swung Emma's small leather holdall over his shoulder and wheeled Susannah's case for her.

Back at their home Luc ushered them inside and went to fetch cool drinks.

Emma looked around her with undisguised curiosity. 'Prinny, darling, you must be working so hard. Your home is beautiful,' she exclaimed. The comment owed more to politeness than honesty. Privately, she wondered how Prinny could possibly bear to live in this tiny little place, after her London flat.

But it was true that the lounge was gleaming and smelt of polish. Liz had been round the same morning, and directed operations until she was satisfied that Prinny could bring her friends to her home and be proud of it.

Prinny found it natural to give the slightest of shrugs and say lightly, 'One has to keep up certain standards.'

Luc followed her unspoken lead. 'Prinny does a wonderful job,' he said as he passed iced tea to Emma and lemonade to Susannah. 'Maman is so pleased that she is here. It is helping her through some difficult days.' He smiled fondly at her and the performance from both of them was so polished that neither Emma nor Susannah saw beyond the intended impression of a hard working and dutiful daughter-in-law who was a great comfort to the woman in the room just along the corridor.

His mobile phone rang and he took it out of his pocket. 'I hope you will both excuse me,' he said. 'But I have to go back to work. I am sure you will all have a lot to speak of. I will be back by seven, I hope.'

'And how is France suiting you?' Emma asked as soon as they heard his car backing out of the short driveway.

Prinny hesitated and Emma looked at her troubled face with concern. 'You do like it here, don't you? It's such a wonderful area. I was saying to Sue earlier, really, there are parts of it which remind me of Provence.'

'It's pretty,' she conceded. 'But it's not what I expected.'

'Oh, darling, you don't have to tell me.' Emma was instantly sympathetic. 'I always thought you'd find it a bore. It's Luc's mother, isn't it?'

She gave the briefest of nods. 'It's so hard, Em,' she admitted sadly. 'If I'd only known, I'd never have come. Even for Luc.'

'Darling, I know you too well. You can't fool me. You'd have followed him to the ends of the earth.'

She gave a despondent laugh. 'You're probably right,' she said. 'But do you know...?'

She leaned towards Emma and lowered her voice. 'Do you know she's actually incontinent? He never told me about that. If he had, I'm sure I'd never have agreed.'

'He absolutely should have told you.' Emma's voice was firm. 'He had no right to bring you over under false pretences.'

But here Prinny was a touch defensive. Emma might be her best friend, but she was not prepared to let all the blame fall on Luc. 'It wasn't quite like that,' she amended weakly. 'I mean, I knew right from the start that she'd had a stroke. Maybe I should have found out a bit more about it before I agreed.'

'What about his family?' she asked. 'Do you like them?'

'Darling, they're horrendous. At least,' she added, 'most of them are. The best one is Marie-Claire, she's his sister. Of course, with the language problem, it's hard to really get to know her properly but she seems pleasant enough. She seems to like me too, or at least, she likes my wardrobe. She did a terrific amount of *'ooh-la-la-ing'* when she was looking at my dresses, and she was positively drooling over the labels. If she'd been nearer my size I'd have given her one of my last season's Dior's, but none of them would come near her, I'm afraid. She's rather a large lady. Her husband keeps the local butcher's shop, and they've got two adorable children, a boy and a girl. Those two just look at me as if I'm from another planet. The language again, I'm afraid. Then there's his brother Maurice, and quite frankly, darling, he's a peasant. He barely acknowledges my presence when we're together, which isn't very often, thank goodness. He's the one who grows grapes.'

'And can't any of them look after Luc's mother?'

'Not Marie-Claire, she's quite obviously too busy. Maurice is married but his wife has walked out on him. Luc thinks she's gone back to Paris but he's not sure. Anyway, she's out of the picture now.'

Her words brought Emma's purpose back to mind, and she seized her chance.

'It's such a pity that Sue hasn't started at medical school yet,' she said, looking significantly at Prinny. 'If she had, I'm sure she could have given you lots of advice. She's sure to study strokes when she starts at Newcastle.'

Susannah stood up and faced her mother squarely.

'Mummy, you really are impossible,' she flared. 'And so totally transparent. You're hoping that Prinny will try and make me change my mind, aren't you? Well, it's not going to work. You know perfectly well that I've decided to be an actress, and nothing either you or Prinny can say is going to change that.'

There was an awkward silence, which Prinny broke by looking at her watch and remarking, 'I'm terribly sorry darlings, but I'll have to leave you for a while. It's time I was giving Arlette her lunch. Unless you want to come with me, of course?'

'Would she mind?' Emma was concerned. 'She might not like two strange English women watching her eat. You said she didn't like strangers.'

'Oh, I don't think so.' Prinny was nonchalant. 'She doesn't want anyone else looking after her, but visitors are different. It will be a change for her. She doesn't see many people now.'

'Yes, I'll come, then, if you really think she won't mind. Then we must think about settling into our gîte. I'd like to get a wash. You know how sticky one gets travelling.'

'Of course, darling. Liz has given me your keys, so we can go along as soon as I've fed Arlette.'

She disappeared into the kitchen, returning presently with a potato topped meat pie, a drink in a plastic lidded beaker and a dish of rice pudding.

'Not exactly cordon bleu cookery,' she said deprecatingly. 'She can only eat, well, sort of mushy things if you see what I mean. She has trouble with food if it's too solid.'

They nodded sagely and followed her into Arlette's bedroom, treading quietly as if somehow ordinary footsteps would be inappropriate.

Arlette looked a little surprised but then acknowledged them with a small lop-sized smile.

The meal did not go well. Emma and Susannah settled themselves in chairs at the side of the room and watched.

After a couple of minutes, Prinny's impatience and Arlette's obvious difficulties combined to result in a brown mess dribbling all down her front. Emma recognized her embarrassment and she stood up quietly and murmured, 'I'll wait in the lounge.'

Prinny nodded, expecting Susannah to follow her, and she was considerably surprised when she said, 'Can I try?'

Prinny handed her the bowl and spoon without a word.

'Thanks.' She carefully held a spoonful of pie to Arlette's lips, and it all went in. She waited patiently until Arlette had swallowed it before she offered the next spoonful. Five minutes later the bowl was empty, without a single morsel being spilt. She calmly offered the cup, again with evident patience and the same success.

Prinny handed her the bowl of rice pudding. She watched Susannah with a mixture of emotions. The first, which she tried hard to push to the back of her mind, was quite frankly a pang of jealousy. In some indefinable way Arlette was hers, and she was piqued to see someone else caring for her. She was also envious of Susannah's easy and calm success where she herself failed, and failed badly, day after day. But then, she thought sourly, this is only one meal. She'd be just as bad as I am if she had to do it day after day. But hard on the heels of this thought was the sure knowledge that Susannah would be as successful as she had been today no matter how many times she did it.

Her innate good manners made her keep her feelings to herself, and she took the empty bowls from Susannah, saying, 'Thank you, darling, that was fine.'

'It was easy.' Susannah was a little surprised to discern that Prinny evidently thought there might be some difficulty involved in so simple a task, and also quite astonished to find that she had actually enjoyed the process. She remained in the room, chatting to Arlette in slow but accurate schoolgirl French and the two of them were soon having a conversation which both of them understood.

'What on earth can I do with her?' Emma said despairingly, as soon as Prinny returned to the lounge. 'Nothing I've said so far has had the slightest effect. She's made up her mind that she's going to some silly drama school or other, and time's running out. She has to confirm her place at Newcastle soon or she won't be able to go. Henry's completely useless, of course. If he had his way, he'd let her do exactly as she likes. You will have a word with her, won't you, darling?'

Prinny was thoughtful. 'I'll certainly try,' she said. 'Do you know, Em, I wasn't sure until now, but she was absolutely super with Arlette. She fed her so much better than I ever manage, and she really seemed to care about her.'

'That sounds more like being a good nurse, not a doctor,' Emma said doubtfully. 'Nursing isn't what Henry and I have in mind for her. She's far too intelligent for that.'

'It's a start, though, don't you think? She really seems to have a knack for caring for people.'

The daylight was fading when Prinny escorted them to their gîte. Emma noticed lights shining through the open shutters of the neighboring house. 'Is someone else staying here?'

'There's an Irish family, they've been here a few days now.' She turned the key and led them into the spotlessly clean hall and through into the lounge.

'It seems tidy enough,' Emma remarked somewhat disparagingly, looking around her. 'I'd much prefer a decent hotel of course, but I suppose it will have to do. It's not forever.'

Orla settled herself on one of the green and white striped sunbeds by the pool. She thought it was a pity that she couldn't swim, as the crystal clear water sparkled in the sunlight and she could imagine how heavenly it would be to dive in. It was surrounded by a white painted stone wall, with long, low tubs of bright geraniums flowering in hues of pink and scarlet. There were wooden tubs containing small palm trees in each corner. The whole place was a heavenly sun trap and she felt peaceful and content. She brought her sunhat down over her forehead to shade her eyes and was soon dozing, her book slipping down by her side.

'Excuse me. Is this sunbed taken?'

She opened her eyes and put a hand up to shade against the glare to see a tall, fair-haired girl standing by her side.

Since it was clearly unoccupied, she said politely, 'No, please have it.'

The girl stretched out long legs and wriggled herself until she was apparently comfortable.

'Such a relief to be here at last,' she said. 'I hate flying, it's such a bore, don't you think, but really there's no choice unless one wants to spend hours on a beastly motorway and book into one of those terrible roadside hotels.'

As the flight had been one of the most exciting things Orla had ever done in her life, she didn't reply. The girl was making her feel countrified and unsophisticated. She looked at her. Her scanty bikini was red with a swirly pattern in white, showing off a tiny waist. The long shapely legs were encased in high heeled red pumps which she slid off and kicked onto the floor.

'And what is this place like? Is there anything to do? Any decent shopping?' The voice was still a fainly bored drawl. Orla battened down her first impression of distaste and tried to remain polite.

'There's Carcassonne. We went there yesterday. At least, we went to the Cité, but I think there are more shops in the town. And there's Narbonne in the other direction. They have a good market there on Thursdays, Mammy says.'

'Oh, darling, not a market. They're full of the most ghastly cheap clothes. I meant, are there any good shops?'

Slightly startled about being addressed as 'darling' by someone she had only just met, she said rather shyly, 'I don't do much shopping actually. Mammy makes a lot of my clothes...'

The girl's eyes widened and she looked horrified but she refrained from comment. Instead she introduced herself. 'I do most of mine in Knightsbridge. I'm Susannah Wade, by the way. And you are...?'

'Orla O'Sullivan.'

'Nice to meet you, Orla.' She held out a hand with pointed, highly polished red fingernails and shook Orla's hand lightly. 'And who's the Adonis I passed just now?'

'Adonis? Who do you mean?' But even as she asked the question she realised that it was an automatic response. She knew very well who the girl meant.

'That gorgeous hunk of a man I passed on my way down here. He looks as if he ought to be the lead singer in a boy band somewhere. Do you know him?'

'That's Martin Saunders. He's staying here with his mother for the holidays.' Her tone was colder than she had intended. She was greatly irritated by the girl's interest in him, and her la-di-da accent was horribly grating.

Quite suddenly she wanted to get away from her, into the coolness of the villa. She picked up her book and walked away. There was no response from the girl.

CHAPTER 11

'Should we have some of those croissant things, do you think?' Theresa was proud of her pronunciation. She had heard Liz refer to them as one of the best options for breakfasts in France.

'Might just as well. They don't seem to have heard of bacon and eggs in these parts.' Declan was felling a little disgruntled by the lack of proper foodstuffs in the village. He was bemused by the hanging tubes of cured sausages, by the long baguette sticks and the bewildering variety of cheeses they had seen.

'Ah, we're on our holidays, Theresa said easily. 'That's what we're here for. To enjoy ourselves, try new things. Orla, my love, you can go to the *boulangerie* and get them for us.'

She was startled. 'What, me? But what would I say?'

'Just ask for them. You can do that can't you? That was the reason you wanted to come, wasn't it? To practise your French? Well, here's a great chance to do it.'

She was still reluctant. 'But I'm not fluent yet.'

'But you learn it up at the convent,' Declan said. 'You must be able to ask for a bit of bread or whatever it is.'

They were both looking at her hopefully now and she hesitated. She realised that she had put them through so much anxiety recently, and here they were with huge expectations that she could do this thing and make them proud.

'OK, I'll go,' she said resignedly.

'That's a good girl,' Declan said approvingly. Theresa searched in her handbag and handed her eight euro coins. 'It won't be any more than that, we only want one each and Padraic might not want a whole one.'

Still reluctant, she pocketed the coins and made her way slowly down the steep hill, taking no notice of her surroundings as she was rehearsing every word of coming transaction, and by the time she reached the *boulangerie* she had it by heart. '*Quatre croissants, s'il vous plait,*' she repeated in her head, over and over. It should be easy enough, but despite the repetition she was nervous when she opened the door.

The first thing that struck her was the wonderful aroma of freshly baked bread, and the next was the people. Everyone seemed to know each other. There were men shaking hands and women greeting each other with two kisses on the cheek. Every time anyone new came in they nodded genially around and said, '*Bonjour messieursdames,*' and everyone said '*Bonjour*' back to them.

The lady at the counter was taking her brown paper bag of croissants and chatting in a steady stream of completely incomprehensible French to the young serving assistant. Startled, Orla's mind flew to the classroom at the convent, and all those hours spent learning irregular verbs. What was it all for, she wondered, if she couldn't understand anything now?

The thought brought her back to her mission and now she was at the front of the queue. To her dismay she saw that there were no croissants left on the counter. The lady with the paper bag had bought the last ones. She panicked now. She had no vocabulary to ask if there were any more croissants, and she could see nothing else on the counter that would be an acceptable substitute. There were triangular slices of cheese and tomato topped pizza, baskets of rolls that looked as if they had chocolate inside them, and behind the counter, propped up against the wall were tall sticks of twisted breads of different thicknesses. She desperately scanned the counter again but it was true. Not a single croissant in the whole shop, and to her horror, the assistant was smiling at her but she was also drumming her fingers on the counter in a way that suggested the need to be quick.

The little French she had almost deserted her. 'Er, *quatre*,' she said, and to point to her meaning she held up four fingers.

'*Oui, quatre, mais de quoi?*' Yes, four, but four of what? the girl was asking.

The question in French panicked her utterly. The muscles in her stomach tightened and she froze.

The assistant was impatient now. The small shop was crowded and she had little sympathy to spare for this girl who didn't know what she wanted. She spoke a little more sharply than she had intended.

'*Je ne peux pas vous aider si vous ne savez pas ce que vous voulez,*' she told her. I can't help you if you don't know what you want.

Suzette was used to helping her father in the *boulangerie*. It was a family business after all and they were glad of the extra income from the summer tourists, but it made life very difficult when she was confronted with customers like this girl who spoke little or no French. She tried to keep the impatience out of her voice but her expression spoke volumes, and Orla was on the point of turning to flee out of this terrible place when a cool, calm voice behind her said, 'Can I help you?'

She spun round. 'Martin! Thank goodness you're here. I was never so glad to see anyone in my life.'

'What are you trying to buy?'

In her panic she couldn't even remember the word. 'It's those half circle things you have for breakfast,' she said in desperation.

'Oh, croissants,' he said. He had a tiny amused smile and he rattled off a stream of fluent French to the young assistant.

'*Ah, oui Monsieur*,' she said and she turned and walked into the back of the *boulangerie*, returning almost immediately with a tray of freshly baked croissants. She filled a bag with four of them and named the price. He gently took her purse from hands that were still shaking and counted out the correct amount.

Once she had her croissants she waited at the door clutching her paper bag until he came out. It would seem churlish to set off back to the *gîte* without him, and besides, she did want to thank him.

'You saved my life in there,' she said fervently as soon as he came out. 'Thank you so much. I was about to run out of the place.'

'Not a problem,' he said easily. He looked at her and his immediate thought was how very beautiful she was. Despite her height, she had a fragile air about her which made him feel somehow very protective. His mother had said she was seventeen, but she looked younger in her pale blue T-shirt and long slim legs encased in dark blue shorts. The hair that was tied back with a blue plastic clip only made her look even younger.

'Where did you learn to speak French like that?' she asked. 'I couldn't do that in a million years.'

'I suppose I've picked most of it here,' he said. 'I come every holiday to stay with mum. She was a French teacher before she retired and of course, I did it at school as well.'

As they walked side by side up the steep hill, he asked her, 'How do you like France? Have you been before?'

'I love it. It's the first time I've ever been anywhere really. Well, only Dublin actually.'

'On holiday?'

'No,' she said quickly. 'No, it wasn't a holiday. I was in a clinic there.'

In response to his questioning glance she explained further, telling him about her anorexia and the treatment she had had. She did not mention Bridget. The memory of her friend was still too raw, too painful to mention.

He glanced sideways at her as he understood the reason for her delicate air and slender limbs.

He did not probe any further, but instead said lightly, 'You see these little cobbled streets? They date back to medieval times. There are lots of ancient villages in this part of France. Personally, I think the best one is Minerve, it's spectacular.'

'I'd love to see it,' she said shyly, 'but Mammy hasn't mentioned going there.'

He hesitated, and then said, 'If you really would like to see it, perhaps we can go together?'

He didn't know if he was being too forward. After all, they had only known each other for a couple of days, but he was overjoyed when her face lit up and she said, 'That would be great, if we could. But how? I mean, is there a bus?'

He was amused. 'No, I was thinking of driving, actually.'

'Really? You can drive? You've got a car?'

'It's not mine,' he admitted, 'but Peter lets me drive his Renault while I'm here. It's not really ideal for two people, it's got seven seats, but he's insured me to drive it and though I say it myself, I am a pretty good driver. I'll take care of you.'

When they reached the top of the hill they passed a restaurant with two ornamental bay trees on each side of the door. She looked up at the sign above the door. *'Les Saveurs.'* What does that mean?'

'It roughly translates as The Flavours, although I admit it does sound better in French. It's one of the best restaurants in the area.'

He stopped and looked at her. 'We could go tonight if you like?'

'By ourselves, you mean?' She was astonished, but extremely flattered that this tall, gorgeous boy was taking such an interest in her. She put her hand up to her cheeks which suddenly felt hot. 'I'd love that.'

'Good, that's a date, then. And if you to go down to the *boulangerie* tomorrow just knock at the door and we can go down together. Mum always gets her bread there so we might as well get yours at the same time.'

She turned into the gate of their gîte feeling more contented than she had done for many months. Martin was such a lovely boy, she thought. It was almost like having a boyfriend. Her only worry was that her mother might object to her going to a restaurant with a boy.

When she went out at home with Kathleen and Lyndsey her parents always wanted to know where she was going, and her father insisted on meeting her at the bus stop when she came home. She remembered how this had puzzled Kathleen, whose own father gambled every single week on the horses and wouldn't have cared if his daughter had chosen to stay out all night. Orla knew all about the constant fights in their house, and how Kathleen was scared that one day her mother would do as she was always threatening and leave.

But even though she appreciated her own parents' concerns for her she was very uneasy. She would feel so humiliated if she had to go and see this boy and tell him that she wasn't allowed to go out with him. Her stomach tensed at the mere thought of asking permission.

She waited until they were all seated at the garden table and Theresa had cut and buttered their croissants before she broached the subject.

'Martin's invited me to go to a restaurant with him. Can I go?'

Theresa and Declan looked at each other. Declan's eyes were wide. 'On your own? On a date, do you mean?'

'Which restaurant?' This was Theresa.

'Yes, on a date,' she said impatiently. She wondered why there always had to be an interrogation on everything. 'To that restaurant round the corner. *Les Saveurs*. Why not?' She was defensive, and looked from one to the other of her parents.

Theresa's experience at the clinic had left her with a nagging doubt as to whether she was to blame in any way for Orla's troubles. A year, even six months ago, a request to go out with a boy would have met with a firm refusal but Doctor Hannigan had let her know, privately, that letting Orla take control of some parts of her life was the best way forward, and she had taken heed.

So now she said, surprising Orla considerably, 'I think that sounds grand. Liz told me it's got a really good reputation, it's supposed to be one of the best in the whole region.' She spoke quickly. 'Declan, would you go and find us some of that apricot jam I got yesterday? It's in the fridge.'

He got up and squeezed past Padraic, and as soon as he was out of earshot, she said, 'Now, you take no notice of what Daddy says.'

'You mean you don't mind if I go?' She was astonished. This had never happened before. She had expected a whole battle with shouting and tears before she got grudging permission.

'No, of course not. You'll have a lovely time, and they say the food is marvellous there.'

'I'm not going because of the food,' she said quickly.

'No, I know that. When did you ever go anywhere for the food?'

They giggled conspiratorially like two schoolgirls. 'I'll tell you what. I'll do your hair for you. We'll curl it, and you can wear that green hair ribbon I got for you.'

'Not a hair ribbon,' she objected. 'I'm not twelve years old. I'm sure he already thinks I look young for my age.'

'Oh, nonsense, it will look gorgeous.'

She sighed. It wasn't worth an argument, she thought, and she knew she would finish up wearing it anyway.

'I found some curling tongs in the bathroom this morning. This place is really well equipped. And you could wear that halter neck dress you brought, the green one.'

She was doubtful. 'Is it good enough, do you think? I mean, it's a posh restaurant. I can't look out of place.' She did not add that she wanted to be dressed nicely for Martin. Let them think it was for the restaurant.

'Oh, it'll be fine. And besides, what else have you got? This is a holiday place, it's not Dublin where everyone gets dressed up to the nines to go out for a meal.'

She was still a little dubious but there was no time to shop for another dress, and in any case she wouldn't know where to begin looking. There didn't seem to be any clothes shops at all in the village. She tried it on in her bedroom and twirled in front of the wardrobe mirror. Not too bad, she thought. Not glamorous, certainly, but good enough.

Back inside, Declan said doubtfully, 'You think she should go, then?'

'Yes, of course I do. This time last year nothing on God's earth would have got her inside a restaurant. Didn't you see how happy she looked? God, Declan, when was the last time she looked happy? After all she's been through, don't you think it's time she had a bit of pleasure?'

'Well, I don't know.' Then he looked up, beaming with delight at the idea that had just occurred to him 'Maybe we should book a table ourselves, just to keep an eye on her?'

Theresa's eyebrows almost reached her hairline. 'Jesus, Mary and Joseph, the child is nearly eighteen. We can't go and sit at the next table and keep looking over her shoulder. She'd never forgive us. No, we've got to let her grow up a bit. The boy is Liz's son and I trust him. He's well mannered, he's good looking and she'll have a great time altogether. So don't be going and spoiling things for her.'

He capitulated. 'It was only an idea,' he said deprecatingly. 'Well, if you think they'll be alright...'

'They'll be just fine,' she said firmly. 'So let's be hearing no more objections.'

'But what about her getting home?'

She closed her eyes in exasperation. 'The place is fifteen minutes' walk from here. She's not going to need a train to get home. Martin lives two doors away for Heaven's sake. They'll walk home. And no,' he said as she opened his mouth to speak, 'you'll not be going out to meet them, either.'

He had to be content with that, and he sighed and took the newspaper he had bought at the airport and went outside to read it in peace.

She was very definitely nervous when the fair-haired manageress showed them to their seats. The awful green hair ribbon was safely in her handbag; she had taken it out the minute she was out of sight of the gîte, and now she looked around her curiously.

The decor of the dining room was subdued, yet it was the most elegant place she had ever been to in her life. The table cloths were dark red with an overcloth of pristine white linen, and each table had an individual red rose in a cut glass vase that tapered out towards the top.

The walls were covered with paintings of buildings, some of which she recognized. That one was the Eiffel Tower, and there was another of a huge white church that she thought she had seen before somewhere. Other paintings were of the local countryside and showed vines, some of them covered in snow. They looked just like rows of gnarled, dead branches but she knew that vines lost their leaves in winter.

A black trousered waiter brought them a menu each. Martin looked at it briefly, and then said, 'Have you decided?'

'To be honest, I don't know what half the things are,' she admitted, and he smiled gently at her.

'There's the *poulet*, that's chicken, and the *canard* dishes are duck. Then the *légumes* are vegetables, and the *riz* is rice....'

'Stop, stop it!' She was laughing now. 'This is sounding like a French lesson. You choose and then I'll have the same.'

'Whatever it is?' he teased. 'And what if I want the chocolate covered grasshoppers?'

Her face lit up as she pealed with laughter again, and Martin looked at her tenderly. She was a different girl when she laughed, he thought.

'If that's what you're having then I'll eat them too,' she said. They both laughed, and she felt totally at ease for the first time since she had come in. Martin was so handsome, she thought. She loved the blonde hair that fell over his forehead and his eyes of such an intense blue they reminded her of jewels. She cast around in her mind for a word that meant sophisticated and she settled on very grown up. Yes, that was it. He was not boyish, but mature like a man.

'What are they like?' she asked him suddenly.

He was confused. 'What are what like?'

'Grasshoppers. Have you ever had them?' Her face was innocent. She really believed him.

'Ah, well, actually, I was joking.'

'Oh. I thought they might eat them here. Daddy says they eat snails and frogs' legs so I thought they might eat grasshoppers too.'

'Not as far as I know,' he grinned. 'At least, I can't find them on tonight's menu.'

The waiter returned with a pad and silver pencil and Martin rattled off a stream of French while he nodded and scribbled.

'I've ordered for you, too,' he said. 'That way it will be a surprise.' His next question surprised her. 'What kind of wine do you prefer? I know you're meant to have red wine with meat, but do you prefer white? Just say so and I'll order it.'

'Wine? Really?' She was astonished.

'Yes, of course. You do like it, don't you?'

She hesitated. She had already admitted that she couldn't understand the menu, she didn't want to appear totally ignorant. But then her basic honesty asserted itself. 'I couldn't say if I like it or not,' she began. 'I've...'

'Never had it,' he finished for her, and he leaned over and took her hand.

'I'm very honoured to be the one who introduces you to our magnificent wines. We'll have a bottle of *Le Clos*,' he continued, his face deadpan. 'That's the best choice to go with grasshoppers. It complements the flavour so well.'

She pealed with laughter at his serious expression, but when the wine was opened and the waiter poured a tiny amount into her glass she looked at him, bewildered.

'Just sip it and nod,' he whispered, and she obediently took the tiniest sip and nodded at the waiter. Then he filled her glass. She had never felt so grown up in her life.

As she was drinking she wondered idly what Kathleen and Lyndsey would be doing now. Probably mooching around the village as they often did, looking into the shops to see what was new. That brought her to thinking of the convent and a huge surge of giggles ballooned up inside her.

'What's so funny?'

'I was just thinking, if Sister Bernadette could see me now. She'd have a fit!'

'Who's Sister Bernadette?'

She told him, and then, the wine loosening her tongue, she continued. 'She's really the reason we're here. She set me off wanting to go on a diet.'

The waiter brought them their starter and she looked at the plate. Before she could put the question, he said, 'It's *foie gras* served on a slice of *brioche*, and that's fig conserve. I've had it before here, it's very good.'

She dutifully took a forkful and her eyes opened wide and she smiled broadly. 'This is fantastic.'

'So it ought to be, this in one of the best restaurants in the whole of the Languedoc.' He gave her a very direct look, and then said curiously, 'Would you like to tell me a bit more about your eating problems?'

'It's hard to explain,' she said wearily. 'At first I just wanted to be thinner, it just seemed like I wasn't as good as anyone else. My legs were too fat, so I started cutting out some foods. I didn't eat fatty things, and then I stopped eating anything at all that was high in calories. And after that I kept a check on everything I ate. I didn't seem to need much food.'

'Pretty hard on whoever was cooking for you,' he murmured, and she looked up.

'Mammy started getting so annoyed with me, and she would force me to eat meals, and so I ate them but then I would make myself sick afterwards. There was no way I could take in all those calories.'

He was obviously puzzled. 'But weren't you hungry all the time?'

'Sometimes,' she admitted, 'I used to feel famished actually, but when I was hungry it just felt as if I was winning in some way. That I was doing what I wanted to do, there was no-one forcing me to eat.' She hesitated, and then went on: 'I used to get so frightened...'

'Of what?'

'I mean, sometimes I thought that the anorexia was going to win, that it was going to control me and that I'd die from it eventually.'

She looked for his reaction, half expecting an instant display of sympathy. Instead, he was silent and he looked very serious.

'Orla, just tell me. Tell me the truth. Don't you think some little part of you liked all that? All the attention it got you? Everyone getting worried about you?'

'No!' The denial was vehement. 'No, of course I didn't.' And then, as he looked searchingly at her, she said, 'Well maybe the tiniest bit, but mostly I wasn't thinking about other people, I was concentrating on getting thinner. Mary kept saying I was upsetting Mammy and Daddy but I didn't believe her at first.'

'Mary?'

'She's my sister.' The tone was very flat, and he probed further.

'What is she like?'

'She's everything I'm not,' she stated very firmly. 'She's the pretty one.'

He raised his eyebrows but waited for her to finish.

'She's the one who's good with her books, she always got good marks and the nuns think I should be as clever as she is. Mammy and Daddy think I should be tidy like Mary, and I should help around the house like M..Mary...' She faltered, as her mood had changed and she felt again all the bitterness that she was carrying around with her.

'But you said it was the Sister at the convent who started you off on your anorexia?'

She nodded, and told him all about Sister Bernadette who had been so horrible to her.

He was thoughtful. Then he said, 'And was she like that with everyone, or was it just you?'

She was eager to tell him. 'She's vile with everyone in our class,' she said. 'Even the people who are really good at history.'

'And yet, the other girls in your class, they didn't think they had to go on a diet because of her, did they?'

'Well, no,' she admitted. 'I think perhaps I might have been a bit jealous of Mary.'

He sipped his wine and carefully placed the glass on the table. 'Even if you were,' he said thoughtfully, 'I can't see why that should suddenly make you want to destroy yourself. There must be something more than that.'

The wine was definitely having its effect on her, and suddenly, a memory stirred. Until now she had never remembered it, but now the hurt and humiliation came flooding back as if it was yesterday. She flushed and Martin said gently, 'What is it, Orla?'

'It wasn't Sister Bernadette,' she said slowly. 'I thought it was, truly, but I think it was someone else, when I was little.'

He waited patiently and she took another gulp of her wine, and then she said, 'I can't remember how old I was. About six, I think, and it was Christmas. I remember looking at the lights in the tree, and there were lots of people in the room. A lady came in and she had presents for us. For Mary and me, and she....' She broke off as the memory surfaced.

'Go on,' he said. 'What happened?'

The words would not come out. She found it hard even now to voice them, but Martin was looking at her so calmly and so gently that she found her voice again. 'She gave Mary a present and then she looked at me, and she said something like, 'What a shame Orla's got so chubby. She's never going to be as pretty as Mary, is she?' I think she was talking to Mammy and I remember her leaving suddenly. Perhaps Mammy said something to her. I don't know.'

Martin was nodding now. 'Yes, I thought there must be something like that,' he said. 'You've been burying that for years, haven't you? And I don't think it's just that, either. I think you want to punish your mother.'

'Mammy?' she was astonished. 'But I don't blame her. Why should I?'

'It could be that you thought your mother was responsible for this lady coming to the house, perhaps?' he suggested. 'And who was she? Can you remember?'

She had a slight frown on her face, and then she looked at him 'I don't know her name,' she said. 'But I remember now, she had a grey thing on her head. I couldn't see her hair.'

'A nun, then?' he said, and she nodded. 'She might have been.'

'And that could be the reason you think this Sister Bernadette is the root of all your problems,' he suggested. 'I think you've projected all your negative feelings about this nun onto her.'

She was watching him with a slight puzzled frown.

'But what I don't understand is why,' he continued. 'Because however pretty Mary is, she can't possibly be a patch on you.'

Her eyes widened. 'Do you really mean that?' She was almost breathless now. This was a completely new idea to her.

'I do mean it,' he said firmly. 'You should never compare yourself with anyone else. You're unique, Orla. There's no-one in the world like you and there never will be.'

She was overcome by his perception and his sensitivity, and she hesitated. 'But, there was Bridget,' she said. 'She was like me.'

'Bridget?'

'She was in the treatment centre with me.' Speaking of Bridget was still hard and she felt hot tears well up.

He said gently, 'Would you like to tell me about her?'

'She...she was the only one who understood. I mean, what it was like to be anorexic. She said I should try and get out if the clinic and then I could decide for myself how much to eat. It would be my decision and no-one else's.'

'And why was she such an influence, do you think? And are you still friends with her?'

The tears spilled over now, and silently, he handed her a tissue. She blew her nose and said, 'Sorry. No, we're not friends any more. She died.'

'Oh, my love, that's awful. But I don't understand why you still seem to think you have a problem with food. Are you doing this because of her? There's such a thing as misguided loyalty, you know.'

'She was my friend,' she said stubbornly. But his words were whirring round in her head. He had called her *'my love!'*

Martin handed her another tissue. 'Here, you'd better take the packet. You know, I never knew this girl but to me it sounds as if she was no friend to you. To be totally honest, she sounds to have been manipulative and selfish. No-one...' He hesitated, and then he carried on with a determined air as if he was going to speak his mind no matter what the consequences. 'No-one who really cares about you would want you to starve yourself. I think you're trying to please her in some way, to persuade yourself that if you follow her, then in some strange way it will make up for her death?'

This last was a question, and she looked at him. She was desperately embarrassed at crying openly in a restaurant, but he seemed unconcerned.

'I suppose it might be that,' she admitted.

'I'm sure it is,' he said firmly. 'And you need to concentrate on yourself now, and try and put her out of your mind if you want to lead a normal life.' He took a forkful of the pâté, and then said, 'Food, you know, it's just a fuel. You take it in, you use it and then you get some more. Like petrol in a car. Your body's much the same. If it doesn't get the right fuel it won't work properly.'

'Yes, they said all that at the clinic. And actually, I did know already.' She waved a fork of pâté in the air.

'Eat it, then, don't wave it about.'

Obediently she chewed it, and then, 'but it doesn't help. Knowing, I mean. In fact, it just makes it worse.'

'How?'

'Well, I mean, knowing that it's so easy. Everyone else can do it, so what's so wrong with me that I can't mange a simple thing like eating? They were forever talking about fuel at the clinic. I think the doctor thought that once I knew what was causing it, I'd be able to stop and everything would be alright again.'

'I can see that. We know what causes a lot of diseases but that doesn't mean we can cure them all. But in your case, I think comparison has something to do with it.'

'What do you mean?'

'I think you're comparing yourself with everyone else all the time, and feeling like somehow you're failing.'

'You do understand a lot about it, don't you? It seems there's a whole host of reasons why I've got it,' she continued a little sadly, 'but none of them mean I'll get over it. I think I'm stuck with it.'

'Oh, no, you're not,' he said very firmly. 'I do have some understanding of the theory of it. I don't have real in depth knowledge of why it affects some people and not others, but I do know that many people do recover from it eventually. It seems to be a state of mind that needs to be changed, and if you can achieve that, the eating patterns will fall into place. And besides, I'm not at all convinced that you do have it. I mean, I'm sure that anyone who is truly anorexic would find it a huge trial to be sitting in a restaurant eating paté, and you look as if you're managing just fine at the moment.'

'You really think so?'

He nodded. 'I'm sure of it. You have been affected and quite badly, but from looking at you now I'd say you've recovered.'

She was non committal. 'Maybe. Anyhow, the paté is gorgeous!' Then she suddenly remembered what Mammy had said about good manners. She had said that it was bad manners to talk about yourself all the time. You should talk about the other person instead, that was the proper way.

Martin was so grown up, and she decided she would try and match him. 'But that's enough about me,' she said, and suddenly she felt very mature. 'Tell me about yourself. What do you do?'

He smiled across at her. 'I'm just a common or garden student,' he said. 'I'm up at Newcastle reading medicine. I'm in my final year, just finished nutrition and respiratory and renal medicine. All very boring really.'

'Just like Mary.'

He raised his eyebrows in surprise. 'Your sister? She's at Newcastle?'

'Oh, no. No, I mean, she's at university. She's reading history at University College Dublin, but I don't know what she wants to do when she leaves. But why are you doing medicine? Didn't you want to do French? You're so brilliant at it.'

'No, not really.' he said slowly. 'French is useful of course, but mainly when I'm here. But as a career I'd rather do something that really helps people. You never know, one day I could save someone's life, and wouldn't that be worth all the years of studying?'

She nodded sagely. Everything he said seemed to make sense. 'Do you come here every holidays?'

He shook his head. 'At Easter and in summer,' he said. 'Christmas and half terms I'm at home...'

'Which is..?'

'Shropshire.'

She surprised him then, by saying dreamily, *'When I was one and twenty, I heard a wise man say, give crowns and pounds and guineas, but not your heart away.'*

252

He smiled in delight. '*A. E. Houseman, 'A Shropshire Lad'*. Yes, I like him, too. I live near Church Stretton and I'm back there regularly. I need to give dad a turn. My parents divorced a few years ago and dad has married again. Phoebe's alright,' he continued, 'but of course, it's not the same as your own mother.'

'Why did they get divorced?' she asked, and then she stopped. 'Sorry, I wasn't meaning to pry.'

'No, that's alright. I don't mind you knowing.'

He smiled at her. 'Although it's not something I would tell everyone.'

He took a sip of his wine and then placed the glass back precisely on the table, as if he were marshalling his thoughts and deciding how much he could reveal. Then he continued. 'It was mainly dad's fault. When I was younger I didn't realise what mum was going through, but I can see now why she left him. He had a major problem with the bottle. Or should I say bottles, plural? More alcohol than the body can reasonably be expected to cope with, and when he was drunk he tended to get violent. He hit her a few times...'

'God, how desperate!'

'Yes, it was, rather. But, he's a reformed character these days, and I must admit Phoebe has had an influence. He doesn't drink at all now and she sees to it that he never will.'

He changed the subject abruptly. He had a sudden memory of how he had lain prone on his bed, an impotent seven year old boy, fingers stuffed into his ears to shut out the terrible screaming that was coming from downstairs. He wanted to block out the memories of his mother's crying, the sounds of slaps, the whimpering and the sudden silence that seemed even worse than the crying.

'But that's enough of my life story,' he said. 'What about you? he asked. 'What are your plans? Do you know what you want to do?'

'Well, Sister Bernadette thinks I should do a history degree like Mary...'

'Oh, Orla, I do wish you'd forget about Sister Bernadette. She's already impinged on your life far too much if you ask me. No, what about you, yourself? What would you like to do?'

'I think Mammy and Daddy would like it if I was a teacher, or maybe a ...'

He interrupted her with more than a touch of impatience in his voice. 'I can't believe you're saying this. First it's what Sister Bernadette wants, then it's what your parents want. I'm not asking what everyone else wants you to do. What do *you* want? This is your life, not theirs. You need to make your own mind up.'

She had finished her starter and she placed her knife and fork tidily on her plate before she said, 'I'm not sure yet.'

'Well, whatever you do decide, remember that it's your decision and no-one else's.'

She smiled at this, acknowledging that he was probably right. During the rest of the meal they chatted easily, and by the end she was feeling happier than she had felt for many, many months. It was as if the shadow of her eating disorder that had plagued her life for years was melting away. She had eaten a full meal without the faintest trace of guilt, and she had enjoyed every minute if it. But she knew that her happiness was only partly the result of her meal. It was Martin who was filling her with joy and delight and she wanted to keep this feeling of pure contentment for as long as she could.

They walked back to the gîtes under a sky that was brilliant with innumerable stars. Orla could hardly take it in that she was here in this exotic place, after a delicious meal in a French restaurant, and by her side was a tall, athletic boy who had listened to her and called her *'my love'*, laughed with her and perhaps, just possibly, loved her?

'Just look at that,' she said in awe, looking up. 'It's incredible. I never knew there were so many.'

They held hands until they reached their gîtes. At her door he drew her close and lifted her head gently, and kissed her. She returned his kiss passionately.

'Will we do this again?' he said, and she was overwhelmed by the intensity of her feeling. At that moment she knew with a certainty that she had never felt before in her life. She loved this man.

The door opened quietly and she crept into the lounge. Declan was lightly dozing in an armchair. His head jerked and his eyes opened as she sat on the sofa.

'Mammy's gone to bed,' he said, speaking softly. 'Did you have a good time?'

'Wonderful,' she breathed.

Declan looked sheepish and his voice was anxious when he looked at her searchingly and said, 'He didn't...he didn't do anything, did he?'

She pealed with laughter. 'Daddy, what do you take me for? No. Of course not.'

He jerked his head towards her significantly, lifting his chin as he said, 'You do know what I'm talking about, don't you?'

She was still smiling broadly. 'Yes, of course I do. There was nothing like that. Nothing at all. Honestly.'

'Shush now, keep your voice down, you'll be having the whole house awake. Well, it's great that you enjoyed it. Get yourself off to bed now, and sleep tight, child.'

He kissed her forehead and she went off happily, thankful to have a little peace and quiet so that she could think about Martin.

In the days that followed, Orla was hardly ever with her family. Martin took her to see the underground *Gouffre de Cabrespine* with its spectacular array of stalagmites and stalactites and the next day he drove them to Rieux Minervois where they parked at the side of the road and walked hand in hand along the Canal du Midi.

They drove up into the Montagne Noire, right to the very highest point at Pic de Nore where they picnicked on chicken wings, paté spread onto slices of baguette, olives, goats' cheese, tomatoes from Peter's vegetable plot and Liz's home made lemondade.

'For a recovering anorexic, you're eating fine!' he teased her, and she grinned back a little shamefacedly. 'It tastes even better up here even than in the gîtes,' she said, biting into her second chicken wing. 'Last year I wouldn't have touched this.'

A buzzard wheeled overhead in wide, graceful circles, riding the air currents before it arced away over the hills. Martin and Orla were sprawled out luxuriously on sunbeds by the pool.

'He's heading for the mountains, I think,' she murmured, shading her eyes as she scanned the azure sky.

'That's Mount Canigou,' he remarked, following her gaze. 'When I'm here at Easter it's covered in snow, it looks fabulous.'

'Could we go, do you think?' She was very eager, but her face fell when he shook his head and smiled.

'It's much further than it looks,' he said. 'It would take us a couple of hours at least, it's way over in the Midi-Pyrénées.' She looked so crestfallen that he added, 'I'll tell you what. We could go over to Narbonne Plage if you like. That's only about an hour or so.'

'Plage? Is that the beach?'

'Wow, you're coming on! Yes, it is. There are lots of resorts along that coast. There's St. Pierre la Mer, but that's a bit smaller. Narbonne Plage has got everything. Massive long beach, shallow water that goes out for ages, plenty of restaurants.' He grinned suddenly. 'We would have to eat in a restaurant, of course.'

'Naturally,' she agreed, and they both laughed. 'That's if I can persuade Mammy to let me go, of course.'

CHAPTER 12

The following day Orla sat on the edge of the pool and looked down into the clear turquoise water. Daringly, she dipped her ankles in the water and made circles with her feet, loving the sunshine sparking on the ripples she made.

Footsteps behind her made her turn her head, and there was Martin in beige swimming trunks. He smiled at her and she returned his smile shyly. He positioned himself at the deep end of the pool, held himself taut and then launched himself into the water. She watched him power his way up and down, his arms thrashing and the water now a turbulent boil.

'Coming in?' He flicked the water out if his eyes and looked up at her.

'I can't swim,' she shouted.

He swam over to where she was sitting and held out his arm. 'Oh, come on in,' he said, 'you can at least splash around.'

'Is it deep?' She was fearful now but not wanting to appear too much of a coward. What must he think of her? Totally ignorant of a French menu and now unable to even swim.

He was laughing now. 'Get in, I'll help you.' He heaved himself out and sat, dripping at her side. 'Hold my hand and we'll get in together,' he said.

If she refused now he really would think her a coward, so she gave him a half fearful, half resolute smile and together they walked down the five steps. 'A bit further, come on, you won't drown, it's only a metre deep here.'

Hesitatingly she waded in further until the water was up to her armpits.

'You need to be able to swim,' he said. 'I can't believe you've got to your age without learning. Look, lie flat now and I'll hold you.'

'You won't let me fall?' She was terrified.

'No, of course not. You'll be fine.' He put his hands around her waist. 'Now, lie flat,' he said again, and this time she let herself go and he held her up. 'Now, practise kicking your legs. Like a frog,' he said and she made a tentative movement. 'That's right, you're doing fine. Now your arms. Put them straight out in front of you, and then make a circle.'

'Wow, I did it,' she gasped.

'Of course you did. Now try your arms and legs together. You're quite safe, I'm holding you.'

She found that with Martin's support she could make the right movements and she laughed delightedly. 'It feels grand,' she yelled. 'I'm nearly swimming!'

'Keep at it, and you'll be a mermaid in no time.'

'I'll never swim as well as you though,' she said deprecatingly and he laughed.

'Oh yes, you will. It's like everything else. Practise, and you'll improve. Had enough yet?'

'I think so, for now,' she said. 'I'll see if I can make it to the steps.' Encouraged by his evident admiration, she struck out purposefully and even managed a couple of strokes before she spluttered and floundered beneath the water and groped blindly for his hand.

'Help me out,' she laughed, and he guided her to the steps. She clambered out and towelled roughly at her hair.

'Could we do this again?' She said she was eager for his answer, but totally unprepared when he caught her round the waist and raised her face towards his. They kissed, gently, and she broke away, confused.

'Could we do *this* again?' he questioned gently, and she flushed.

'I'd love to,' she said, and she really meant it.

The next day he drove them both to Narbonne Plage. There were hundreds of people on the beach, but the miles of golden sand accommodated all of them with no suggestion of overcrowding. Family groups sheltered from the heat underneath bright parasols and laughing children teetered and splashed at the water's edge.

He was dozing on his back, his blond hair falling over his brow, and Orla was on her front, idly flicking the pages of the Elle magazine she had bought at the tabac on the beach front. Or at least she was looking at the advertisements. After the morning's confusion in the *boulangerie* she wanted to improve her French, but somehow the magazine was not helping. It was full of words she had never learned at the convent, and the vocabulary she already knew was missing from the pages. Still, she recognized many of the designer clothes and perfume labels. You didn't need French for that, she thought with satisfaction.

At her side, Martin stirred and sat up slowly. She rolled over to face him. 'Goodness, but it's hot,' he said, gazing at the sea. 'I think I'll go for a dip. You coming?'

She raised her head and looked across at the sea where heads were bobbing up and down in the water and a couple of teenagers were doing their best to stay afloat on top of a large blow up dolphin.

She smiled. 'It looks brilliant, yes, let's go.' She scrambled up and stuffed her magazine into a plastic bag.

'Don't leave your things here,' he cautioned. 'Bring the bag with you.'

She scooped up her beach bag containing her clothes, Martin's car keys and their mobile phones and together they ran over the hot sand to the water's edge where it lapped in gentle rushes over their feet.

She teetered into the tiny waves and shrieked. 'Ooh, it's freezing!' Martin was in up to his ankles and he looked back at her and laughed.

'Rubbish! It's warm enough when you get used to it. It must be at least twenty degrees.' But she was hopping about frantically.

'Who's a little wimp, then?' She looked at him, stricken, but then she saw his teasing smile and she laughed.

'You go in if you like but it's far too cold for me, I'm going back,' and she turned and scuttled back across the hot sand and sank down, waving to him.

She watched as he waded in, arms high above his head and then he was splashing his upper body. Finally, he struck out and swam with powerful over arm strokes. At last he was no more than one of the many heads in the water, too far away to be clearly visible, and she rolled over onto her back and closed her eyes.

Monsieur Pierre Girard was in his early fifties, and the proprietor of a jet ski hire business which had been thriving until a few year ago but was now in decline. He was grizzled, overweight, bearded and cantankerous but he could be charming enough when it suited him, and it suited him when customers presented themselves in the office wanting to hire one of his jet skis and a wetsuit.

Today he was in an even worse mood than usual. He had woken up aching all over, especially his legs, and he was both hot and shivery at the same time.

It was nearing the end of the season and business was not looking promising. He had taken a chance this year and with the help of a bank loan he had bought three new jet skis at the staggering cost of nine thousand eight hundred euros each. Almost thirty thousand euros, he thought dismally, and he was hiring them out at twenty-eight euros an hour. His total fleet of jet skis was fifteen now, and although there was a bit of profit in hiring out the wetsuits, the overall picture was looking gloomier by the day. He repeated the calculation that he did at least five times a day, just in case the figures looked a bit more promising with repetition. But they didn't. He would be lucky to break even he thought, and he was wondering what he could do during the winter to bring in a few more euros.

Worse still, two of the jet skis were out of action awaiting repair and if he didn't get them sorted soon the profits would slip even further.

He struggled to sit up, but sank down almost immediately. His legs were too wobbly, he knew they wouldn't hold him if he tried to stand. Claudine was up already and he could hear the gurgle of the coffee machine coming from the kitchen. She would be cutting the baguette into slices now, adding two pain au chocolate rolls and getting out the pot of her homemade strawberry jam and spooning it into the green leaf shaped dish with its matching spoon. Since their wedding day thirty years ago the routine had never varied and the breakfast table had always looked exactly the same with her own hand embroidered mats and the pale green crockery she always used. He usually enjoyed the meal but today the thought of breakfast almost turned his stomach.

He closed his eyes, meaning to get up in five minutes, but he was deeply asleep again when Claudine came into the bedroom.

'Pierre! Aren't you getting up? It's half past seven.' Then she looked at his flushed face. 'What's the matter, don't you feel well?'

'I think it's flu,' he groaned. 'I'm aching all over.'

'Well, stay in bed, then. I'll bring your breakfast in here for a change. You can have a good sleep afterwards.'

'No, I've got to get to work.' He glanced out of the window at the faint heat haze that was shimmering over the garden. 'It's going to be hot, it'll be a busy day...'

'You're not going anywhere in that state,' she said firmly. 'After your breakfast...'

'I'm not hungry. Where are my trousers?'

'You won't need them, you're staying where you are today,' she said firmly, hauling the duvet back over him. 'You'll just have to miss a few days at work, that's all.'

'I can't,' he groaned. 'The beach will be crowded, there'll be a lot of business.'

'I'll ring René,' she said. 'He might be able to step in for a few days until you're better.'

René was her brother. He lived in the village, existing on the government's minimum payment scheme for those out of work. He had never had a steady job since leaving the Lycée in Carcassonne, and spent his days hanging around the village, smoking and drinking wine with a band of friends.

'He hasn't a clue, he'll be hopeless,' he muttered.

'Do you have any better ideas?' She was impatient now. 'You're in no state to drive, let alone work, so if you've nothing better to offer then I'll ring him and at least the place will open.'

He heard her on the telephone in the hall, and then she poked her head around the door.

'He says what's in it for him?'

Pierre groaned again. This was going to cost him a fortune if he was in bed more than a couple of days.

'Tell him fifty euros for the day,' he said weakly.

There was a long conversation before Claudine's head appeared around the door again.

'He'll do it for a hundred a day,' she said, and even she seemed a little startled. She had thought that René might offer to help out, but evidently she was wrong.

'Seventy five, and tell him that's final,' he said. He was tired now and wanting to sleep. Resigned now to the fact that he would have to pay René, he snuggled under the still warm duvet and drifted off to sleep, but his dreams were troubled.

Three hours later he awoke, startled out of his dreams. He knew there was something. He levered himself upright and leaned over to find his slippers. He still felt very trembly but he managed to put on his fleecy dressing gown and made it to the telephone in the hall. He punched numbers in feverishly and waited. 'Come on, pick it up, you idiot,' he muttered, but there was no answering voice at the other end. When he was prompted, he left a voicemail message. *That's all I can do*, he thought, *he'll pick it up soon.* With a sense of having done all that was possible, he made his way back to the bedroom and was asleep five minutes later.

Over at the beach, René was smoking his tenth cigarette of the day when two young men approached. He stubbed it out and switched on his smile to greet them.

'Yes, are you wanting a jet ski?' He was very welcoming. 'It's fifty euros an hour.'

The two boys looked staggered. 'But we came last year and it was only twenty-five,' the first one said. 'Wasn't it, Louis?' He was tall and althletic, with bulging arm muscles. Louis nodded in corroboration. 'Why is it double this year?'

'Ah, it's my brother-in-law,' René told them. His voice was very regretful. 'He's had to put the price up. It's the cost of the fuel, you see.'

Louis looked at his companion, who shook his head, saying, 'Not at that price. We could do beach volleyball instead. That's free.'

Both of them turned and started to walk away but René cut in urgently. 'I'll tell you what,' he said. 'As you're old customers, I'll do it for forty-five. How's that? My brother-in-law will kill me if he finds out, but what the eye doesn't see, eh?' He winked at them conspiratorially and he saw the first man was weakening.

'I don't know,' he said slowly. 'It's still a big increase on last year.'

René appeared to consider deeply. Then he said. 'Look, just for you two, I'll come down to forty. I can't go any lower than that.'

They were still a little reluctant but finally they agreed, and René grinned at them. 'Let's get you kitted out with your wetsuits, then,' he said, and they followed him to the back of the office where rows of wetsuits in different sizes were hanging on rails.

Once they were suited, he took the eighty euros and handed them to keys to the first two jet skis in the bay. 'Have fun,' he told them, and they waved at him as they slid into the water.

Out on the water his two clients were powering through the sea, the wake surging behind them and the stiff wind hitting them in the face. Shouting to one another, they twisted and turned, expertly steering their craft and exhilarated by the power of the engines and the sting of the surf.

Louis wound round in a huge circle, twisting his head around to watch the curving arc of spray as it whipped up in his wake. He braked to go into his turn, but he felt his stomach tighten and lurch when the machine did not respond. He swung the wheel hard over but to his horror, he carried on in a straight line. He was headed towards the beach. He yelled out frantically as Marc's jet ski whipped in front of him.

'I can't stop!' he yelled, but Marc was already past him and curving away on his next circuit. He tried to stay calm but the fear was too great now. He slammed his foot on the brake, pushing down as hard as he could but the machine carried on at the same breakneck speed. There was no way he could stop.

To his horror he spotted a head in the water and knew with a sickening clarity that he was in the path of a swimmer. He yelled his loudest but a second later the machine bounced and continued to hurtle towards the sand. He could see the people on the beach standing up now, staring in disbelief at the speed of the approaching jet ski. They scattered in panic as they realised what was happening, and a second later he came to a juddering halt as he hit the sand. The sudden stop sent him flying out of the machine and his body thudded onto the sand. He heard the snap of his ankle bone at the same time as the agonizing pain shot through his body. He lay there, winded and panting and he was surrounded by a crowd of people all shouting instructions.

'Turn him onto his side!'

'No leave him. Don't move him, it's dangerous!'

'Ring for the Samu!'

Louis squirmed in agony, clutching at his ankle with both hands to try to lessen the pain. His breath was coming in short gasps and his head was pounding.

A woman forced her way to the front of the crowd and knelt in front of him. She held a tin cup to his lips. 'Drink,' she said, and she tipped the cup forwards. He tasted the brandy and a warmth stole through his body. He gasped out now, 'The swimmer, there was someone swimming.'

'Don't worry. Try to keep calm now.' It was the woman who spoke again. Her large breasts hung over him, barely contained by her sagging bikini top. 'They're picking him up. Here, finish this.'

The rest of the brandy hit his throat. The terrible sharp pain in his ankle was now a huge throbbing ache but it wasn't as unbearable as a second ago.

Orla was only dozing lightly and the sudden commotion on the beach roused her. She sat up and shaded her eyes. The shoreline was crowded with people shouting and gesticulating. Some were even swimming out with strong strokes, and a group of people were huddled over a black machine. She heard screams and shortly afterwards the sirens of a police car and ambulance as they halted by the roadside.

She looked around her, scanning the long beach for Martin. He must be around somewhere. If he had swum any distance he may have come to shore further along the beach, and she screwed up her eyes against the sun, expecting to see the tall figure any minute. She was curious abut the commotion by the seashore and she stood up and went to join the back of the crowd. She couldn't see clearly, there were too many people blocking her view, but she knew by now that a jet skier had been injured.

A noise from behind parted the crowd and she nipped quickly aside as a motorboat was pushed towards the shoreline by three burly lifeguards. It splashed into the water and the motor roared as it sped off. The crowd was suddenly hushed now. Two ambulance men came running from the roadside with a stretcher and they lifted Louis and bore him across the hot sand to the waiting ambulance.

She was starting to panic now and she looked around wildly. Where was Martin? He should have been back ages ago.

She picked up her plastic beachbag and walked along the soft sand, scanning groups, looking for his familiar face among the crowds, but he seemed to have vanished into thin air. She knew she shouldn't go too far away. If he returned to their sunbathing space then she should be there when he came back, so she turned and made her way slowly back.

She couldn't understand why the crowd by the sea had not dispersed now that the injured man had been taken care of, but she suddenly saw the bright orange of the motorboat. It was riding the swell of the waves towards the sand and another two of the ambulance crew were waiting by a stretcher. She was near enough now to see clearly, and in a moment of horror, she knew who it must be.

'Martin! The word tore out of her and she slithered across the hot sand, pushing people out of the way until she was at the very front. She sank to her knees beside the stretcher and saw him.

He was lying very still. His face was white, and his lips were a ghastly blue colour.

One of the ambulance men took her gently by the arm but she wrenched it free. 'Let me go! Is he alive? Oh, Martin, please, please don't die!'

'Il n'est pas mort,' the ambulance man said. 'He is not dead'. She was crying so much now that she could hardly speak. The two men started to lift the stretcher and she got to her feet and watched helplessly as they slid it carefully into the back of the ambulance. One of the two open doors slammed shut and before they could close the second she had a terrifying thought. 'Stop! Oh, stop! You have to stop!' The second man turned to her and spoke, rapidly, urgently, and in French. She didn't understand a word, but she grabbed at his sleeve. 'I have to go with him,' she cried. I can't get home, he has the car!'

The man frowned at her. Evidently he was impatient. It was his job to get this injured boy to hospital as soon as possible and this hysterical girl was holding things up. What was wrong with her?

She was frantic by now. If Martin went off in the ambulance she would be stranded, miles from home and with no way of getting there.

She racked her brain for the right French to explain all this and from somewhere, a few words came. She pointed to Martin. '*Pas de voiture*,' she said desperately. 'No car,' and she shook her head vehemently in an effort to be understood.

'Ah!' The few words and her urgency was enough to convey her meaning, and the ambulance man pointed at the open door of the ambulance. '*Montez*,' he said. 'Get in.' Thankfully, she scrambled into the back of the ambulance and she sat on the long seat, never taking her eyes off Martin's pale face.

Oh, dear God, she thought, *don't let him die. Please let him be alright. I'll eat properly, I promise I will, only please let Martin be alright.*' Her thoughts whirred in her head and her eye never left his face as she gabbled a decade of the Rosary.

If she hadn't been so worried about Martin she would have cried from pure fright when they arrived at the hospital. She scrambled down from the ambulance and followed the stretcher as it was wheeled through the large swing doors. She tried to follow but the ambulance man shook his head at her.

'*Restez ici*,' he told her. 'Stay here.' He turned away from her as he wheeled Martin to a cubicle where a doctor was waiting to examine him and she was left alone in the reception hall.

She was desperately embarrassed, standing there in a bikini, with bare feet which still trailed grains of sand whenever she took a step. People were looking at her and then turning away with either a contemptuous glance or a snicker of amusement. It was like one of those nightmares, she thought, where you dreamed you were naked in a crowded shop. Except that this was real.

She spotted a sign just along the corridor, thankful for the logo which clearly indicated the women's toilets and she made a dash for it.

Once inside the cubicle she tried to control the tears that were sliding down her face as she hastily scrambled into her sandals, t-shirt and shorts. She took several deep breaths, and opened the door. She made for a wooden bench in reception and sat down, thankful now for her relative anonymity.

The respite did not last long. The terrifying reality hit her now. She was stranded here in a strange hospital, she had no idea where Martin was and she had no way of getting home.

She looked around her, scanning the anonymous people who were going about their own affairs, nurses and doctors and ward orderlies, all of them walking past her as if she didn't exist. She was desperate for help from somewhere. Anywhere. There was a woman in a glass cubicle on reception, and she walked over to her and rapped on the glass. The woman looked up, eyebrows raised questioningly. She had no idea where to begin. She spotted the telephone on the woman's desk and jabbed a finger at it.

'I need to telephone,' she said desperately and in English.

The woman replied in a stream of French. Without understanding a single word, she knew that the answer was negative, and her heart sank. Would she be here all night? Would she ever get back home again?

The nightmare was getting worse by the second, and suddenly the strain of the last couple of hours overcame her and she burst into tears.

The woman in the glass cubicle was alarmed. She hurried out of the door and put her arms round her, addressing her in yet more French that sounded more sympathetic, even if Orla didn't understand a single word of it. She led her to a bench and sat beside her. Then she took out a pager from her uniform pocket and spoke into it.

She heard the word '*docteur*,' but that was all she could understand. She was still sobbing hopelessly when a white coated doctor approached her and the lady from the office stood up and gabbled to him, pointing to her and gesticulating.

'*Anglaise*,' was all she said, nodding her head at her.

The doctor spoke, and she could have hugged him as she heard her own language, even though it was heavily accented.

'What is wrong?' he asked carefully. 'Are you ill? Do you have pain?'

Immensely thankful that she could now explain, she shook her head. 'No,' she said breathlessly. 'It's not me. I came with.....' She hesitated, and then said firmly, 'I came with my boyfriend. He's called Martin Saunders. I don't know where he is and I can't get home. I have to phone my mother.'

'Ah!' The doctor gave a nod of complete comprehension and spoke rapidly to the receptionist.

Evidently all was clear, for she took Orla by the arm and led her into the office and pointed to the telephone.

Thankfully, but with fingers that were still shaking, she dialled.

Over in Caunes-Minervois, Theresa was expecting Martin and Orla to wander in at any minute after their day at the coast. When her mobile phone rang, her first feeling was exasperation. Surely they weren't going to be late?

When Orla gabbled the news her hands flew to her mouth in horror. 'Is he badly hurt?'

But before Orla could reassure her, the door swung open and Liz pelted into the hallway. 'They've just rung me from Narbonne Hosptial,' she gasped. 'It's Martin. He's been hit by a jet skier!'

'Oh, Jesus, no! He's not...?' She found she couldn't say the word, but to her relief, Liz shook her head.

'They think he's concussed,' she said. 'They're keeping him in,' and then she

274

remembered. 'But what about Orla? Where is she?'

'She's just ringing me from the hospital.'

She spoke rapidly to her. 'Listen, Orla, try not to worry, do you hear me? We'll come and pick you up as soon as we can. Have you had anything to eat at all?'

'No. I'm not hungry.'

Where have I heard that before? Theresa thought dismally, but for now she was too concerned about Martin and Liz to say anything about food.

'Stay where you are,' she cautioned. 'Don't go out of the hospital.'

'Oh, Lord, Mammy, where on earth would I go?' She was impatient and her anxiety over Martin made her tone sharper than she had intended. 'Of course I'll stay here.'

'Have you seen him at all?'

'I came with him in the ambulance, but they've taken him to one of the cubicles now and they wouldn't let me in.'

Liz said urgently, 'Theresa, go and get a jacket or something. We'll have to get off as soon as we can to pick Orla up.'

'But Declan won't know the way. He's terrible about finding places, and in the French car and everything...'

'I'll run over to Prinny's. She and Luc know Narbonne. One of them will take us.'

She turned around and was racing down the path. She looked back over her shoulder and shouted. 'Get Declan, will you? We'll get off as soon as we can.' With that, she turned out of the gate and was gone.

Thankful to have something practical to do, Theresa shouted to Declan to come in from the garden. He could see by her face that something was seriously wrong.

'What's happened? Is it Orla?' For one panic stricken moment, his mind flew to the terrible time when Orla was in the hospital. Please God nothing had happened to her.

'No, it's not Orla.' She saw his face relax, but then his mouth opened in horror when she said breathlessly, 'It's Martin. There's been an accident. A jet ski's hit him. Orla's on her own at the hospital, we need to go and pick her up. Make sure everything's locked up, will you, and hurry up about it.'

A few moments later Luc's car was at the gate and as soon as Declan and Padraic came pounding down the path and hurled themselves in, they were off.

Martin opened his eyes to see his mother, Peter, Orla and her parents and little brother in a cluster around his bed.

'Martin! What happened?' It was Liz, sounding more anxious than they had ever heard her. Theresa looked at her and took her hand gently.

'There was a jet ski,' he said hazily. He was still weak and dizzy and had only the faintest recollection of the events of the last few hours.

'What on earth were you doing swimming out so far?' she said sharply. 'There's a designated area for jet skis, you know that, surely? You've been swimming there before.'

'I wasn't,' he protested weakly. 'I was near the beach.'

'You mean, he hit you deliberately?' Peter said. 'If he did, then that's attempted murder. He could go to jail for that.' He looked round them all as if waiting for corroboration, but no-one replied.

'I don't know, I don't think he meant to. To be honest, I don't remember much about it, only that he was coming towards me and then I woke up here.'

'Have they told you what's wrong exactly?' Liz asked fearfully.

'They don't need to. I know. I've got all the classic symptoms of mild concussion. I was sick as soon as they brought me in, I'm dizzy and I'm tired. He must have just glanced off me. If he'd hit me head on I wouldn't be here talking about it.'

Liz shuddered and learned over and kissed him. 'Thank God it was no worse.'

'Very odd, really,' he mused. He put his hand up and touched his bandaged head very gingerly. 'We've covered all this at Uni. Now I know what it's like first hand. I just hope there's a question on it in the finals.'

'You're being very brave about it,' Peter said.

'Not much else I can do, is there? I'll be fine in a few days, if the textbooks are right.' He managed a faint smile, but they could see that he was exhausted.

Padraic, who had been silent up until now, boldly walked to the bedside.

'Does it hurt?'

Martin managed a weak grin.

'I've got a thumping great headache, but it will soon be better.'

'You need some magic cream,' he stated with authority. 'They'll have some here. You should ask them for some.'

'Padraic, for the love of God be quiet,' Declan growled. 'Martin can do without your chatter.'

Liz turned to Orla. 'And you, my dear. You poor little thing, you must have been terrified, seeing the accident and then being left all on your own here.'

'Oh, Orla will have coped fine,' Theresa said. 'She's got her head screwed on right.' She nodded to emphasize her words and Liz smiled faintly.

Orla felt that there was no need at all to elaborate on how exactly she had felt. The desperate moments of sheer panic were something she strongly felt were best kept to herself.

At that moment a nurse came in to take Martin's blood pressure and temperature and Liz addressed her in a stream of French that left the rest of them gaping. She nodded her head at the explanation and then said, 'There are no serious injuries. He has some bruising to his forehead and they want to keep him in overnight, but he should be discharged tomorrow afternoon if there are no complications.'

'*Il faut que vous partiez maintenant,*' the nurse told them. '*Il doit se reposer.*'

'She says we have to go now, he needs to rest,' Liz translated for them. She leaned over and kissed him again. 'We'll come back in the morning,' she said gently, and he was already asleep before they had left the room.

Pierre Girard was not expecting any callers. He felt well enough to leave his bed and he was now in the lounge in his dressing gown and sipping the hot whisky and lemon that Claudine had brought him. The loud rapping at the door startled him so much that he jerked the whisky glass and it spilled onto the tiled floor.

He heard Claudine answer the door and the loud tramping on the floor, and then the two men entered. He was startled. Gendarmerie. What could they want?

The two officers stood facing him. 'Monsieur Girard?'

He cautiously nodded acknowledgment, and the officer continued. 'Are you the owner of the Plage Jet Ski Club?'

Pierre stared at them. 'Yes, that's me. Why? Who wants to know?'

'There's been an accident at the club this afternoon.' This was the second, younger man speaking.

He consulted a black notebook that he took from his pocket. 'A swimmer was hit by a jet ski at about three o'clock this afternoon,' he said. 'Were you on the premises at the time?'

Before he could finish speaking, Pierre heard the word accident and his stomach turned over. It had to be René. He had hired out the faulty machine!

'No,' he mumbled. 'I wasn't there. My brother-in-law was standing in for me.'

'And his name is....?

'René Hortois.'

'Do you have a telephone number?'

'Just a minute.' His heart was thumping and he felt faint and nauseous. 'Claudine,' he yelled, and when she appeared from the kitchen, 'Where's René's number?'

Her mind was racing as she went it look for the small black notebook with telephone numbers. What did they want with René? She found it after rifling through the drawer in the kitchen table and took it back to the two officers. She handed it to the taller one silently.

'You have no idea where your brother will be now?' This was the second officer, and she shook her head mutely. She had a terrible feeling that René was somehow implicated in this accident they were talking about, and the less she said, the better. It was not the first time he had been in trouble with the police. When he was fifteen, he and a group of friends had been caught shoplifting in Carcassonne. It was a particularly idiotic thing to do. They had chosen to steal from a supermarket, the fools. A supermarket protected by overhead cameras. Small items: a couple of video games and a pair of small headphones.

She remembered her mother's pale, worried face when the gendarmerie had called at the house, and René's vehement denials. He hadn't even been in Carcassonne he blustered. He would never do a thing like that, not stealing. His mates might have been there, but not him.

Then came the search; two officers in his bedroom, while René had stayed downstairs, his face immobile and then the rush of furious, red faced denials when they confronted him with the evidence. Could he produce a receipt for the items? Why had he lied?

It was years ago now but the sight of the two officers brought everything back. Her mother's wails and René's cries of pain when their father had thrashed him, using a belt until the boy's back was a mass of welts.

So now she remained silent. The first officer noted René's number and they left, with the stern warning that Pierre may be required to give evidence if the case went to court.

CHAPTER 13

Peter gazed down into the pool, satisfied with its sparkling clarity. He replaced his pH and chlorine testing kit in its place just inside the small shed that housed the pool pump before settling himself in a deckchair. It would be a rare moment of peace after the anxiety of the last few days.

Martin had been discharged two days ago and he insisted that he was feeling fine, although he knew that Liz was still concerned about him. She was over at Prinny's now, giving her a French lesson.

He had barely sat down before the headline jumped out at him. *'Local man fined for faulty jet ski.'* His eyes opened wide as he read the short article stating that Monsieur Pierre Girard, of Carcassonne, had been fined twelve hundred euros for hiring out one of his jet skis that later proved to be faulty. An unnamed swimmer had been injured in the accident.

Liz returned half an hour later.

'She's really making an effort,' she said, pleased. 'I thought she was going to be really difficult but she's throwing herself into it. She reminds me of the second years actually. She's about that standard, and if I can persuade Luc to speak to her in French it won't be long before she can cope with most day to day things.'

Peter didn't comment on Prinny's progress, but instead, he thrust the opened newspaper at her.

'Here, read that.'

She took it and read through the article, frowning as she finished it. 'Twelve hundred euros,' she exclaimed. 'That's a joke. He should have got a prison sentence.'

'Ah, now, Liz, be reasonable,' he soothed. 'It was an accident, like the paper says. Martin just happened to be in the wrong place at the wrong time, that's all.'

She was not at all mollified. 'He was damned lucky not be killed,' she fumed. 'There's no way that man should be free to operate a business if he can't make sure the equipment is safe.'

He could see that nothing he could say would persuaded her otherwise, so he changed the subject.

'Is he back yet?'

'No,' she said shortly. 'He's gone to Minerve with Orla. I didn't want him to go. I think he should be resting more but he won't listen. They should be back any minute. I'll have to get tea sorted out. He's asked if she can eat here tonight.'

'He seems very keen on her, doesn't he?'

'Oh, he'll forget about her once they leave.' She was very sure, but Peter stroked his short beard and remarked, 'I wouldn't count on that if I were you.'

She was startled. 'But he's a medical student. He's got the whole of the university to choose from. He'll finish up marrying a nurse or a sister, or maybe even another doctor. That's what most of them do. Look, I can't stand here talking about Martin, I'll have to get on.'

She flung the newspaper with its offending article back onto a spare deck chair and hurried away. Peter made a long arm and retrieved it, shaking his head slightly. He was not as convinced as Liz about the temporary nature of Martin's affection for Orla, whom he still thought of as 'that skinny little Irish girl in Les Jonquilles.'

Martin twisted his head round to ease Peter's car into the one remaining space in the car park just outside the village of Minerve.

Together they strolled across the arrow straight stone bridge that was the only entrance and exit to the village. They peered over the parapet to the dry river bed far below them.

'It's amazing,' she breathed. 'I feel dizzy just looking down there.'

She joined hands with him and together they gazed out across to the close huddle of ancient stone houses jutting out from the surrounding rock. Beyond the village across the haze of shimmering heat was a rugged landscape of olive groves and vineyards tucked between great expanses of limestone gorges.

'We can get down to the riverbed if you'd like to go,' he said. 'It's pretty steep, though.'

They found their way through the narrow streets to the cobbled pathway leading down to the river. It was bordered on both sides by picturesque sturdy stone cottages, built to last for centuries. One or two of them bore the circular green *'Gîtes de France'* logo and most were fronted by a small garden bearing succulent plants and tangles of trailing alyssum sprouting from low walls. Here and there were clumps of brown tipped leaves of long dead irises and wind blown roses tumbling across shuttered windows. They spotted small, blind-eyed gargoyle figures perched on small rocks.

'It's like walking through a Hans Christian Andersen story,' she said in wonder. 'Imagine real people living here.'

As they walked, he told her a little more of the history of the village.

'There was a group of Cathars here, they took refuge after the massacre at Beziers...'

'When was all this?'

'Oh, centuries ago, in 1210 I think. They thought they'd be safe here, because the village is so easy to defend, but Simon de Montford's army set up four catapults and held them under siege for ten weeks. They surrendered eventually, and over a hundred of them were burned alive when they refused to give up their faith. One of the roads up in the village is called *Rue des Martyrs*, and that's where they're supposed to have walked on their way to the stake.'

She shuddered, despite the intense heat which was causing small damp patches under her arms. She wiped the back of her neck with her handkerchief. 'It sounds horrible.'

'It was a long time ago.'

'That doesn't make it any better, though, does it? How can people be so cruel?'

'It's amazing what people are capable of when religion is involved. And especially in those days when religion was a whole way of life. If people didn't conform to what was wanted then they paid a terrible price. But then I suppose we're all prisoners of our own society. Perhaps we should be thankful that ours is a bit more tolerant than theirs was.'

'Mmm.' She was thoughtful for a moment, and then she said a little sadly, 'I'm Irish, remember? I don't think times have changed that much.'

'Perhaps not,' he said, 'but I rather think it's a bit more complex than you imagine.' He put his arm around her waist and gave her a little hug. She was unlike any other girl he had ever met. He loved her for her naive simplicity, her artlessness and total lack of duplicity. There was no-one to compare with her. He thought for a moment of his fellow students at Newcastle. Naturally, some were attractive, but he had never gone out with any of them for more than a couple of months, and he had certainly never met anyone he felt he would like to spend the rest of his life with. Until Orla. He wondered if she had the slightest idea of how he felt towards her.

They passed under a low stone archway, where the houses gave way to an even steeper twisting cobbled path which they negotiated slowly and very carefully, before finding themselves at the bottom and treading across an expanse of river-smoothed pebbles.

They made their way across the riverbed to the other side and sat down, thankful to be in the shade and resting their backs against the massive prehistoric boulders.

After a five minute rest, he stood up and put out a hand to haul her to her feet. They walked back up to the village by an easier route which took them past gigantic rocks, smoothed and hollowed out over millennia.

Back up in the village they made their way back to the car park, pausing only to inspect some of the tiny shops on each side of the streets. In one window they spotted the same stone gargoyle ornaments they had seen in the gardens, and they went inside to wander round.

The interior was gloomy and smelt of leather. The only light came from the open doorway and a tiny rectangular window high up in the wall behind the owner's counter, where he was sitting completely absorbed in meticulously carving a tiny gnome with oversized bat-like ears. They crept around the shop, as if any loud footsteps would disturb him. It was a treasure trove of fantastic artifacts. There were mirrors with wooden borders of sculpted gnome-like creatures and twisting serpents, grapes and tiny toadstools. The walls were hung with brightly coloured leather bags and purses, beaded necklaces and they could barely move for the tables packed with highly glazed pottery, hair ornaments made from carved leather and stands with rings, bracelets and earrings of silver, set with softly gleaming stones of amethyst, topaz, rose quartz and jasper.

Orla stood in front of it, mesmerized but very hesitant. Theresa had given her a twenty euro note, but with strict instructions not to spend all of it and the smallest of the rings was twice that price.

Martin was beside her. 'Here, try this one,' he urged her, and he selected the smallest ring he could see and slipped it onto the third finger of her right hand. She wriggled her fingers, admiring the three tiny amethysts.

'It's gorgeous,' she said, 'but it's far too expensive.'

'I'll get it,' he said easily, and when they emerged into the bright sunlight she was wearing not only the ring, but a matching silver and amethyst pendant.

'Thank you,' she said softly. 'They're beautiful.'

He took her hand and together they walked slowly back across the bridge to the waiting car.

On the following afternoon Susannah spent half an hour smothering herself in sun cream, reapplying her nail varnish, combing her hair and selecting her newest blue and white bikini before she set off towards the pool. She was a competent swimmer and the water looked very inviting. Martin was lying face down on a sunbed with a heavy open book in front of him.

She looked down at him and smiled.

'You look comfortably installed there,' she said. 'Care for a swim?'

He opened one eye and screwed up his face against the sun. 'I wasn't intending to, actually. I'm supposed to have read this wretched book before I get back to Uni, and I'm only half way through.'

'Oh, have a break.' Her voice was persuasive. 'It's the holidays now. You'll have plenty of time for that when it's raining. Enjoy the sun while you can.'

Teasingly, she leaned over him and picked the book up. '*Essential OSCE Topics for Medical and Surgical Finals,*' she read aloud. 'How can you possibly concentrate on that on such a gorgeous day?'

'Hey, give that back.' He sat up now, annoyed by her interference, but doing his best not to show it as he suddenly remembered that she was a much needed guest in his mother's gîte and it would never do to upset her.

She passed him the book and tried once more, saying in a wheedling, high voice, 'Just a teeny tiny dip?'

He was resigned. He could see there would be no peace until he agreed. 'Oh, alright, if you insist. Half an hour at the most, though. I still have to make some notes on chapter six.'

'Now that's better. The water's twenty-eight degrees. It´ll be fabulous.'

Declan and Padraic were splashing about, Padraic a little hampered by his armbands but doing his best to cover some distance in a clumsy doggie paddle, and Declan was encouraging him. He was no brilliant swimmer himself and the prospect of Martin and Susannah getting in and showing him up was enough to make him yell, 'Right, son, see if you can get to the steps now, it's time to get out.'

He was instantly aggrieved. 'What for? I want to stay here.'

'No, no, you've had long enough. Out you get now.'

Still visibly reluctant, he splashed his way to the steps, closely followed by Declan who towelled first Padraic and then himself before the two of them set off back to the gîte.

Martin swam lazily around while Susannah circled around him, sometimes in her back and sometimes doing an elegant breaststroke. After twenty minutes she had had enough and she caught up with him. 'Shall we go for a walk?' she suggested.

He shrugged. 'If you like. If you don't think it's too hot?'

'Oh, we'll be fine. Just give me a few minutes to get out and get changed and I'll meet you by the gate.'

Reluctantly, he swam over to the steps and heaved himself out of the pool. As promised, ten minutes later she was by the gate, fresh and crisp in white shorts and halter neck t-shirt in a bright red, her shiny hair now piled up in a bun on top of her head and held by a red rose clip.

'I know absolutely nowhere in these parts,' she told Martin when he appeared. 'I'm leaving it to you to be my guide.' She held it a hand to him and he took it politely.

'We could stroll down to the market.' He was not enthusiastic but she took him up on it immediately.

'Oh, that sounds simply lovely! I just adore markets. Especially these little country ones, everything they sell is so fresh.'

'We can cut through the vineyards, it's much quicker.'

'Do you think my sandals will stand it?' She held up a long leg for him to inspect her high heeled leather pumps and he smiled. 'As long as you're careful, it should be fine.'

They set off towards the vineyard. The lane was bordered by wild almond trees, heavy with suede skinned brown nuts, and fronds of fennel splaying out above their heads. Tangles of brambles showed the promise of juicy blackberries to come and in the distance rose the undulating hills of the *Montagne Noire*. As they passed, flurries of birds flapped out of the undergrowth and soared high above them, and a massive buzzard floated and wheeled high above them in graceful circles.

In the vineyard they trod carefully between the tall rows, brushed now and then by leafy tendrils which had escaped their restraining wires and lay in their path. The grapes were glistening purple, tightly packed in bunches, almost ready now for the imminent harvest.

Back in her gîte, Orla was lying on her bed reading an Elle magazine. She was so impressed by Martin's easy command of French that she was determined to try and improve her own.

Her mother's voice, a little impatient, interrupted her. "Orla, can you go and find Padraic please? Tea will be ready in fifteen minutes from now and he'll need a wash. He's out playing somewhere.'

She closed the magazine and flung it onto the bedside table. 'Yes, fine. What are we having?'

'Salad. It's too hot to be cooking a meal, and I've got some of that great crusty bread they have. Pity we can't get it at home, it's the best bread I've ever tasted.'

'OK, I'll go.' She was glad to be doing something. Padraic would most likely be in the garden somewhere, and she made her way across the neat gravelled paths.

He was nowhere to be seen. She tried down by the pool but the gate was closed and locked. Mammy was going to be greatly annoyed if she didn't find him soon, and she went to the gate and peered out into the vineyards. If he wasn't in the garden, he had to be in there somewhere. The afternoon sun was ferocious and she had forgotten her sunhat. Her head ached faintly, but going back to fetch her hat would take ages, so she continued into the tall vines, tramping down one row after another to see if she could spot them.

The end of the row of vines was bordered by a high dry stone wall, and as Martin and Susannah walked by it she stepped on a stone, lost her footing and slipped sideways, shrieking as she hit the ground and sprawled awkwardly.

'Are you OK?' He held out a hand to pull her up but she winced when she twisted her body to try and stand.

'I've hurt my ankle. Oh, God, it's killing me!' She half sat up and leaned forward, gingerly caressing her injured ankle.

'Let me have a look at it.'

She stretched out and eased off her sandal and he felt carefully around her ankle, his fingers exploring for swelling and his concentrated gaze looking for any bruising.

'It's just a sprain,' he said finally. 'It will hurt for a while but nothing's broken.'

She was very doubtful. 'Are you sure? It feels as if it might be broken, it hurts so much.'

'Yes, I'm sure. You may have torn a lateral ligament, and in that case it will swell and you'll have some bruising but the bone is fine.'

'Most people would just say sprained,' she said ruefully. 'You sound just like our doctor.'

'That's what I should be next year, hopefully. I'm a medical student.'

'Really? If you'd asked me, I'd have said you were a singer in a band.'

His face stretched in amusement. 'God God, no! Why on earth should I be a singer? I'm practically tone deaf. They threw me out of the school choir after a week. And I wouldn't be contributing much to society even if I could sing.'

She stretched out both legs and gingerly moved her injured ankle a fraction. 'Could we just sit here for a while? I don't think I could make it to the market today.'

'If you like. We'll have to get you home, though. Can you stand on it?'

'I'll try in a minute, but let me rest it for a while. She turned to face him. 'Tell me a bit more about yourself. Where are you studying?'

'I'm up at Newcastle.'

'No? Honestly? I've been accepted there too!'

'Really? For medicine?'

'Yes.' She leaned forward and gently massaged her injured ankle. 'Ouch, it still hurts.' The stab of pain lent an additional bitterness to her voice as she continued. 'I'm not going, though. I'm going to do a drama course in London.'

She sounded sulky and he said, 'Just out of curiosity, could you tell me why?'

'That's what I've always wanted to be. Don't you think I'll make a good one?' She looked up at him, anticipating enthusiastic agreement, but instead he made a slight shrug and only said, 'If that's what you want.'

At that moment, Orla approached the dry stone wall from the opposite side. She heard voices, and with a sudden shock she recognized Martin's. She had no desire whatsoever to meet up with them, and Padraic or no Padraic, she thought, she would sit down by the wall until they went.

She had not intended to listen, but Susannah's question came clearly.

'And do you like her?'

His voice was disparaging. 'Goodness, no, not in the least. She's forever on a ridiculous diet, although to be honest she needs to be. She's overweight and she does zero exercise. I've been out with her a couple of times, but only because she pestered me.'

Susannah's high pealing laugh reached her and she felt sick. He had to be talking about her, and to that terrible girl of all people, and he thought she was fat! Her mouth opened in horror but she kept perfectly still; even her breathing was arrested, until she heard Susannah's voice again, saying, 'I think I can try and walk now. It feels a bit better. Give me a hand up, will you?'

There was a scuffling noise as he hauled her to her feet, and then their footsteps receded until finally she heard no more. Suddenly, she turned over onto her side and she vomited violently onto the hard ground.

For a few moments there was nothing except her own misery, and she felt dizzy and weak. Everything around her was focussed into a clarity she had never yet known and would forever associate with a feeling of despair in the years to come. An ant, scurrying towards its destination, a squashed grape bursting its sticky juice on the ground, dry sticks broken from the vines and littering the hard ground. Sweat was pouring down into her eyes, from both the sun and the effect of her retching, and she closed her eyes. She felt betrayed and humiliated. All thoughts of Padraic were completely forgotten. All she wanted to do was to cry out her anguish.

She waited until the feeling of weakness and panic had lessened slightly, and she stumbled unsteadily to her feet. There was no sign of Martin and Susannah. She wanted to lie down somewhere cool and dark, and she turned towards home. Suddenly, she hated the place; the merciless glare of the sun beating down on her, the strange landscape of vines, the isolation of the decaying stone buildings she could not identify. All of it seemed a million miles from the comforting gentle landscape of home and she wished they had never come.

She stumbled into the house, and the first thing she saw was Padraic, sitting at the table placidly forking ham and slapping it onto his bread.

'Ah, there you are.' her mother cried. 'Where on earth have you been?'

'Nowhere,' she muttered.

'Well, come and sit up, for Heaven's sake. Padraic wasn't out playing after all, he was in his room, he didn't hear me calling him.'

'I'm not hungry.'

Her mother stared at her and even Padraic glanced up.

There was alarm in her mother's voice. 'You must be hungry. You've not had a bite to eat since lunchtime, and that was only a couple of sandwiches. Come on, now.'

'You're not listening to me! I said I'm not hungry!' Her face registered her fury, and Declan and Theresa looked at each other, appalled. She tore out of the room and ran into her bedroom. The door slammed and she threw herself face downwards onto her bed and broke into a storm of weeping.

Declan opened the door and strode across to the bed. 'Orla, get up this minute. What's wrong with you, child? What are you crying for?'

'Oh, leave me alone, can't you?'

'Now, don't take that tone, there's no need for it. Do you hear me? Now sit up like a good girl and tell Daddy what's wrong.'

'You wouldn't understand. And I wish you'd stop talking to me like I'm seven years old.'

'Orla, when you're a big grown up lady with children of your own, you'll always be my little girl and I'll always love you.' He sat down on the bed and patted her hand. 'And I might understand. You wouldn't know until you tell me.'

Very reluctantly she sat up her face was streaked with tears and he put his arm around her shoulders.

'He thinks I'm too fat,' she said, and with the memory of it the tears started to fall again.

Declan was bewildered. 'Who does?'

'M..Martin. He told that girl...Susannah. They were talking about me, and he said I was overweight...'She could not bring herself to relate the rest of the words that had hurt her so deeply. The dreadful knowledge that he had only taken her out because she had 'pestered him.'

'What! Oh, he couldn't have said that, child, you must have misheard him. I mean, just look at you. You're still as thin as a lath. I know you're eating now, but there's no way you're fat, nothing like it. I'll be having a word with the lad myself...'

'Daddy, no! Don't you dare!' She was outraged. 'I should never have said anything. I'll die if you go and see him. Promise me you won't.'

'Alright, alright,' he soothed her. 'But you must be wrong. He must be blind if he thinks that. Now then, dry your eyes and let's be hearing no more about it.'

She swung her legs to the floor and stood up. Declan put his arm around her shoulder as they walked back to the dining room. 'You know, child, it's a terrible thing for a parent when they see their children unhappy. In a way it's worse for Mammy and me, because we feel so useless...'

'Daddy! You're not useless.'

'Helpless, then,' he replied. 'We hate just standing by and watching you go through all these troubles.' He stopped and looked her in the eyes. 'For our sakes, child, for Mammy and me, could you try and stop these silly ideas you've got in your head about being too fat?'

The love in his voice brought the tears to her eyes once again but she tried valiantly to stem them. 'I'll try, Daddy,' she said. 'Really I will.'

'That's a good girl,' he said. 'Now come on and let me see you eat a good tea, and try to put this boy out of your mind. I'm sure he didn't mean anything.'

By eight o clock on Friday evening the barbecue was in full swing, and the atmosphere far more relaxed than the previous week. Liz tried hard to forget that when these guests had gone home, there would be no more bookings until a week in late September.

Last night she had slept badly. The worries over their finances had snaked around in her head, until finally she dozed off just before four o'clock. Peter, she noticed, seemed to sleep much as usual, and now he was handling the spluttering sausages with an easy skill, flicking them over and from time to time feeding the fire with the sticks that were kept on a shelf below the barbecue. At least everyone seemed to be enjoying themselves. Or at least, nearly everyone. Orla, she noticed, had a face on her that would sour the milk and she wondered vaguely if the girl was alright.

She cast a surreptitious glance at Susannah, whom she had mentally classed as a little madam from the moment they met. She had extracted a gold plated mirror from her clutch bag and was touching up her bright red lipstick.

She had taken the seat next to Martin. He looked across at Orla opposite and gave her a faint, apologetic half smile, but she met his gaze with a stony face and refused to smile back. Puzzled, he turned his attention to Susannah, offering her a selection of salads. She laughed as she dropped a spoon on the floor and he bent down to retrieve it for her and then left to find her a clean one. She thanked him with a soft smile.

Orla was watching her with narrowed eyes, hating her. The air was humid and her own hair was starting to frizz, but Susannah's was still smooth and silky. Unreasonably, she hated her for that too.

Padraic was running around the table, heedless of gentle remonstrances to sit down, until Declan caught hold of him by the tail of his shirt as he attempted to pass.

'That's enough, now,' he said. 'You sit still for a minute and let's all have bit of peace, shall we?'

'But I saw an animal,' he protested, his voice high with excitement. 'It ran away.'

Liz laughed and indicated a length of about six inches with her index fingers.

'Was it about this long?' she asked him, 'and did it have long tail?'

'Yes.' Padraic nodded vigorously and beamed up at her.

'That's a lizard,' she explained. You watch out for them, there are lots of them about, and sometimes they climb up the walls.'

'Can I catch one?' he asked eagerly. 'To take home with me?'

'Oh, they're pretty fast,' she smiled. 'They're very hard to catch but you can try if you like.' She caught sight of Theresa's face, definitely concerned, and added hastily in a lower voice, 'He's highly unlikely to catch one. Don't worry, you won't be taking one back to Ireland with you.'

Theresa laughed in her turn. 'I was having terrible thoughts of unpacking the child's suitcase and picking out dead animals,' she admitted.

'I will catch one,' Padraic insisted.

He had a determined look on his face, and to distract him, Liz said quickly, 'Listen can you hear that noise?'

They were all momentarily silent as Padraic cocked his head to one side. In the near distance they could hear an incessant chirruping.

'Are they birds?'

'No, not birds, they're insects,' Liz told him. 'They're called cicadas, and believe it or not, they're quite small. The noise they make is quite disproportionate to their size.'

Then she added, 'If you're very quiet and look carefully, you might just be able to spot one of them on the trees over there.'

He was evidently fascinated, as she had expected, and still chewing on his burger, he set off down the garden.

'Ah, it's very good you are with the child,' Declan said appreciatively, and Liz smiled. 'As long as he's interested, it's a pleasure to tell him about the life we have here.'

'It's totally different from home, that's for sure,' Theresa said. 'He'll remember this holiday for a long time.'

Peter was coming round with a large wooden tray filled with pizza slices, hamburgers and sausages.

'What can I give you?' he asked when he stopped beside Orla.

'Nothing, thank you. I'm not hungry.' She was barely polite, and Peter's eyebrows lifted slightly.

'You're sure?'

'Yes, honestly, I couldn't eat a thing.' She couldn't keep the bitterness out of her voice, and Declan and Theresa exchanged glances.

Peter's eyes narrowed slightly and he stroked his short beard; small gestures that his former pupils would have recognized immediately, but he kept a tight rein on his annoyance. The girl had been almost rude in her refusal, but, he reminded himself sternly, she was not a member of his sixth form, she was a badly needed paying guest. Things were different now. Even so, he was finding it hard to adjust from a role of authority to one of genial host. He smiled at Orla briefly and passed on.

Theresa was furious with her. In this public place it was impossible to say anything that would cause a scene, but the look that she gave Orla spoke volumes. Martin was watching carefully, not fully comprehending but aware of a tension around the table that was almost palpable.

Emma too recognized that something was wrong and she made an attempt to lighten the atmoshere by asking Liz about the strange stone buildings that dotted the surrounding fields.

'They're called *capitelles*,' Liz told her. 'You wouldn't have seen them before. Not many of them are in use now, but in the past they were used as shelters by the *vignerons* who lived up in the mountains. They would eat there and keep their equipment in them. You see, they wouldn't have had cars in those days and it was too far for them to go back home to eat, so the *capitelles* were a useful little shelter. And of course, we can get some quite violent storms here in the summer and they could stay in them until it passed. Keep your eyes open and I'm sure you'll see a lot of differences between here and England. For instance, if you look out for…'

Emma was never to find out what she should look out for, since at that moment Prinny hurtled through the gate and in a second she was amongst them. She was dishevelled and wild eyed. Her heavy mascara was streaking her face, making her look grotesque, and she was babbling incoherently. They heard the words 'Arlette' and 'pills,' but none of them could make any sense of what she was saying.

Peter slammed his barbecue fork down and took her arm, leading her to a vacant seat next to Padraic.

'Prinny, what's wrong?' he asked urgently. 'Here, sit down. Calm yourself now. What's happened? '

For a full minute she couldn't speak. Instead, she sobbed, her breath coming in great gulps. Liz was beside her now. She pulled a tissue out of her handbag and handed it to Prinny, whose sobs were diminishing a little as she blew her nose and wiped ineffectually at the mascara still staining her cheeks.

Theresa and Declan exchanged appalled glances, and Liz looked over at them, groaning inwardly at this chaotic interruption to what was meant to be a convivial evening for her guests.

'Prinny, you must tell us. What's wrong? Is it Luc? Are you ill?'

She shook her head, and then Peter urged her. 'You must tell us, Prinny. What is it?'

Visibly, she made an effort but her voice was still trembling as she said,

'It's Arlette. She's taken....I mean, I've given her too many of her tablets.'

'Which ones?' Martin's voice came crisply and they all turned towards him. He pushed his chair back and joined Liz and Peter.

'It's very important, Prinny,' he said. 'What were they?'

Emma was by her side now. She put her arm around her friend and spoke to her urgently.

'Darling, calm down and tell us what's happened. Take some deep breaths now.'

She bent over Prinny and she almost recoiled when the unmistakeable smell of whisky hit her. She glanced up and looked at Peter and Martin. Would they have noticed?

Prinny did her best and took a gulping breath, before she sobbed out in a strangled voice: 'They were her...her...sleeping pills.'

'How many has she had?' His voice was very curt and she answered weakly, 'I...I'm not sure.' She was twisting the handkerchief round in her hands, and Liz's face changed from exasperation to open mouthed horror.

Padraic sidled up and tried to get closer to the weeping Prinny, but Theresa grasped him by the hand and said firmly, 'Padraic, you go back into the house. This minute, do you hear me?'

With evident reluctance he walked away slowly, turning back to look over his shoulder at the scene.

Martin took her arm and gently raised her to her feet.

'Prinny, we have to go now. There may still be time if we hurry.' She stood up a little unsteadily. Emma supported her at one side and Martin at the other as they made their way as fast as they could out of the gate.

Theresa stood up and said in a low voice, 'Declan, we'll go back to the house. They won't want the whole crowd of us there.' And then, to Orla, 'Where are you going? Come on, we're all going back to the house.'

But she was talking to her retreating figure as she raced along the path to catch them up.

'Let her go,' Declan said. 'If he doesn't want her there he'll send her back.'

As they hurried along, Prinny began to babble. 'I didn't mean to. I just couldn't remember if she'd had one already.'

'How long ago was it?'

'It wasn't long ago. She was still awake when I left her, and then I remembered I'd left my magazine in the bedroom, so I went back in, and she...she didn't look right, and I couldn't wake her up.'

'Is that when you left?'

'Y..yes. I didn't know what to do.'

'You should have got Luc to ring for an ambulance straight away if you couldn't wake her up. Why didn't he do that? Where is he?'

She was tearful once more. 'He's not at home, he's gone to Guillaume's. He said he'd help him with his camper van. Do you think, I mean, will it be too late?'

'I doubt it, if she's only had a couple of tablets.' He looked at her sharply and asked, 'Has she had any alcohol?'

'No. No she hasn't.'

But you have, Martin thought grimly. He wondered how on earth this situation had got so out of hand. How anyone so unreliable as Prinny could possibly be trusted with a sick lady. But then he pulled himself up. It was none of his affair, but if they hurried, he knew what he had to do, and he only prayed that he would be in time.

He approached her bed, closely followed by the others who crowded round him.

'Stand back, all of you,' he said peremptorily, and then, to Susannah, 'would you please give me some room?' Deeply offended, Susannah moved back a few paces, and then he addressed Orla.

'Go and get me a cup of hot water with two teaspoons of salt in it.' And then, to his mother, 'Call the SAMU, mum. Let them know it's an overdose of sleeping pills.'

He picked up a small bottle from the bedside table and looked at the label. 'It's temazapam,' he called over his shoulder, and Liz nodded quickly at him as she began to speak in rapid French. They heard her give the address, and then she said, 'They're on their way. It will be about ten minutes, they said. Will she be alright?'

'I hope so,' he said grimly. 'If I can get a drink into her.'

Orla sped off to the kitchen, her hatred of Susannah completely forgotten for the moment. She found a kettle, quickly washed a grubby glass that she found on the draining board and feverishly hunted through the grimy cupboards until she found the salt. She carefully ladled in the two teaspoonfuls that Martin had asked for and carried it back to the bedroom.

Martin was examining Arlette. He was worried by the pallor of her face and by the weakened pulse, but he tried not to show any alarm and his voice was calm as he thanked Orla for the water.

Supporting the woman under her shoulders, he levered her into a sitting position and tilted her head back. She was not completely unconscious and he poured the hot salt water into her mouth, waiting for her to swallow before he laid her back down and turned once again to Orla.

'Help me to roll her onto her side,' he said, and between them they managed to lever Arlette over onto side. There was a retching noise, and Arlette coughed and gasped as she vomited.

'That's better,' he said quietly. 'Now, if she can just do that again...'

He was rewarded by the sound of choking vomiting as Arlette spewed out the stomach contents that had threatened her life.

No one noticed when Susannah slipped out of Arlette's bedroom. She made her way back to their own gîte, thinking about what she had just witnessed. Suddenly, she was overcome with jealousy. It should have been herself that Martin turned to for help instead of that skinny little Irish girl. *She* should have been one of the principal participants in the drama, for drama it surely was. And not on a screen. This was real life.

By the time she reached her own bedroom she had set the scene in her mind, and she lay face upwards on the bed and let the images flood over her. There would be a terrible accident, a traffic pile up, maybe, and she would stop her car and rush onto the scene.

'Let me through, I'm a doctor,' she would say, and her voice would carry such authority that the crowd would part and give her the space she needed. There would be gasps of astonishment, and low mutterings that this girl couldn't possibly be a doctor. She was too young, far too glamorous. She could be an actress, but not possibly a doctor, they would say. But she would pull out her black medical bag and start work, leaning over the injured man on the pavement and administering.....here, the exact details became a little vague, but one day she would know. There would be a paragraph in the papers regretting the terrible incident on the M25, but praising the efforts of Doctor Susannah Wade whose presence at the scene had undoubtedly saved the young man's life.

She rolled over and sat up, preparing to redo her make up before tea. It was only in her imagination, she knew, but one day it could really happen. When she was a doctor.

It was less than ten minutes before the rest of them heard the screaming siren of the ambulance. Quickly the two paramedics took in the situation. Martin filled in the details and in a few moments, Arlette was on a stretcher and on her way to Carcassonne hospital.

'Declan, for the love of God would you speak to the child. She ate nothing at the barbecue last night and now half a crumb for her breakfast. She's starting it all over again.'

'What can I say? She won't listen to me.' He was startled by Theresa's vehemence.

'You could try. She takes more notice of you than she ever does of me, that's for sure. I don't know what in earth's got into her. I thought all that was finished. She even went to a restaurant with Martin, for Heaven's sake.'

'Ah, I think that could be at the bottom if it all.'

'What do you mean?'

'It seems they've had some kind of lovers' tiff. She'll get over it. Just leave her alone and she'll come round. She'll eat when she's hungry enough.'

Theresa placed the cleaned plates carefully on the dresser, and then asked, 'How did you know?'

'Ah, she was a bit put out the other night.' His tone was casual and he refrained from telling Theresa the exact nature of the quarrel. Much better to leave things vague, he thought. Heaven only knew how she would react if she got the impression that Orla was depressed again.

'Well I surely hope that's all there is to it. Where is she, anyway?'

'Gone for a walk.'

Orla at that moment was on her way back up from the village, where she had been pacing around, the memory of Martin's overheard words filling her head until she hardly knew where she was going. She felt hot, dizzy and confused, and several passers-by had to skirt around her as she failed to make way for them on the pavement.

She barely reacted even when she heard her own name being called, and then the voice came again. Insistently this time, and she looked across the road to see Martin waving to her, a big cheerful grin on his face. She looked away and began to hurry up the street.

'Orla! Wait!' He looked quickly from side to side and then crossed over the road to join her. 'Didn't you see me? His voice was teasing and she knew that he expected her to be thrilled to see him. She ignored him and continued up the hill, increasing her pace until she was almost running.

Plainly, he was astonished. He caught up with her, grabbed her by the arm and swung her round to face him. 'What's wrong?'

'Nothing.'

'Don't be silly. Obviously something's upset you. What's the matter? I thought you might like to go around the vineyards with me.'

And then as there was no reply, he looked searchingly into her face. 'Come and sit down on this bench,' he said, and he almost pulled her up the street to and empty seat. 'Now,' he said firmly. 'Tell me what's wrong.'

'Nothing's wrong, I've told you.' She was still very mutinous.

'You've said that once and I'm not buying it. Has someone upset you? Is everything alright at home? What is it, Orla?'

She stared at him, looked directly into his eyes and said shortly, 'You should know, if anyone does.'

'Me! What have I done?' Genuinely bewildered now, Martin was also beginning to be annoyed with her. 'Look here, Orla, if I've done or said anything to make you feel like this then the least you can do is explain.'

'You know what it is,' she blurted. 'You think I'm fat. I heard you say it.'

He looked aghast, and then the anger showed in his face and in his voice, when he said, 'and just when exactly am I supposed to have said that?'

'You said it yesterday. In the vineyard. You were talking to ...to that girl.' She found that she could not even say Susannah's name. The memory of the conversation was still too painful.

'You mean Susannah?'

'Yes, of course I mean her. Who else could it be?' she snapped. 'You were talking about me and you told her I was overweight and that I was p..pestering you.' Her distress was now evident in her stammer, and to her surprise, a slow smile played about his lips.

'If you think it's funny,' she began furiously. His head lowered, and he looked at her, quizzically.

'And what makes you think I was talking about you? Did you hear me say your name?'

'No. No, but...there's no-one else, is there? You must have meant me.'

'And that's why you've decided to stop eating, is it?'

'Not really, no. I just wasn't hungry, that's all.'

'Oh, no, don't give me that, Orla. You've got your parents worried about you....yes, you have,' he stated, as she started to protest. 'They're every bit as worried now as they were when you were really ill. And is that what you want?'

'Of course not.' Her head was low and the easy tears were starting to form.

'You needn't start crying, it won't help,' he said remorselessly. 'I can tell you now, Orla. You're behaving like the worst kind of stroppy teenager at the moment. Something's upset you, so you decide to worry everyone by refusing to eat properly.' He stopped, and then added. 'Although that's not entirely true, is it?' With a wave of his hand he indicated a young couple strolling past on the other side of the street

'*He's* not worried about you, and neither is she. They couldn't care less if you live or die. No, the people you've decided to harass are the people who love you most...it's beginning to look like emotional blackmail, Orla, and it's a despicable thing to do.'

'Why did you go for a walk with her, then?' A part of her was still consumed with anger and jealousy.

'I was only being polite, that's all.' The exasperation was clear in his voice when he continued. 'Think about it for a minute. Who does she have to talk to here? She's only here because her mother wants to visit Prinny, and let's face it, you haven't shown her much friendship so far, have you? And in any case, *she* asked *me* to go for a walk. I didn't ask her.'

'M'sorry,' she muttered.

'And another thing,' he continued remorselessly. 'I know no-one's said anything, but you did upset mum and Peter quite a lot, you know, at the barbecue. Peter puts a lot of effort in, and you were almost rude when you wouldn't eat anything.'

The tears were streaming down her face now, and he pulled a packet of tissues from his pocket and handed it to her.

She fumbled with the polythene wrapper and pulled one out and blew her nose. 'I didn't realise,' she said in a small voice. 'I didn't mean to be rude.'

He grinned. 'That's what I told mum.'

'God, I feel awful. Please tell Peter I'm sorry. Will you?'

'Might be better to tell him yourself,' he suggested. 'Or better still, eat everything on the table at the next barbecue.'

'I will, I promise. Honestly.'

'That's a bit better. Now look at me.'

She looked up and to her relief, his expression was kindly once again.

'When I say the people who love you, that means me as well, you know.'

Still not entirely convinced, she ventured, 'Who...who were you talking about? I know it wasn't me, but.....'

Again, he smiled. 'She's my stepmother Phoebe's daughter from her previous marriage. She's sixteen and naturally, we live in the same house, or at least some of the time when I'm on holiday. She's called Mandy and she's most definitely overweight. Her mother loves cooking and her favourite food is sausages and chunky chips. In no way is she a rival to you, so don't think you can go back to your anorexic excuse and stop eating again.'

She was outraged. 'It wasn't an excuse! I was anorexic. I was in hospital.'

Martin stayed calm and spoke reasonably. 'But that was quite some time ago now, though, wasn't it? Since then you've put weight on, you're eating normally....or at least, you were until you decided that life was treating you badly and you needed to go back to childish tactics to retaliate.'

'I will eat properly again.' Her voice was very low. She felt very humbled, and ashamed. She hated the idea that Martin found her childish.

'I know it's still a struggle for you. Really I do. I've been on an anorexic course at Uni, and it's a horrible disease. But there are people who are much older than you who've struggled with it for years. Sometimes it never really goes away, even for people who *look* normal. But that's not your case, Orla. You're young and you've been in control of it for a long time now.'

'I still think about it a lot,' she ventured, hoping that he wouldn't immediately accuse her of childishness again. But he didn't. Instead, he said, 'Of course you do. That's to be expected. But I do want you to promise me something. Promise me that you'll never use food again as a means of exerting pressure on other people.'

Her head was low and her voice trembled a little as she said, 'I promise. Honestly.'

He smiled at her now and took her in his arms. Ignoring the passers-by who stared at them disapprovingly, they kissed.

Martin stepped out of the shower and wrapped a large towel around his lower body, before padding across to his room. Once there, he found his shorts, neatly pressed by his mother, and an orange t-shirt. He dressed and lay on his back on the bed, looking up at the ceiling. He needed the peace of his own room to define his thoughts.

He was utterly convinced now that he loved Orla. Everything about her was perfect. He loved her shy smile, her lack of affectation. He loved the way her long auburn hair glinted when it caught the sun, her beautiful, achingly vulnerable face and her tall, slim body with legs that were now tanned to a pale brown.

But his thoughts turned to practicalities. They were both on holiday here. It smacked of a temporary holiday romance, and he was quite sure that her parents would never agree to her moving to England to be with him. Equally certainly, he could not uproot himself and move to Ireland. He had to finish medical school. But once he had his degree, he would be free to go where he chose. He had already researched all the hospitals within a radius of Orla's vicinity, and if could land a job in one of those, he would be in a position to marry.

Marriage to Orla. He had never wanted anything more in his whole life. He knew that she was the perfect partner for him, and he was half dozing as he imagined their lives together. There would be children, he was sure. A slow smile spread across his face. Orla was Catholic; would that mean a whole string of children? How would they cope? And how would her parents feel about him, nominally a Protestant, although he had no strong religious persuasions.

The smile faded abruptly as he heard a muffled noise coming from the next room. Surely it couldn't be? He got up and moved to the door, opened it and listened again. Yes, it was. The awful sounds of his mother, sobbing. His mind flew back to the last time he had heard her cry, when he was only eight years old and his father had hit her so hard that she had staggered backwards, screaming in pain. Surely it couldn't be happening again? Oh, dear God, he thought, let it not be Peter. His affection for the big, grizzled man had grown with the years, and he regarded him as more of a father than his own had ever been.

He went to her door but hesitated. Should he go in? Would it be better if she didn't know that he had heard anything? But then he decided. The last time he had been far too young to take any kind of action. But this time he was a man. He pushed the door open.

Liz was lying face down on her bed, her whole body shaking with the violence of her sobs. He went over to her and laid a gentle hand on her shoulder.

'Mum?'

She started at his touch and jerked upwards. 'Martin! I thought you were out.'

'Sit up, mum. What's wrong? Has something happened?'

'Oh, it's nothing, love. Just a fit of the blues. We all get them sometimes.'

She sounded so low, so forlorn, and he put his arm around her shoulder.

'This is more than that,' he said. 'I know you, mum. You don't get all worked up over nothing. Do you want to talk about it?'

She lifted her face towards him, and when she spoke it was with great difficulty.

'It's nothing for you to worry about.' She seemed on the point of saying more but then shook her head.

'You let me be the judge of that. How do you know, if you won't tell me?'

He was gentle, and his kindly tone brought the tears streaming down her face again.

She groped under the pillow, brought out a clean handkerchief and blew her nose. 'Oh, it's just money really. It's the gîtes. We can't book them out, no matter what we do. We've tried everything, and if we don't get more guests in I don't know what we're going to do. We've worked so hard on this place.'

'I know you have.' His voice was quiet. He sat beside her on the bed. 'Are you sure you've looked at all the options? There's always an answer, you know, and it's not like you to be defeated.'

He was thinking now of the far off days when his mother had shown just how decisive she could be. There had been one more of those terrible rows which had shrivelled him up inside. He had wanted to hide, not to hear the screaming and the sounds of slaps, of yells of pain and the sight of his mother staggering backward, hands up covering her face, and her terrible cold fury when she had packed suitcases for both of them.

Finally, she had picked him up and carried him out to the car. He remembered so distinctly, as if it had happened yesterday, how he had looked back from the drive and seen his father at the window, watching them go with a look of utter desolation on his face, and tears coursing down his face.

They had climbed lots of stairs, until his legs were aching and finally she had pushed open the door into an immense room. It was teeming with women and children in groups, the women sitting in chairs, children playing with battered toys scattered around the floor. That was the beginning of a life which seemed to stretch for months, and he had not gone to school. Then, finally, they had moved again, this time to a small flat, and he had had his own bedroom once more.

He jerked himself out of the past, as Liz was speaking again. 'I'm not defeated. No, it hasn't got to that yet. It just came over me. I felt so helpless. I just have no idea what we're going to do. The money's almost gone. In a few months we'll have nothing to live on.'

He could see how desperate she was, even though she was trying to sound as light as possible. Her voice was wobbling dangerously again.

'What about selling up and going back to England? Wouldn't that be better than staying her and worrying? You and Peter could go back into teaching.'

She shook her head dismally. 'It's not as easy as that. For one thing, even if we wanted to, it could take forever to find a buyer for this place, and we'd run out of money long before that. I just don't know where to turn. Whichever way you look at it, it's hopeless.'

He searched around in his mind, trying to find something to say that would not sound like empty sympathy; to give her some concrete help.

'Couldn't you get a job here, either of you?' he suggested. 'Something to tide you over?'

'I've looked at that. There's nothing. We're so isolated here. There's only Carcassonne, and in any case, there's so much unemployment already. Most French firms wouldn't even consider an English person.'

He thought, and then had a burst of inspiration. 'But mum, you speak French. Why don't you do some private teaching? You could stick notices in some of the local shops. Why not give it a go?' He was eager to offer some practical advice, but to his dismay she was not enthusiastic.

'It wouldn't be enough,' she said sadly. 'I could teach the whole day long and it still wouldn't cover all our costs. Besides,' she continued. 'Most of the children round here, at least the boys, are going to be *vignerons* in the end. Why on earth would they need English for that?'

In his turn he was dismayed. 'Yes, I can see that. But listen, mum, please try not to worry. You say yourself often enough that things have a way of working out. You know you do.'

She managed a wan smile. 'Yes, I do, don't I? But then the things that needed working out were not usually as desperate as this.' She sat upright now and smiled at him, her face normal again. 'But you're right. I am being a bit defeatist.' Then her smile widened. 'At least I've got you. There's not every mother who's so lucky, having a fantastic son.' Suddenly, she reached out and hugged him close. 'Love you, pet.'

He hugged her back, quickly, and then released her. 'I love you too, mum.' And suddenly, he felt a lump in his throat. She had already suffered so much, and he couldn't bear to know that she was so unhappy. He decided to turn the conversation, even though he hadn't intended saying anything so soon.

'Mum, there's something I've been meaning to tell you.'

She scanned his face, a look of alarm in her eyes. 'You're not in any trouble, are you?'

He laughed softly. 'No, nothing like that. It's...well, it's about Orla.'

Her eyebrows lifted. 'The Irish girl?'

'Yes, of course.'

She said slowly, 'What about her?'

'I love her, mum,' he replied simply.

She turned to face him and looked at him with a slight worried frown. 'Oh. Martin, are you sure? She's here on holiday, like you.'

'Mum, *please* don't tell me it's just a holiday romance.'

'But love, that's exactly what it is.'

'Only in the sense that we met here, that's all.' His tone was gentle but firm. 'You're trying to denigrate it, simply because we're on holiday. I love Orla and I want to spend the rest of my life with ever. It's as simple as that.'

She stood up and bent over to smooth the duvet cover and plump up the pillows. 'We'll talk about it at teatime,' she said finally. 'Peter needs to know, if you feel so strongly about her.'

She laid the table in a silence which Martin mistook for disapproval, but which was, in reality, simply her way of coming to terms with the fact that he had meant every word. She knew him too well to mistake the sincerity in his voice and she wondered how Peter would react.

She ladled the carrot and onion soup into the yellow and white bowls which she had brought with them. It was lucky, she reflected wryly, that they also had all Peter's crockery and cutlery still packed up in boxes, because they simply could not afford to replace even a broken plate at the moment.

Over the meal, Martin told Peter much of what he had previously related to Liz, adding, 'and please don't tell me I've got the whole of the university to choose from, because it simply isn't true. Lots of the girls have already got boyfriends and even those who haven't are usually working so damned hard they don't have time for anything else.'

Peter said, 'Look, Martin, I do believe what you're telling us, and I know I'm not your father, but I do need to ask you; are you quite sure about this? Have you thought about practicalities? You live in England, Orla lives in Ireland. She'll be going back home soon, so what happens then?'

Martin regarded him with slightly raised eyebrows and then said patiently, 'In a few months I'll have my degree, and I'll be applying for jobs in Ireland. Oh, mum, please don't look like that,' he said hastily as he caught Liz's distraught look. 'I'll come back here whenever I can, so don't worry about that. I'm not thinking of emigrating to Australia. There are flights from Dublin to Carcassonne, you know that.'

Liz nodded but her expression was still serious.

'I'll get a job,' he continued, and when Orla has finished her education then we'll marry.'

Liz and Peter looked at each other, both their faces still showing concern.

'And what about Orla?' Peter asked. 'Does she know how you feel?'

'Yes, of course she does,' he said with a touch of impatience. 'We've discussed it, and she's going to talk to her parents tonight.'

'From what I've seen so far, she might have a hard time convincing her mother,' Liz said. 'She doesn't strike me as the type to be thrilled at a holiday romance carrying on when the girl gets home. Oh, yes, I know, you've said it's not, but I bet you anything her mother will see it like that.'

CHAPTER 14

Prinny made herself a cup of strong coffee and took it out into the garden. Arlette was due back today after an overnight stay in the hospital where they found no lasting damage from her overdose.

She was deeply ashamed that she had come so close to killing Luc's mother and she knew that her drinking had reached the point where, if she continued, there was a real possibility that she would harm someone.

Resolutely, she left her coffee on the garden table and marched into the salon. She knelt down in front of the cupboard and took out three bottles of whisky. Holding one in each hand with another under her arm, she went into the bathroom. It was without a single pang of regret that she opened them one by one and watched the contents gurgle down the sink.

Slowly, she went back outside into the hot sunshine and sat down with her coffee.

No-one had openly blamed her for what had happened, but she knew what they must all be thinking of her. She had been especially hurt by the look of utter contempt that had shown in Liz's face as Arlette was being wheeled to the ambulance.

She knew that Liz must surely despise her as a wanton spendthrift, totally useless and incapable of managing even the most basic household tasks, let alone look after a sick woman and she was surprised to find how much the thought upset her.

Previously, and without being conscious of any snobbery involved, she had mentally classified both Liz and Peter as being 'from the North', which in her London life would automatically have disqualified them as real friends, unless of course they happened to be from a limited number of aristocratic families, but it came to her, suddenly and with a pang of real anguish that she would give a lot to have Liz's respect.

She cast her mind back to what Liz had said to her. She couldn't recall the long word that she had used. What was it? Something about doing things for people, but the essence of the conversation had stayed with her, submerged in her mind until it surfaced now.

For the first time in many years, she began to think about herself in terms other than her appearance and her once all important London social life. She tried to think logically, rationally, and to give herself honest answers to the questions that she had so far avoided thinking about.

Why had she come to look after Arlette? Did she really feel sorry for the woman? A month ago the answer would have been a resounding no. Most definitely, a few weeks ago she had felt no pity at all for the woman who had lost so much in the few seconds it took for the stroke to rob her of her health, her job and her independence, but day after day of watching the woman struggle with her food, listening to the almost indecipherable mutterings and witnessing her ever present frustration had left a mark. Yes, at this particular moment she was most definitely sorry for her. She would rather have died, herself, than live such a life.

Luc was more relaxed than he had ever been in London. England had been a massive, bold experiment and it had overwhelmed him. Like an uprooted plant, his was a nature that withered when it was taken outside its natural environment. This was his home and he was so much happier here. He had fought her desire to remain in London and he had won.

But what about herself ? Was she a winner or a loser? What did she have here? She hated the tiny, cramped house they were forced to live in, she felt lost and vulnerable when she couldn't understand the conversations around her.

And then there was Emma. What did Emma think of her? The answer hit her with an unexpected jolt. How much did she actually care what Emma thought of her? The response came with a sudden shock. She knew now that Emma belonged in London with the smart sophisticated set that she herself was once a part of, and that her own life had changed irrevocably.

And Susannah? With a small shock she suddenly remembered that she had not fulfilled her promise to Emma. She was supposed to talk to the girl, to try and persuade her that medicine was the best career for her. This, at least, would be a start. She would have a chat with Susannah as soon as she could. It would be a beginning, something to do that could help another person.

She might even feel better about herself if she tried.

Susannah was lying on her back, an open magazine by her side, and apparently asleep, but when Prinny's shadow fell over her she opened her eyes, shaded them with her hand and looked up.

'Sue, do you have a minute?'

Since she was so blatantly doing nothing at all except lie in the sun, there was only one possible answer but she was rather bemused when she sat up and said, 'Yes, of course,' and she waved a hand at the next sun lounger, inviting Prinny to sit down.

But Prinny shook her head and said, 'If you don't mind awfully, I'd rather go over to the house. I've left Arlette on her own and I'd rather be there in case she needs anything.'

Susannah could hardly object to this, but she was still mystified. 'Yes, fine. Just give me a couple of minutes to get into something decent. I can't very well parade across the village in a bikini.'

She levered herself up, and Prinny took her place to wait, but also to think carefully about what she was going to say. She knew that Susannah could be as headstrong as Emma and she sighed inwardly. All she could do was try, she thought philosophically, and if it didn't work then at least she would have done her best.

Susannah appeared in less time than Prinny expected, now dressed in a long floaty blue skirt, white sleeveless top and high heeled sandals.

As they walked out of the gate, Susannah's curiosity was evident when she said, 'Is something wrong, Prinny?'

'No. No, nothing's wrong exactly. It was just that I wanted a word with you, that's all.' She matched her steps to Susannah's long legged strides, and shortly afterwards they were out of the glare of the sun and sitting on the sofa in Prinny's lounge.

'Well, don't keep me in suspense,' Susannah said. 'What is it?'

'Look, I don't want to interfere,' she began. She was obviously embarrassed, and Susannah's eyebrows were raised now as she began to realise what Prinny might wish to talk about. She was about to come back with a sharp retort, but something in Prinny's manner stopped her and she remained silent.

Prinny made an effort and continued. 'It's just that...well, have you quite decided what you want to do with your life?' She was floundering now. 'I mean, Emma says...'

She got no further, as Susannah interjected, 'So Mummy's been getting at you, too, has she?'

'Not exactly getting at me. But she did just wonder if you've absolutely decided on acting?'

'When she and Daddy want me to do medicine, you mean?'

'Well, it is a good career,' she said. 'That is, if you've got the brains for it.' She paused for a moment and looked at Susannah, before she said earnestly, 'And I know that you have. Emma tells me you're predicted really good grades in your A levels. Not like poor little me,'

327

she added with a wry laugh. 'I never even got to A level standard, I left school well before then. But it's different for you, Sue. You're easily bright enough to be a doctor, so why not do it?'

Susannah was not entirely unaffected by the compliment to her intelligence, and her expression was perplexed as she said, 'I did want to be an actress, but now I'm not so sure.'

'I was really impressed with the way you coped with Arlette, you know' she went on. 'You were far better than I am. You seem to have a natural ability to deal with sick people. I just think it would be a pity to waste your talent, that's all.'

'That was just feeding someone,' she said sullenly. 'And I'm talented as an actress, too. Mummy and Daddy both thought I was terrific as Juliet when we did the school play.'

Prinny glanced across at her. Susannah's lips were a thin line of annoyance now and as she had no intention of antogonising her she simply said, 'Do give it some thought, Sue. It's what everyone wants for you and it would be a fantastic career.'

'I'll think about it,' was all the rejoinder she got, and she had to be satisfied with that. She sighed to herself as Susannah bent to kiss her and left.

Liz took the pile of washing into the small room off the kitchen. They called it the utility room, although in fact it was nothing more than a former garage which now had shelves the length of the room holding an assortment of pots and bric-a-brac which they couldn't find room for in the house.

It was large enough to accommodate the small chest freezer which they had brought with them, and the washing machine which they had bought in France. Although both the gîtes had top of the range dishwashers, it was a luxury they themselves decided they had to forego until there was more money.

It was a beautiful drying day, she thought, and she would get the clothes out as soon as she could and iron them before lunch.

She bundled everything in and turned the dial. Instead of the usual swish of water, all she heard was a dreadful grinding noise, and suddenly there was the acrid smell of burning rubber and at the same time, a cloud of grey smoke belched out from behind the machine.

'Peter,' she yelled, and in a minute he was beside her. Between them they tugged the machine out from the wall and Peter was bending over the back of it.

He shook his head and wrinkled his nose at the smell. 'I think it's had it,' he said finally. 'There's no way I can fix this. Either we call a plumber out or we'll have to get a new one.'

'It's the middle of July,' she snapped. 'There's no chance of getting a plumber to come out.'

He knew that she was perfectly right and he nodded glumly. The worse time of year to have any sort of emergency was July and August when most of the working population was on holiday. They had even heard that being ill or having a baby were to be avoided if possible during the peak holiday season.

'In any case, if it's the motor that's gone it will cost nearly as much to fix as getting a new one. We might as well just buy one.'

He was totally unprepared for her furious reaction.

'And how exactly are we going to do that?' she exclaimed angrily. 'We haven't even got enough for the next electricity bill, let alone a new washing machine.'

She scooped up the pile of washing and stormed into the kitchen. 'I'm going to have to do this lot by hand,' she fumed. She grabbed a pile of underwear and flung it into the stone sink.

Peter followed her and he said tentatively, 'You could use one of the machines in the gîtes, couldn't you?'

She looked appalled. 'They're not ours.'

'Of course they're ours,' he said irritably. 'We own them, don't we? Why shouldn't we use them?'

'Oh, Peter, talk sense. The gîtes are let out. And besides,' she added, 'they'll be locked. The Irish family went out this morning and those two from London left about ten o'clock. I saw them go.'

'We do have keys,' he said, and they looked at each other.

'I couldn't possibly,' she said finally after a long moment. 'I mean, imagine if they came back and found us there. Technically, we'd be trespassing. Although to be honest,' she added, 'I don't think Theresa would mind if I asked her, but we can't go in there without permission. I'd feel terrible, and what if they went home and told people? None of their friends would ever come to a place if they thought the owners were likely to break into the place any time they fancied.'

'Don't be so melodramatic,' he said, irritated in his turn, 'It wouldn't be breaking in.'

'Whatever you want to call it,' she retorted, 'I'm not doing it. It wouldn't be right.'

'Have it your own way, then, if you want to wash by hand.'

'I don't *want* to,' she shouted. 'What else do you suggest I do?'

But she was talking to his retreating back as he stalked off. Angrily, she filled the sink with water and started rubbing the clothes as viciously as if they were the real culprits.

After a few moments of banging at the clothes, self pity began to overcome her anger, and she thought bitterly: *No dishwasher, no money and now no bloody washing machine*. Suddenly, it was one crisis too many and she started to cry.

She hated it when she and Peter had any kind of disagreement, and it was happening now on a regular basis. At heart, she knew that it was only because they were both so terribly stressed, but at this particular moment the logic failed to lift her spirits and she continued to weep silently, brushing the tears away with wet, soapy hands.

As she twisted and slapped at the first batch of washing, she heard the front door open and Peter say tersely, 'She's in the kitchen.'

She knew immediately who it was, and she hastily did her best to adjust her expression to a welcoming smile, but it was no use. There was no hiding her emotions and suddenly Prinny was beside her, her eyes questioning.

'Liz, are you OK?'

She tried to make her voice sound normal, but the words came out on the verge of a sob. 'It's nothing,' she said in a dull voice. 'Just the stupid washing machine's broken, that's all. These things happen.'

Prinny was bewildered. 'So that's why you're doing this?' And she indicated the sink, before she said sympathetically, 'and you can't get another one delivered, you mean? That is such a bore.' Then she added quickly, 'But there's no need for you to do this. I have a washing machine. Take your things over to my house, darling.'

'That would be great, Prinny' she said thankfully and she began to search for a plastic bag to put the washing into.

'So when is the new one coming?' she asked idly. She watched as Liz continued to pile clothes into bags.

'It isn't,' she said shortly.

'Oh, darling, can't you find the one you want? The shops here are absolutely hopeless, aren't they? I've been looking for an induction cooker everywhere, but can I find one? You wouldn't believe it, Liz,' she prattled on, 'but I've actually bought a recipe book. Luc says he's tired of eating beans on toast every night and he's going to teach me to cook. But the cooker here is just hopeless. It must be fifty years old at least. I know exactly the model I want, but the only place I've seen it is in London. Luc says they won't deliver it here but I'm going to ring them. I'm sure I can persuade them to ship one over. It's just a matter of speaking to the right person.' She failed to notice Liz's mounting exasperation and she continued artlessly, 'Why don't you do the same, darling, if you can't find the one you want here?'

She was totally unprepared for Liz's reaction. She turned to face her and her hands flew to her hips, her face red with anger. She suddenly overcome by an almost uncontrollable urge to slap the woman in the face. It was impossible to control herself and her voice was shaking with fury as she shouted, 'You have absolutely no idea what I'm talking about, do you? It's not about choosing a washing machine, you.....' She only just managed to stop herself from calling Prinny a stupid fool, but she controlled the impulse, before she yelled again.

'I can't *afford* a washing machine. I would never expect you to understand that in a million years. You're living on a different planet to everyone else. Money means nothing at all to you, does it? You've had as much as you want your whole life.'

She stopped, and glared at Prinny, who was looking horrified.

She was totally unable to stop herself from continuing. 'Just let me tell you something, Prinny. Some of us have to live in the real world. We have to budget, we have to count every single euro, and sometimes even that's not enough. Sometimes we just can't make ends meet, no matter how hard we try. We've tried so hard, both of us, and it's just not working and it never will be.'

Her voice broke as the surge of emotions overwhelmed her, and she started to cry.

Prinny was appalled. She had never seen Liz other than totally calm and controlled, capable of anything. Liz was the one who sorted everything out, and it was such a terrible shock to see her in this state. Tentatively, she reached her arm out to the weeping woman, but Liz shook her off impatiently.

'Don't touch me,' she said roughly. 'I can't stand it if you touch me. I'll....I'll be fine in a minute. Just leave me alone.'

She was already bitterly regretting her outburst. She fully expected Prinny to walk away, and she was considerably surprised when the high voice spoke again.

'No, Liz, darling. If you don't want me to touch you then of course I won't. But please,' she added, and her face was crumpled with concern, 'Please come home with me and we can sit down. We need to talk.'

This time she offered no resistance. It was as if her spent rage had exhausted her and drained away her will. She allowed Prinny to gently steer her out of the house and along the road whilst she tried to compose herself, taking deep breaths to steady her nerves, and making no attempt to shake off the protective arm around her waist. They arrived.

'Liz, you're perfectly right, I have no idea about money. I've always had as much as I want and more, so it's hard for me to put myself in that situation of not having enough.' Then she brightened. 'But honestly, if that's all that's worrying you...'

'All?' Liz was shocked at how little Prinny understood, and her voice rose. 'It might seem like nothing to you but we're at the end of the road. There isn't even enough in the bank account to cover the next electricity bill. Can you even begin to understand how that feels? And you know what it's like here. This is not England. One unpaid bill and you wake up with no electricity.'

She was ashamed to be pouring out her woes to this pretty butterfly, but now she had started she couldn't stop herself. She barely noticed that Prinny was rummaging thorough a beige leather handbag, murmuring, 'Oh, these bags, you can never find anything. Ah, there it is.'

For all her wealth and privileged background, Prinny was far from selfish. At school the girls had always been taught to think of those less fortunate than themselves, and were often involved in activities which supported local and national charities. It came to her, as quite a shock, that Liz and Peter fell into this category, and she knew how she could help them.

She pulled out a cheque book from Coutts Bank. 'I know you'll probably say you don't want this,' she said as she scribbled, 'but I'd really like you to take it.'

She tore out the cheque and handed it to the astonished Liz. She gaped at it, stunned by both the gesture and the amount of money staring at her. She looked at it for a long moment, and then she passed it back. 'Prinny, this is so very, very kind of you. I can't tell you how much I appreciate what you're trying to do, but I really can't accept this.'

'No, I insist, Liz,' she said firmly. 'If you like, you can count it as payment. You've done so much for me.' She took Liz's hand and pressed the cheque into it, gently closing her fingers around it. 'It's not very much in any case,' she said, 'and it should sort out the immediate issues. At least you'll be able to buy a washing machine. Take it, Liz, please.'

The amount was ten thousand euros. Liz opened her hand and stared at it with a mixture of amazement and total fascination.

'You must, Liz. Please. Do it for me, just to make me happy. No-one's been very pleased with me since I gave Arlette those tablets. And don't forget that it was Martin who saved me that day. I owe him something, too. You know she could have died if he hadn't been there.'

Liz was silent for a long moment. She kept on looking at the cheque and her mind was racing. Finally, she said in a low voice, 'I'll pay it back. I swear you'll get every euro of it back, if it's the last thing I ever do.'

'Forget it, and it's not a loan. You're welcome to take it as a gift.'

'But it's so much...'

She was unprepared for Prinny's gentle laugh. 'You were right, you know, when you said we live in different worlds. Believe me, when you cash this, I won't even notice that it's gone.'

Liz was genuinely bewildered by this. 'What about Luc?' she asked. 'Won't he mind?'

'This is my own account, not Luc's,' she said firmly. 'And it's something I want to do.' She paused, before she added, 'It's something I can do with no effort at all, you know. There's no sacrifice involved anywhere. I'm not giving up any of my time, as you did for me. Now please, put it away.'

Liz slapped the steaks on the table, and followed them by fried onions, chips, mushrooms and a light pepper sauce.

'What's all this?' Peter was amazed and far from being pleased, his annoyance was very evident in his voice. 'Steaks, Liz? Do you know how much these cost, for Heaven's sake?'

She smiled widely but made no answer. Instead, she waited until he sat down and then she slid Prinny's cheque over to him.

'What's that?' Martin asked. Silently, Peter passed it over to him, his face registering his shock.

Martin scanned it and his eyes widened. 'Mum, you can't! You can't possibly take this. Not from that woman.'

'Don't call her that woman,' Liz flashed. 'She's our neighbour.'

'And suddenly she's your closest friend, apparently,' Martin said, and the sarcasm in his voice made her flinch.

'So what if she's not? She's given me this and I for one, am very grateful, so don't start casting aspersions on her.'

Peter had his hand over his mouth. 'No, Liz,' he said gently. 'No matter how badly off we are, we can't rely on charity. It's not right.'

'This is not charity,' she shouted. 'I've done a lot for 'that woman' as Martin so rudely called her. All she's doing is paying me for it.'

'Don't be daft, love,' he replied, but not unkindly. 'No-one gets paid to the tune of ten thousand euros for just helping someone around the house.' He paused. 'And besides, I'm not at all happy about taking any of her money.'

Liz sounded truculent now. 'It doesn't mean anything to her. She told me, she won't even notice it's gone out of her account.'

'That's it exactly, Peter said. 'She's a bling princess with a Coutts bank account. Money means nothing at all to her. And her type are apt to get temperamental. She's handed it over on a whim and she's just as likely to ask for it back on another. You'd never be secure. No. Give it here.' He stretched his arm across the table, and before Liz could even cry out, he ripped it in two.

The sight of the torn up cheque unleashed all Liz's pent up frustration of the past few weeks. To her, the cheque represented the kind of security they had never known since moving to France. It meant freedom from the terrible gnawing nightmare of going completely bankrupt, of having their services cut off one by one, and the dreadful terror that came to her during the night of there being no money left for even basic food shopping. Everything she had dreaded could have been avoided, and with the sound of the ripped paper, she screamed out,

'What the hell do you think you're doing?' She lunged across the table and tried to grab the torn pieces, but Peter closed his fingers around them and screwed them into a tight ball in his fist.

'Mum, I think you should know, I'm with Peter on this one,' Martin said. 'I think Luc might object to his wife giving half a fortune away, too.'

'He won't care,' she yelled. 'She said it's her money and she does what she likes with it. Don't try and use him as an excuse.'

'Don't be naive, love,' Peter said, not unkindly. 'Of course he'll care. Everyone knows he married Prinny for her money.'

'But he didn't,' she protested vehemently. 'He's got a job.'

'That's the impression he's trying to give,' Martin said firmly. 'No man would want people to say he's living off his wife. But he's got a Porsche, hasn't he? You're not telling us he bought that out of his Christmas bonus, are you?'

In fact they were both wrong, and Luc would have been a little upset but not at all surprised if he had heard them speaking like this.

He had always feared that people would judge him, and in fact his wife's wealth was something of an embarrassment to him. He still met up with friends from his youth. Generally they were *vignerons* today, with simple, uncomplicated lives and tastes, and Luc did not wish to be excluded.

He knew that there was nothing Prinny liked better than shopping, and when she had presented him with a Porsche for his birthday his pleasure had been just slightly tinged by a presentiment that here would be a cause of jealousy amongst his small band of friends. They occasionally went for a drive in it, but when he went to work, he continued to use his second hand Citroën.

Liz was silenced for a second, but she was in no way appeased. She was still livid with both of them.

'He's always dressed in top quality clothes, too,' Peter put in. 'I'm sure Prinny wouldn't have it otherwise, but I bet you anything she buys them for him.'

She jerked her head at him, thrusting out her chin. 'So what if she does? That doesn't mean a thing. And I suppose you've got some magic plan of your own to get us out of this mess, have you? Because if you have then I want to hear it.'

The steaks were untouched, the fat starting to congeal.

'Listen, mum, I'm going into my final year in October. Providing I get my degree, and there's no reason why I wouldn't, then I'll be starting work. A junior doctor's salary isn't enormous, but I'm sure I'll be able to give you something when I start earning.'

Peter too had started eating now. With a reasonable, calm air, he said slowly, 'We need to discuss this.'

'What's to discuss?' Liz flashed back. 'You've just thrown away our only hope of surviving the next few months.'

'And that's all it is. Another few months, and if Martin's willing to help us out a bit then we'll manage.'

'Of course you can. Look, mum, if I can give you four or five hundred a month, and you get a few more bookings for the gîtes then you'll have enough to live on. It might be a bit tight but it should be enough. And that's a much better idea than taking any money from Prinny.'

She looked bewildered. 'But you'd never be able to afford that out of your salary. What about your own bills? You'll be paying rent, and you'll need a car.'

'Don't be looking for obstacles, mum,' he said firmly. 'I'll be sharing a flat probably. That's what most junior doctors do, at least for the first couple of years, and in any case rents in Ireland are not what they are in England.'

Orla was secretly very relieved when Susannah and her mother left to go back to England. Mindful of Martin's remonstrances, she managed to say goodbye very politely on the Saturday morning as Luc was loading their suitcases into the back of his car.

Henry was there to meet them at Stansted. The two weeks' respite had calmed him and he was all affability as he kissed them both before leading the way to the car park.

Susannah was very quiet during the drive back home, only contributing an occasional comment and barely listening as Emma recounted the horrors that Prinny was facing in her daily life.

As soon as they arrived, she dragged her small case upstairs to her room. Without pausing to unpack, she sat at her desk and downloaded a form from the Internet. Fifteen minutes later, a single click sent the form on its way. She had decided on her future.

Downstairs, Emma and Henry were in the lounge, both sipping a pre dinner sherry.

'I really do think Prinny has influenced Sue,' Emma said enthusiastically. 'You should have seen the way she coped with Arlette...'

'Who?'

'Prinny's mother-in-law...'

'Oh, yes. Yes, of course. Why? What was so special?'

'She just seemed so natural with her. Prinny had no idea how to feed her, the food was all over the place, and Susannah just took over. She's going to make a fantastic doctor, Henry. I'm just so glad that we went over.'

'Well, that's a relief,' he said. 'Problem solved, then.'

'I knew this holiday was a good idea,' she said with a satisfied smile. Then she continued seriously, 'I just wish that Prinny could find some sort of solution. She can't go on like that for the rest of her life, she'll go insane. She's absolutely miserable there, no matter how much she tries to hide it.'

'Well, it was her choice, wasn't it? No-one dragged her over there.'

'Even so, she'd be much better off if she came back. The trouble is, as long as Luc's there, she'll stay. I know she will.'

Back in France, the O'Sullivans were nearing the end of their stay. For Orla, the weeks had flown by in a heady mixture of excitement, discovery, pain and sheer joy.

She stretched up and lifted her suitcase down from the top shelf of the wardrobe and slowly filled it. She did not pack her amethyst pendant or her ring. She wore them both constantly, and now she sat on her bed and turned the ring around rather sadly. She had to go home, of course, but the sadness of this was mitigated by Martin's words to her.

'You'll have another ring just as soon as I'm qualified,' he had told her the previous evening as they were sitting in the fading sunlight by the pool. 'For your left hand.'

She smiled now, as she knew that Martin too was feeling low at their imminent parting, and she would try to be as brave as she could, for both of them.

There was, naturally, one huge gnawing anxiety left. She would have to confront her parents and she was expecting an almighty battle. It was no longer begging for permission to go out with her friends, or to wear a little make up.

Daddy would be the easier of the two of them to convince, she was sure of that, and it was with a sense of trepidation that she went in search of him.

'Oh, child, are you sure about this? It's not something to take lightly, you know. Once you're married, that's it. It's for life, there's no going back.'

'Yes I know, Daddy.' She was earnest, her eyes seeking his, trying to convince him. 'But I love Martin and he loves me, so why should we wait?'

'But what about your studies, child? Don't you want to go to university like Mary?'

'No, not really. Just because Mary went it doesn't mean I have to do the same.'

'No, no, of course not, that's not what I mean,' he said hurriedly. 'Only, I don't want to see you making a mistake, that's all.'

'Don't you like Martin? Is that it?'

'Oh, he's a grand lad all right. Don't get me wrong, I've nothing against the fellow. But Orla, child, you're still so young. You could meet anyone. Anyone at all. Just because he's the first fellow you like, it doesn't mean you have to get married. You need to live your life a bit more first. Finish your education, get a job.'

'I've already met him, Daddy,' she said gently. 'I love Martin and we want to get married.' To her relief she saw the worried frown disappear and he looked calm again.

'Well, you should know your own mind. If you're sure about it then I'll not be objecting. I don't know what your mother will say, though.'

Orla herself was worried on this point. She hardly knew how her mother would react, but, deep inside, she knew with a certainly that she hardly dare admit to herself, that one of her reasons for marrying was to get away from her mother. She cast her mind back and thought of all the years of being an obedient daughter, of wearing what her mother said she had to wear, of keeping her hair long because her mother liked it that way, and of not staying out late like her friends.

Declan gently pressed her head to his shoulder, and he stroked the auburn curls. 'Don't you worry, my pet, it'll all work out. You'll be fine.'

Theresa wanted to leave the gîte in an even tidier state than they had found it, which proved to be almost impossible until she looked in the kitchen cupboard.

'These glasses should have been organized properly in order of size when we arrived,' she announced in a pleased voice as Orla came in and sat at the table. 'I can't think why they weren't. Everything else was so tidy.' She turned round to her, saying 'Now, have you finished your packing yet? Give your case to Daddy and then go and help Padraic with his, will you? We have to be off early tomorrow morning and we can't be hunting around the place for anything.'

Orla didn't answer and she was distinctly annoyed. 'Didn't you hear what I said?'

She swallowed nervously, before saying, 'Mammy, I have to tell you something.'

Her eyebrows lifted. 'Well, what is it? Be quick, now.'

'Do you think you could leave those glasses for just one little minute and listen to me?'

Startled by her unusually sharp tone, Theresa pushed the last glass into place and sat down by her side. 'What's wrong?'

'Nothing. Why do you always think something's going to be wrong with me?' She took a deep breath, and then said quickly, 'It's just that….well….Martin and I are going to get engaged.'

She looked at her mother and waited for the storm of outraged protest that she was expecting. Instead, Theresa's voice was quiet when she said, 'Child, he's not the boy for you.

You're far too young to be thinking about that sort of thing. And besides, he's not a Catholic. You can't marry a Protestant.'

She glared at her mother. 'Will you *stop* calling me a child! I was a child when I was three, when I was ten, for Heaven's sake. I'm nearly eighteen now and I can make my own mind up about who's for me and who isn't. And we've talked about religion. He's perfectly willing to bring up any children as Catholics, so you can't use that as an excuse.'

She frowned. 'But isn't he a student up at a great big university with hundreds of girls in it? He's just flirting with you. You're taking it all too seriously. He'll forget about you the minute you leave here.'

'Oh, no I won't.' They both looked up, startled at Martin's voice. He came towards them and sat down, uninvited and he took Orla's hand.

'I am definitely not a flirt, Mrs. O'Sullivan,' he said firmly, and Theresa's face flamed with embarrassment and annoyance. 'Orla is perfectly right when she says that we'll be getting engaged. And I will look after her, I can promise you that.'

'We'll see what her father has to say about that,' she said coldly.

'Daddy knows already, and he's fine with it,' she said.

'Mrs. O'Sullivan, you can't control Orla for the rest of her life. She's right when she says she's no longer a child. You've directed her whole life up until now. You've told her what she has to wear, what she has to do, what she has to study at school. You've even told her what she can spend her pocket money on, and it's time it stopped. She's a grown woman with her own life to lead.'

Seeing the evident hostility in her face, he stopped short of telling Theresa what he had long suspected, that it was she who was the principal cause of Orla's anorexia. It would be cruel and there would be no point at all in saying anything now.

Theresa's voice was shaking with anger. She jerked her head at him now and said icily, 'I can't see what business it is of yours how I choose to bring up my own child...'

'I'm *not* a child...'

'She's right about that.' He was angry now in his turn. 'And it *is* my business since I intend to marry Orla as soon as I can.' He stopped for a moment and they glared at each other.

Suddenly they both jumped as Orla banged her fist hard on the table. 'Stop it!' she cried. 'I can't stand this. Will you stop fighting with each other.' She put her head down on the table and broke into a storm of weeping.

'Now look what you've done!' she snapped. She stroked Orla's hair and said in a gentler tone, 'Come on, now, stop all this. It'll be alright.'

'Leave me alone!' she yelled. She lifted her head up and turned a tear streaked face to her mother. 'Martin's right. I'm not yours to boss around for the rest of my life. I'm sick and tired of you telling me what to do. And if you want to know...' She stood up now and pointed a finger at Theresa's face. 'It was *you* who started me off on my anorexia. It was your fault. You never let me choose anything on my own.' Her voice dropped and she sobbed now. 'I chose the only thing that I could, the only thing left to me that you couldn't control.'

Theresa stared at her uneasily, and Martin groaned softly.

'Orla, stop it,' he said. 'That's going too far.'

But it was too late. Theresa's face had the blanched, bleak look of someone completely defeated, and she said weakly, 'That's not true. You can't blame me for that. All I ever wanted was for you to be happy...'

Her voice tailed off and she suddenly rushed for the door. They turned to each other as they heard it slam, and he took her in his arms and kissed her.

'She'll never forgive me,' she sobbed.

He was soothing as he caressed her. 'Oh, yes, she will. She's your mother, isn't she? That's what mums do.'

Orla and Theresa avoided each other for the rest of the day. Theresa busied herself with the packing, but her mind was in turmoil. Finally, she zipped Padraic's case up and went to the bedroom. She sat down heavily on the bed, and the pent up frustration and emotion overcame her and she started crying softly. The tears slid silently down her cheeks and she put up a hand to brush them away angrily.

Her mind flew back to the last time she had cried, when she was sitting by Orla's bed in the hospital, praying that she would live. Slowly, she began to reason. Was it her fault? Perhaps, just possibly, Orla could be right. Perhaps she had wanted to control her too much.

Declan came in with a pile of towels over his arm. 'Do we wash these, do you think, or do we...?' He stopped and his face changed as he saw her.

'Has something happened?' he asked anxiously. He threw the towels onto a chair and sat beside her. 'What's wrong?'

Desperately, she told him what had happened. 'She thinks it's my fault,' she said miserably. 'She's blaming me for her anorexia.'

He was greatly distressed to see her in this state. 'Ah, now, don't be getting yourself all upset over that,' he said. 'She's sad to be going home, that's all. She'll get over it as soon as she's back with her friends.'

'No, Declan, she won't,' she sobbed. 'I was totally wrong. It must have been my fault.'

'No, no, it wasn't,' he soothed her. 'What did they say up at the clinic, now? They said it could have been anything at all that set her off. Don't you remember how they talked to us about it? No-one up in Dublin thought it was your fault.'

'Martin thinks it was, I bet that's what he's been telling her.' She refused to be mollified.

'Sure and what does that fellow know about anything at all?' he said gruffly. 'Isn't he at his books the whole time? Never done a whole day's work in his life. Don't you take any notice of what he thinks, now.'

She sighed deeply and he was gratified to see that she appeared calmer.

'We'll, let's finish the packing, shall we?' She sounded resigned as she collected the towels from the chair. 'I'll get these in the wash, they'll be dry before we go.'

Theresa and Declans's suitcase was packed and in the hallway ready to be loaded into the car the next morning.

On the dining table lay a small gift of three teatowels, each one printed with a different image of County Limerick. She had chosen these carefully, as Mona Kelly had told her it was the correct thing to do.

'Nothing too expensive,' she had said crisply, 'and nothing you've noticed is missing in the gîte. They would take that as a criticism. Just something small nicely wrapped up.'

Bearing this advice in mind, she had chosen a green and gold paper and tied it up with a gold ribbon. Now she wrote a small floral thank you card which she slipped underneath the ribbon.

The parcel was ready now, and yet she was very reluctant to take it over to Liz's house. She would have to take the keys back, of course, but her mind recoiled at the thought of meeting Martin.

She turned the parcel over and over in her hands, thinking of his bitter words. She could send Padraic over with it, of course. Surely that would do? But then, she suddenly decided. She would go over herself, this very minute, before her courage deserted her. She left the package where it was. She would do as Mona said and give it to them tomorrow just before they left.

Liz was in the kitchen, grating cheese over a pizza.

'You haven't come to give me back the keys yet, have you? It would do just as well tomorrow morning.'

'Ah, no. Actually, it was Martin I wanted to see. Is he at home at all?'

Liz had an idea why she wanted to see Martin, but she kept her suspicions to herself. He had barely spoken to them last night and they could see that something was on his mind, but neither of them broached the subject. As Peter said, the lad was a grown man now and if he wanted to tell them something he would do it in his own time.

She wiped her hands on a cloth and said, 'He's in the back garden, he's just getting me some carrots for tea.'

She led Theresa over to the back door, from where they could see Martin bending over a clump of feathery stalks.

She nodded her thanks and walked over to him. He straightened up at her approach and his face flamed.

'Martin.'

'Mrs. O'Sullivan.'

They both spoke together, and she rushed on, her face creased with anxiety. 'I came to say how desperately sorry I am about yesterday.'

He interrupted her. 'No, please. I...I shouldn't have said all that, it was so rude of me...' He shook the earth off the bunch of carrots, and then said, avoiding her eyes, 'It's just that...well, I really do love Orla, and...'

'Yes, I know,' she said quickly. 'And you were right, you know. I did try and control her too much. I realise that now. And it was my fault she started dieting, I can see that now.'

He shook his head and looked earnestly at her now. 'Not necessarily,' he said quietly. 'I studied it last year at Uni, and honestly, the causes are far from clear. It could have been any number of things that set her off, and most probably a combination of lots of different unconnected events.'

She was eager to placate him. 'At any rate, she seems to be getting over it now,' she said, 'and I do know that you've helped her so much. She would never have gone into a restaurant before.'

He smiled. 'She actually ate everything, you know, and it was quite a heavy meal.' He paused, and then said cheerfully, 'I'd better get these carrots in the kitchen. Mum likes to get the meal prepared well in advance.'

Theresa was definitely approving of this, and Liz was considerably surprised when Theresa came back inside with Martin, both of them seeming now completely at ease with one another. She was racked by curiosity about what had passed between them, but, she sighed inwardly, much better not to ask.

CHAPTER 15

The dining table gleamed and the small salon had a pleasant scent of beeswax polish. Prinny had scrupulously followed Liz's instructions on the order in which to clean a room, and she was highly satisfied with the results. She was almost preening with pride when Luc came home. His shirt was damp with sweat and he sank down onto the sofa.

'Well, do you like it?' She beamed round at the salon.

He was unsure. 'Do I like what?'

'This. The salon. I've spent hours cleaning it.'

'Ah, yes,' he agreed, without so much as casting his eye round the room. 'It is good. You must have been busy.' He leaned over and kissed her, but sensed that all was not well. She pulled away from him, patently offended. Her lips were tight now, and she got up and went into the bedroom. When she returned she had changed into a flowery summer dress. Luc was flicking through the television channels.

'Do we have to stay inside and watch TV?' She spoke lightly, but Luc heard the underlying tension, and he grabbed the remote and turned it off.

'No. There is nothing worth watching, I think.'

'Let's have a drink in the garden, then. Your mother will be fine, she's resting.'

Once installed comfortably in the garden, Prinny did not launch straight into what was uppermost in her mind but started by saying, 'I do wish I could get someone in to do the cleaning. No-one in this place seems to want a job any more.' She spoke lightly, but her voice belied her real anxiety. She would cope far better without the endless round of chores which was completely alien to her.

'Why not ask Liz?' he suggested, but she made a wry face and admitted, 'I already have, but she says she hasn't got time. It's understandable, I suppose. She has got three houses to look after and she says she wouldn't have time to take on anything else.'

She waited until they were in their dessert before she finally said, rushing a little, 'Luc, I've been thinking. Looking after your mother, I honestly can't do it for much longer, it's driving me insane.'

'But, but she has to be looked after,' he stammered.

'By someone,' she said firmly. 'Of course I know that, but surely it doesn't have to be me? Yes, I know you said she wanted a member of the family, but let's face it, I'm not related to her in any way.'

She rushed on, determined to make him understand that she was not prepared for a lifetime of looking after his mother.

'I need some help with her,' she said. 'She's your mother, not mine, and I think it's time you took a turn at caring for her.'

He looked aghast, which was the reaction she had expected, but she pressed on. 'When you come home from work in future,' she said firmly 'she's your responsibility. I don't mind during the day, I can manage that, but it's so unfair to expect me to do everything.'

She gambled now, on the fact that if he had to choose between his mother and her, that she would win. She hardly dared to say the words, but knowing that if she didn't, she would regret it for the rest of her life.

'It's your choice, Luc,' she said quietly. 'Either you start helping me, or I go back to London. I can be gone by the end of next week. You have to decide.'

She felt terribly guilty over the subterfuge but she knew had no choice. She watched him out of the corner of her eye as he paced about the room. His handsome face was twisted with emotion as he wrestled with the bombshell she had dropped. She could almost see him coming to a decision, and finally, he said,

'I have let you do everything for my mother, and you are right, it is my turn to help you with her.'

She gave no sign whatsoever of the relief that was flooding her. All she said was, 'Thank you Luc.' She was already planning the next part of her strategy. She would give him two weeks at the most, and then she was sure he would be ready to listen to her next proposal.

It didn't take two weeks. At two o'clock in the morning they heard her calling. He half raised himself in the bed and looked at Prinny. She stirred, and turned over but did not waken.

Very reluctantly he heaved himself out of bed and wrapped a brown towelling robe around himself before walking into her room. The was a stench that made him wrinkle his nose, and his mother looked at him, her eyes blurred with sleep and she said, 'Luc, it's you. Where's Prinny?'

'She's sleeping. I don't want to disturb her.'

'You're sure?' You'll need a bowl of warm water, and the pads are in the top drwaer.'

On his way to the kitchen, treading softly so as not to wake his wife, he fully appreciated how much Prinny must hate this life, and when he had finished cleaning his mother and fetched her some fresh water and finally got back into bed himself, he came to a decision.

He said nothing in the morning; it was always a rush to eat his croissants and drink enough coffee before driving to work, but in the evening, he came home earlier than expected.

Prinny had prepared an appetizing stew from a recipe that Liz had given her, and she watched as he ate with appreciation. When he had finished and they strolled out into the garden with their coffee, he said in a carefully nonchalant voice, 'I think we need a professional nurse for Maman.'

She hardly dared to breathe and was very careful not to betray the elation she was feeling. Instead, she said cautiously, 'I'll pay for someone to live with her if that's all that's stopping you.'

He spread his arms wide. 'So, you will pay? Yes, this is good, but there are other problems. This nurse, where will she sleep? We do not have enough rooms.'

The problem had occupied him nearly all day. Last night had been horrendous and he dreaded the thought of having to do that nearly every night until Prinny took over what he thought of as her duties once more. Now, finally, he could see why she was so adamant that she would not continue. He knew that unless they found a solution, she would do as she had threatened and go back to London.

Before she could answer, they both turned their heads at the sound of approaching footsteps, and Luc stood up. 'Liz,' he began, and then he noticed the expression on her face and he faltered, 'Is something wrong?' Liz's face was stony and her eyes were cold. She accepted the chair that Luc was indicating and then she said flatly,

'I came to tell you...' She stopped, as if it was too difficult, and then she recovered herself and continued. 'I came to say that Peter has torn up your cheque. He says we can't accept it.' Her tone was bitter.

'Torn it up! But darling, what on earth for?'

'Prinny, it's so hard to say this. You'll think we're the most ungrateful people in the world.'

Prinny's expression changed from dismay, to a searching stare, and she said, 'No, of course not. But why doesn't Peter want to take it? Isn't it the best solution?'

Liz twisted her wedding ring round and round on her finger, and she did not meet either of their troubled gazes when she said in a low voice, 'He thinks it's charity.'

'Oh, really, Liz, that's just too absurd!'

Luc was looking puzzled, the problem of his mother shelved for the moment. 'What are you talking of? What is this cheque?'

Prinny was unruffled. 'It's not important, darling. I gave Liz a tiny cheque just to help her out a little, that's all.'

'You didn't tell him?' Liz said incredulously. 'You mean, you were ready to give me all that money without even letting Luc know?' She looked from one to the other of them, fully expecting an outburst from Luc, but to her surprise, she saw his face break into a slow, gentle smile.

'Prinny does as she likes with her money,' he said easily. 'It is not mine. If she wishes to make a gift then it is her decision.'

Liz was struggling to come to terms with this attitude, and he continued, saying, 'I have my salary, from my work, you understand? And Prinny, she has her own money. No-one will ever say to me that I married my wife because she is rich.' His tone had changed now and he sounded slightly embittered. 'That is what everyone thought. Even Guillaume has said this to me, and Maurice.' He warmed to his theme now, and he flung his arms wide in the air. 'But no, I say to them. I love my wife before I know that she has much money. It is the woman I love, not her bank account.' He looked appealingly at Prinny. 'This is true, *n'est-ce pas*?'

Prinny laughed. 'He's right, actually. Mummy never believed it, but he is the one in a million who wouldn't do that, aren't you, my love?'

She reached over and kissed Luc on the forehead. He stroked her face, with no embarrassment and for the moment at least, Liz was distracted. Both she and Peter had privately voiced the opinion that all Luc wanted was Prinny's money, but from all she was hearing it seemed as if they were wrong.

Luc turned to her now and said, 'But I am not polite. It is a hot evening and I offer you nothing to drink. What would you like? There is orange juice, lemonade...' He was well aware of Liz's antipathy to alcohol, and he rose to his feet as she said, 'Orange juice would be lovely, thank you.'

'So, Liz,' Prinny said as Luc disappeared into the kitchen. 'If Peter won't accept my cheque, what will you do?'

Liz stared out across the garden without seeing it. 'I have absolutely no idea.'

'And Peter? Has he any suggestions?'

She shook her head. 'No, my dear, nothing at all,' she said bleakly. There are the gîtes, of course, but we still have hardly any bookings. When the Irish family go, we've nothing at all until a week in September. Peter,' she added bitterly, 'seems to think that if we don't mention it, somehow everything will work out fine. Well, maybe he'll change his tune when we haven't got enough money for the groceries.' Then she continued, shamefacedly. 'I shouldn't be criticizing him, I know. He really is the best man in the world, but I just can't get him to see how serious things are.'

Prinny was silent for a time. She felt sorry for Liz, but so helpless. If Peter wouldn't take money then she was at a loss.

Luc returned with a tall glass of iced orange juice, and Liz took it from him with a murmured, 'Thank you.' She took a sip and then she looked up with a wan smile and said, 'I am so sorry, you two. I'm boring you both to death with my petty problems, and here you are with Arlette to look after. How is she? Has there been any improvement?'

Prinny gave a wry smile. 'No, not really. Some days she seems to be a little better with her speech and then it gets worse again.'

'That's so hard for her,' Liz murmured. 'And for both of you too, of course,' she added hastily.

'Luc seems to think that she needs a full time nurse,' she murmured. 'But this house is not big enough. We could have someone during the day but she often wakes up during the night. She sometimes needs changing, or else she needs a drink, and one of us has to see to her.' She did not mention that now it was Luc who was getting out of bed instead of herself, but instead she continued, 'We need to find a solution that suits everyone. If we could do that I think everything would be fine.'

'But, my dear, why don't you and Luc have a house built? You could look for a plot of land somewhere close, and then Arlette can have a nurse. You'd be near enough to visit her regularly. Why not give that some thought?'

Prinny turned to face her, and for the first time there was hope in her voice. 'Do you know, I never thought of that,' she said eagerly. 'You're right, it would be possible.' Then her face clouded. 'The only problem would be, we'd need to stay with Arlette while it was being built, and that could take months. Oh, Liz, I really don't think I can take months more of this.'

After a full minute's silence whilst she contemplated her polished fingernails, her head suddenly flew up and she clapped her hands to her mouth. 'Liz, I've just thought! Oh, God, why on earth didn't I think of that before?'

Liz was startled. 'Think of what?'

'Your gîtes, of course! Oh, how stupid can I get? I should have thought of that ages ago!'

'Prinny, what are you talking about?'

'We can rent one of your gîtes, of course.' Her eyes shone. 'They're going to be empty soon, aren't they? Don't you see? We can pay you rent for one of them, and Peter can't possibly object to that, can he? There's no way he can say that's charity. Luc and I can live there until we can get a house built, and we can get a nurse for Arlette as soon as possible. She can live in the house with her, and we'll be so near we'll be able to visit her every day.' She was smiling broadly now. 'Two birds with one great big stone, don't you think? It would give you and Peter the income you need and give us some space at the same time.'

Liz's face lit up. 'My dear, that is the most sensible thing I've heard from you in a very long time.' She beamed at the woman she now counted as one of her dearest friends. 'From everyone's point of view, I don't think you could do any better.'

'Luc, what do you think?'

361

Her eyes were shining and he caught some of her enthusiasm. 'It sounds to be a very good proposition,' he said carefully. 'We will think about this, of course, but I cannot see a reason why we should not do it.'

Secretly his own relief almost matched Liz's as she thought of the rental income that would mean financial stability and put an end to the months of strain and worry.

He beamed round at both women, and announced, 'Tomorrow, we will begin to search for a good plot of land.'

Orla dragged her suitcase behind her and her face was wet with tears as they arrived at the crowded Carcassonne airport. Declan went straight away to the announcement board to check that the Dublin flight was on time, and didn't see Orla's face suddenly light up with joy as she waved frantically out of the window.

'He's here!' she shouted, and she bolted out of the door.

'Orla, where are you going?' Theresa turned her head to shout after the retreating Orla, but got no reply. She followed her into the bright sunshine, scanned the crowds and then she understood.

Martin and Orla had said their goodbyes at the house, but on a sudden impulse, he legged it round to Peter's Renault and followed them, arriving on a couple of minutes after them.

She flew into his open arms and they embraced, and then he turned and led her away from the crowds to the lesser used car park which adjoined the massive runway perimeter fence. Here they were relatively private, and they kissed once more.

'It won't be long,' he said, and his own voice was choked with emotion. 'Here,' he said, handing her a tissue. 'Mop up.'

She obediently dabbed at her streaming eyes, and he held her close. 'I want you to promise me something.'

'Anything,' she sobbed.

'Work hard for me,' he urged her. 'Get your qualifications, and don't ever go back to your anorexic times. Please promise me, my love.'

'Yes. Yes, of course.'

'Ring me when you get home?'

'The minute we're in the door,' she said. And then she looked at her watch and realised that Declan would be panicking by now. 'I have to go now.'

He nodded, and they clung tightly to each other for a final moment before she turned and left him to join her family for the flight back to Dublin.

EPILOGUE

Doctor Monica Lewis felt the cold night air on her face as she left the hospital. She wrapped her woollen scarf around her mouth and pulled up the hood of her coat as she scurried to the car park. It had been a busy shift of twelve hours and she was exhausted. She was well aware that she was barely sufficiently alert for safety, but it was late, there was little traffic about and she drove slowly and carefully until she reached her flat on the outskirts of Newcastle.

Her eyelids were drooping but she made a cup of black coffee and flicked on the television before she sank down onto the sofa. She simply could not miss this programme.

It was another half an hour before her face broke into a delighted grin as the announcement was made.

'And this year's BAFTA award for best supporting actress goes to.....' There was a protracted pause before screaming applause rang out to the the words.... 'Susannah Ward.'

A few hours later and the morning routine was in full swing at Newburyport Hospital. It was one of the few hospitals in the County Limerick which had an anorexic unit attached, and Doctor Martin Saunders was heading there now, a sheaf of notes under his arm and a plastic cup of vending machine coffee in his other hand.

In the eight years that had passed since his memorable holiday, he had changed very little. The shock of blond hair was just a little thinner and he knew that he would have to pay careful attention to his weight if he wanted to avoid his slightly bulging stomach developing into a paunch which was testimony to his wife's excellent cooking.

He would have to hurry. The case study meeting started at half past two and it was twenty-five past already. As he walked briskly down the long corridor, he mentally rehearsed his notes, knowing that the other doctors relied on him for a succinct and precise account of the progress of each of his patients. There were six of them in the unit at present, all of them severely undernourished. Their treatment would be complex, but he was sure that all of them were capable of making a complete recovery, even including the sixteen year old girl who had been admitted twice in the last year. She would need a highly specialized and personalized diet to boost her triglycerides and her immune system, but he had complete faith in the team's recently appointed nutritionist. He smiled as he passed her door which held a new brass plaque, simply inscribed: Doctor Orla Saunders.

By the same Author

Clouds over the Montagne Noire

When tragedy strikes Lynne and Alex Stevens they decide to make a fresh start in an idyllic wine producing village in the South of France. But even before they move in they unwittingly make enemies. Who hates them enough to vandalise their property?

Lynne takes classes in the local Lycée, and her influence will change the course of one of her pupil's lives forever.

In the village, falling wine sales force one château owner to choose between the woman he loves and financial security, and when the owner of the local shop discovers a terrible secret about her brother she faces an agonising dilemma.

A compelling story of the hopes and aspirations of a community in the Languedoc region between the Montagne Noire and the Pyrénées.

http://www.amazon.co.uk/dp/B009QIC4PQ